EVERY
LAST
BREATH

RUSHDAN

sourcebooks
casablanca

Published by Sourcebooks Casablanca, an imprint of Sourcebooks, Inc.
P.O. Box 4410, Naperville, Illinois 60567-4410
(630) 961-3900
sourcebooks.com

Printed and bound in Canada.
MBP 10 9 8 7 6 5 4 3 2 1

No need to waste a bullet.

Vivaldi's *Stabat Mater* filled Aleksander's ears, the violins and countertenor's falsetto dampening the muffled cries of the woman bound and gagged behind him. He didn't want her life, just the use of her third-floor bedroom. Then he and his son, Valmir, would be on their way.

A wisp of a cool breeze rustled the ivory lace curtains, taunting him from the three-inch hole he'd cut in the window. Seated with his legs on either side of the tripod, he stretched his neck, letting the joints pop. He tucked the butt of the high-powered AX50 rifle into the pocket of his shoulder, pressed his cheek to the stock, and adjusted the scope for a proper zero.

Sweat gathered on his brow, sliding down his temple in a sticky trickle as he waited. Three more minutes passed like a painful thirty. He gnashed his molars, fingers itchy.

Putting a slug in a man's skull was never easy, but every profession had its challenges. He'd learned long ago, the same way he'd taught Val, to push through. To distill the unpleasantness of necessary things. The work became normal. Pushing and distilling a habit.

But this wasn't a job. This time, the endgame was personal.

Aleksander sighted through the scope, his focus fixed and every sense alive. His position was ideal and the line of sight golden. *Come on*, he silently urged, though his quarry adhered to a strict schedule. Two bodyguards left the upscale town house across the quaint road. One stood beside the doorway. The other went down the steps to the curb, where a chauffeured car arrived at 7:15 on the button.

The detailed dossiers Aleksander had purchased from the information broker had been worth the exorbitant cost. He'd waited, planned, saved, made the right connections, seething for seventeen years—an eternity that could drive a man insane. Very soon, he'd have what he yearned for most in the world, the reason he'd sold his soul to the devil. *Ah, yes.* They would pay.

He controlled his breathing, slowed his pulse.

The front door opened again. Twenty seconds. That's all he'd have for a clear shot—and all he'd need. He licked his lips in anticipation and thumbed the safety off his rifle as Val came up beside him.

Blackburn emerged in the doorway across the street. A cold resolve settled over Aleksander at the sight of his target.

One. Two. With his finger on the trigger, he drew in a breath and exhaled slowly. *Six. Seven.* He lined up the crosshairs, lasered red dot on the center of the forehead. *Eleven. Twelve.*

A smooth squeeze of the hair trigger and stout recoil. The .50-caliber hollow-point round spat from the end of the suppressor, swallowing any sound. The back of

Blackburn's head burst in a spray of pink mist as he pitched backward and dropped onto the sidewalk like a sack of potatoes.

One down.

Relief hummed through him. It had begun. *Finally.*

Val gave Aleksander's shoulder a little squeeze. Yes, they'd see this through until the end—together. No matter what it took.

Aleksander removed his earbuds and packed the AX50 with quick, mindless efficiency—muscle memory gained from many years of practice.

"The chartered plane is ready and waiting at Heathrow."

"Excellent," Aleksander said, thirsting for the next step. Hell-bent on reaping revenge.

GRAY BOX HEADQUARTERS, NORTHERN VIRGINIA
12:30 P.M. EDT

Digging deep—beyond guts and the sublimation of physical pain—to survive a Gray Box mission was tricky enough. Doing so unscathed was impossible.

Maddox Kinkade hung her towel in her locker and threw on her underwear and bra, gritting her teeth.

Fucking up wasn't her style. She was a go-getter, had an unblemished record—until now, with the covert op in Iran that'd spiraled from dicey to hell in a handbasket.

A hot shower had done little good, but her aching muscles screamed thanks after a quick rub with liniment. As she shoved into her jeans, relishing the soothing tingle and scent of menthol, there was a knock on the women's locker room door. "Yeah?" she called out.

The door swung open. Gideon "Reaper" Stone, her best friend and wet work specialist—fancy term for CIA-bred assassin—met her eyes. His ice-blue gaze didn't veer for a second to her exposed cleavage or the right side of her torso, which resembled battered meatloaf.

"Ten minutes," he said. "Conference room. The DGB wants you on a priority op."

After losing their asset, blowing critical data retrieval, barely escaping a Quds hit squad, and crossing seven time zones, she'd been stateside less than three hours. She needed an IV drip of fluids, painkillers, and solid sleep. But what the DGB—director of the Gray Box—wanted, he got.

"I'll be there in five." She checked her smartwatch. "Grab me a coffee?"

"Sure." Voice flat, face deadpan, his titanium veneer never softened. Not even for her.

She pulled on a compression tank top, easing the irksome throb in her side, slipped her arms through the loops of her shoulder holster, and shoved her Gray Box–issued Maxim into the rig. Unlike a standard 9mm, this one had a built-in suppressor.

She slid extra mags—one round shy of max capacity to preserve the springs—into slots on the holster and put on her lightweight blazer.

Peering in the mirror, she whisked on makeup, covering a purple contusion on her cheek, undereye shadows, and sallowness in her golden-tan complexion, for a fresh game face. An art she'd mastered doing in a jiffy. She corralled her damp brown spiral curls into a ponytail and stuffed a lipstick tube housing tear gas gel spray in her pocket before glancing at the almost decade-old torn photo strip taped inside the locker.

Nikolai held her on his lap, snuggled close as she laughed. The only man she'd ever loved. Beyond reason or measure. The memory of that soul-deep happiness and the never-ending grief was a fist around her heart, squeezing—an ache she'd learned to live with, like a sore tooth she couldn't pull.

The guilt of his death had made her better suited

for this job in a strange way. At twenty-nine, she had
nothing else to live for, nothing more to lose.

———————   ———————

Powering down the hall, she passed Alistair Allen, former
MI6 officer, and Sean "Ares" Whitlock, the team's other
wet work pro. They were no doubt headed out of the
subterranean compound for well-deserved time off after
busting their butts as her backup.

"Drinks should be on me." Considering this fail
rested on her shoulders. "Sorry, guys."

"We heard," Ares said, implying the priority op.
The one thing about him darker than his hair, eyes, and
badass presence was his precision in killing. "Don't party
too hard without us."

Party being a bizarre euphemism for trying not to die
while getting the job done.

"We're blowing up your bar tab at Rocky's." Alistair
winked, his smirk wry. With his faded jeans and slicked-
back hipster haircut, he was the antithesis of James Bond.

John Reece, their demolition expert, hustled over
and slung an arm around her shoulder in a side hug.
His ball cap read *Another Day I Didn't Use Algebra.*
"Eau de Bengay. How sexy. Grrr." He purred like a
tiger and flashed a dazzling smile worthy of a toothpaste
commercial.

She elbowed his ribs, quashing a grin. "It's Icy Hot."
As if that sounded better.

Their team's rare bond ran deeper than friendship and

was the glue holding her together. The blood they'd shed for one another was thicker than water of the womb.

She waved to Alistair and Ares, a tiny part of her wishing to go with them. More than that, though, she was hungry to tackle another op. Make up for her failure and reaffirm she belonged here as one of the anointed.

The glass walls of the conference room had been electrically frosted opaque for the brief. Reece pushed through the door, holding it for her. Plowing through exhaustion, she craved caffeine worse than a junkie in need of a fix. She strode up to Gideon, who was standing rather than sitting, a sign the briefing would fly at warp speed.

Gideon handed her a cup of hot java, and she hummed her thanks.

Castle towered over the head of the glass table like a mountain of muscle. Tough guy, prick extraordinaire, and, as luck had it, her big brother. "The DGB is busy, so you're stuck with me." The harsh, clipped tone he'd perfected as a Navy SEAL could crush a diamond. "We've learned that in fifty-six hours, weaponized smallpox will be sold to arms dealers via closed auction."

Her stomach pitched.

Christ.

This kind of op—and keeping it quiet—was the Gray Box's bread and butter. Their off-book special-activities outfit had a black budget never meant to see daylight and was sanctioned for direct action on foreign and domestic soil to prevent exactly this type of doomsday scenario.

"The heavy hitters on the short list are the worst of the worst. Blackburn in England. Reinhart in Germany.

Kassar—the faceless arms dealer whose whereabouts are unknown. And the top two based right here in the great USA, Clive Callahan and Ilya Reznikov."

A chill spilled down Maddox's spine, raising goose bumps. Ilya was a monster she wouldn't piss on if he was on fire, and the hatred was mutual. It was hard to believe he'd almost been her brother-in-law.

Once upon a time, she would've done anything to marry Nikolai Reznikov.

She fixed a stoic look on her face and swallowed past the rising lump in her throat.

"Retrieve and recruit Cole Matthews." Castle brought up blurry photos of a guy on the touchscreen tabletop. "Six-one, black shoulder-length hair, scar on his left cheek, tattoos on both arms. In his early thirties and rides a black Kawasaki Ninja. With his ties to Reznikov, he's our only way into the auction. According to SIGINT reporting, the Russian embassy wants him for unrelated reasons. Real-time chatter indicates they have imminent plans to bag him. We're tracking his cell phone. Get to him first." Castle's gaze locked in on her.

Although they shared their mom's sea-green eyes, his were sharper than broken glass.

She glanced at the out-of-focus pictures splashed across the digital display. A peculiar tightening crawled through her chest.

"The asset is hostile to government agencies and considered dangerous. Use your import/export cover. The story is we have a pharmaceutical company that is an interested buyer looking to profit from a new vaccine for this supposedly deadlier virus strain."

No-brainer why the chief wanted her on this. Maddox was fluent in Russian, asset recruitment was her forte, and her personnel file noted her past familiarity with the Reznikovs.

Familiarity was a pasteurized, watered-down version of the truth that only Castle was privy to and she never wanted the others to know. Especially not her boss. She shook off whatever it was that had coiled her muscles and let out the breath she'd been holding.

"Questions?" Castle asked.

"We've got it," she said.

Her brother folded his action-figure arms. "Keep it simple. Get it done."

Simple and easy were rarely the same, but this job was do or die trying.

ROSSLYN, VIRGINIA
12:35 P.M. EDT

Everyone loved vacations. People worked hard most of the year so they could unplug for a week or two on a sunny beach on a tiny island. Burning through money, clogging arteries with decadent meals, filling dead time thinking about the holes in their lives, lazing about with no sense of purpose—all in the name of freaking *fun*.

Everyone except Cole Matthews.

He exited I-66, and the iconic spires of Georgetown University came into view. Hitting the Key Bridge, an artery connecting northern Virginia to DC, he crossed the Potomac River.

The hot thrum of his motorcycle echoed his simmering annoyance. This was his first day of vacation since he'd been a graduate student. One week of forced leave per the boss's orders after Cole had lost his temper and mouthed off to a douchebag, a.k.a. a wealthy client who refused to follow his security detail's instructions, endangering not only himself but Cole's men.

Cole had called it straight. The boss knew it. But for appearances' sake, and since the client was always right even when clear-cut wrong, Cole's penance to appease the rich putz was unpaid downtime. Or anger management—the one thing that sounded worse than a damn vacation.

He glanced at his side mirror, checking his six—an occupational habit—and would've sworn the same white SUV he'd spotted two blocks from his Arlington town house was now three cars behind him.

Was someone tailing him?

He wasn't sure. The SUV didn't ease too close on his rear, giving him plenty of space, keeping other cars between them and preventing him from catching the license plate.

Controlling security and neutralizing threats was how he earned a living at Rubicon Inc. Best way to identify a tail was to do an SDR—surveillance detection route—with a spotter verifying you were being followed. On his own, he'd have to bait them into giving themselves away. Stall at a green light, take four consecutive right turns, enter a one-way street going in the wrong direction. Something to test their patience and coax them to slip up.

Exiting the bridge, he cut left onto Canal Road NW, headed away from his originally planned destination. The picturesque neighborhood of Foxhall was a cluster of densely packed million-dollar homes laid out in a triangle. Plenty of bottlenecks and light midday traffic.

Cole snaked deep into the heart of the neighborhood. He passed charming Tudors and immaculate lawns. Taking two sharp rights, he swerved down a street that choked into the kind of cul-de-sac that snuck up on you. Parking in front of a walking path sandwiched between two houses at the curved bulb end of the street, he waited.

He lifted the helmet's visor and sat, with the engine idling. The soft growl of his bike washed through his ears. His eyes stayed trained on the intersection and his grip tightened on the handlebars, squeezing so hard his fingers grew numb.

No cars passed. No white front bumper edged to the corner, giving the driver a peek.

Heat radiated from the asphalt in palpable, bubbling waves. The sweltering June sun roasted him in his leather riding jacket. Perspiration licked down his spine like a warm, slimy tongue, to the pocket of skin between his kidneys.

Still, he waited, his annoyance cranking to a quick boil.

The heavy beads of the Buddha prayer necklace he wore on days when he didn't carry a gun were like an anchor against his chest, grounding his focus.

Maybe he was being paranoid. Mandatory leave

was screwing with his head, but it was just the first of ugly things to come. Every unfortunate event that'd happened in his life had occurred in threes, an escalation from bad to worse to epic shitstorm that threatened to put him in the grave.

And always during a godforsaken heat wave.

Cole wasn't superstitious, but he had an uncanny ability to scent trouble on the horizon. He sensed it in the atlas, the topmost vertebra between the skull and spine, like an arthritic joint sensed rain in the wind.

Right now, he had a hairline tingle in the back of his head, juicing up, sparking. He slammed his helmet visor closed and rode down the paved walking path, too narrow for a car to follow. After a quarter mile, the footpath opened into the mouth of a public library parking lot. He hit MacArthur Boulevard, navigating the grind of traffic aggressively, until crossing onto M Street.

The *dry-cleaning run*—a counter-surveillance tactic to shake any ticks—to his Georgetown destination took a vexing, overheated hour.

No sign of the tail, but there was no reason for anyone to follow him. Not after years of exercising painstaking care, cutting every warm-blooded link to his past, and living like vapor.

He nabbed a spot in front of his favorite café. It served authentic Russian cuisine and wasn't frequented by anyone in the Bratva, the Red Mafia. He pulled off his helmet and jacket, surveying the area. Smoothing his long hair behind his right ear, letting the left side screen the scar on his face, he tugged his tee down over the Browning blade sheathed and hooked to his waistband.

The weight of the Ka-Bar knife strapped to his ankle was an added comfort.

His gaze snagged on a white SUV parked down the block, on the other side of the street.

It was possible multiple teams were on him and one had leapfrogged. But that would mean he'd been surveilled for several days without noticing.

He never took the same route or came and went at the same times of day. Anything to avoid establishing a pattern. But Rubicon headquarters, his town house that he'd turned into a veritable fortress, and this café that reminded him of his mother's cooking were predictable places in his routine.

A sixtyish woman carrying shopping bags dashed across the street, a key fob in her hand. The headlights of the white SUV flashed. She hopped in and pulled off.

He let out a breath. *Stop overreacting. Take a chill pill.*

But the persistent electric niggle at the nape of his neck refused to ebb.

He dug in his pocket, grabbed a cable looped at the ends, and ran it through his jacket's sleeves and a clip on the helmet, securing his gear to the bike with a U-lock. Then he strode into the cozy café, cosseted by the familiar smells of cooked cabbage and warm spices.

The blond waitress, Anya, greeted him with an eager smile. He glimpsed Olga, the brunette, disappearing into the kitchen without giving him her usual wave. He looked over the handful of patrons. No one stood out.

The hole-in-the-wall joint had ten tables and a second egress point through the kitchen into an alley.

He sat with his six to the wall, giving him sight lines of the entrance and hall to the kitchen.

Anya sashayed to his table, throwing too much sway in her hips, nibbling her pink lip. She twirled a loose strand of blond hair around a delicate finger. "Summer borscht today?"

The thick beet soup, served cold in the warmer months, was the closest he'd found to his mother's recipe. The ultimate comfort food. He could taste the tangy sweetness on his tongue, and with the memory, others surfaced—but he didn't want to think about his family, of everything he'd lost and the blood he'd shed.

And he certainly didn't want to think about the woman who'd taken a wrecking ball to his life and left his soul bleeding.

A knot bunched in his chest. "No borscht today. Any specials?"

"Beef Stroganoff."

His mouth would've watered if it hadn't been dry as sand. "Sounds perfect for my first day of vacation."

"Mr. Workaholic on vacation?"

He mustered a shallow grin, sweeping his gaze over the door and street. "I find it hard to believe too."

"Tomorrow, how about you come to my place for a homecooked dinner?" Anya blushed, her moss-green eyes gleaming. "I'll serve anything you want." She pressed her voluptuous hip against the table and tapped a pencil on the plump swell of her breast.

He took in her inviting smile and soft curves.

If only he was interested in curling up with her rather than a bowl of borscht. But he'd learned through trial-by-fucking that casual sex had a way of making the emptiness more acute. He wanted a woman who set him on fire, warmed his heart and burned on his mind, without torching his world to ashes.

"Very generous offer, but I have to pass." His gaze fell to his hands, so like his father's had been. Rough, callused, bloodstained. The hands of a killer. "I'm going to be busy." Doing laundry. Working out. Dodging imaginary tails. Trying not to go bananas. *Vacation-palooza*.

"A big, strong hottie like you still has to eat."

Nice of her to think him attractive considering his hideous scar.

With a nervous giggle, she jotted something on her pad and set the sheet on the table. "If you change your mind, call me. No reason to eat alone while on vacation." She strutted off.

He glimpsed her wiggling ass and swung his focus to the door and street.

Another spike of alarm he couldn't explain or shake keyed up his synapses to high alert.

He slipped off the Buddha necklace and rubbed the solid beads. One hundred and eight steel ball bearings threaded with galvanized aviation wire and strong as hell. The decorative tassel and dharma wheel pendant added the distinctive touch, making a deadly tool seem a harmless instrument of prayer.

Some might consider it sacrilegious. To him, it was smart. "Anya."

She spun around, hopeful excitement beaming on her wholesome face.

"I'll have it to go. And add borscht to the order."

Her mouth flattened and the light in her eyes died like a blown bulb, but she nodded.

Olga made a beeline to his table and set a glass of ice water down. "Is very hot today," she said with the thick accent from the Urals. "Anya always forget to give you water."

"*Spasibo*." Thank you in Russian. His throat was parched from the oven-baked ride. He pounded half the glass, drinking past the taste of chlorine and old metal in the tap water. If he had intended to stay, he'd get bottled. "Are you feeling okay, Olga? You seem a bit off."

She wiped shaky hands on her apron, her gaze jumpy. "I'm sorry." Her voice dropped to a whisper. "They threatened to take my visa. Close my uncle's restaurant." She met his eyes.

The fear in her face gripped him by the jugular. Lowering her head, she ran to the kitchen. His gaze dropped to the glass of water, and his blood turned to slush.

No telling what the water had been spiked with or how long he had before it took effect. Cole stood, and the room spun. His vision blurred, then cleared.

Shouting erupted in the kitchen. Dishes clattered to the floor. Outside, a white SUV double-parked in front of the café, blocking his bike. Diplomatic plates, YR. *Russians*.

Damn. Russian intelligence was worse than if the mob had come for him on their own. Also explained how those ticks, who lived and breathed tradecraft, could've been crawling all over him for days without him noticing. Clever of the Bratva to use them.

Three men in black suits hopped out of the SUV. Three more entered the main dining room from the kitchen and pushed past a flabbergasted Anya.

Cole's pulse went ballistic, but his mind locked on one thing—self-preservation. He war-gamed options. None boded well for him.

He clutched the tassel, wrapping the Buddha necklace once around his hand, letting the rest of the beads dangle, and unsnapped the sheath of the blade at the small of his back.

The men drew closer, cutting off his exits. He was cornered.

With muscular cords protruding from their thick necks, wide jowls, and buzz cuts, they looked like a pack of Dobermans ready to tear into him.

Fortunately for Cole, he was a different breed. More werewolf than dog.

Two bruisers flanked him. "Time to go home," one said in Russian.

Cole swung the necklace, whipping it hard across the face of the man on the right. The crunch of his jawbone breaking was audible, and the guy crashed into a table.

Whirling left, Cole lashed backhanded at the other man's arm, stopping him from reaching into his jacket for a weapon. Not hesitating for a second, Cole thrashed the guy's head with a powerful one-two wallop of the beads, sending him spilling to the floor.

Rubbery weakness pulsed in Cole's legs. Dizziness washed over him. He pulled his blade and kicked the table into two others, desperate to stay on his feet.

Darkness edged his vision. His throat tightened,

heartbeat slowing when it should've been skyrocketing, thanks to the drug flooding his system.

He had one minute to do as much damage as possible.

Then his knees would buckle, it'd be lights out, and he would be as good as dead.

03

GEORGETOWN, WASHINGTON, DC
1:50 P.M. EDT

T wo blocks from the target's location," Maddox said as
Reece zigzagged through traffic on M Street.

The unease prickling her gut since the briefing hadn't
subsided.

Something about this op was wrong. From the
grainy, out-of-focus pictures of Matthews that looked
as if they'd been taken by an incompetent drunk to the
shoddy intel. Proper recruitment of an asset meant a
one-inch-thick dossier to analyze and time to find the
best angle to exploit. It was a delicate process convincing
a target to cooperate, to possibly turn against friends or
even their country.

A cold approach with little preparation was the riski-
est. Finding the right opening and building rapport
quickly with a stranger all had to be done on the fly.
Working someone after establishing a genuine emotional
attachment of friendship—or something stronger—
was the best way. The CIA had trained her to read
and manipulate people and to handle tricky situations.
With a bioweapon capable of starting an epidemic in the
mix, her only option was to get this done by any means
necessary. Extra special care was needed for a dangerous

asset who was hostile to government agencies, not to mention wanted by the Russians.

She'd give Cole Matthews the soft, kid-glove treatment. Persuasion was preferred over coercion. But if he wasn't willing to play nice and things got violent, she could handle it.

Being able to hold her own physically against an opponent who'd most likely outweigh and outmuscle her was a requirement that came with black ops territory.

For two years, Nikolai had taught her Systema, a brutal martial art used by Russian Special Forces. The Agency had broadened her skills with Krav Maga, but the DGB had sharpened her talents to a lethal edge on the Gray Box whetstone.

She glanced at the flashing red dot on the handheld GPS tracking unit pinging Matthews's cell. "The asset should be in the building second from the corner, this side of the street. A café, according to Google."

"Black Kawasaki Ninja parked out front," Reece said from the driver's seat. "Maddox, white vehicle. Russian diplomatic plates."

In the back seat, Gideon cocked his gun, chambering a round.

Hers was already prepped to fire, but she had no intention of using her sidearm.

She looked over her shoulder at Gideon. Pale-blond hair, electric-blue eyes, heartbreaker looks—a beautiful, unfaltering killing machine. How the DGB loved deadly things in pretty packages.

"No shoot-outs with these guys," she said. "They're probably Russian intelligence. Protected by diplomatic status. A high visibility incident and cops swarming would be bad all around. Nonlethal force only. Follow my lead."

They both acknowledged the order with a nod.

"Reece, the map shows a back alley. Cover the rear of the café. Reaper, with me."

As they approached the corner, Reece slowed the SUV. She and Gideon hopped out and darted across the street, dodging traffic. Reece veered right, heading toward the alley.

Although they wore fingernail-sized comms devices in their ears, Maddox directed Gideon with a quick hand signal to sweep around the far side of the white SUV. Training dictated he'd check the vehicle for potential hostiles and close in on the other side of the café door.

A loud commotion came from inside the restaurant. Wood crashing, glass breaking, fists hitting flesh. Sounded like a nasty brawl. Suddenly the noises flatlined, as if the scuffle had ended.

"A second vehicle with diplomatic plates parked by the kitchen door," Reece said in her ear. "Vacant. I'm going in through the back."

"Use extreme caution," she said, but with his Delta Force background, that was a given.

The café door swung open. Two men in suits dragged out an unconscious guy wearing a tee and jeans. His chiseled, ink-wrapped arms were slung over their shoulders. The man had a bloodied silver Buddha necklace wrapped around his hand, and his head hung with long black hair obscuring his face.

Cole Matthews.

"Four men down inside," Reece said.

"Asset is outside," she said low. "Gideon, take out the tires."

Gideon nodded through a tinted window from the far side of the white SUV.

She approached the closest guy. Six two. A solid two-forty. Built like a bull with a wide neck and powerful torso, no doubt he knew how to handle himself.

If he was right-handed, she'd have the advantage. Encumbered with Matthews's limp weight on his right side, he'd be slower to draw a gun and maneuver to fend off an attack.

His gaze swept over her. A cursory side glance, and he dismissed her. As expected. All he saw was a woman—attractive face, wide eyes, a spot of cleavage. A nonthreat.

She closed the gap to four feet as the men hit the curb. Any second, it'd happen. Another glance, this time cautious and scrutinizing, followed by a defensive posture.

Then she'd have to be quick. Precise. He'd anticipate a blow targeting his soft tissue areas. Nose, throat, groin. She couldn't go for those first.

Their eyes met. Her focus tunneled to action.

His expression hardened. "Get him into the car," he said to the other man in Russian.

Less than two steps between them, he disentangled himself from under the weight of Matthews and reached into his jacket.

It was now or never. Maddox moved fast. She drove her heel down into the side of his kneecap and slammed a hammer fist on his arm, stopping him from pulling a gun. He staggered, trying to recover his balance. She raised her right arm across her chest and spun, sending the hard, flat part of her forearm into his windpipe with all her strength.

He clutched his throat, strained for air. Stunned.

Gritting her teeth against the bite of pain in her bruised side, she hooked the back of her ankle behind his calf and shoved him over backward. He went down hard to the ground, wheezing. She flicked off the cap of the lipstick in her pocket, whipped out the spray, and hit him in the eyes and open mouth with one burst. He was toast.

The second man had dumped Matthews onto the vehicle's back seat but hadn't noticed the slashed tires.

Reaper was still lurking somewhere out of sight.

Maddox leapt between the parked motorcycle and another car, closing in on the white double-parked SUV. The Russian pulled his gun from a shoulder holster and spun, leveling it at her center of mass.

A bolt of cold arrowed down her rigid spine. No matter how many times a gun had been aimed at her, that visceral reaction was always the same.

She raised her palms, still holding the spray in her fingers, maintaining eye contact.

The good news was that this guy wasn't an untrained civilian with a twitchy trigger finger.

"He is a Russian citizen," he said in English, gesturing to Matthews. "Now on premises belonging to Russia." He implied the car, referencing the articles of the Vienna Convention. "Premises and transport of diplomatic mission have immunity from search and requisition."

The muggy air seemed to thicken with tension. She needed to get closer. *Six more inches.*

"Yes, you're correct," she said in unaccented Russian, daring to step those six inches. She set fear aside, focused only on the next move to retrieve Matthews. Without getting shot.

"Decoy. Three seconds," Gideon said in her ear as if reading her mind. "On your left."

"Immunity should be respected," she said. Two feet between them, arm's reach. An electric buzz hummed in her blood, firing her muscles. "But it doesn't mean it can't be violated."

Gideon whistled on her left, drawing the Russian's aim.

The guy pivoted, redirecting the SIG Sauer. Maddox snatched the muzzle. She torqued it counterclockwise with her left hand while driving the heel of her right palm into the inside of his wrist, popping the gun free of his grip. His phalanx bones snapped, with his finger caught on the trigger. At almost the same time, she kicked his groin, smashing her shin up into his crotch.

He crumpled to the blacktop beside the rear wheel, holding his privates. Poor guy wouldn't even need tear gas to stay put.

Reece belted around the corner in the GMC Yukon, tires squealing on the hot asphalt, and slammed into park behind the white SUV. Gideon threw open the rear door on the driver's side of the Russian car, grabbed Matthews's upper body, and hauled him out.

The asset's head hung forward, chin to chest, a sheet of black hair curtaining his face.

Maddox tossed the SIG into the front seat of the white SUV, stepped over the Russian writhing on the ground, and hustled to their vehicle.

The scent of melting rubber peppered the air.

Maddox climbed into the back seat, opened the other door for Gideon, and helped him load Matthews inside, tugging the unconscious man by the shoulders. Once Gideon hopped in, sandwiching Matthews between them, Reece cut into the snarl of traffic. Horns blared and another car screeched to a halt. He made a sharp right out of the congested artery and gunned it down a clear road.

She was shaking from the high of the retrieval, the rush flooding her system, but the hardest part was yet to come—getting inside the target's head and figuring out the right buttons to push.

Cole Matthews was slumped over, head on her shoulder. She tilted his chin up and pushed his hair aside. A sudden knot in her chest forced all the air from her body as her hand fell from his face.

For a staggering moment, the shock couldn't have been more brutal if she'd been blindsided by a speeding bus.

The world warped in a shattering upheaval. Sent her careening into the impossible.

It couldn't be. Yet it was.

Longer hair, but the same pristine black of a starless sky. Tattoos befitting a killer on his arms—those were new. His body a marvel of lean muscle honed by dedication. The jagged scar added a savage touch to his brutally handsome face, but without a doubt, it was *her* Nikolai.

"Maddox," Gideon said, jump-starting her brain. "What's wrong?"

"It's him." Her voice was a ghost of a whisper. "Nikolai…" His name tasted of bittersweet ash on her tongue and words failed her.

"Your fiancé?" Gideon peered at him.

Her best friend had seen the picture in her locker many, many times, heard the name—first name only—although he didn't know the whole story. Recognition ignited in his blue eyes.

"Holy shit." Gideon recoiled with an uncharacteristic crack in his composure. "I thought he was dead."

The knot twisted. "So did I."

SHADY OAK, VIRGINIA
3:47 P.M. EDT

Cole stirred to consciousness, his brain swimming in murky water. He opened his eyes.

A blur of golden light flickered like a meteor shower. Maddox's face floated toward him through the buttery haze of dancing light.

Beautiful.

She knelt, looking up at him, and pressed a palm to his cheek. Solid and warm. So real.

Too real.

His vision came into sharp focus and his brain cleared in a mad rush of blood to his head. He flinched as if struck by a high-voltage cattle prod.

"Maddox." His voice was raspy. It sounded as if his

larynx had been raked over gravel, but it was a wonder he could breathe. The air in the room had turned dense as mud. "You're real?"

"I could ask you the same."

Pain slashed through her eyes, faster than lightning splitting the darkness, before it was replaced with a distant emptiness.

He went to reach for her, suddenly that naive twenty-four-year-old fool again, but couldn't move his wrists and ankles.

Shit. He was bound to a chair. A steel chair that was bolted to the floor.

What the fu—

"I gave you an IV drip of a special cocktail to help combat whatever mickey the Russians used to drug you." Maddox unscrewed the cap of a water bottle and tipped it to his lips. His Buddha necklace, clean and sparkling, was wrapped around her wrist like a bracelet. "But your tongue probably feels like sandpaper."

He guzzled the water, eyeing his surroundings. Sunlight filtered through trees into a first-floor window, casting shadows in the left-side corner of the small room. The unfurnished bedroom faced south.

"Better?" She wiped his mouth with her thumb.

Standing, she eased back into the piquant sunlight. Maddox, in the flesh. He took her in with such vivid clarity, his eye sockets burned.

Time had twisted him into a monster while sculpting her into a masterpiece.

Her light-brown skin was smoother, the taper of her waist narrower. A tank top hugged fuller breasts. Those striking eyes, the color of the Bering Sea in winter, were clearer yet deeper.

She was *more* of everything that'd once brought him to heel. He'd been an eager-to-please puppy who'd have chased after her into highway traffic.

He caught himself staring, the sight of her ripping a tender scab from his heart. She'd nearly killed him once. If he wasn't careful, he wouldn't survive her a second time.

"What happened to the Russians?" Best to attack a rattlesnake before it shook its tail. He yanked at the flex-cuffs and sensed someone move behind him. "Why am I restrained?"

Two men strode into his periphery, coming up on either side of him. Fit and lean, they carried themselves with self-assured, stealthy gaits. An edge radiated from them that had diddly to do with the big-ass guns in their shoulder rigs.

A white heat filled Cole's chest, rising until he tasted his anger.

Ex-military, if he had to guess. Some brand of special forces, but they didn't give off the overbearing fetor of mercenaries.

Both guys eyeballed him, sizing him up. Pure posturing. They'd already done the once-over while he was unconscious and had appraised him as a potential threat. Hence the restraints.

"You took down four armed, well-trained men in close quarters," said the man with dark hair, wearing a ball cap. "We wanted to make sure you could tell the difference between friend and foe when you woke up disoriented and defensive."

"From where I'm sitting," Cole said, cutting his gaze to Maddox and ignoring her muscled motley crew, "Frick and Frack don't look too friendly."

"That's Reece." She nodded to the dark-haired guy. "Gideon." She pointed to the pretty-boy blond.

Frick and Frack would do. Cole wasn't in the market for bosom buddies who had a penchant for bondage.

"They helped me get you away from the Russians." Her gaze was direct, assessing. Her stance tense like she balanced on a tightrope over an abyss. "Why are they after you?"

Better questions: How had she found him? Why did she have backup? Why was she questioning him while he was restrained?

Fate was playing a cruel joke on him today.

Cole shrugged. "I guess the Bratva in the Motherland heard I was alive and pulled strings to have the pleasure of my company. The Lazarus trick seems to have put me in high demand."

"They heard all the way in Russia while I've been clueless right here in the Beltway." Hurt glinted in her eyes, but her tone remained cool. "I guess the only thing worse than being the last to know is never knowing."

The air stuck in his chest. They'd been as close as two people ever could be. He'd lived for her, killed for her, and, in a million ways, died for her.

He unlocked his lungs, drawing a breath, and shoved the cloying memories into his mental bunker. Needing to get a handle on this situation, he dropped his gaze and caught the gleam of his necklace on her wrist. The beads glimmered like a lifeline just out of reach.

"Would you mind returning my prayer beads? They have a calming effect. And how about freeing one of my hands so I can scratch an itch?"

"Tell me where you itch." Her bedroom eyes held him, her butter-soft words tickling his underbelly. "I'll scratch for you."

His mind went tailspinning into the gutter, which was inevitable if he was near Maddox. Proof you could be attracted to someone you hated, but it didn't take long for him to course-correct his thoughts with her armed sentries in the room and flex-cuffs chafing his wrists.

"And when did you become a monk?" She fingered the beads. "From what I recall, you had the most ferocious appetites."

"I saw the light after the woman I was going to marry almost got me killed." His tone was sharp enough to sever a carotid artery. "A near-death experience can make a man turn to prayer."

An indefinable look settled on her face, not giving anything away. She watched him as one would an adversary. Her question had been loaded, and he'd taken the bait. She was poking around for something. But what?

Nine years, two weeks, and a heat wave since he'd last seen Maddox, and she was on a fishing expedition while failing to give him his due.

No apology. No explanation for why she'd ruined them. No tears of joy and I-missed-you kiss, although he'd have to be suicidal to let those lips touch his. Not one irrefutable iota she gave a damn he was alive, except for whatever she wanted from him.

Oh, he was way beyond ticked and was so pissed that

he was shaking. Hell, he wanted to shake *her*, maybe even strangle her. His restraints might be necessary, or anger management. Anything but this fucktastic vacation.

"How did you find me?" He glanced at Frick, who tipped up the bill of his cap. Frack leaned against the doorjamb chewing gum, hands in his pockets, looking as if his body ran ten degrees lower than Maddox's reptilian temperature. "What am I doing here, wherever 'here' is?"

"We have a situation," she said. "Our employer needs your help with a problem."

Here it comes—the shitstorm Cole needed to avoid. Aside from his job, he dodged involvement, had no attachments, and was resolved to serve his sentence in peace.

Getting ensnared in another soul-shattering Maddox mess was not on his wish list.

A bitter laugh bubbled out of him, and he leveled a glare at her. "Who's your employer, and what's the problem?"

He wanted the answer as much as he wanted a snake-bite in the balls.

From the looks of her, he was about to get one anyway. Maddox was coiled, tail rattling, fangs bared and poised to strike his gonads—then something in her shifted. Shuttering her gaze, she flattened her mouth in a grim line and folded her arms.

"I need to speak to him alone," she said to Frick and Frack. The men exchanged glances and gave her a questioning look. "Two minutes. Please."

They nodded and left, closing the door. Heavy footsteps drew away out of earshot.

She crossed the room and crouched between his legs. "I never wanted you restrained, but they insisted." The note of sincerity from her struck a sensitive chord in him he despised.

Holding his gaze, she patted down his legs, working toward his shins.

Her hand froze on the hilt of his knife. "Nice to see some things stay the same."

She wriggled his pant leg up, pulled the Ka-Bar, and cut the flex-cuffs on his ankles. Casting a furtive glance toward the door, she hustled behind his chair and freed his hands.

Cole leapt out of the chair and whirled, pinning her against the wall with a hand on her throat, not hard enough to hurt her, only to compel a straight answer from her fork-tongued mouth. But an electric frisson skipped over his skin, stilling him. That magnetic pull to her revived. No matter how much time had passed, it'd never been extinguished.

Talk about fucked up.

"Don't crowd me," she said low and controlled, not a flicker of fear in her fiery eyes.

"Or what?"

Tapping on his inner thigh drew his gaze down. She had the tip of his Ka-Bar pointed at his groin. He glanced lower, noticing her shoes.

She wore black tactical field boots. The cushy, expensive kind, same as Frick and Frack.

Who had she become? "What's going on, Maddox? Why are you with those men?"

"We don't have much time before they come back."

Her gaze darted to the door. "You won't be able to take the three of us."

The words had an unexpected sting. "That's the first time you said *us* not meaning you and me." Damn, had that been his out-loud voice?

An unguarded look broke on her face, vulnerable and somber. "You're the one who left and never looked back."

She was the one who had wronged *him*. Every action he'd taken since had been justified. Still, there was a pathetic niggle of regret.

He forced his grip to slacken and stepped back.

She flipped the matte-black blade in her hand like a badass, handle pointing to him. A shimmer of pride and a hint of alarm seeped through him.

He took the knife and shoved it in the ankle sheath. As he stood upright, she draped the beads around his neck, fingers caressing his collarbone, and handed him the key to his bike.

"I had them get your motorcycle. It's parked on the west side of the house. Go out through the window. Lay low until nightfall, somewhere the Russians won't find you." Honest concern shone in her eyes. "Then come to my place. My address is written on a piece of paper in your pocket. You'll be safe there and I'll explain everything."

She pressed her palms to his chest, her expression softening. He couldn't help soaking in the bittersweet familiarity of her touch and the intimacy in her gaze. Emotions he'd buried in an unmarked grave in DC, where his previous life had ended, resurrected with a ridiculous kick.

"I need your help. It's a matter of life or death.

Please, come." Her emphatic tone tugged at him, and he needed a swift boot heel to the head to snap out of it. "I'll answer any question."

"Any?" Just like that, she had him hooked. For him, *any* condensed to one. Why had she betrayed him?

She squeezed her eyes shut for a breath, the faintest quiver running through her, and nodded before glancing at the door. "Hurry, before they come back."

He hesitated. Would she be okay alone with them?

It was insanity to be concerned for her. Then again, she'd always triggered his protective instincts. At one time, his entire world had revolved around Maddox, and her safety had been more important than his own.

He would've sworn by now he was immune to her, but she was an incurable disease out of remission and might put him six feet under for real.

He gritted his teeth against the prickle of sentiment. She'd be fine—shed her skin and slither out of trouble.

He unlatched the window, opened it, and climbed out. The small house appeared to be isolated in the woods. For a heartbeat, he stood quiet, listening to be sure neither man had wandered outside, then ran. West side, hugging the wall, through grass, where he found his bike.

Frick and Frack would be alerted as soon as he cranked the engine.

Unease kept nagging at him. Fool that he was, he couldn't help hoping they wouldn't take it out on Maddox.

———————   ———————

The roar of the motorcycle split the air. Emotion seesawed through Maddox. She clenched her jaw and ignored her churning stomach. This asset needed delicate development.

Jeez. Did the term *asset* apply here, considering he'd been the love of her life?

She slammed the safe house window closed and locked it.

Reece opened the door, entering the room. "Are you sure this is the right play?"

Nikolai Reznikov was alive, back from the dead with a new name and life, and he wanted nothing to do with her. The red-hot poker of such an unfathomable reality jabbed between her ribs, leaving her unsure of anything. So she was following instinct. Her gut had never steered her wrong.

"Positive." She took her blazer and holstered gun from Gideon, who'd trailed Reece inside. "As soon as I mentioned our employer, he iced over. Would've gone better if you two had listened to me and not zip-tied him to a chair."

"Based on the carnage I saw in the café," Reece said, "we had a tiger by the tail."

She'd taken down guys twice her size, but her combat skills were useless with Nikolai—Cole—whatever the hell he was calling himself. Nine years ago, he'd been deadly.

Today, he looked sixty-nine shades of lethal.

"Your history with him is complicated," Gideon said, "and things ended badly. You hadn't seen him in years. No telling what he was capable of besides extreme violence."

The walls pressed in on her. Cole obviously despised

her enough to let her grieve and suffer with the torment of thinking she was responsible for his death.

Reece pulled off his cap and raked a hand through his scruffy dark hair. "After the Russians jacked him, he would've been geared to butcher first and take names later."

Okay, caution had been the right call. Cole was furious, hurt, defensive. Hated her.

After baiting him, she'd seen the loathing in his eyes. He'd never forgiven her and might not even help her. Not that she was entitled to it, after what she had done to him and his family.

"How can you be sure he'll show tonight?" Reece asked.

Cole had curled his hand around her throat as though he meant to strangle her, but then his touch had softened. A different kind of spark had kindled in his eyes. There was so much more simmering beneath his rage.

"He has questions only I can answer. He'll come."

And when he did, she wouldn't smell like an old lady slathered in arthritis cream.

Reece rubbed his chin. "What if you're wrong?"

Beaded sweat chilled on her skin. She couldn't afford to be wrong. "You usually have my back, Reece. What's with the twenty questions?" And the utter lack of faith in her judgment.

"If I didn't have your back, your ex would still be strapped to that chair. Not out of our custody, on his bike. The DGB is going to grill us on what—"

"I'll explain to Dad." A nickname for the DGB they used with affection and respect, albeit never to his face.

"I put a roving bug on Cole's phone." The bug would allow her to activate the microphone on his cell. She could listen in on his calls, remote eavesdrop on any conversation within the vicinity of the phone. And if he tried to turn his cell off, the malware would mimic a shutdown while keeping the phone on. "We can stay abreast of his plans and keep him on a short leash."

"We'll give him a three-mile tether and stay off his shadow while you get Dad's blessing on this COA," Reece said. Any course of action that impacted the mission this much needed to be sanctioned.

Fear of another failure clawed up her chest, but she wouldn't yield an atom to self-doubt. She'd harness the stress bubbling in her core instead, use it like a battery charging.

"Easier to keep our finger on the pulse of this if we monitor his phone," Gideon added.

True. Maddox handed him the handheld device that had the roving bug app. "Don't let him spot you. If he doesn't come to me or tries to run, I'll go to him and use a coercive approach."

Which would be an absolute last-ditch recourse, after she'd exhausted every other possibility. Cole was not the type of man to bend under intimidation.

04

After they landed, Aleksander slid into the passenger's seat of the rental car that welcomed them on the tarmac. Val loaded the packed rifle and their gear in the trunk and started the vehicle. They'd cleared customs on the plane, no waiting in lines, no hassle with luggage being searched. The privileges of flying private were a necessity with their jam-packed schedule.

"How will I do it?" Aleksander asked, testing Val, ensuring he was switchblade-sharp.

Determining the *how* was always the hardest part. The slightest miscalculation meant the difference between success and failure.

"Bodyguards surround Callahan at all times and he's rarely exposed in the open for more than five seconds," Val said. "The front of his house has a porte cochere, providing cover as he leaves and gets into a chauffeured car with bulletproof windows. Security is too tight at the warehouse where he runs day-to-day operations."

His son's thorough assessment of the target was spot-on. "Continue."

"Callahan goes to his casino in Fishtown every night, where the car is left unattended. You'll do it there. Outside." Val punched the location of the casino into the navigation system without waiting for confirmation. He was so self-assured—and quite correct.

"You memorized the address?"

"Of course. All the details on each target."

Aleksander schooled his face, smothering a grim smile, his soul aching. His son was a fine man. Resilient, smart, capable of handling the unpleasantness of the necessary things ahead with focus and a cold tenacity.

His mother and sister would've both been proud. Anguish washed over him so hard and fast he fought not to gasp, but he embraced the pain. His grief gave him strength, his sorrow fortified his resolve to never stop until he got payback.

ARLINGTON, VIRGINIA
4:55 P.M. EDT

Handling himself in a physical fight, even when outnumbered, was one of Cole's gifts.

To get trapped in a disastrous scenario he couldn't overcome, then to be rescued by a person who suddenly needed his help—that was destiny giving him a chance for closure. Or fate, probing to see if he was a glutton for more pain.

Sure as shit wasn't a coincidence.

He stormed through his town house, throwing clothes, technical gear, and his gun into a backpack. His body was strung tight, wired to spring into action.

Daring to go home even for five minutes was risky, but if the Russians were still looking for him, they would've placed their bets on his workplace. Going home would be stupid, and they knew he was no fool. So he'd taken the chance, armed with the knowledge of a rooftop exit no one would expect, and parked his bike two blocks over.

He took out his cell and called Linda at Rubicon. No one was better at digging up dirt on someone. "Hey, it's Cole. Do me a favor, and I'll bring you a box of the chocolates you love."

"What do you need, sugar?" she rasped, sounding as if she'd spent the last thirty years smoking exhaust fumes from the tailpipe of a Harley.

He slipped a blade in his waistband sheath, replacing the one he had lost in the café. "It seems the Russians are looking for me. Might have to put your ear to the ground for 'Nikolai Reznikov.'" Nobody at Rubicon knew his birth name. He'd been burned trusting the wrong woman before, but Linda had been like a mom to him the last few years and he was short on options. "Verify the threat is real."

Fool me once, shame on me. Fool me twice, I might have to bury Maddox if she orchestrated this. Right after I get answers.

"Also run a background check on Maddox Kinkade." He'd longed to look her up during more sleepless nights than he could count, the ghost of her plaguing him. Every time, he'd been too chickenshit to face the agony of knowing. Now that Maddox had opened the door and shoved him across the threshold, there was no turning back. "I need it super fast."

"It's slow here. I'll put the team on Kinkade. We'll be quick, discreet. How deep to dig?"

"Make it thorough. If you hit any walls, go around them, down to who she's fucking."

Linda cleared her throat. "Pretty deep, sugar. I'll get to it. Never heard you so fired up."

That's what Maddox did to him—crept under his skin and fired him up hot as napalm.

"Thanks, Linda." He clicked off, his blood simmering, his thoughts spinning.

Maddox had killed their chance at happiness. He'd left her behind, so pissed at her betrayal he couldn't set eyes on her but he had also needed to protect her. He'd been haunted by her every day since. What he wouldn't give to be free, to purge her from his thoughts, and his heart.

To extinguish her from his soul.

He had to see her, ensure she was safe after cutting him loose, and get answers for closure. That was all. If he got caught up in her mess, allowed himself to get sucked back in for any reason, it would be a one-way ticket from limbo straight to hell.

GRAY BOX HEADQUARTERS, NORTHERN VIRGINIA
5:20 P.M. EDT

A cold vein of anger pulsed in Maddox's head.

She'd been set up by her own. Cole Matthews turning out to be Nikolai Reznikov was so far beyond the realm of coincidence, it landed smack-dab in the quagmire of the perverse.

Granted, he looked different. His *rebel with a cause* charm had given way to something savage. He had a barely leashed readiness for violence running through him like a live wire. But no matter how different he appeared, if there'd been one clear photo, she would've recognized his face. The DGB had wanted her going in blind.

Was Castle in on it? Would've taken elephant-sized balls for him to look her in the eyes and send her off clueless.

Maddox swiped her badge through one of the electronic turnstiles on either side of the metal detector in the Gray Box lobby. Amanda Woodrow, who'd picked her up from the safe house, was at her side, wearing a trademark pantsuit that telegraphed she didn't take fashion too seriously. Maddox had recruited Amanda from the Drug Enforcement Agency after a joint operation, where she had worked under the guise of Homeland Security. The DGB didn't waste any time adding Amanda to his prized collection of flawed elite. He had the vision to tap those once misemployed or disavowed and put them to better use.

They'd become close, fast friends, being the only two women in the Gray Box with operational field experience. Although Amanda had requested desk duty as an analyst after her son, Jackson, was born, that instant bond of mutual understanding had never gone away. As a woman, smaller than the others in black ops and most of the baddies she encountered, she had to be faster and sharper and work twice as hard physically to hold her own.

Undoubtedly, Amanda sensed something awry in the uncommon thick silence between them but knew not to ask about a mission outside her purview.

Maddox lifted a stiff hand hello to the two armed plainclothes security guards behind the curved, richly veined white marble desk. They gave curt nods. Amanda's heels struck the polished concrete floor in a staccato like gunfire, echoing in the lobby.

An iris scan gave them access to the elevator, and Maddox slapped the button for the operations floor. Green laser beams from a state-of-the-art TSCM— technical surveillance countermeasure—scanner swept for unauthorized devices, from personal cell phones to bugs. Their encrypted cells that they used in the field were allowed in the building, but no mobile phone functioned in the subterranean facility.

Once cleared, the elevator lowered in a smooth motion toward the sixth-floor sublevel, a bunker so protected it could withstand a nuclear explosion. Working here, being a Gray Box officer, had been everything for Maddox. It was the sole thing of consequence in her life. Until today.

Her temples throbbed, the slightest quiver ticking in her leg at the thought of him. *Cole Matthews*. The man was an epoch-making juggernaut who had defined her life. BNE—Before Nikolai Era. ANE—After Nikolai Era. Now was the fricking Age of Cole.

The elevator hummed to a stop, and the doors whispered open.

"When this mission is done," Amanda said, "we'll grab a glass of wine and talk."

Maddox had been the shoulder Amanda leaned on after her boyfriend had dumped her at eight months pregnant and again three years ago when her son was diagnosed with leukemia. Maddox had stepped up as her birth partner and become auntie to little Jax, but she was nowhere near ready to divulge the secrets buried inside her.

Amanda elbowed her. "Or we could just drink and skip the heavy talk."

As usual, her friend read her too well. Amanda flashed a supportive smile, making her look ten years younger than forty. The woman never seemed to age, could eat anything without packing on the pounds, and had girl-next-door freckles dusted across the bridge of her nose— attributes Amanda credited to the genetics on her mother's side. But it was her untiring rainbow optimism, regardless of how harsh the storm, that left Maddox in awe.

She nodded her thanks to Amanda and marched down the carpeted walkway separating the Intelligence side of Operations from Black Ops. Silvery-blue partition walls lined the path. Chatter from the nine TVs in Intel tuned to news networks from CNN to Al Jazeera faded into the background.

She couldn't wrap her head around why the DGB had set her up. The humiliation of being treated like a mark, denied professional courtesy, pissed her off enough to spit railroad spikes, but she rallied an iron demeanor. Shrouded the wrinkles of angry disappointment behind a calm veil.

Janet Price, the DGB's executive assistant and right hand, came around the corner. "Maddox, glad I found you. Reece is on the phone for you." The middle-aged brunette had the disposition of warm syrup and a voice to match. She went out of her way to take care of every-one, from pet sitting when they deployed to bringing in scrumptious home-cooked snacks.

"Mind if I take it at your desk? I need to see the big guy right after."

"Sure. Castle is in with him, but you can go in once they're done."

Great. Kill two birdies with one stone. Maddox steamrolled past her, gunning for the combat zone. The administrative offices divided the expansive floor into two separate sections: operations on one side, and the common areas, such as the conference room, break room, gym, soundproofed range, and supply where they stored their gear and gadgets, on the other.

Sybil Parker sashayed by, working her Louboutins and chic body-hugging dress with serious prowess. She gave Maddox the once-over with those shark eyes. The woman stayed in motion, circling, sniffing for blood in the water. Put the great white in *Jaws* to shame.

Parker was the one person in the Gray Box the DGB hadn't handpicked and couldn't fire. Only the DNI, the director of national intelligence, could touch the insider threat monitor. Her sole responsibility was to keep an eye on personnel, communications, and networks, ensuring everything stayed aboveboard and no one misused access.

Every government agency had ITMs. Considering the Gray Box was plugged into the networks of the CIA, FBI, and every other alphabet-soup agency, Parker's position carried hefty weight. She knew it, too, and needled the DGB whenever possible, igniting epic battles.

Maddox hurried to Janet's desk and picked up the line with Reece on hold. "What's up?"

"He's verifying the Russian threat is credible and running a background check on you."

Cole had resources to tap. Not good. Meant he wouldn't need her for a safe place to stay.

"I think you're right that he'll come to you. He wants his investigator to find out who you're fucking."

So Cole still cared about her on a primal level. Even if it was only a testosterone-fueled, territorial one. "Anything comes up, any issues, bring it straight to me."

"We've got your back. Always. But cover our asses and get Dad's blessing."

Castle opened the door, leaving the big guy's office.

She lined up her thoughts like ammo in a magazine. "Will do. Got to go."

Meeting Castle's gaze, she searched his face but found the usual stony blockade. Then the oddest thing happened. He smiled, throwing any read on him into left field.

"How did it go?" His voice was off, too light, too airy. "Did you get lucky?"

"In a *Twilight Zone* way, yes." She kept her tone calm. "You took those shitty photos of him, didn't you?"

He dragged a hand over his bald head, the one telltale he was uneasy. "Yeah. I did."

Castle didn't know how empty she'd been for near a decade, but he'd witnessed the Reznikov train wreck, knew what she'd lost. She nursed her simmering anger but reined in the urge to punch him. Losing her temper, regardless how righteous, was a luxury she didn't have.

"That's low," she said, level, controlled. "Even for you."

"We all have our trials. I chose to follow orders. No matter how difficult." Castle folded his arms, flexing big bear muscles. Not the cuddly teddy-bear type either. "Buck up. The only easy day was yesterday."

"Are you ever going to stop being a dick?"

"Yep, got it marked on my calendar. It's the day you stop being a candy-ass."

Painting on a careful smile, she said, "Thanks for the heart-to-heart, Castle."

"Anytime, buttercup."

Sad truth, that was probably the most intimate chat they'd had in years. He kept everyone at a distance. Something ugly had happened to him on his last mission as a Navy SEAL, something so painful it led him to the Gray Box. Something ugly and painful had led most of them here.

She pivoted and strode into the DGB's office.

"Close the door. Take a seat," Bruce Sanborn said from behind his black glass-top desk.

Her boss had the look of a natural-born covert operative—hunky build, above-average height, a face resembling someone you knew or wanted to, but no one you quite remembered. The perfect camouflage of ordinariness.

She shut the office door and sat.

"Castle opposed my decision not to tell you Cole Matthews's true identity." Sanborn leaned back in his leather chair. The gray sprinkled along the sides of his dark hair, the patience in his warm brown eyes, the timeless bow ties he wore, gave him a sense of elegant wisdom.

But she questioned his judgment this one time. "Why was the truth kept from me, sir?"

"There wasn't much information in your personnel file on your association to the Reznikov family, besides a brief liaison with Nikolai." His low, gritty tone and relaxed demeanor echoed his managerial philosophy: authority speaks, but real power whispers and carries a bazooka. "I squeezed Castle to see what he knew. Discovered your file has gaping holes. It appears your relationship had been more than brief and casual. That you feel responsible for what happened to the asset."

She held her boss's calculating gaze, making sure her eyes gave away nothing. "I am responsible." She would've done anything for Cole, anything to be with him, to silence her father and prove him wrong. And she ended up destroying any chance they might've had.

Sanborn hit a button, frosting the glass of his office to an opaque silver. "Castle gave me the impression your prior connection to the asset was…rather intense."

Intense? A delicate, cautious word that didn't skim the surface of the bond they'd shared—like calling a hurricane a breeze.

She gave a subtle nod.

"It's my job to know my operatives and understand in which conditions you each work best. I was concerned you'd overthink things, allow emotion to cloud your judgment. But if I tossed you in the deep end, blindfolded, instinct and experience would take over. You would swim. I was looking out for your best interest. Telling you would've hurt you out there."

Sanborn's keen attention to detail and no-nonsense approach kept his operatives breathing. His shining attribute was loyalty. The welfare of his people came first, everything else second. He protected, guided, and sometimes reprimanded—as any good dad would.

"I understand." And she did, although she didn't like it.

"Where do we stand with him?"

"The Russians had grabbed and drugged him, but we squirreled him away to the safe house. There were concerns about the danger he posed. We restrained him, but that, combined with the two other swinging dicks in the room," she said respectfully, assured he appreciated her candor, "caused him to clam up when I broached the subject of needing his help. So I cut him loose."

Sanborn steepled his fingers, studying her.

She clasped her hands in her lap, wearing confidence like armor. "Strong-arming him won't work. Appealing to his conscience with a plea about the greater good won't persuade him. I need to soften him, in private. Take a personal approach and mend a broken bridge first."

It was true, but she neglected to mention how she'd have to give Cole what she suspected he wanted most. An explanation and an apology—to open a vein and let him see her bleed. If he didn't believe she'd also suffered and been hurt in this, he would never help her.

"I asked him to come to my apartment later so we can talk. I offered him a safe place to stay. If he's going to help us, he must feel it's his choice."

"How are you monitoring him?"

"Roving bug on his phone. Gideon and Reece are on him. Three-mile tether."

He gave a slow nod as if mulling over her words, weighing options, listing pros and cons. "Your approach has the potential to be very effective. Intimacy breeds a sense of responsibility and trust. How you accomplish that tonight, I leave to your discretion."

Sleeping with an asset wasn't condoned nor discouraged. The reality was it sometimes happened. It was only when an operative forgot sex was a tool and became emotionally involved that things became complicated and objectivity flew out of the window. Since Cole still had a regrettable hold on her, sex would prove ruinous. While he was an asset, she couldn't sleep with him, no matter how much she was tempted. Their chemistry had once been incendiary, and they hadn't been able to keep their hands off each other, going at it two or three times in one day.

She crossed her legs at the abrupt, stupid tingle in her thighs. After the op was finished, they could reconnect with no holds barred, explore the possibilities. Maybe find a way to forgive.

"Why is the Russian embassy after him? He's an American citizen."

"He was born here, but his parents were Russian nationals and filed the forms to have his Russian citizenship recognized. Cole must've done something pretty big to upset the mob there."

Nikolai had wiped out the Bratva transplanted to DC in a single day, making headlines, spawning Cole. Probably ticked off powerful people in Siberia who wanted his head on a pike.

Guilt pricked her conscience, but she swatted it away as one would a riled hornet, certain it would snap back far more viciously later.

"Putin's power is founded on both his links to organized crime and the way he rose through the ranks of the former KGB. The mafia must have called in a favor to get Putin to pull strings. If Cole helps us, I'll do what I can to fix his problem with the Russians."

If anyone could, it was Sanborn. He'd been known to pull off a miracle or two akin to parting the Red Sea. "How did you find out he was alive?"

"You're now cleared to access his file. Dig as deep as you want into his current life. The CliffsNotes version is his mother died last year and he went to the funeral."

His mom was kind, loving, would've made a perfect MIL if Maddox hadn't blown it.

"He kept his distance at the cemetery, never took off his helmet, but the FBI was crawling all over the place. Followed him. Loaded photos in a database of known associates."

"How did he drop on our radar?"

"Willow found him."

Overachiever Willow Harper. Tightly wound loner, analyst, techie—pure savant.

"Willow learned about the auction to sell smallpox by hacking into the dark web on her time off. When she was researching ways to get us in, she went through the database of associates for the invited arms dealers. She drilled deep for connections, found Cole Matthews—a man with no history. She ran his picture through facial recognition and got a hit on Nikolai, Ilya Reznikov's brother. Once she learned his true identity, his prior association to you popped up from your personnel file."

"Great work on Harper's part." She controlled the quaver of sarcasm in her voice. "Is this op the reason you rushed my assignment in Iran?" The accelerated timeline had forced Maddox to push her asset before she was ready. "Sent Alistair and Ares to extract me?"

"Recalling you was the best COA, despite the loss of your asset. Especially considering the Russians' last-minute involvement we picked up in SIGINT traffic."

If she'd had one more week to complete the assignment, her asset would still be alive, and she would've gotten the data they'd needed.

"An hour ago, Willow intercepted chatter on the darknet. Each arms dealer was sent an auction passcode via messenger. Convince Cole to get the code from Ilya." He looked at his watch. "The auction begins in fifty-two hours. It's imperative we get our hands on that bioweapon."

Or thousands could die—here, possibly abroad. "I understand what's at stake."

"Maddox, I know this op is a challenge for you. Cole was someone you loved, hoped to marry, somehow wronged. Thought him dead. Then on top of all that, you suffered a late-term miscarriage."

Her throat cinched. She tried to swallow against the dry knot, but it only tightened.

She'd fallen so hard and deep for Cole, the kind of love you go all in on. After believing he'd died, she'd failed to hang on to the only piece of him left, the child he didn't know about. Somewhere along the way, she'd lost herself.

Checking every red flag of body language, Maddox disconnected, like pulling a plug, and wiped her mind blank. She willed herself to mirror Sanborn's unflinching composure. He was gauging her ability to handle this emotional powder keg without blowing up the mission.

"The strongest steel is tempered in the hottest fire," she said, quoting him.

He softened, flashing an apologetic smile. "If you feel the least bit conflicted, I'd say it's understandable, considering. It'll be tough to get close to Cole without getting entangled."

Try impossible. "I assure you, I'm capable of doing my job."

"Glad to hear it." He took on that protective, fatherly expression she knew well. Despite being in his late forties, he looked far too young and vital to be her dad. She often wondered why he didn't spend less time in the office and a little having a social life. He'd make some lucky lady a great partner. "But if you encounter any hiccups, you can come to me. I won't view a setback as a failure in this."

Nodding, a little choked up at his support, she had no intention of ever taking him up on such an offer. Running to him with a problem meant she couldn't handle the situation, and that wasn't going to happen.

"There is one more thing. Don't blow your cover. Based on the asset's psychological profile, he's unlikely to cooperate with this agency or any federal organization."

"That's an understatement." Cole would rather swallow rusty razor blades than help the CIA, FBI, you name it. As the son of a Russian crime boss, his family had been endlessly harassed. He'd had a disdain for law enforcement ingrained in him at an early age.

"Maintaining your cover as a buyer for Helios is key," Sanborn said.

The front of Helios Importing and Exporting provided a solid cover for their constant travel, the fleet of vehicles, and the tricked-out helicopter Sanborn had squeezed from the DNI.

Except that Cole had a gift for smelling lies, a survival skill cultivated out of necessity, growing up around gangsters. Even as well trained as Maddox was, he would sniff one out from her. "Leveling with him, being honest—"

"Honest?" Sanborn's shrewd eyes narrowed, tone going quiet. "With a man who let you believe he was dead, moved on, without a word to you in nine years? He isn't worth the gamble of honesty."

A dull knife twisted in her heart, but she didn't so much as flinch.

Sanborn strode around his desk and sat on the edge. "Your cover is the best safeguard you have." With a gentle smile, he leaned in and put a reassuring hand on her shoulder. "If you're honest, he's less likely to help you and more likely to endanger you. Trust me. I can't stress enough the tightrope you have to walk here." His compassionate manner was a comfort. "Mend the bridge. Only get as close as necessary to persuade him and don't blow your cover."

This wasn't just about her duty, safeguarding national security and saving lives, although each mission drove her with the crack of a bullwhip. Sanborn had plucked her from a floundering desk job at the Agency, given her a purpose, groomed her, believed in her, forged her into one of his best. She owed him nothing less than her all.

She owed them both a win.

"I'll get it done, sir."

05

Val drove past Callahan's Navigator, parked in a VIP spot directly in front of the casino. The area buzzed with constant traffic, millennials dressed to party and gamble through the night. Light casino security milled about, derelict in their vigilance. Val parked the sedan on the edge of the loading zone at the far end of the circular drive as Aleksander had instructed.

They got out in tandem. Val grabbed the hard-shell golf travel case that had the rifle, tossed Aleksander the key fob, and went off to execute his part in the main parking lot. Aleksander hiked the lightweight backpack containing a brick of Semtex explosives on his shoulder.

A warm breeze off the river carried the stench of urine. A ghost moon was rising in the north. Striding past a row of taxis the color of crushed daffodils, Aleksander glided as if cloaked in shadows. He strolled into the VIP parking section, surveilling the area. No eyes on him.

He hit the alarm button on the key fob.

The high-pitched *dee-doo dee-doo* siren sounded, drawing outside attention away from him. Whipping the bag off his shoulder, he dropped to the blistering pavement and slid underneath the Navigator. He clicked the remote once more, killing the noise. The fit beneath the undercarriage was cramped, giving him inches to work within, but he was slender and had maneuvered in spaces more confined than this.

He removed the wired explosives from the backpack. His sweat-dampened hair stuck to his forehead. Perspiration gathered in his armpits, running in ribbons down his long-sleeved shirt, his clothing clinging in the boiling air, but he ignored the distractions. Singular focus.

Attaching the explosive device to the chassis near the gas tank took less than a minute. He'd done it so many times, he could've been blindfolded. He hit the alarm button on the remote key again, and the shrill sound pierced the air once more. As the gazes of everyone followed the noise, he scooted out from under the vehicle. A quick brush of his sweaty clothes, and he strode toward the sedan.

Val intersected his path. "Black Dodge pickup. Third row. Sixth in."

Aleksander handed his son the key fob and detonator. "If I'm not at the rendezvous by 0900, go ahead without me. You can handle the next target. I'll catch up."

Val nodded.

A casino security guard standing beside their sedan said, "Whose car is this? It can't be parked here."

"Sorry," Val said with no trace of a Slavic accent. "I'm an Uber driver. I was looking for my customer."

Aleksander hung back until the guard had moved on and then exchanged one last look with his son before heading into the main parking lot. He located the Dodge pickup that Val had hotwired for him, the engine running. He jumped in the cabin of the truck, resting a hand on the rifle case, and spotted his son moving into a position with lines of sight to the Navigator and the front doors of the busy casino.

Val would wait for Callahan to get into the car and clear the casino before detonating the bomb. Amateurs rushed, making careless mistakes. Val would be patient, focused. The way Aleksander had trained him.

Aleksander drove out of the casino parking lot and hit the highway, I-95 south, for his two-hour drive. His fingers tingled. There was so much left to do, but with each step, they drew closer. This was everything.

He would have retribution, come hell or high water.

And make no mistake: he would be the hell, and his son the high water.

06

VIENNA, VIRGINIA
6:45 P.M. EDT

Cole picked the electronic smartcode dead bolt of Maddox's apartment in twenty seconds. Technically, he cheated. He hooked a hi-tech RF signal disruptor to the lock's touch screen, scrambling the Z-wave—if he correctly recalled the geek speak on how the gadget worked. The pricey off-market tech was a challenge to acquire, courtesy of his boss as part of his job.

Once inside, Cole shut the door and locked it. Beyond the long entry hall, he glimpsed a living room.

He stalked into her place, past a console table with a small crystal bowl, absorbing the upscale, tidy environment. Neutral beige and calming blues, blank walls. Plush furniture that enticed him to kick off his shoes and settle in. Experience taught him to peel back the seductive superficial layers to see the butt-ugly truth.

After Maddox had hijacked him from the Russians and strapped him to a chair, the tension that'd been abrading his nerves was scratching deep.

He rounded the corner, prowling into the kitchen. Empty red wine bottles filled a recycling bin. Half-eaten takeout containers and protein shakes lined the fridge. The freezer wasn't better, with waistline-friendly dinners, gelato, an unopened bottle of vodka. The good stuff. A barren pantry had a few boxes of pasta, soup, scotch—more of the good stuff—wine, and freaking MREs. Meals ready to eat, only consumed in the pinch of a combat zone.

Drifting into the living room, he soaked in the details. No Blu-rays in the entertainment center. No keepsakes. No mail, no bills, no magazine subscriptions.

No photos of her with friends, her parents, a man.

The cozy place had the warmth of a corporate apartment and personality of a hotel suite. It was clean, empty, like his or anyone who needed to bolt at a moment's notice.

He wandered into the bedroom and stilled. Above her bed hung a framed photo print of the Kogod Courtyard ceiling at the National Portrait Gallery in DC, where they'd met. A phantom fist dragged him to a time that'd broken more than his heart.

On breaks from MIT, he'd avoided family business and spent time gazing at the ceiling of the Kogod Courtyard—an architectural marvel of glass and steel that floated, catching the sun, setting the imagination afire. But seeing Maddox for the first time had set his entire body alight.

It felt as if someone had combed the recesses of his dirty mind and created this young, alluring woman just for him. Curly brown hair, light-brown skin, mesmerizing eyes. A mouth made for sex and hips meant to cradle a man. She'd been perfection, squeezing the air from his lungs.

But her looks were only the half of it. He'd learned fast: she was bright, had a wicked sense of humor, a feisty spirit, and no clue the power she wielded with her guile-less sensuality. He'd been a moth drawn to a blowtorch.

Damn it. He still was.

He shoved the torturous memories into the bunker and moved to Maddox's bureau. Neat rows of lacy underwear. Yoga pants, running shorts, tees, tanks. He rifled the right nightstand, recalling she preferred the side of the bed closest to the bathroom. Top drawer had a phone charger, vibrator, and condoms. Closing the drawer quickly, he realized he might not be ready to face all of this.

A large velvet case sat in the bottom drawer. Thumbing the latch, he flicked it open. A sweet set of kunai throwing knives sent a flutter of surprise through him. The black stainless-steel blades jibed with the new Maddox. The woman who wore tactical field boots, handled a knife like a professional, had kidnapping as a hobby, and was savvy enough to discern his Buddha beads weren't for prayer.

The deeper he dug, the louder his shitstorm meter screamed *mayhem a-coming*.

If she had these blades, high probability there was other stuff. He kept sweeping her condo, snooping under the mattress, shoeboxes in the closet, coffee cans in the kitchen.

Thirsting for pay dirt, he unearthed nothing. No secret compartments, no false bottom drawers. Not even a laptop. Besides the throwing knives, the only other out-of-place thing was a spool of fishing line in a kitchen cupboard.

In the living room, his gaze fell to the gas fireplace. He dug out a flashlight from his backpack. Shining the light inside, he scanned for signs of tampering, any indication something might be hidden within. Nothing odd stood out.

He unscrewed the vent plate anyway. Inside were the usual knobs, metal tubing, and wires. A patch of darkness in the far corner snagged his gaze.

Most people would've dismissed the slight oddity. Not him. He reached in and felt around.

Bingo. A black courier bag made from a scaly, high-heat-resistant fabric. He dumped the contents. Passports in fake names, bundles of cash in a variety of currencies. His gut tightened.

With Maddox's mixed heritage—African American on her dad's side, Swedish and French on her mom's—her ethnicity was impossible to discern. Her dad had worked for the State Department, bouncing their family from one embassy posting to another. Maddox had a knack for linguistics and spoke four different languages. Five, counting the Russian Cole had taught her.

The powerful combo of her looks and being multi-lingual enabled her to blend in and disappear in almost any country of her choosing. The question was, why would she need to?

What was she caught up in? Was she in some kind of trouble? Or was *she* the trouble?

Again.

After the FBI raid that had taken out the big gathering of the Bratva families discussing expansion, he'd called her to see if she'd told anyone about the meeting. He'd hung up once she'd said yes, too furious to hear the why. The only thing that'd mattered was cleaning up the fallout.

The soft shuffle of footsteps in the outer hallway stopped right outside. His gaze snapped to the front door and dipped to the slight crack at the bottom. There was a shadow of someone standing on the other side. His pulse zipped up a notch.

It wasn't Maddox. She would've unlocked her door and come inside. Whoever it was stood still, as if listening. Or trying to figure out how to circumvent her smartcode dead bolt.

A whisper of a rustling sound, then a second shadow appeared, sending a wild kick of adrenaline surging through him. He chucked the passports and cash into the courier bag, stuffed it beneath the fireplace, and tipped the vent plate back without wasting time screwing it in place. He scrambled from the floor, yanking his Beretta Storm out of his backpack, and took a defensive position in the kitchen.

If the Russians had tracked him down, they wouldn't get the drop on him twice in one day.

———————————

Maddox's skin crawled. Standing still as death in front of her apartment, she stared at the doorknob as though it was coated in ricin. Her instincts vibrated like a hard-struck tuning fork. An intruder had been in her apartment and was possibly still inside. Even if her gut was wrong—and it seldom was—proof lay on the ground.

The small piece of monofilament fishing line she placed between the strike plate and door every time she left her apartment wasn't there but on the threshold. A simple method of detection, no elaborate bells and whistles, but effective, easy on her government-salaried wallet, and unnoticeable unless a potential intruder knew precisely what to look for.

She had set down her groceries with the barest rustle of plastic. Her mind spun, retracing her steps. Had anything seemed odd, suspicious on the street? No one loitered near her building, no unfamiliar cars that didn't belong, and Cole's motorcycle hadn't been parked out front.

Drawing her gun, she tapped in the code on the touch screen. She twisted the knob slowly. Inching the door open, she eased inside and crept down the hall. She snuck a quick glimpse over her shoulder to be certain no one was closing in from the coat closet behind her.

The air in the condo shifted. She sensed someone's presence. Danger lurked somewhere in her home. Whoever had violated her sanctuary was going to get a bullet for their stupidity.

She skirted deeper, stiff spine against the far wall, giving her a clear view of the empty living room. Her finger rested on the trigger guard, never the trigger until she had sights on a target and was prepared to shoot.

A floorboard creaked in the kitchen. She sidestepped, rounding the corner, gun aimed, and came face-to-face with her intruder.

Cole held a gun leveled at her head, prepped to blow a hole in her. A wired energy thrummed from him, crackling in the air. He stood with the barrel trained on her, keyed up, riding a perilous edge.

She holstered her weapon. "Unless you're going to shoot me, put your gun down."

Eyes darker than a nightmare stayed narrowed, lean muscles bunched, poised to launch into explosive action. He lowered his gun, slowly, as if debating whether or not to put a bullet in her. He blinked twice, settling a hair.

Releasing a breath, he flipped the safety on, stuffed his gun in a pack, and tossed it on the sofa. The bottom vent plate on the fireplace slid to the surrounding marble with a clank.

She whipped a cutting gaze at him. "You rummaged through my things?"

"Can you blame me? You did kidnap me with no explanation."

In a day, he'd fought off four armed men and been drugged and abducted—by her, no less. She couldn't blame him. "I rescued you—big difference. *And* I told you to wait until dark to come."

Reece and Gideon were probably having a laugh over this one. At least she was confident they'd give her the professional courtesy of not spying on their conversation.

"I'm not much good at following orders." He shrugged out of his riding jacket, revealing those sculpted arms covered in tats he'd acquired in his new life. One where she didn't exist.

Had he kept his first ink on his back or covered it with something that didn't remind him of her?

"So I've seen." She collected the groceries from the hall and locked the door.

The rubber-band tension in him eased, and he no

longer looked ready to snap, but his eyes were wild and wary. He leaned against the counter, arms folded, ankles crossed, looking kick-ass cool. Her gaze snagged on the long, tantalizing line of his ripped physique, and her heart did a silly flip.

She wanted to slap herself for having the same old physical reactions to him. Better yet, slap *him* for pretending to be dead and putting her through the agony of mourning him.

"Are you hungry?" She forced a tone of nonchalance while unpacking the food and putting away the handful of perishable essentials in the fridge. "I can cook you something. Or order takeout."

"How pedestrian." He pushed off the counter, grabbed her forearm, and spun her around as he kicked the refrigerator door closed.

She bridled her defensive reflexes, flowing with his crisp actions as if they were dancing.

"I didn't come for dinner." He caught her by the back of the neck and with the two forceful strides that sent her feet scuttling, she allowed him to box her into a corner.

Pressing close, he clasped his hands to the counter on either side of her. Much closer than they'd been in the safe house. So close, the heat of him bore down on her, and she smelled him. Leather and musky salt. The rest was pure him. No cologne. No aftershave.

The scent she'd sucked in, face buried in one of his T-shirts, night after night, grieving, regretting, until the smell of him on the fabric had died too.

They were too close with him invading her space. If

she could smell him, then he could smell her parfum de Icy-Hot. "I don't like being crowded."

His eyes locked on hers, hard as granite. "I remember. Frankly, I don't give a damn what you do or don't like." The frost in his tone chilled her blood. "Tell me why you did it."

Deep inside, she flinched but outwardly, she stilled.

"I made a mistake." Her body drew tense when she needed to soften, raze her walls, exhume her suffering to abate his anger. But she couldn't. "I'm sorry." Such feeble words.

"The last night we were together…"

Cole had brought her home for one of many Sunday suppers with his family, hadn't hesitated to throw the doors to his world wide open and usher her in. Whether he'd marry her hadn't been a question, only when. But that night, his brother had sat at the table with them.

"My mother forced Ilya to sit with us because she loved you like a daughter," he said. "I turned on my brother, defending you."

Ilya had asked to be godfather to their half-breed children. Cole's temper had flared and he had broken his brother's nose before the second course had been served. Instead of excusing himself, Ilya had stayed, with his head held up, a snow-white napkin turning crimson as it soaked up his blood. Vodka had flowed heavily, and the conversation had turned to business.

"My father spoke freely in front of you. Because *I* trusted you."

A meeting had been set for the heads of the Vory

families. Ilya had voiced concerns about the Reznikovs not attending. No one ignored the call of the Bratva without consequences, but their father hadn't wanted to drag the family into human trafficking.

"I let you in where no one ever got close. How could you?"

She wanted to uncork her remorse, let it overflow, but she was congested. Her throat, tear ducts, her very pores clogged long ago by heartache.

He snatched her by the arms. "Why?"

"Because I was greedy." The only way she could vomit the details was to steel herself with her self-hatred. "My father ambushed me, attacked you, your family. He was relentless."

Her father's voice rang clear as a bell in her head.

You're gifted, special. You want to piss away our money on an art degree, squander your God-given talents to be a curator, fine. But I'll be damned if you waste your life on Russian mobster trash. Not after the sacrifices I've made for the Agency, this country. Over my dead body!

"Nothing new from your father," Cole snapped. "You were used to it."

No one got used to her father's intimidation. They weakened under the strain.

"He gave me an ultimatum. Demanded I break up with you, or he'd cut me off. Forced me to choose." As if there was ever a choice.

Cole's face pinched in a scowl. "You needed Daddy's money? Was that it? Ye of little faith. I would've taken care of you."

"He threatened to cut me off from my family. Castle

would've turned his back on me. My mother would've had to sneak around to see me like I was a dirty secret, treating our children like dirty secrets, her heart breaking every time she looked at me because I had chosen you over family. Once my father laid down the law, nobody dared go against him. He was—"

"I know." His voice was quiet. Too quiet. He loomed, sucking up the air around her.

Her lungs shriveled to peanut shells. She shoved her hands up in between his arms and rotated, breaking his hold, needing space to finish. Needing to be free of his grasp. A muscle knotted in his jaw. He didn't touch her, but he also didn't give her breathing room.

"I thought once he heard about the big meeting, how your father refused to participate in human trafficking, wanted to legitimize, it'd prove my dad wrong. That he'd give us a chance."

She sucked in a sharp breath, not wanting to exhume the things she'd long ago buried, but had to now, for him. He'd loved her, trusted her, and had lost everything because of it.

"Then I could've had a big wedding, my father walking me down the aisle. My parents beside us as our children were christened. You arguing with Castle at Thanksgiving while our fathers watched football and our mothers played with the kids. Don't you see?"

The crushing burden pressed down, and something in her chest splintered.

"I believed my father was a pencil-pusher for the State Department." Agency? Sacrifices? She'd been naive, dismissive about the little things her father had said.

The anger and shame and misery of the past nine years jammed her throat, and she wanted to choke, but needed to finish.

"I didn't know he was CIA. I never imagined he'd take the information to the FBI."

He rocked back on his heels, stumbling away and shaking his head. His expression slid from shock to disdain to hurt.

"I would've chosen you over the whole world," she said low, her insides clenching in the struggle not to unravel. "I'm so sorry."

Cole had been in a room with her dad four times and it was clear there was more to her father than him being a low-level diplomat. Built like a Mack truck, Robert Kinkade had a wary way about him, picked up details a Joe Blow would miss, carried a concealed gun—at least in Cole's presence.

But CIA?

Jeeeeesus! The worst exploiters. Absolute lowest bloodsuckers. Willing to cross any line.

"Nikolai, I didn't mean to betray you. To kill us." Her eyes were somber, but there wasn't a flicker of the agony he'd endured showing through her tempered surface. "I loved you, Kol."

There was a sudden God-awful twinge in his chest, the rage he had carried as his sole companion decomposing into something more corrosive.

Those with a foothold in his past inner circle had called him Nik. His family used the loving Russian diminutive Kolya, but only Maddox had ever called him Kol, a nickname straddling the two worlds that had divided him.

Cole was the only name that fit his new identity.

"Can you forgive me?" she asked, shutting her eyes. "For everything? For your father?"

He could never forget. Or forgive. Knowing why she did it changed nothing.

His father was dead because of her, and he was now a different man. He hated the selfish weakness that had driven her to spill his family's secrets. Hated how the fallout had turned him into a killer, like his own father. Robbed him of the life he'd wanted with her.

He tried to convince himself he hated her. If only he didn't miss her smile, the fire in her eyes, the sound of her voice. Crave her like a man possessed.

And he hated that most of all.

She gazed up at him in the strained silence choking the air. He couldn't utter any absolution, and she seemed to pay a dear price, holding his stare. The raw intimacy shared in the look, as if they were lovers again, cost him also, for there was no going back.

"What happened to you?" she asked. "Did you really take out thirty-two men? Alone?"

He drifted into the living room, looking at those blank blue walls. His family's absence at the Vory gathering had caused waves, but the FBI raid the same day had painted his father a traitor.

"My father was murdered because they believed *he*

snitched, Maddox. They marked all of us for death. I did what I had to. Erased the threats to my family."

He and Ilya had trained in the martial art of Systema since they were boys, brought up learning how to use a knife, a gun, hell, a fucking barstool to defend themselves. Ilya had lacked discipline and focus, choosing to rely on bodyguards, whereas Cole only wanted to rely on himself. His father had forged him into a lethal weapon. Vengeance had put that weapon into play.

"I knew word of what I'd done would reach powerful ears in Russia. So I had to die, to protect anyone close to me." *To protect you.* "But I have more questions of my own."

His cell buzzed in his pocket. He looked at the screen. Linda from Rubicon.

"I need to take this." He waited, giving her a hard glance that spoke volumes.

"Oh." She lowered her head. "I'll freshen up. Give you privacy."

She went into her bedroom, shut and locked the door. The shower started a second later.

"What did you find?"

VIENNA, VIRGINIA
8:05 P.M. EDT

"The threat of the Russians is serious as a heart attack while scuba diving," Linda said in her croaky voice. "Big mafia bosses want you hacked into little pieces on Russian soil."

A terrible dread gripped him. The bitter decade he'd spent a condemned soul, damn dead man walking, deprived of a real life, had been for what?

"Perfect start to my vacation. What did the team find out about her?"

The timing of Linda's call couldn't have been better. He'd have the truth to weigh against the story Maddox intended to spoon-feed him.

"Not sure you're going to like that either."

Whatever Linda had found better explain the passports and cash. He'd lost his way over the years, had done dark things he wasn't proud of, but he only wanted Maddox to be safe, even if they couldn't be together. "Tell me."

"She likes privacy. No social media footprint. Mail goes to a PO box, which made getting her address tough, but you know us." Linda gave the address of the apartment he was in. "The condo is one of a few properties under the name of a limited liability company established by her late father. The LLC is owned by her, the mother, and a brother. We figured out which property was hers because there's one utility in her name. Never been married, and if she's fucking, it's no one steady."

The news came with a strange sense of relief, but he had zero intention of psychoanalyzing why.

"For almost six years, she's worked at Helios Importing and Exporting for Bruce Sydell. He specializes in black market goods, from stolen antiquities to nasty stuff that kills and maims."

With her art history degree, he'd envisioned her selling paintings in a gallery, not trading death on the black market. This wasn't the life meant for her.

Had his leaving sent her spiraling down a horrid path? Was she trapped in some shady business because he never came back for her?

"You're right. I don't like it."

"Helios currently has a lucrative contract with a big pharmaceutical company."

"Any arrests, federal wiretaps, signs of coercion?"

The feds had harassed his family for as long as he could remember, tossing their house every time a warrant gave them an excuse. His father—a Vory boss, a high-ranking member of the Russian mafia—had been untouchable. Until Maddox.

"No. But there was something else."

He plunked down on the sofa, bracing himself. "What?"

"Someone worked very hard to erase something from her past."

The hairs on his nape bristled. "I hate suspense. Spill it."

"Nine years ago, she was hospitalized for three days. But I don't know why."

His thoughts ricocheted in his head like ball bearings in a pinball machine, hitting every horrid possibility. "When?" He cleared the tightness in his throat. "The date?"

"She was admitted September nineteenth."

Three months after she'd betrayed him and he'd killed anybody threatening the ones he loved, then faked his own death. He'd done it to appease the Vory, to safeguard his family. Especially her.

The news of his death must've been a shock to her at first. She was supposed to heal and move forward. Had she tried to hurt herself?

"There's more. Our whiz kid found it, wanting to impress you, his superhero." Tom was a techie genius who sliced through digital layers like a virtual surgeon. "Someone with resources buried it real, real deep, never meant to surface."

A sickening feeling rained over him as if the bottom of his world was about to drop. "Tell me."

"Afterward, she spent time at Privé Solace in Canada. One of those uber-private mental health places disguised as a spa, for depression, anxiety, PTSD."

Slamming his eyes closed, he pinched the bridge of his nose, struggling to get a handle on the information rattling around in his skull. As soon as things had gotten tough, he'd bailed on her. He'd promised to always be there for her, but the situation had been a quagmire he'd barely escaped with his life. All because she couldn't be trusted with his family's secrets.

Fuck! "Anything else?"

"Nope. All I could find."

That'd been plenty. "Thanks. Never mention Nikolai Reznikov to anyone. I owe you."

"Stay safe, sugar. I want my box of chocolates."

His fingers twitched like he had caffeine jitters. He couldn't wrap his fists around this. The hell Maddox must've gone through, believing he was dead.

He grabbed his wallet and pulled out the frayed, torn-in-half strip of snapshots taken of him with Maddox in a carnival photo booth. They looked so young, so in love.

The memory was a splinter embedded in his brain. Her throaty laughter, her curtain of ringlets tickling his cheek, the pear scent from her shampoo, the grounding weight of her head on his shoulder, her smile—a punch to the gut.

She had been the flame warming his soul.

With her, he'd found something he'd never known before. Comfort. No judgment. No conditions. No expectation for him to change or be anything other than who he was, even though she was way too good for him. And for that, he wanted to be the best man he could—for Maddox.

A gummy thickness tightened in his throat.

He put the photos away, unable to bear remembering. Unable to ever forget.

The shelf life of his responsibility to her had expired long ago, but no matter what, he couldn't stomach the idea of her in danger. He had promised to take care of her, to keep her safe. He could make good on at least one.

If she was in such deep trouble with her employer,

this Sydell, that she'd gone to the effort of tracking Cole down, then things didn't bode well.

Regardless, he'd help her. If nothing else, to ensure she wasn't on the Russians' radar.

His instincts were still hardwired to protect her, his body programmed to lust after her, but he'd get a lobotomy before getting involved with her again.

Loving her had been the greatest danger. The biggest damn mistake.

Maddox zipped through a shower, lathering and exfoliating with a textured loofah—no need to shave, since she was religious about waxing—moisturized, and redid the makeup covering the bruise on her cheek. Lickety-split. Standing in front of her bureau, she contemplated attire. After her inability earlier to carve out her heart and serve it to him bleeding on a silver platter, she needed to show him a hint of softness, a willing vulnerability.

The aqua lounge set she picked out matched her eyes. The pants clung to her curves. A soft cami with lace trim accentuated her cleavage without flaunting it. Not sleeping with him didn't mean she couldn't reel him closer with the bait God had given her. He was a man, she was a woman, and their magnetic attraction had been so wickedly powerful, it'd altered the orbit of her world.

I'm a pro. I've got this. She unlocked and opened her bedroom door.

Cole sat on the sofa, shoulders slumped. His head tipped up, and he looked at her, taking her in from top to toe in a slow perusal. His gaze stroked her with the intensity of a physical touch.

A shimmer of awareness licked her spine, but when his eyes caught hers with undeniable interest, her toes curled. She snatched her gaze away and headed for the kitchen. "Want a drink?"

"No. I want answers." He lunged off the sofa and stalked up to her. "How did you know I was alive? Why did you rescue me? What does your employer, Sydell, want from me?"

Shit, the background check came back fast. *Don't break your cover.*

"I could use a drink." She stepped around him.

Activity centered her. Making a drink would give her hands something to do and her eyes a focal point other than his savagely handsome face.

"Still slithering through cracks when faced with slippery questions." He swooped in front of her, slapping a hand to the wall, blocking her. "Be honest. What the fuck is going on?"

She dropped her gaze to the buttercream carpet, collecting her thoughts, and he snapped his fingers in her face, forcing eye contact.

He pressed two fingers to her carotid artery, sending her pulse skittering. A manual technique to monitor her heart rate and breathing to better detect lies. Was he serious?

"Is this necessary?"

He cast her a distinct *hell yes* look. "Are you in trouble? What are you caught up in?"

Her training fired the perfect, calculated words to mind in a tight-shot group. He was primed to accept her cover story. Even with his innate ability to sniff out lies, his intimate knowledge of her inside and out, if she could beat a polygraph, she could beat him.

Problem was she didn't want to.

They had once laid themselves bare, not a secret between them. He had treated her as though she'd been the most important person in the world, had worshipped her body and appreciated her mind and admired her spirit.

Cherished her completely. Before she'd ruined it.

Reducing him to nothing more than an asset made him a pawn. Desecrating the memory of their rare connection with a lie was the kind of wrong that went against the laws of nature.

"If you're in danger," he said, "you can tell me without zip-tying me to a chair. I won't run."

Ha! "You might. You've no idea what you're dealing with. Don't make promises you won't keep. Not again."

His mouth set in a hard line. "I deserve that. I swore to always be there for you. To stand by you, no matter what. And when the shit hit the fan, I—"

"Cut and run," she taunted, feeling him out.

The tic in his jaw popped. "Don't. It wasn't that simple." His voice vibrated with tension. "You dug me up somehow for a reason. Put all your cards on the table, and I swear, I'll help you."

For him to swear was no trivial thing, but he had no good reason to bind himself to help. Not one. Guilt indebted her to him, not the other way around. He owed her nothing, while she owed him an entire life.

She hadn't even been able to slice open a vein, hemorrhage her pain, and wheedle him to forgiveness with her remorse. Yet still, he was willing to help her?

"Why?" After all this time of playing dead and pretending she didn't exist—nine years of not giving two shits about her. "What do you want in return?"

He cupped her neck with a familiar and fierce tenderness, bringing their bodies flush, their gazes clashing. For one insane and reckless moment, she thought he'd kiss her. Even more insane and reckless, she hoped he would.

"I want closure. To be free of you."

The barb punched home with painful accuracy.

Before she'd met Cole, she'd been ignorant that anything had been missing in her life. Being loved by him had redefined the meaning of happiness, and losing him had left a gash in her soul.

Now here he was, within reach. And he wanted... closure.

Her heart squeezed, and everything inside her hurt like one giant exposed nerve. "You've been free of me for nine years."

"What I wouldn't give for that to be true."

They'd once vowed to be honest, no matter how brutal the truth. So nice of him to remember.

He skimmed his thumb along her jaw, coaxing her chin up, and his eyes seared into hers.

"Tell me what it is, Mads." His tone softened to black velvet.

The way he said her name, *Mads*, an intimate caress, had her dissolving. She was once again that susceptible girl who'd been hopelessly in love. He was no longer hers, but a part of her would always be his.

A palpable energy saturated the air, an electric current teasing her skin. Standing this close, his proximity was a call demanding an answer. Desire to touch him, to taste him tugged at her like gravity.

He bent his head, his breath kissing her cheek. His thumb ghosted across her lips.

She shivered, fingertips aching, and couldn't stop herself. "I'm CIA."

Sugarcoating the bitter pill wouldn't make it any easier for him to swallow. Not that she was CIA anymore, but she couldn't tell a civilian about the Gray Box.

He stilled and, a breath later, recoiled with appalled urgency, as though she'd confessed to having leprosy.

"You're a scum-sucking spook?" A volatile storm brewed across his face. "You followed in his footsteps after what he did? What it cost me? Became one of them?"

Them. The word was a sandbag in her chest.

She'd never blamed her father. He'd had an unwavering ethical compass. An admirable vision of right and wrong. He had died serving his country in a terrorist bombing overseas seven years ago, shifting the way she'd viewed him and his job. When the Agency had approached her in college, pursuing her old dream—a career in art acquisitions—had seemed selfish after her father's sacrifice. What could she say to Cole that he would understand?

A gleam sparked in his eyes similar to light glinting off a blade. "This whole thing has been one elaborate setup, hasn't it?"

"No, Cole." She reached for him.

Lightning reflexes launched him into the living room. He snatched his bag from the sofa. "Son of a bitch." He screwed his eyes shut, mashing his lips like an ugly idea had crawled into his head. "You figured out I was alive somehow and leaked it to the Russians." His voice iced over. "Fucked my life up all over again. Then swept in to the rescue. Make me feel indebted, grateful enough to forgive you, so I'd go back to being your lapdog. Is that it?"

Her stomach soured. Could it have happened that way?

Sanborn was known as the Black Ops Whisperer. He had a talent none of them fully understood but wholly respected. He was spoken about with awe in small, private, powerful circles. But the delicate timing necessary, the intricate level of precision he'd have needed to both orchestrate and thwart a risky Russian bag and drag was not only beyond his capability, it was also beneath him to deliberately jeopardize someone's life.

"We'd never do that."

"We!" His upper lip curled. "You people most certainly would."

Whoa. "You people?"

Okay, if push came to shove, they might put a potential asset in a bind for leverage, but not under these time-sensitive conditions. Not with so many moving parts out of their control and a bioweapon on the line. That would be insane, and Sanborn wasn't a lunatic with a god complex.

"You have to trust me. We didn't—*I* didn't—sic the Russians on you."

"Trust you?" His pitch-black gaze boiled. "A liar who destroyed my life once already? The CIA deserves you, honey, if they're stupid enough to entrust you with their secrets."

Oh no, he didn't. What a bullshit buckshot.

She'd seen and heard plenty in the two years they were together. Never stuck her nose in, never pried. Never said a word about his family's business until one stupid moment of weakness with her father. Cole had no idea who she was today, what she'd endured. She'd become a Sisyphus, rolling the boulder of Gray Box missions uphill every day as punishment.

Her facade of equanimity teetered, but she mustered her iron composure. She'd been forged in the CIA, recast stronger in the Gray Box. "Please, listen. Give me a chance to explain everything."

"A chance to spin a sticky web of lies?"

She just threw herself into this meat grinder because she didn't want to lie to him. "No, of course not."

He stormed to the kitchen and grabbed his jacket. "How long have you known I was alive? Have you been surveilling me in tandem with the Russians? Tag-teaming ticks."

She wasn't playing with fire, Cole was a nuclear warhead on the brink of detonation. "I had no idea you were alive until I saw you today."

He hunched over the counter, clutching the granite in a white-knuckle grip, chest heaving like someone had ripped out his lungs. "You must think I'm a fucking fool."

Her nerves stretched tight, skin turning to shrink-wrap. "The Agency hid the truth." She pussyfooted into the kitchen, giving him space to decompress. "You're not just an asset to me." *You're the one man I'd sacrifice anything to be with.*

Hell, she was jeopardizing a mission because of him.

Curses in Russian exploded from him. Nasty things, too fast for her to catch every word. He snatched his stuff from the counter and headed toward the door.

Reading people, using feminine guile, pushing buttons, pulling strings—those were some of her strongest talents. The five little words to stop him dead in his tracks itched on the tip of her tongue, their flavor acrid.

"You swore to help me." Hating herself for pushing that button, she took a deep breath through the queasiness bubbling up.

His word was his bond, yesterday, today. Always.

He froze in front of the door. The sound of his harsh breaths filled the dead air between them. "What do you want?" A pained whisper.

She ignored the quick twist of guilt in her gut. "Cole—"

"You have thirty seconds," he said, keeping his back to her.

Taking tentative steps, she needed proximity and eye contact. "Please look at me."

"Twenty."

This was shaky ground and she was losing her footing. She swallowed hard, straining to think of the right thing to say next.

"Fifteen seconds to spit out how you want to turn my life into a pile of steaming shit."

"In two days, a bioterror weapon is going to be

auctioned on the black market. You have to be invited to the auction. Ilya is on the short list. I need his passcode."

Lowering his head, he pounded a fist on the door, barking a scathing laugh.

"Does Ilya know you're alive?"

A weighted silence settled around them. The quiet felt massive, the seconds like an eternity.

"Yes," he finally said, sounding withered. "But I haven't seen him since…"

That bastard Ilya was in on it. She had asked him point-blank nine years ago if Cole was truly dead, and he had lied to her face. She really was the last to know. Damn, it hurt.

She eased behind him as one would a caged animal that might tear her apart. "It's weaponized smallpox. A new strain. Thousands could die in the first wave alone. If uncontained, it'll start an epidemic." She dared to put a hand on his shoulder. "We need you to prevent it."

He whirled on her with such swift rage that she stumbled back. Her heart beat harder and faster than a war drum, but she stilled, gauging what he was capable of. Then she saw in his eyes the hurt outweighing the anger. She was in no physical danger from him. Of that, she was certain, but the situation was slipping through her fingers faster than grains of sand from a busted hourglass.

"Don't. Touch. Me." Anguish slashed across his face, and her breath caught.

God, that look—that look would haunt her forever.

"You should've put me out of my misery and let the Russians take me. Damn you."

He tore out of her condo, slamming the door.

Panic snapped along her nerves.

Years ago, an explosive argument would have led to even more explosive, sheet-clawing sex. But neither had ever walked away when they fought, much less stormed out.

She roped her arm around herself against the vicious ache. "I never saw a wild thing sorry for itself," she whispered the D. H. Lawrence poem. "A small bird will drop frozen dead from a bough without ever having felt sorry for itself."

Raising her chin, she summoned self-possession, getting her shit together, and went to call Gideon and Reece.

08

MARYLAND
11:56 P.M. EDT

Gunpowder-gray clouds roiled across the black tarp of sky, occluding the spotlight of the moon and legion of stars as Aleksander paddled the stolen canoe into Whitehall Bay.

The water was calm, no waves buffeting the small boat. Darkness of the lazy night enveloped him like an old friend in welcome. The luxury homes sprawled along the shore had expansive parcels of forested land in between. One man's myopic desire for absolute privacy had paved a path slick as black ice for Aleksander to put him in the grave.

He moored the canoe in the shadow of an overhanging oak. Spanish moss draped the low boughs with dense webs, and a damp resinous scent perfumed the thick night air. Wrapping the rope from the boat around the tree trunk, he tied a clove hitch knot. He pulled the hood of his camouflage suit over his head. The lightweight, polyester mesh ghillie was covered in over a thousand synthetic leaves patterned after deep, shady woodlands.

Silent as fog rolling in, Aleksander waded through high grass, weaving past trees. The army had taught him how to blend in and disappear. He had thirty years practice in vanishing.

His footsteps were light, his movements ghostly. A massive oak tree on the wood line, with wide outstretched branches like the gnarled fingers of a giant, gave him a clean sight line to the back of the gated mansion where the bedrooms faced the bay and pool. He took out a night vision monocular with laser range finder and confirmed the distance. Fifty meters.

Longest shot he'd ever made was at two thousand, and he made every shot he took.

A deadeye.

He slung the rifle strap over his shoulder, climbed the tree, and situated himself on a sturdy limb in a prone position. Pulling the charging handle, he chambered a round. He used his pack to support the barrel and rested the butt on a beanbag, eliminating any concerns of muscle fatigue.

The leaves shivered around him, the breeze whispering across the grass. *More interminable waiting.* He emptied his mind and visualized the Osumi Canyon, the river running through his mountainous hometown of Berat. Mild white-water rapids, pockmarked slopes of the canyon, small caves, verdant vegetation so picturesque, heaven had reached down to kiss the limestone cliffs of the gorge. The Grand Canyon of Albania. His wife's special place.

He flinched as the images invaded. His wife, Sonia, and little Mila, his beloved darlings. He always pictured them as he'd last seen them. Broken. Bruised. Bloodied. In pieces.

Not only were they murdered, but his memories of them had also been butchered.

The demon in his head seethed. Eyes dark like two pits of charred earth, it foamed at the mouth. Rabid to rip out jugulars. It begged. Oh, how it begged to be unchained, to make the world its playground and bathe in blood.

No, no. Aleksander couldn't free it. That wouldn't be payback. It'd be madness. He hadn't fallen so far down the slippery slope not to discern the difference.

Shhh, Levik. Some men named their cocks. He had named his demon.

Aleksander inserted earbuds and played a little Handel to center them. Sarabande.

He'd feed Levik soon, when the target strolled the property for his morning wind bath before a swim. Aleksander would be one step closer, but neither one of them would be fully appeased until D-day.

09

MARYLAND
THURSDAY, 5:25 A.M. EDT

Sunlight fractured the concrete sky. Cool air rushed over Cole.

After riding all night on the I-495 loop, the Capital Beltway—a sixty-four-mile stretch of freeway encircling Washington, DC, winding through Virginia and Maryland—the roar of his bike had anesthetized his bitter rage. A long, hard ride was the best form of self-medicating, more addictive than booze. But his thoughts still whirred as if his mind were caught in a blender.

His attempt at shut-eye in a dingy dive motel in Silver Spring had been torture. Every time he closed his eyes, he saw Maddox. She'd baited him. Lured him to her apartment under questionable and possibly reprehensible circumstances. Where he could *stay and be safe*.

CIA code for fuck him, then fuck him over getting him to do her bidding?

Those scum suckers were master manipulators.

She'd sashayed from her bedroom, smelling of rose water. That sexy getup clinging to her curves had been an insane tease yanking his leashed gaze, drawing his body tight as a steel cable. But he'd done what he considered a sensational job not regressing into a devoted puppy drooling for her treats.

Nope. Never again.

Such bravado. A part of him craved her in the worst way, and he cursed the damned Pavlovian response.

Pure craziness to have touched her—hell, to get within ten feet of her. The woman was biological warfare incarnate, wreaking havoc on his common sense and self-control.

Shit. He hadn't volunteered for this war. He'd been drafted and wasn't even sure who the enemy was anymore.

Riding round the interstate loop, he had no idea where he was going until he exited on to Route 50, to Annapolis. Ilya had sold the family home in DC, no surprise. Their father had been shot on the front steps. What had stunned Cole speechless was that Ilya hadn't taken the opportunity to legitimize the business. He'd propelled it to new illegal depths instead, adding arms trafficking to their list of sins. Everything Cole had sacrificed to keep his mother and brother safe, to free them from an illicit life under constant guard, had been wasted.

Cole rolled up in front his brother's multimillion-dollar gated compound. It sprawled across several acres facing Whitehall Bay. He hit the intercom button.

"Yeah. What can I do for you?" said a voice he didn't recognize.

Cole lifted the visor on his helmet. "Is Vitali up?"

Vitali had been the family's head enforcer for as long as Cole could remember, and the only other person besides his mother and brother who knew he was alive. Ilya would never get rid of Vitali. The loyalty ran too deep.

"Yep. What's it to you?"

"Tell him it's Nikolai." He all but choked on his real name. It'd been nine years since he'd referred to himself by it, and he felt like an impostor. The truth was he no longer belonged there. A part of him never had.

"Nikolai who?"

"Just tell him." He rubbed his eyes, fatigue stinging his retinas.

On a subconscious level, he must revel in being tormented by Maddox. It'd brought him here, when not even the love for his mother had done that.

What were the long-shot odds the woman who'd upended his life by spilling secrets would become a damn spy? That bombshell had been worse than a boot heel to the groin.

Looking at it deeper, she might have the right skill set in spades. Her compassion endeared her to others—had won over his reticent father easily. Had Cole sharing secrets in the darkness between the sheets. And any good spy needed the ability to get others to confide.

She had book smarts to match street sense, was multilingual, and could handle herself. He'd made certain of the last one, teaching her devastating strikes, kicks, submission holds. She'd learned with the ease of a natural. Her fluid efficiency was impressive, but her ballistic speed and precision were her strengths.

No hesitation. A fighter's heart. Fearless. And fierce.

Freaking CIA. He removed his helmet and spat the disgust from his mouth onto the driveway. Why couldn't he hate her and be done for good?

Last night, he'd seen flashes of sorrow and regret

in her. None of that emotion had burned through her tough-girl facade, but he'd sensed her heartache, the loneliness. He had recognized the second he'd wounded her, for the sake of closure. And hurting her, even to save himself…

Excruciating pain wrenched his chest, worse than a knife between the ribs. It was as though his feelings for Maddox were a thoroughbred stallion that had a broken leg. He had to find a way to put a bullet in its head and spare himself further misery.

"Who the fuck is this?" Vitali said in Russian over the intercom.

Looking up at the camera pointed at him, Cole pushed the hair from his face. A moment passed. The wrought iron gates swung open.

He put his helmet on and sped up the winding, tree-lined drive to the massive stone house.

Blood money had paid for the expansive grounds, the mansion, the sports cars parked to the side.

Men like his brother and father had built their wealth off the graves of others. Although Cole had never had a hand in the family business, he was accountable. He'd saved Ilya and given him a chance to spread more misery.

If he could help stop a bioweapon from killing innocent people, he had a responsibility. Maybe, just maybe, his karmic debt would be paid.

He parked the bike near the four-car garage, catching a glimpse of the pool in the back. Stiffness riddled his leg muscles from the long ride. He stretched and walked toward the front, past two armed guards. Gravel crunched under his boots.

Vitali opened the front door and greeted Cole in a bear hug. "It's been too long."

The burly man looked him up and down and patted the left side of Cole's face with affection. Vitali's wrinkles and scars were stories engraved by seventy-five hard years. His hair was thinned and gray, his skin leathery. Time had shown him little kindness. His mobility was dulled, but the old guy probably still packed a mean right hook.

"I bet that scar hasn't hurt you with the ladies."

A hollow smile tugged at Cole's mouth. He didn't have a problem getting laid whenever he needed to take the edge off, but it'd been a while. Not since he had moved back to DC.

"Come in." Vitali beckoned him to enter the house.

Taking a tour of his brother's lavish blood-money mansion wasn't on the agenda. "I need to speak to Ilya. Now."

Vitali huffed, propping his fists on his hips. "He's sleeping. Won't be up for a couple of hours. Come in. Have coffee. Tell me about your life."

The warmth in the old guy's eyes and the love in his voice slayed Cole, but he wasn't here to socialize. He didn't have the stomach to reminisce.

"Wake him. I'll wait around back near the pool." Turning, Cole strode away before Vitali protested.

Curses in Russian spewed behind him. Then a door slammed.

He needed to confront Ilya, get the passcode for Maddox, and get gone. He'd help her, even if he was helping the CIA. Keeping a biological weapon out of the hands of a terrorist wasn't too different from the work he did at Rubicon. Or so he told himself.

The back of the house overlooked the bay. Mist blanketed the water and silvery dew coated the grass. Small flowering trees and a garden of azaleas and delphiniums and peonies—his mother's favorites—were planted beside the lap pool. The rising sun warmed the sky to a powdery blue. Serenity. The quiet seclusion and charming beauty of the property stilled the restless energy winding through him and, at the same time, amplified his turbulent thoughts.

He didn't begrudge Ilya a nice view or a large house. He had a taste for the finer things himself. The difference was everything Cole had, he'd earned through honest hard work and smart investments. Ilya had built this palace trafficking in violence and death.

Their father had been an *ubiytsa*, an assassin, who'd risen through the ranks of the *Vory v Zakone*, Russian mafia. The underworld brotherhood had gotten him and their mother out of Russia, but there was a price. The debt had built the illicit Reznikov empire, but it was his love for his wife and children that had driven him to strive for a legitimate legacy in America.

How could Ilya dishonor his memory like this?

A tingle sparked at the base of Cole's skull. He glanced over his shoulder, staring at the bank of trees on the south side of the property. He had an eerie sense of being watched.

He scanned the thicket for anything that didn't belong.

Leaves swayed in the whistling wind. Blades of grass danced. The scent of evergreen was heavy. Gossamer shreds of mist coiled and drifted like phantom fingers tickling the earth.

The tingle deepened to a throbbing tightness that was impossible to ignore.

No birds. At this hour, there should be the rustle of wings, the busy activity of feeding. It was nothing major, but his instincts geared him to full alert.

A patio door opened. "Nikolai?" Ilya stepped outside under the wisteria-covered pergola and stared at him a second. "Kolya!" He waved him over, then disappeared inside.

Cole sighed, dreading the conversation, and traipsed toward the house. He snuck another glance over his shoulder. Nothing stirred; all appeared peaceful. He passed the pool and grabbed the handle of the open solarium door. Hesitating, he promised himself he wouldn't stay long. A sudden strange urgency prodded him to get inside, across the threshold. He entered the sunroom and shut the door.

"Back from the dead," Ilya said with a sleepy smile. "I can't believe it. I called Vitali a liar when he said you were here." Ilya stood in the solarium, wearing silk pajama pants and a matching robe. On his bare chest, the eight-pointed stars of the Vory had been inked.

Ilya gave him a one-armed hug.

Patting his brother's back in return, Cole steered him deeper into the room. The solarium wasn't much better than being outside, its high glass walls fit for a menagerie. At least the six-feet tall ficus plants scattered along the periphery provided some screening.

The prickling throb in the base of his skull tightened.

He peered between the plants outside at the woods. Wind brushed away the mist, but he still didn't see any cause for alarm.

"What have you been doing with yourself all this time?" At thirty-six, three years older than Cole, gray hair salted Ilya's temples and he'd already packed on a paunch.

"I'm pretty sure not as much as you." Atrocities always followed in the wake of an arms trafficking deal. A Reznikov deal.

"This is nice, huh?" With the foliage-lined walls, pots of blooming flowers, and soft morning light for a backdrop, Ilya grinned, arms extended, waltzing around the room, oblivious to Cole's contempt. "Momma loved this place," Ilya said. "At the end, when the cancer got bad, she talked about you a lot. She wanted to spend one more day with you before she died, making your favorites. Blinis. Borscht."

Cole's regret at losing a chance to hug his mother once more was another on a mounting pile.

"I caught a glimpse of you at the funeral." Ilya slid his hands into his silk pockets. "Knew it was you, even at a distance with that *beautiful* face hidden behind a helmet."

The sarcasm cut deep, but Cole met his brother's eyes with unflinching coldness.

"Vitali! Bring us some coffee," Ilya said, averting his gaze.

"Is your *guest* going to grace us with his presence long enough for coffee?" the old man sneered from the hall.

"No." Cole threw the word like a dagger.

"Pssh." Always willing to play with fire, Ilya waved a dismissive hand. "He stays for coffee." He pranced around the room as if he were a king. "So, are you back to take your place at my side?"

Cole folded his arms across his chest. "I'd rather shit glass."

Ilya threw his head back with a grating laugh, the noise shredding the air. "Kolya, you always had a flair for the dramatic. All those people you gutted nine years ago. Come on, *bratik*." He called him *brother* in Russian. "You have to admit, that was pretty dramatic."

Not once had Cole ever shed blood because he enjoyed it. Violence wasn't imprinted in his DNA like it was for Ilya. Their father had been gunned down for something he didn't do. A bull's-eye had been smeared on the rest of their backs—including Maddox. Not a day went by he didn't think about the blood on his hands. Taking lives to protect those he loved was the second hardest thing he'd ever done.

Leaving Maddox behind to keep her safe topped his list.

For Ilya to joke about it sickened him. He shot a warning glare at his brother.

Ilya held up his hands, feigned self-reproach painting his slim face. "Don't get me wrong, it was necessary. I owe you my life. You did what no one else would've been able to and in a very short amount of time. When you get pissed, watch out."

Ilya threw a one-two punch in the air, hopping on the balls of his feet. "A force to be reckoned with. My crooked nose is a daily reminder." Ilya tapped the indentation of the bridge that slanted to the left. "Unbelievable. You broke my nose in front of Momma over that bitch, Maddox."

Those sloppy words lit a primal fuse in Cole and he strained not to detonate. "Watch your damn mouth. You're not good enough to speak her name."

Ilya rolled his eyes, flashing a tight-lipped grin. "That piece of ass still gets you worked up? She came to see me after you *died*, asking if you were truly dead. I enjoyed consoling her."

Cole charged across the room. Ilya staggered back, his smile faltering. Cole snatched his brother by the robe's lapels, slamming him into a ficus, smacking his head against the glass. Ilya stood taller by an inch, with a muscular frame, but there'd never been a contest between them in this department.

Fury whipped white-hot through Cole, constricting his thoughts into laser focus. "Did you touch her?" Cole shook his brother, hoping to knock some decency into his head. Why hadn't Maddox mentioned she'd gone to see him? "Did you lay a finger on her?"

A vile grin spread across Ilya's mouth. Cole cocked his fist and punched the smirk off his face.

Ilya yelped, throwing his hands up. "Shit, *bratik*! I didn't touch your fucking *pizda*."

Cole nearly collapsed from the profound relief. Ilya hadn't hurt Maddox, and Cole didn't have to butcher his mother's firstborn. Maddox was capable of kicking Ilya's ass, but Ilya was the type of disgusting lowlife who would've had others hold her down for him.

"Breaking your nose obviously didn't teach you the fucking lesson. If you call her a bitch, piece of ass, *pizda*"—cunt in Russian—"or anything else disrespectful, I'll break your jaw so it'll be wired shut."

A tortured expression stamped Ilya's face. "Want to know why I never liked her?"

Cole jammed his fist under his brother's chin, against his windpipe. "I know. You're a prejudiced bastard."

Ilya snorted a laugh that curled up and died in his chest. "I see you. So clearly. Yet you don't know me at all, Kolya. It was never about the color of her skin."

"Bullshit. You said the vilest things. After I smashed your face in and broke your nose, you screwed every whore with a shade of brown skin just so you could talk about what you did to them and make your sick implications." How his brother had run through prostitutes to ensure his gross point hit home had disgusted him.

Cole's fists shook at the recollection, acid eating at his stomach. He jostled Ilya, knocking his head against the glass wall. "Did you think time would erase my memory?"

"I thought you'd end it with her if I got deep enough under your skin." Ilya tilted his head and his gaze fell.

"I loved her." Clenching his jaw, Cole shoved him. The glass vibrated like it might break. "Why would you do that?"

Ilya's eyes sliced up to his. "If her father had been a gangster instead of some white-collar Dudley Do-Right from suburbia, I would've embraced her like a sister."

The words slapped Cole dumbstruck.

Ilya's jaw tightened. "I never thought you working on that hoity-toity master's degree would stick. You'd never be an architect. I knew that whole fantasy life you dreamt of would fade away eventually, because I see who you really are. Deep down, you're just like Papa."

The stone-cold tongue of fear licked Cole's spine,

and he let his brother go. There was something terrible prowling inside Cole and he fought to keep the darkness in check, but he wasn't a monster.

"You're one of us." Ilya wiped blood from his mouth. "But when she came along, I knew I'd lose you. To the suburbs and your fantasy of a legit life. And then I lost you anyway."

What Ilya said made sense, in a twisted way. He had seen her as a threat, as the one thing that could truly sever Cole's connection to the family, but it didn't justify his grotesque behavior.

Turning his back on his brother, Cole crossed the room. He'd never told Ilya the raid had been Maddox's fault. Even in the middle of the shitstorm she'd caused, he'd protected her.

Vitali came in, carrying a tray of coffee. He set it down on the glass table in the center of the room and left in stubborn silence.

Adjusting his robe, Ilya smoothed down the shiny fabric.

"Why the fuck are you wearing stars?" Cole raked his hair back with both hands. "You swore you were done. You looked me in the eye and gave me your word. Instead, you became one of the most notorious arms dealers on the Eastern Seaboard."

Ilya shrugged. "With you and Papa dead, the big dogs back in Russia were willing to forego further retribution, but the other three families getting busted put a major crimp in the cash flow. I had to step up and bring big money in or be put down six feet under."

The ripples of Maddox's mistake had killed the

possibility of Ilya going legit. But he had accepted the role with too much zeal to make Cole believe this lifestyle was an unwelcome burden.

"Who would've guessed you'd be an overachiever," Cole said.

Ilya laughed, picking up a cup of coffee, and wandered toward the glass doors.

The itch to leave niggled under Cole's skin. "Look, I'm not here to rehash history or give you a hard time about the choices you've made." *Not today, anyway.* "I need a favor." He followed his brother toward the back of the room. "I'm here because of the auction tomorrow. I want your passcode. I need you to step aside in this."

Ilya froze, facing the doors overlooking the pool. Slowly, he pivoted on a velvet-slippered heel, brows knitting. "How the fuck do you know about that?"

"How doesn't matter. I know. You're going to leave it at that, because I'm your blood."

Ilya eyed him hard, like he wanted to reach into Cole's head and rip out his thoughts. "When did this become your field of interest? Whatever I spend at the auction, I can make up threefold on the open black market. I already have a buyer lined up. Why should I do this?"

"Because I've asked it. Because you *owe* me."

Ilya stared at him for a long, long time.

All traces of the brother Cole knew faded away in that look, leaving the true face of the cold-blooded gangster Ilya had become. Ilya's gaze fell as he drifted to the chairs by the door with a view of the bay, sipping his coffee. "Vitali!" He sat in a high-backed lounge chair and propped an ankle on his knee. "Bring me the envelope that came by messenger."

Cole strode to his brother and leaned a shoulder against the glass wall. The plants providing the only cover were on the other end of the room, probably to give an unobstructed view of the water from this part of the solarium.

He rubbed the back of his head at the unease crawling over him, and his gaze veered toward the woods.

As crazy as it seemed, he couldn't shake the sense they were being watched. Confronting his past demons must be frying his instincts.

"You should stay and wind bathe with me," Ilya said, referring to walking around outside naked. A practice of cleansing the pores, passed down from their father. "Nothing like the air licking your balls in the morning. Other than tea-bagging the mouth of a pretty young thing." He cackled.

The prickle along Cole's skin had him turning to stare back outside. "Can't. I have to go."

Vitali came in, carrying a five-by-seven envelope. He handed it to Ilya and cut his eyes at Cole before disappearing down the hall.

"This makes us even, *bratik*," Ilya said. "My life debt to you is paid."

They'd never be even, not in this lifetime, and Ilya would never understand why.

Surveying the grounds, Cole stood upright. "Thank you for the passcode."

"It's not a passcode."

Cole's gaze swung to his brother. "What do you mean?"

"Here, see for yourself." Ilya stood with the envelope extended, his back to the woods.

A flicker of light glinted in the trees over Ilya's shoulder. Cole tensed, ignoring the envelope Ilya offered. He tipped his head at the unnatural glimmer that had winked in the trees, the wrongness of it, trying to identify the source.

There it was again. A dot of light danced, then held steady. Sunlight reflected off glass. Light hitting the scope of a sniper rifle.

Cole lunged for his brother as the wall shattered in a spray of shards. Another bullet whistled past his ear.

But the next hot slug struck him with a searing burn.

10

VIENNA, VIRGINIA
7:13 A.M. EDT

Humidity saturated the dense, sticky air. Fire flared in Maddox's lungs as she sprinted the last yards of her short, three-mile run back to her building. Her legs shook, thighs burning, right-side ribs aching in protest.

Herman, her neighbor's Vizsla–terrier mix, galloped at her side, his tongue lolling from his mouth. Stopping at the front steps, she checked her smartwatch. Twenty-three minutes. Not shabby.

She mounted the stairs inside leading to the second floor and knocked on her neighbor's door. Mrs. Saunders, an African American retired schoolteacher with rheumatoid arthritis, had adopted the dog from a shelter after her husband died. A beautiful copper-brown, he was an affectionate companion but needed lots of exercise.

The door opened, and Mrs. Saunders greeted her with a cheery smile.

"Herman was a great buddy as usual." Maddox handed over the leash.

"Such a short run."

She usually did a six-miler before or after work when she was home, fitting it in every day without fail. Her banged-up body moaned gratitude for today's dialed-down intensity. "I felt like taking it easy. It's pretty hot out."

"Thanks so much. I appreciate it and so does Herman."

Maddox scratched behind the dog's floppy ears, and he licked the sweat from her legs. "My pleasure."

"Honey, if you don't mind my saying"—Mrs. Saunders painted on a grave look—"you should dump the SOB who beats you."

This wasn't the first time Maddox had been seen with unexplained bruises. The contusions on her cheek and upper thigh exposed by her running shorts were obvious. She'd tried the patented excuses in the past—*I fell, it happened in self-defense class, my job is hazardous sometimes*—garnering raised eyebrows and a smug nod, adding credence to the assumption she was being abused and hiding it.

The supposition was natural, and Maddox had long since stopped trying to change her neighbor's mind.

"Thanks for your concern." She unlocked her apartment door directly across the hall and waved goodbye, swallowing the words *I gave as good as I got*.

She locked her door, kicked off her sneakers in the bedroom, and started the shower.

Reece had texted a situational report at 3:00 a.m. Probably assumed she was sleeping and didn't want to disturb her with a call. She'd dozed, in between icing her bruises, but the few z's she had nabbed couldn't be classified as sleep.

According to the SITREP, Cole had left a budget hotel after staying two hours and resumed more laps on I-495 while they maintained the three-mile buffer. His ring-around-the-Beltway must've driven Reece batshit crazy. Gideon, on the other hand, took such things in placid stride.

They would check in again at nine. If Cole hadn't contacted her by then, plan B.

She stripped, dumping her sweaty clothes in a heap, got in under the water spray, and lathered up.

Cole would simmer down, process things with a filter of rationality, sooner or later—she was gambling on the long shot of sooner—and do as his conscience dictated. The right thing.

God, it needed to be sooner. As in before she was forced to take drastic measures, triggering him to go from an ugly DEFCON 3 to an apocalyptic DEFCON 1.

The more she tossed over how last night had played out, the more she despised the acrid taste in her mouth. She'd fucked up. The findings of the background check he'd run had primed him to swallow her cover story, lock, stock, and barrel. And she'd fumbled. Let sappy nostalgia and foolhardy hopes of a second chance drive her to a madcap decision.

This should've been about the mission from A to Z. No room for anything personal.

She shampooed, conditioned, and hopped out of the shower. As she squeezed water from her hair with a towel, a shadow moved in her peripheral vision.

Quick.

Quiet.

Someone was in her bedroom.

A pins-and-needles sensation flooded her fingers. She itched to grab a gun.

Fight mode switch flipped, she wrapped the towel around her body and crept to the lower bathroom cabinet. She took out the box of tampons. With her pulse at a sprint, she pulled her loaded Boberg XR9 shorty from inside. Thumb-flicked off the safety.

Small and lightweight, the gun had the same stopping power as a Glock. Hard lessons and the scars they'd left had taught her there was no such thing as being overprepared.

She eased toward her bedroom, slipped through the crack of the door, and pressed into the corner of the room to her left.

A man stood on the other side of her bed, looking out the window.

Cole.

The tension in her chest slackened. As she lowered the gun, he turned, facing her.

"Holy shit. What happened?" She rushed to him and looked at his arm. His jacket was frayed as if pierced by a bullet. The blood on his shoulder stilled her.

Did he get into an altercation with Ilya?

Weariness hung heavy on his face, his solemn gaze a weight on her shoulders. "Flesh wound. Sniper bullet caught Ilya in the chest. Second bullet hit me."

The news rocked her back on her heels as if it'd been a physical blow. He'd gone to see his brother because of her and had almost been killed. By a sniper? She touched his shoulder where the bullet had shredded a hole in his jacket, and he winced.

"Is your brother okay?" She couldn't believe she was asking, but Ilya was his family.

"Not critical. If I hadn't gotten him out of the way, it would've killed him."

And the world would be a better place. "You're probably glad you were there for him."

He clicked his tongue. "Not so sure."

She met his eyes, a question tap-dancing on her tongue. Did he get the passcode?

It hung between them, smothering other words. But asking him would only fuel his distrust.

He grasped her chin between his thumb and forefinger. "What happened to you?" He stared at her cheek, his brows creased, mouth in a hard frown.

Sweet of him to be concerned when he was the one bleeding on her account. "Occupational byproduct. Looks worse than it feels." She put her palm to his chest and absorbed the thudding of his heart, grateful for the rock-steady beat. "Let me clean you up."

She hurried to the bathroom.

Not only had she roped him into this mess, but she'd almost lost him for good. Again. Hands trembling, she tucked her gun back into the box of tampons, pulled out the med kit, and took it to the bedroom.

She stilled, down to her fingertips, in the doorway. He sat on her bed, waiting. Bare to the waist, legs spread wide. The striking tats on his muscle-corded arms held her spellbound as she tried to absorb the sight of him.

Her belly tightened with awareness, sparking an inappropriate tingle.

But the blood on his shoulder revived her urgency, and she tore her gaze away.

"This is what you want." He held out something in his hand.

A white envelope with elegant gold script across the top that read *Ilya Reznikov*.

Triumph burst in her chest like fireworks. Cole had gotten the passcode with plenty of time to spare. They'd be able to access the auction tomorrow. Thank goodness. She wanted to rip open the envelope and verify the contents, but his cold stare pinned her.

Calculating, measuring her response. A test.

Something inside her quivered with desperation to pass.

She eased between his legs. Ignoring the envelope, she opened the med kit and set it beside him. Her damp curls fell, dripping on his chest.

A twitch coursed through him, dragging her gaze down the chiseled landscape of his body.

"Sorry." She corralled her hair over her shoulder out of his way.

"I don't mind." His voice was husky and low. Thick with promise.

Or maybe it was just her desperate imagination.

Cole set the envelope on the nightstand next to her cell phone, ran his hands down his legs, and gripped his knees.

Her mind warred with her heart, and her mouth was mired somewhere in the middle. Words were usually effortless when she was on the job. This time, not knowing the right thing to say, she bit her tongue.

She put on latex gloves, set out gauze and saline solution. Cleaning the wound would burn like hell. "This is going to hurt."

"When it comes to you, I'm accustomed to pain."

The sting of his words bled through her, but she didn't let her equanimity falter.

"Whatever doesn't kill you makes you stronger." She squeezed the saline into the wound.

He gave a sharp hiss and tightened his jaw.

The bullet had clipped his deltoid, but there wasn't any damage to the axillary nerve. She tore open a packet of Celox, a grainy blood-clotting agent that didn't burn like some others and would help him heal faster. Rubbing a little powder deep in his wound, she worked quickly to minimize his discomfort. She pressed clean gauze to it, wrapping it with a pressure bandage.

"There. Should be good until we get you stitches. Lucky there's no major damage."

"You're pretty good at that." He nodded down at his arm.

She tugged the gloves off. "I've had a lot of practice." Patching up herself and battle brothers in the field was her only hobby. No time for anything else in her life.

His gaze found hers and his dark eyes held her ensnared.

The dangerous edge running through him, drawing her in, had always been the backbone of the young man she'd fallen for. But the wear and tear of time looked good on him, worked in his favor. A sophisticated accessory. As did the arresting refinement of his body, hard curves and sharp angles. More tempting than ever.

Brutally gorgeous. He'd been hers once. She'd give anything to have him again. For a day. For an hour. Damn, she'd take ten minutes.

She caressed his cheeks, leaning into the warmth of

his body. A tremble of longing shivered through the center of her, and she didn't hide it.

He brushed his knuckles over her bruised cheek. Her skin tingled, nerve endings awash in the muscle memory of his strong hands sweeping over her in the darkness, their limbs inexorably tangled, his strained breath in her ear, sweat coating their skin.

The heat in his eyes burned bright and hot as a signal fire, inviting her home. The knots in her stomach loosened as new ones bunched in her chest. Old scars growing sore as a fresh wound opened. The years she'd spent piecing herself back together, trying to recover from the agonizing loss of this—while he was out in the world, alive and well all along.

She swatted the thought away, not wanting anything to spoil those ten minutes.

He cupped the back of her leg, caressing bare skin, pulling her closer. Her thighs quivered and her breath grew shallow. He slid his palm to cradle her head, guiding her lips toward his.

The suspended moment whetted her anticipation. Her toes curled into the carpet, heart palpitating wildly like hummingbird wings in her throat.

His mouth claimed hers, or hers claimed his. She didn't know, didn't care, lost in the shocking relief of the kiss.

Like being submerged under water, fighting for air, drowning in the abyss, lungs too tight. Then busting through the surface into sunlight, gulping in a life-giving breath.

That's what it was like kissing Cole.

Cole couldn't stop Maddox coming in for a kiss any more than he could turn away from watching a six-car pileup. If she needed to get this out of her system, fine, he'd oblige. He'd take what she tossed at him and swing it right back. Prove to her and himself he wasn't going to let her have him by a leash. Not again.

Then their lips touched.

God, the sweet ache of his insides jump-starting after nine years trapped in limbo. Not quite alive. Not quite dead. Starved for affection for so, so long.

He tried to rally his inhibitions, but they dispersed. He was an open box of dry tinder tossed in the air, and she set everything ablaze.

Maddox put her knee on the bed, straddled his thigh, spread her toned legs wide, and rocked her towel-clad curves against him. Torturing him.

His skin burned with a need he'd denied for almost a decade, seared down to the bone.

Against his better judgment, he did the stupid-est thing possible—deepened the kiss. He took total command of her mouth, intent on drawing out her pleasure with every erotic stroke of his tongue. He slid his hand up under her towel and gripped her bare backside.

She wound her arms around his neck, her fingers diving into his hair. Her cool wet curls caressed his hot skin. A soft groan escaped her, the wicked vibrations shooting to his groin.

His body tightened, strained with want. He hadn't

been with a woman in three years, but the only one he'd
ever hungered for was her.

He longed to rip off her towel, give in to the raw
urge, and take her, but kissing her was like running
in quicksand. Each caress and taste sucked him deeper
into the ravening intensity, with no traction to be
found in the millions of grains, threatening to swallow
him whole.

He damn sure couldn't sleep with her.

The cell on the nightstand rang.

She went rigid, her mouth leaving his, gaze whipping
toward the phone.

He glanced at the screen. "Helios Importing and
Exporting." The employer's name that Linda had found
in the background check. "Code for CIA?"

The phone continued to ring, but she didn't reach
for it. Probably her boss checking to see if she'd made
headway with the *asset*. More like a puppet, and she was
pulling his strings.

How had he let it happen?

If he didn't screw his brain in tight, they might not
make it through the auction alive.

Helios Importing and Exporting. Code for CIA?

Fury had lit his eyes, biting sarcasm had chewed
through his words, and Maddox cringed on the inside.

Cole stood, nudging her away from him.

Grasping the top of the towel, she longed to cover

up with the thickest pair of sweats she owned. Back to square one. The phone stopped ringing, and she exhaled.

"You should open the envelope," he said, his tone icy.

She eyed the gleaming gold letters on the envelope and was torn. *A to Z, the mission first*, her head prompted, but her body and heart won by majority.

This was an opportunity to clear the air she didn't want to lose. "The passcode can wait."

"It's not a passcode." Cole's expression was closed down, hard and frigid. "You asked for my help. From the looks of things, you're still going to need it. And when this is done, we can be done."

Everything seemed to slow down—her breath, her thoughts. Everything except for the way her chest pinched and the ache that flowed. "Is that what you want?" Her voice came out a thread of sound.

He stared at her, letting the question dangle, like the blade of a pendulum over her throat. She dreaded him leaving again worse than dying.

The NOC—nonofficial cover—cell phone rang again. She wanted to smash it.

"You better answer that." He turned and grabbed his backpack.

The tattoo was still on his back. Her ink. Unaltered. A dazzling serpent swallowing its tail etched on the length of his spine in a double ouroboros infinity loop. Her birthdate, the Chinese zodiac year of the snake, hidden in the stunning mosaic of the colorful body.

Till I Die inked across his traps.

The punch of seeing it might as well have been a fist to the solar plexus, leaving her breathless.

She cleared her throat and answered the phone. "Yes."

"Can you speak?" asked a tinny female voice.

"Is this Harper?"

"Yes. You need to know what's happened. Blackburn and Callahan are both dead."

Two of the biggest players in arms trafficking, two of five invited to bid at the auction. "What? How?"

Cole threw on a fresh tee from his bag, coming toward her.

"Blackburn took a bullet to the head yesterday in London," Harper said. "Callahan went up in a car bomb in Philadelphia last night."

Maddox stared at Cole's injured shoulder. "Someone went after Ilya Reznikov this morning, but he's alive."

Cole stood close, shy of contact. Heat suffused her face and slithered down her chest, forcing her to look away from him.

"Did you get the passcode?" Harper asked.

Maddox picked up the envelope. The weight of the paper was heavy, pricey. She opened it and took out a thick card, gilded in gold.

"Fuck." The word left her mouth in a whisper. She looked up at Cole, who wore an *I told you so* expression.

"What is it?" Harper asked.

"It's not a passcode. They're coordinates. 39°13'23.8' N, 76°29'22.6' W. The invitation says *black tie, no weapons or a penalty will be issued. Free to bring a guest for your comfort.* And the auction has been pushed up. To tonight. I'll be there as soon as I can." She hung up.

"We'll be there." He snatched the invitation and

slipped it into his jacket pocket. "Wherever you're going on this, I'm going."

"You've already done more than enough."

She couldn't ask him to risk his life further. He'd almost been killed this morning. Endangering herself was part of her job, but this wasn't his problem.

"I'm happy to see you're done using me and ready to toss me aside so quickly, but since this auction is taking place in person, you'll need a Reznikov with you."

He was right about the latter part, but the pigheaded gleam in his eye warned her not to debate the former.

For now.

11

NORTHERN VIRGINIA
8:48 A.M. EDT

Cole followed Maddox on his Ninja.

Un-freaking-believable. After getting what she wanted, she had tried to dump him on the curb like a bag of trash. Insult to injury.

The only thing more unbelievable was the big-ass truck she was driving.

They exited the George Washington Memorial Parkway and hit a service road. A quarter mile through an isolated area along the Potomac River, a gated compound came into view. By the time they drove past a sign that read *Helios Importing and Exporting*, Cole was ready to spit battery acid.

Maddox stopped beside a stone gatehouse the size of a Metro station booth, perched in front of the gated compound. He idled behind her, taking in the perimeter. Nothing drew unwanted attention—no guard towers, no razor wire atop the ten-foot brick fence. Smart.

Yet odd. This wasn't the massive, in-your-face, overt CIA complex at Langley.

Maddox rolled down the tinted window of her Toyota Tundra and hiked a thumb back at him as she spoke to a guard in plain clothes. He was definitely packing heat.

The guy threw a quick glance at Cole and gave her a nod. She swiped a badge or card on an identification reader and punched in a PIN. The solid black gate slid open. From the thickness, Cole gathered it was armored.

She drove in at a snail's pace and he trailed behind. Six-foot concrete barriers with reinforced rebar edged the path for the first four hundred yards. A posted sign warned against exceeding thirty-five miles per hour.

Twelve-inch-diameter shiny silver disks dotted the road in a familiar pattern. Those were retractable pneumatic bollards—electrohydraulic stainless-steel pillars—that'd pop up from the ground if triggered by high-speed velocity. Or, he guessed, a security lockdown protocol. Enough of them could stop a tank. And there were a buttload.

Trees shrouded the road after the barriers—giant sycamores, sweeping oaks, dense willows, and a bunch of others. The drive in under the thick canopy of greenery was quite idyllic.

He knew this location—or about it anyway. This had been the planned site for a swanky housing complex. He'd been impressed as hell by the online renderings as a teenager with a budding love for architecture. Designed around a verdant park, the compound had been intended as the quintessential suburban community, with necessities at residents' fingertips. The project lost funding and someone anonymous scooped it up a few years after 9/11.

Around the bend on the asphalt path sat a large building, shaped like a giant gray box with massive stone columns. Down the road behind it was a smaller-sized hangar. Trees broke up the parking lot in front of the gray building, giving it a helter-skelter look. The limited aerial exposure made the setup a covert agent's wet dream.

He followed her to the far end of the lot and parked next to her. As he removed his helmet, tucking it under his arm, she climbed out of her truck.

"Never figured you for a truck gal."

"I'm not. That's mine." She pointed to a red Hyundai SUV. "It didn't start. I think it's my alternator, but I haven't had a chance to deal with it. This"—she gestured to the pickup—"belongs to Knox. He's deployed."

"Are you sure your boyfriend won't mind you driving his wheels?"

She stepped up close, a tease of a smile on her full lips. "Knox is better than a boyfriend. More reliable too. He's the deputy here, like a brother to me. And I'm *sure* he won't mind."

Something in her silken tone, the gleam in her eyes as she talked about the dude had Cole disliking Knox no matter what the nature of their relationship.

"You can't bring your cell phone inside." She held out her hand. "Well, you could, but you'd have to leave it at the security desk. The elevators won't work if an unauthorized cell is detected. Also, no weapons allowed for you."

Narrowing his eyes, the questions in his head mounted. He put his phone, knives, and gun in his backpack and handed it over but hung on to his helmet.

"Bruiser beads too."

After he proffered his necklace, she tossed it in her car and strode off at a clipped pace.

"Care to explain?" He swept an arm at the compound, strolling beside her.

"What?"

"This isn't Langley, baby."

Her eyes cut to him. "I hate it when you call me *baby*."

Still? Good. "Yeah, I remember. Baby."

She looked straight ahead and kept walking. Hips swaying in a pair of painted-on jeans, she wore a sexy V-neck that spelled *all woman*, despite the boots made for stomping in heads and a lightweight jacket covering her weapon. Maddox packing heat still boggled his mind. And from the bulge, hers was bigger than his. Go figure.

He snatched her arm, forcing her to a jerky stop. "Explain, or I don't go in."

"Technically, I'm not CIA anymore. I'm this." She pointed a finger at the gray building. "We're an off-book outfit designed to do what other agencies can't and to give plausible deniability to higher-ups."

That was about as clear as if she'd spoken in Tagalog. "What do you do here?"

"I take care of problems."

He quirked an eyebrow. "What exactly is this?" He pitched a thumb at the building.

"Let's go inside. I called my boss in the car to tell him I was bringing you in. Sign the NDAs, then we'll talk. Okay?"

Not his first rodeo with a nondisclosure agreement, but this was *not* okay. "Who in the hell are you, Maddox? What've you become?"

Squaring her shoulders, she gave him the iciest look he'd ever seen from her. "I could ask you the same."

Touché. If that's how she wanted it, he could play this

game. "All right, Miss Secret Agent, lead the way." He dropped his hand from her arm.

"In the CIA, MI6, *this*"—she gestured to the building again as they headed toward it—"we're officers. It's a common mistake. Agents are foreign assets for us. Unless we're talking about the FBI or DEA."

"I'm glad we cleared that up," he quipped, following her to the front door.

Inside, Maddox swiped her badge along an automatic turnstile, opening the retractable barrier flaps while a metal detector screeched as Cole passed under the rectangular arch.

"His helmet must've set off the alarm," Maddox said to two more plainclothes guards. "He's clean."

"Then your guest is cleared, Kinkade," said one of the guards.

"Thanks." She waved as they headed for an elevator.

Security sat behind an elegant, curved white marble desk veined with gold and grayish blue. The floors and walls were dark concrete polished to mirror perfection. *Pretty sweet.*

Crossing the lobby, her gaze floated upward. He followed her look to a balcony filled with rows of shelving units. As he scanned the second floor, the base of his skull tingled, his shoulders drawing tight.

At a biometric reader mounted on the wall, she lined her eye up with the ocular identifier. After an iris scan, the elevator doors opened.

This level of security was the kind he encountered at billion-dollar companies safeguarding proprietary rights against corporate espionage.

"A crazy budget paid for this. You guys must be rolling in government dough."

"The spare-no-expense budget that created this agency and facility came as a response to the Patriot and Bioterrorism Preparedness Acts after 9/11. Over the last few years, funding has dried up. We still have enough to stay operational and pay for our topside security contractors." She nodded to the plainclothes guards. "They don't have access to the facility below."

"Below?" He followed her into the elevator.

She hit the button for the sixth floor, and the doors closed. Green lasers scanned them—for listening devices and unauthorized signal waves, at his best guess—and then the elevator lowered in a mad-money-smooth motion.

Into a sub-facility. *Underground*.

Now, he was really impressed. Restricting access for topside security was also the type of smart recommendation he'd make to someone dealing with sensitive information.

"Working here, I'm surprised you don't live in a fortress," he said.

"Or perhaps a gilded tower fit for a princess?"

"Nope. You killed my fairy-tale illusions of you a long time ago." Her gaze cut to the doors, and he decided to finish his point. "Only took me twenty seconds to break in."

"When did B&E become your hobby?"

"Since I started working as a consultant for Rubicon Security."

She eyed him hard. "You used illegal off-market tech to get into my place, didn't you?"

He shrugged. "Are you going to dime me out? I know it's not beneath you."

"I never would've figured you for that kind of work," she said casually, ignoring the low blow. "Doesn't sound like you."

"Ditto, baby."

She rolled her eyes. He loved getting under her skin, even if it wasn't the way he craved.

"After the auction, do you plan to pull a disappearing act? Go back to playing dead?"

The doors opened, and she marched off.

Catching up to her, he said, "Let's get something straight. *You* resurrected *me*, to use me for your job. And after you roped me in, I got *shot*. I took a bullet. Playing this game with the CIA—or whatever the hell you are now—isn't on my bucket list."

She went straight as a lightning rod, picking up the pace. "The bullet grazed you."

"Grazed?" As if it'd been a scratch. A freaking bullet put a hole in his arm!

"It's a flesh wound," she said with frigid nonchalance, but her eyes snapped with fire. "Would you like me to kiss your *boo-boo* and help make it better?"

"Listen, you can kiss my—"

"Fine. You win the poor-me award. Should we have your trophy engraved?"

As infuriating as she was and as livid as he was, damn if this new ball-breaker side to her didn't turn him on like a floodlight. "Are you kidding—"

"Shit happens."

Her teasing tone tickled and goaded him at the same time.

"Whatever doesn't kill you makes you stronger,"

she said. "And I'm not talking about the playing possum kind, where you let your fiancée think you're dead. The only easy day was yesterday. So suck it up, *baby*."

A nice guy would've let her have the win, but standing in super-spook central, he wasn't inclined to concede an inch. "You weren't my fiancée. I never proposed."

She stopped so violently, it was as if she'd plowed into a wall. She whirled on him. A thousand emotions flashed in her eyes, condensing to one that ripped a hole in his gut.

They'd talked about marriage, made plans for a future. He'd had every intention of hitching himself to her until death, the kind that'd actually put him in a casket, but he'd never popped the question. Never gotten her a ring.

"You're right." Her voice turned soft as cotton, an unearthly composure falling over her. "I wasn't as important as a wife or a fiancée. You would've come back for one of those."

He was officially an asshole. He reached for her, but she stepped away. His gut burned.

She was unreadable. Only her eyes telegraphed scathing pain before hardening to steel.

"Maddox," said someone, drawing both their gazes.

A woman with a cello-shaped figure and bright eyes that screamed *on high alert* stood posted outside a conference room, its glass walls tinted an opaque gray. She ducked her head inside the room. Then a guy in his late forties, maybe early fifties, waltzed out. Despite the snazzy suit, he didn't look like a desk guy. He had the sharp presence of someone used to being in the thick of the action.

"Thanks, Janet." He patted the woman's shoulder, and she left. "I'm Director Bruce Sanborn, Mr. Matthews. Or would you prefer Mr. Reznikov?" He extended a hand.

"Cole works." Tightening his grip on his helmet, he stuffed his other hand in his pocket.

"We appreciate your assistance, Cole." The guy lowered his hand. "This is time-sensitive and of the greatest importance. You'll be read into mission details, but there are nondisclos—"

"I'm up to speed about the NDAs."

"You don't mince words and you don't waste time." Maddox's boss flashed a smile bright as a bare bulb and just as empty. "You'll fit right in."

Cole tugged on a cold, tight grin. "Trust me, Mr. Sanborn, I won't."

"Simply Sanborn is fine."

"Before I help you people any further, I need to know—are you responsible for the Russians finding out I'm alive?"

The coincidence stank of a setup. Maddox also stared at her boss as if keen for an answer.

Sanborn wiped the smile from his face. His demeanor relaxed, gaze unwavering. "We don't have the luxury of living in a black-and-white world with binary simplicity. It's gray. Our job boils down to what's necessary to safeguard this nation. Without apology. But no. We didn't orchestrate Russian interference. You're too important. You're our only way into this auction, and it would've been impossible to ensure your safety. Okay?"

The point-blank spiel wasn't what Cole had expected

from the poster boy for *Spies R Us*, but no tells of lying pinged in him. Not the faintest worrisome niggle in his gut. In fact, Sanborn's stark honesty was a bit unnerving. Cole nodded his satisfaction with the response.

"Would you wait in the conference room while I speak with Maddox in private?"

Cole glanced at her, longing to apologize. Not as if he'd muster the words in front of the slick operator in the suit, but her gaze roamed everywhere except to him.

Swearing under his breath in Russian, he pushed into the conference room.

Maddox steeled herself, refusing to let Cole mess with her head. Or her heart.

Sanborn waited until the door closed behind Cole. "Great job getting us in to the auction. You're free to wash your hands of this now. Castle can take point."

Acid burned up her throat. She'd roped Cole into this, nearly gotten him killed for real. She wasn't going to leave him hanging. Sure as hell wasn't giving Sanborn's protégé her mission.

"This is mine." She filtered angry desperation from her voice, keeping her face stoic, not letting him see how much she needed this. "You can't take this away from me."

She was battle-tested, capable of shooting, stabbing, and breaking necks with the best of them. Busted her butt proving herself, volunteered for assignments that didn't require a pretty face, took bullets and beatings, and endured unspeakable things to be one of Sanborn's elite.

"This mission is perfect for me. It's exactly what you trained me to do. I'm qualified—"

"You're more than qualified. I'd prefer to send you to the auction over Castle." The smooth gravel of his voice coupled with his soft gaze lightened her anxiety by ten pounds.

His stamp of approval and getting the job done were all she had. Even if what she wanted most was sitting in the conference room.

"A security detail will look at Castle or Reaper and tap four men to cover them," Sanborn said. "With you, they'll just see that face of yours. Won't suspect you're capable of putting down four of them. You're my secret weapon." He flashed a smile brimming with pride. "I asked a lot of you emotionally, and you delivered. If you want to pass, it's fine."

"I can handle this." Working with Cole would test her, a new trial by fire, but she'd figure it out. Get the job done.

Sanborn gave a warm nod. "Glad to hear it."

Yes.

"Considering your personal history with Cole, it's best if Castle is on this too."

Damn it. Maddox plastered on her best professional smile. "Castle is a hardcore operator. Excellent in the field, but—"

Emily "Doc" Duvall strolled up to their huddle in a hurry. Her long, fluid skirt swished about her ankles and her hair flowed back as if there was an invisible wind machine on her. "Oh, I'm glad I'm not late for the briefing. Willow headed to the conference room fifteen minutes ago, but I was still preparing," she said, bright and cheery, always like an interminable ray of sunshine.

Maddox smothered a sigh.

"You're right on time." Sanborn slipped his hands into his pockets with an uncharacteristic zippy little rock back on his heels. "As our resident expert on bioweapons, I would've waited for you."

"Sir." Daniel Cutter approached them.

Sanborn shifted his gaze and totally missed the killer smile Doc threw at him right before she strode into the conference room.

For months, Maddox had caught the flirty little looks Doc tossed at Sanborn. And for months, the best spy on the planet had been oblivious.

"I heard the op has taken an unexpected turn. I thought you might want an extra analyst on this." Good ole Cutter, always eager to volunteer. Gung ho on steroids due to his time as a Marine Corps analyst strapped to Force Recon.

"As a matter of fact, I want you and Amanda to sit in on the briefing," Sanborn said.

Cutter gave a curt nod and hightailed it toward the analysis section.

Sanborn's attention swung back to her. "Castle stays." The grit in his tone was coarse. Final. "Part of your backup, with Reece and Reaper, who are already in the conference room. That's your team." He flashed his best pro smile, smoother and brighter than hers by far. "If you still want it."

She pulled on her good-soldier expression. "Of course, I want it." At least she'd have her battle brothers. For Reece, you support your friends and keep your word, or you're not worth your weight in salt. And Gideon was the guy you wanted at your six, never in your face. Both were rock solid, would have her back. They were family in an unfailing way she didn't have with Castle.

"Castle knows you in a way the rest of us don't," Sanborn said. "I've lost officers who've gotten emotional on a mission before. I won't lose you down a rabbit hole. Are we clear?"

Sanborn didn't have the faintest idea the havoc he was about to wreak, assigning her brother as her babysitter. "It won't work. Castle and Cole can't—"

Yelling erupted inside the conference room. They exchanged glances and rushed into the room just as Castle flung his chair behind him into the wall and charged around the conference table.

Planted in a wide stance, Cole stood, gaze locked, razor-sharp and lethal. He gripped his helmet like it was a bowling ball, ready to swing.

They'd always rubbed each other wrong, but it'd never escalated to violence.

Fists cocked at his sides, Castle was a mountain in motion. "If you think you're going to waltz back in, fuck my sister, and piss all over her life again, you're mistaken."

Her stomach lurched. She'd never seen this fiercely protective side of her brother. Reminded her of her father, in the best and worst ways. Cole didn't know what she'd gone through after he left, about the baby she'd lost or how the emptiness had broken her. She never wanted him to know. But Castle had a front-row seat to her misery.

Gideon and Reece jumped in front of her brother to stop him, wrangling him by the arms to hold him back.

Doc sat stunned and wide-eyed. Willow Harper hunkered in her seat, clutching a notepad to her chest.

Maddox glanced around to find Sanborn standing behind her, looking cool and collected. Meeting her gaze, he shot her one of those go-handle-it looks. This was her team, but she fired a this-isn't-my-mess-to-clean-up look right back. Sanborn had lit the fuse to this shit bomb.

"If you can't lead them in here, what are you going to do in the field?" Sanborn asked.

"I'm going to knock that arrogant look right off your damn face, Reznikov." Growling, Castle drove forward, not letting anything, not even four hundred pounds of resisting muscle, stop him from crossing the room.

———————   ———————

A big guy could be taken like any other, but fired up, Castle appeared to be a worthy opponent. He'd make Cole work for a win.

Maybe Castle had a right to be angry. Despite his damned good reasons, Cole had left Maddox behind to deal with grief brutal enough to send her to a private psych facility. And he'd been drowning in his own crap at the same time, impotent to check on her.

Letting his shoulders drop, Cole lifted his chin and prepared to take one hit. One.

Castle yanked free of Frick, or was it Frack—fuck it, *Reece's* arm, and a ruthless fist slammed into Cole's cheek. Pain bloomed. The salty taste of blood hit his tongue.

"I owed you one." Cole ducked, sidestepping the next blow. "I won't give you another."

Snarling, Castle lunged. Cole blocked the fist with his helmet and gave Castle a swift kick to the shin. He swung the helmet to the back of the knee. Castle dropped but recovered with quicksilver speed.

Fuck, all he'd done was poke the ogre. Last thing Cole wanted was to use real force.

As Castle grabbed Cole by the jacket, Maddox jumped in between them. A part of Cole wanted the beatdown he probably deserved, but he wasn't equipped to lose.

Maddox shielded him with arms outstretched. "What are you doing?"

"You're going to let him back in, aren't you?" Castle clenched his jaw, chest heaving.

She stood rigid, eyes hard. "We have a mission and lives to save. We need his help."

Of course, she was protecting the *asset*. Cole straightened, drawing everything inside tight. He was such a dumbass to think for one second that he was anything more than a means to an end.

"Communication is the first step in building an effective partnership." Sanborn strode to the head of the black glass-top table. "As of right now, you're one team. There is one fight. Retrieving a bioterror weapon before it can be used. Take a seat."

Guarded, in slow motion, everyone sat. The tension in the room was thicker than a setting slab of wet concrete.

Maddox clutched Cole's forearm. "Are you okay? You took a pretty hard blow."

Castle expelled a heavy sigh, reeling in everyone's attention. He shook his head, mouth twisted like he was chewing on words made of jagged metal.

"I'm fine." Cole pulled his arm away.

Sanborn sat and typed something on a touch screen on the smart table. "Cole, several NDAs should be on the screen in front of you. Read and sign while we go through the briefing. If you have questions, don't hesitate to interrupt. This is Willow Harper." He gestured to a petite young woman. "One of our analysts. She'll give us an update."

Just then, a man and woman entered.

"This is the rest of our analysis section. Amanda Woodrow is our lead analyst."

A lean, lanky, attractive woman sat beside him and said, "Lead just means I get to handle the boring admin stuff like performance reports."

Cole noticed a small white clump matted to her chestnut locks. "You've got something in your hair."

She pulled it out and brushed it from her hands. "Part of Jaxi-bear's breakfast. Oatmeal."

"That's Daniel Cutter." Sanborn nodded to the one in need of a shave and sporting a rumpled suit. The young guy had a rugged build and looked like he should be out riding a wave or a bucking bull rather than sitting in the conference room.

"Happy to take any of those admin duties off your hands, Amanda," Cutter said.

The woman sighed as if she'd heard and rejected the offer many times before.

"Proceed, Willow." Sanborn gestured with his raised mug.

She cleared her throat and tapped the black glass-top table, bringing up a digital built-in screen. The brunette had a sexy librarian vibe with her tight bun, pencil skirt, silk blouse, and pearls. "The coordinates from the invitation are to Sparrows Point Shipyard in Maryland. It's a forty-minute drive from Ilya Reznikov's compound, which leads me to believe this isn't the final location where the auction will take place but a pickup point."

Cole paid attention as he went through the digital paperwork and signed. Apparently, this place was called the Gray Box and even its name was classified. Posh setup they had here. Although the federal ESIGN Act made an electronic signature legally binding, most places still used paper.

"Considering the other bidders live all over the world," the analyst said, spouting information like water from a spigot on full blast, "I think everyone was given a specific meeting location within easy reach. I suspect whoever shows up for the auction will be transported to an alternate site from there."

A satellite image popped up in front of everyone—a patch of bare land surrounded by small roads, adjacent to I-695 and the Patapsco River. "This is the shipyard. It's been closed for some time. No structures to provide coverage for the backup team."

"I've called in drone support, so we can monitor the situation at a distance," Sanborn said. "Cole, you already know Castle. You've met John Reece." He threw a nod at the guy with the dark hair and face partially hidden by a trucker hat that read *Drinks Well with Others*.

"And Gideon Stone, also known as Reaper around here." Sanborn lifted his mug toward the one with all-American, apple-pie looks. "He'll pilot the helo for the backup team. This"—he smiled at a strawberry blond, who had the aura of a flower child—"is our resident CDC scientist and part-time medic, Emily Duvall, but everyone calls her Doc."

"Sorry to meet you under such circumstances," Doc said, blue eyes radiating warmth.

"Any idea how we'll be transported from the pickup site?" Maddox asked.

"It's anyone's guess." Harper shrugged. "The river runs into the Atlantic. Air, ground, and water transport are all viable. Oh, and a video was posted on the darknet this afternoon. The biological weapon we're dealing with is ten times worse than we suspected, but Doc will explain."

"Simpler if you guys watched first." Doc tapped a few buttons on the table, changing everyone's individual screen.

A video played, showing a male, midtwenties, restrained to a metal-framed bed and hooked up to an IV. Filthy room. Paint-chipped walls. Somewhere abandoned. No audio. A person wearing a hazmat space suit held up a French newspaper, *Le Monde*, dated one week ago.

The camera zoomed in on a small canister beside the young man. A timer counted down for ten seconds. The container opened, dispersing a fine mist throughout the entire room.

The video jumped to four hours later. Large red

pimples speckled the man's face and arms. One day after initial onset, a rugged landscape of red blisters and bubbling pustules covered the guy's body. Three days later, black blood ran from his nostrils and ears. The man was dead five days after exposure, the body incinerated with a flamethrower.

Cole's blood turned to ice and he suppressed the urge to heave. He'd seen a lot in his life but nothing so vile. Aside from shifting her gaze from the screen, Maddox appeared unfazed, but he knew better. His hand was on her back, rubbing in small circles, before he had the sense to stop himself. Just couldn't help it.

Not even Superman had the misfortune of being attracted to his kryptonite.

"This is proof of product, sent before the auction," Doc said.

Maddox's brows drew together. "The timeline on the video doesn't match how the virus is supposed to work. It should take two weeks for symptoms of small-pox to first appear. Not four hours. Much less death in five days."

While Maddox shared her concerns, holding the attention of everyone at the table, Doc fiddled with her coppery-blond hair, brushing it back from a shoulder. Sanborn's gaze zeroed in on her from the quick, little gesture and held for the tiniest beat too long as he rubbed a knuckle across his lips.

The look was subtle, but the spark of interest was unmistakable. No one else seemed to catch it, probably because it didn't last. An instant later, he was engrossed in his coffee.

"You're right. This bioweapon has been altered." Doc brought up a chart depicting differences between the strains. Cutesy charms dangled from a bracelet that complemented her bohemian top.

Everyone focused on their screens, except Sanborn, who stared at Doc. There was no lechery in his eyes. Cole recognized the loneliness and longing. Sanborn looked like a kid staring in a shop window at one of the shiny, unobtainable toys on display.

Although there appeared to be a fifteen- to twenty-year age gap between him and Doc, Sanborn was fit and most women would probably find him appealing, but Cole sensed a *look but don't touch* energy from him.

"We're calling it smallpox-M," Doc said. "The M is for *magnified mutation* in this terror-borne strain. It's a biosafety level 4 virus that attacks and cripples the immune system within hours, causing the accelerated onset of symptoms. This hot agent is extremely contagious and, from what I can tell, far deadlier than anything we've encountered."

"How does it spread?" Cole asked.

"It's airborne—a cough or a sneeze is enough."

Sanborn threaded his fingers. "Fatality rate?"

"Natural smallpox has a fatality rate of thirty percent. I can't be certain with this since I don't have a sample to study. But based on the video of the victim, who was young and appeared healthy, and the severity of the symptoms that overwhelmed his immune system like a viral blitzkrieg, I'm estimating that this mutated version will have a much higher fatality rate." She blew out a long breath. "Possibly ninety percent."

There was a sudden heaviness in the air.

"There's no known vaccine or cure," Doc said. "Those few who survive will be horribly disfigured from the scars left by the lesions. This has potentially devastating consequences. Worldwide."

Fan-freaking-tastic. The M might as well have stood for *monstrous*, elevating the stakes and risks. What else should he have expected—he was on vacation in the middle of a heat wave.

"Thank you, Doc." Sanborn turned to Harper and gave a nod.

She tapped a button. Pictures of two men he didn't recognize came up on his screen.

"Blackburn and Callahan were killed in the last twenty-four hours," Harper said, fiddling incessantly with a pen.

Sanborn leaned forward. "I believe Blackburn's murder might've triggered the seller to move up the auction."

"As far as we know," Harper said, "Ilya Reznikov in Maryland, Kassar, whose whereabouts are unknown, and Reinhart in Germany are still alive."

"Ilya was attacked this morning." Maddox gently touched his injured shoulder. "Cole was shot saving him. Doc can give you stitches. For the flesh wound." Dropping her hand, she gave him a side-eye that had him both clenching his jaw and squirming in his seat.

"Well, you did the world a favor." Reece rocked back in his chair, wearing a sarcastic grin. "A real solid, saving an arms trafficker responsible for countless deaths."

The comment hit worse than a sucker punch because it was true, but instinct had made Cole lunge for his brother. "Well, that arms trafficker got you this." He whipped out the auction invitation and tossed it on the table. "And since all *you people* care about is the mission, I'd say I did everyone in this room a real *solid*."

The words hadn't been aimed at Maddox, but her gaze fell as she tensed.

"Golly gee, thanks." Reece handed the invitation to Harper.

"Around here, we do care about the mission." Gideon rested his forearms on the table. "If you have a problem with that, Castle would be happy to resolve it with you in the break room. And if he needs any assistance, I'd be pleased to help."

Castle's jaw tightened, veins in his temples throbbing as though he itched to get back to duking it out street-fight style.

"This is my backup?" Cole hiked a thumb at the three tough guys across the table.

"We're backup for Maddox," Castle said. "Not you."

The air needed to be cleared. A street fight wasn't a bad way to do it either.

"You three are to cover Maddox and Cole." Sanborn's voice was quiet yet implacable, arresting everyone's attention. His eyes darkened. "If you're not up for this, I can call Alistair and Ares in early from R&R to replace you."

No one responded as butts shifted in seats.

"Cole will infiltrate the auction as his former self, Nikolai Reznikov, standing in for Ilya," Sanborn said. "The attempt on Ilya's life earlier is the perfect excuse. Maddox will go as your wife and business partner. A spouse won't raise any vetting alarms and the business angle would explain her presence. Apprehend the buyer, seller, and secure the weapon. Any questions?"

He'd pretended she was his wife in his head more times than pride would let him admit. Doing so to save lives wouldn't be an issue, even if he was working with some supersecret government agency that left a bad taste in his mouth.

"We've got it." Maddox stood to leave. "I'm going to supply to gear up."

Cole wanted to stop her. Say something that didn't come out sounding like *Assholese* or *Shitheadish*, but the words were beyond him right now.

"Do I get gear?" Cole asked Sanborn while his gaze stayed fixed on Maddox as she strutted out of the room alongside Amanda.

The three musketeers trailed behind her, eyeing Cole on their way out.

This is going to be fun.

"Nope," Sanborn said. "No gear for civilians, but we can provide a tux that should fit. I believe the card said black tie."

To hell with that. He didn't go anywhere unarmed. Not even into the spy central bunker. His helmet had proved useful when he'd needed it. "I left my prayer beads with my stuff outside. I'll need those—they relax me. Help me to focus."

"No problem," Sanborn said.

"One more thing." He snagged Harper's pen. "Mind?"

"U-uh, yes." Her eyes went wide, and she stiffened,

like he'd shifted the delicate balance of the universe instead of taking a nondescript ballpoint pen.

"Thanks," he said, ignoring her response. He clicked the pen a couple of times and shoved it into his pocket.

Experience had taught him almost anything could be used as a weapon.

12

CENTRAL VALLEY, COSTA RICA
2:30 P.M. EDT, 12:30 P.M. CST

Camouflaged by the white curtain in the master bedroom window, Aleksander watched Kassar do laps down in the garden-side pool. A lush oasis of manicured bushes, blooming flowers in an array of striking colors, and a carpet of trimmed grass surrounded the azure water.

"Natalia, bring me a towel?" Kassar climbed out of the water, bronzed and fit, skin and hair glistening in the bright sun.

Known as the faceless arms broker, he was the only weapons trafficker to build a network and clientele base strictly through the darknet. Also the only one to forego any security.

Perhaps he thought anonymity would keep him safe.

"Natalia! Maria!" Kassar plodded into the villa, wet feet slapping on the Spanish tile.

A balmy breeze carried the sweet scent of jasmine and incoming rain. The sound of Spanish cartoons filled the open villa. Aleksander peeked into the bathroom where Kassar's wife and daughter lay bound and gagged in a bathtub large enough to fit four.

He put a finger over his mouth. "Shh."

When possible, he avoided killing women. Not

because they were the fairer sex or weaker or somehow undeserving of death. None of those lofty ideals. It was the prospect of accidentally taking a mother's life, prematurely separating her from a small innocent. Mothers were gods for their children. Such sacrilege made his stomach roil as though he'd swallowed live eels.

He'd taken a contract on a woman once. A fellow assassin, and if she'd had any wee babes, she'd hidden evidence of them well. But he never killed children under any circumstances.

Fatigue snaked through his shoulders as he shut the bathroom door. He'd slept on the flight, but hopping time zones and the constant need to stay on the razor's edge of his game were catching up to him. A power nap and an espresso from the gleaming machine in the kitchen once Kassar was done should give him the pick-me-up he needed.

"Maria, *dondé está?*" Kassar trotted up the stairs. "Are you and Mommy playing hide-and-seek? I don't have time today. Daddy has to leave soon."

Aleksander leaned against the doorjamb as Val slipped behind the open bedroom door, pulling the garrote from his pocket. His son extended the handles, drawing the fiber wire taut.

Kassar strode into the bedroom and froze, alarm wrinkling his face.

Val glided up behind him, quickly, silently, overlapping the handles of the garrote around the neck and tightening the wire. He rammed a knee into Kassar's lower back.

Tug and hold.

Horror exploded in Kassar's bulging eyes. The natural phases of impending death streaked across his face—fear, denial, concern for his family.

"Your wife and daughter are fine," Aleksander reassured. "The housekeeper will find them."

The wire dug into Kassar's neck, crushing the trachea and cutting off blood flow to the brain. Not as quick as a bullet, but a silent, clean death in thirty seconds.

Kassar gagged, scratching at his own throat, kicking at air. They always struggled. No use, but they tried nonetheless. Air rasped from Kassar's lips—those last sounds of life squeezing out always stung Aleksander's ears. A few seconds longer, then the body went limp.

Val dropped him on the bed next to the laid-out tuxedo and slipped the garrote back in his pocket. "You look tired. Would you like me to make you an espresso, *Baba*?"

Such a good boy, taking care of his father. "After we finish preparing, yes."

Aleksander picked up the five-by-seven-inch heavyweight linen textured card lettered in gold. Out of all the invitations, this was the easiest one to get his hands on, so he'd saved it for last. Impersonating Kassar required no effort, since no one knew what he looked like. With the others, he needed to pick off the competition, keep the price of the bioweapon down. The arms dealers had much deeper pockets, while his resources were finite…

Eliminating them was a means to a justified end. There hadn't been time to get them all. He'd had to be selective. Losing Reznikov still vexed him. He'd been positioned with a clear shot, waiting for his opening. Then the scarred man on the motorcycle had appeared.

There'd been a moment Aleksander swore the man had looked right at him. And when Ilya Reznikov proffered the invitation to Scarface, Aleksander had to take the shot. Kill them both. Lined up in his sights, no breeze, no obstructions, Aleksander went for Ilya Reznikov first. But Scarface had moved fast as a gust of wind, robbing him of the kill. Ruining his perfect record.

Taking out the other invitees with the deepest pockets helped, but three of five was not what he'd endeavored to achieve. He swallowed the loss, the taste bitter as cyanide.

Val hauled out the suitcase stowed under the bed. He removed the false heels of the men's dress shoes, put on gloves, and packed the cavities with the rest of their Semtex. This explosive was better than C-4, both malleable and waterproof. Aleksander set the detonator—already hidden in an empty lighter case— beside a pack of Delta cigarettes. With no way to know what they were walking into at the auction, they needed to be ready for a multitude of scenarios.

The two 160mm e-cigarettes Aleksander withdrew from the suitcase were the longest and widest he could find. He'd removed the wicks, inner tanks, and batteries, keeping the tiny springs and rigging them with No. 10 scalpel blades. A slight press on the battery button and the ultraslim soldered blade would eject. Two inches in length, so he and Val would have to be close to the targets, but the surgical precision of the instrument would do the heavy lifting.

No one ever questioned a smoker. They could have

cigarettes, nicotine gum, and an e-cigarette without raising a single eyebrow.

The Tourbillon Skeleton watch Aleksander wore everywhere was a chunky, classic timepiece that was broken but still served a vital function. He tested the crown. The push-button knob, typically used to wind the mainspring, ejected the black stainless-steel side of the case, revealing double-strand fiber wire that the artistic skeletonized dial concealed. The two-inch section of steel and the rest of the watch acted as handles. A homemade garrote, carried for luck.

Like a perfected aria, it was a magnificent piece of artistry. Aleksander handed the well-used watch to his son. Val would be his good luck and the watch his son's.

Val cradled the watch in his palm and smiled. He was the one bright spot in Aleksander's life.

"Thank you, *Baba*," Val said with a hint of reverence.

Aleksander nodded. His burner phone hummed in his pocket. It could only be the information broker, who'd helped him orchestrate this. The untraceable phone was for emergencies. Aleksander had a standing agreement to pay for any intelligence that could compromise him or help further.

The broker had global resources, spies planted everywhere. The dossiers on the bidders and the auction host had been thorough, making possible everything he'd accomplished in the last thirty-six hours. The text shouldn't have surprised him, but the message was shocking.

Informant on inside has relayed: undercover Gray Box agent to attend auction.

Details to follow after additional payment received. Intel solid.

13

SPARROWS POINT SHIPYARD, MARYLAND
5:00 P.M. EDT

Maddox sat in the SUV, knuckles pale from clenching the steering wheel of the parked car for the past half hour.

Once dressed in her gear, she'd fortified her focus. Didn't matter how irresistible Cole looked seated beside her. Or how the tux molded to his body despite the lack of tailoring. Didn't matter his aura of danger and sex appeal were ramped to the max. With his lush black hair swept in a tight, low man bun, and bruiser beads draped around his neck, everything about him screamed *pure warrior*.

But it didn't matter. She was dialed into the mission.

She ran her hand over the large turquoise stone centerpiece of her necklace.

Inside was a hidden camera, giving the team real-time eyes and ears. Faux diamond earrings housed a one-way communication device, so she could hear them in return.

She and Cole hadn't exchanged a word since she told him the team could hear a pin drop.

Silence was good.

She didn't have to look at Cole to know he was staring. His gaze was heavy as a physical touch, stripping her bare, tangling her belly into knots. Pressing a hand to her midsection, she prayed the sensation subsided. If only he'd take his eyes off her for five minutes.

He wanted her—the dark desire in the air between them was thick as honey—but he didn't want to be *with* her.

And that stung. It cut her to the quick. She wished he was interested in starting over, that this was a date to explore possibilities instead of a mission. Which was as juvenile as the stutter of her heartbeat every time his gaze slid over her.

She fiddled with the belt hanging loose around her waist to give her hands something to do. She must've lost a few pounds over the last couple of days.

The belt was designed to go with a variety of outfits, including the fancy full-length dress she wore. Castle and Noah, another battle brother of hers out on assignment, worked with a talented weapons expert to get them their gear. The chunky buckle on this one contained a mini flashbang grenade and had gotten her out of more than one jam.

"Helicopter inbound from the east," Reece said in her ear. He and Gideon had crashed on the sofas in the break room that afternoon, snatching a few winks, but she'd been too wired to contemplate a catnap.

The sound of rotor blades *thwopping* through air grew louder until a helo came into sight.

Nausea nipped her stomach. Preop jitters she'd learned to compartmentalize. "Ready?"

Cole clicked a pen and shoved it in his suit jacket. "Always."

The sleek white helicopter touched down near the SUV and they climbed out of the car.

Time to earn her paycheck. If only it came remotely close to compensating for the danger.

The spinning rotor blades whipped dust into the air. She wobbled as they walked to the chopper, the dirt ground throwing off her balance. The dress shoes had literal titanium spikes in the high, narrow heels, covered with material to match the uppers, and the flat, finished tips popped off to reveal lethal points. Their weapons expert was an innovative woman.

The chopper pilot approached them. "Good evening. May I see your invitation?"

Cole withdrew the invite from his inner jacket pocket and held it up. "I'm Reznikov. This is my wife." He wrapped an arm around Maddox, cupping her waist.

The pilot's face was hard, his eyes shielded behind shades, but he waved for them to get in.

Cole patted her ass as if she belonged to him. "Let's go."

She bit the inside of her cheek, offsetting the sharp pleasure of his touch. "Careful," she warned.

"With you?" A sly grin curled his mouth, a wildness burning in his eyes. "Never."

The man was insufferable. Eager to sleep with her but entirely prepared to walk away once this was done. Made her want to slap him and kiss him and crawl all over him like a cat against a scratching post.

With a deep inhale, she packed away her emotional baggage and climbed into the helicopter. Cole hopped in, closing the door. The uber-luxury helicopter screamed money with the quietest cabin and no need to wear noise-reduction headsets.

Cole wrapped a strong arm around her shoulders and moved in, pressing his leg against hers. "Stay close, darling."

First time he had ever called her *darling*. Under different circumstances, she would've laughed, but it was better than *baby*.

"You two okay?" asked the pilot. "Long ride ahead."

"We're great." Cole tightened his grip on her. "Happy newlyweds. Inseparable."

Her insides clenched. She shut her mind to the memories rippling the surface. "How long of a ride?"

"Orders not to say. Settle in, get comfortable."

They lifted into the air. Heading east, they flew over the narrow strip of the Patapsco River.

The team would track the helo with the drone flying high enough to remain undetected. With an unknown flight time, they'd need to follow in person as well, at a distance. They were excellent operatives, and there was no one more skilled at directing field missions than Sanborn. Her backup would be there when she needed them.

The landscape shifted, and they coasted in the air over the great blue expanse of the Atlantic Ocean. Nestled against Cole, keeping up their cover, she hardened herself. Meditation had helped her get through the Farm, the covert CIA training facility at Camp Peary, Virginia. She'd learned the tools of espionage and how to recruit assets, sharpened the self-defense skills Cole had taught her.

Now she cleared her mind, concentrating on breathing, letting the edginess rev inside. No distraction. Her focus crystallized.

Cole settled against her, body tense, his gaze on the water.

Hours later, fading sunlight winked across the amber water in a backwash of diamonds. The helo approached a leviathan luxury yacht shimmering on the horizon. Two hundred feet of glass and steel gleamed like something out of a Bond movie.

The helicopter descended as her nerves rose.

Maddox scanned three decks. Six guards in black suits patrolled the main level, automatic weapons for accessories. There'd be more bodyguards on the other levels.

The chopper touched down on a helipad. Training hammered her instincts, every muscle tight. Two guards carrying HK MP7s—serious firepower—hustled to open her door.

Outnumbered and outgunned, the odds were seriously stacked against them.

Every mission was a gamble. The outcome came down to training and determination. She had both. And this time, she had Cole, a man who redefined the very nature of beating the odds.

————————   ————————

INTERNATIONAL WATERS, ATLANTIC OCEAN
7:10 P.M. EDT

Briny air prickled Cole's senses, ratcheting him up on high alert.

He extended a hand, helping Maddox out of the

helicopter. A warm gust of wind caught her dress and sent the side slits billowing, flashing her long, lissome legs. She'd covered the bruise on her thigh with makeup. Brown ringlets were piled on her head in a fancy updo, tendrils brushing her strong, slim shoulders.

The dress was provocative yet classy. In it, she was the most elegant, jaw-dropping creature alive. Having her on his arm, even as they walked into the lion's den, filled him with inexplicable pride.

Two armed guards in black suits greeted them with instructions for them to lift their arms for a pat down. The guys had the rough and tough look and stench of mercenaries.

Cole went first, extending his arms. He'd been frisked before, but these guys were thorough, venturing closer to his crotch than any in prior experiences, even checking inside his shoes. The pen in his jacket pocket garnered a casual glance before it was returned, and his prayer beads were dismissed entirely.

There wasn't much clothing on Maddox to check. The guard kept a neutral gaze, running his hands down the sides of her rib cage and over her flat stomach.

Cole's whole body tightened as he resisted the urge to clock the guy just for putting his hands on her. The bottom of her dress danced and twirled in the wind, displaying too much skin for his comfort. The guy did a double take. Cole moved in, roping a possessive arm around her waist.

The guard checked Maddox's purse, removed a lipstick, and felt the handbag's lining. Once satisfied, he returned her things and said, "This way." He escorted them down a flight of stairs to the main deck and opened glass doors to the interior of the yacht.

They strolled into a swanky room that dripped money, boasting leather seating, an art deco dining table long enough for twelve, a crystal chandelier, plush carpet, and a gleaming ebony piano.

Off to their right, a wrought-iron spiral staircase led to the lower level.

Four bodyguards armed with submachine guns, slung over their arms under their jackets, circulated through the room. They were spread far apart. If necessary, Cole could pick one off and secure a weapon. The furniture in the room was solid, would provide cover under fire.

He noted anything in the room he could use as a weapon. Lead crystal ashtray. Champagne flute. Decorative marble obelisk on the side table. Cord from a lamp. Dining chair.

What Systema martial arts lacked in artistic fluidity it made up for in cold, buttery efficiency.

Piano music floated through the luxurious space from the far side of the room. The haunting melody tugged at his mind. Something familiar. The open top of the Steinway obscured the face of the musician, but Cole zeroed in on another exit behind him that should lead to the front of the yacht.

A stocky guy paced beside the piano, drinking champagne. His poorly tailored tux was atrocious. Looked as if a bicep might bust free any minute, while the jacket draped his plump midsection rather than being tapered to fit. The extra girth would slow the guy in a fight. Cole could take Nervous Guy with little effort, but he had a beefy companion built like a brick shithouse. Probably plus-one security. That guy would require work, but Cole would have speed on his side.

The oaf in the ill-fitted tux caught sight of Maddox, stopping in his tracks. He ogled so hard and long, his gaze Velcroed to her body, Cole felt violated for her. Any excuse would do to introduce the guy to his fist.

A third man with an athletic build, about their age—early thirties—prowled the room with singular focus. He made no eye contact with Cole, unnatural purpose in how he observed the room. Not as if afraid but as though completely resolved and considering when to strike.

That guy would be a problem.

Maddox stroked her neck, playing with the stone at her throat. Looking bored, she scoped out the room with the finesse of the spy she'd become. A part of him still had difficulty accepting that truth.

Movement near the bookcase snagged Cole's attention. Another man seemingly materialized out of thin air.

How long had he been there watching them?

Slender and sinewy, in his fifties or sixties, the pale man glided in like a ghost. He surveilled the room, exuding something confident. Capable. This was a man proficient in delivering pain.

Cole's shitstorm detector pinged *beware*.

The man crossed the room as smoothly as a shadow would into the light. Salt-and-pepper hair framed a hardened, weather-beaten face. Dark crescents stroked under the same beetle eyes as the younger guy. There was nothing clumsy or indeterminate about him.

The eerie man raked a glance over Cole, sizing him up. Quickly, too quickly, as if he already had a bead on Cole. Then the man swung his predatory gaze to Maddox, dissecting her in a way completely devoid of sexual interest.

Cold unease welled in Cole's stomach.

Staying loose, he turned so only Maddox saw his lips and put his hand to the small of her back. "No matter what happens, stay away from those two men."

She stepped closer, bringing them cheek to cheek, and whispered, "Who? The horror movie creepers?" Her tone was easy-breezy, but goose bumps prickling her skin told him she'd registered the threat.

"There are about ten men in this world I wouldn't care to go up against one-on-one. Two are in this room." He drew back, narrowing his eyes at her. Didn't matter how much training she had—it was easy to think you were the best at something until you met the person who taught you otherwise. "Promise me you'll stay away from them."

She pursed her lips into a thin line. "Not a promise I can keep."

His pulse throbbed in his temple. Beneath his muddled emotions for Maddox, there was one thing as certain as a compass needle: his determination to protect her. "Damn it, woman—"

The music stopped, and he turned toward the piano, swallowing the rest of his words.

A puff of teased white hair rose from behind the Steinway, attached to a small, lean man in his midsixties with wire-rimmed glasses. He approached Cole and

Maddox in a self-assured, leisurely manner, the cut of his expensive tux flawless.

The stocky guy should take notes.

"Mr. Reznikov, welcome. I am Alexander Van Helden," he said in a European accent, possibly Austrian. He smiled, hand extended.

Shit. Cole had come across the name once at Rubicon. This man was throwing the party, but he wasn't the seller. He was a middleman who facilitated the tricky sale of illegal products. The guy had a firm handshake.

"Nikolai Reznikov. This is my wife, Maddie."

"And business partner, darling." Maddox leaned closer to Cole and tucked a wayward strand of hair behind his ear. "We make all big decisions together," she said to their host.

"Enchanté," Van Helden said to Maddox as a white-gloved butler came over carrying a tray of glasses. "Would you care for champagne?"

"Thank you." Maddox took a Baccarat flute.

"Nikolai. Not the Reznikov I expected." Van Helden ran a finger across his top lip. "I heard you were dead."

"I'm back from the grave to help my brother. He was shot this morning and was no longer inclined to attend."

Van Helden's eyebrows raised and he shook his head. "I abhor violence. Mr. Blackburn and Mr. Callahan won't be joining us either. Unfortunate. I'm sure the final price would've been higher if they'd participated."

"Perhaps that's the reason they're not here." Maddox risked flashing a dazzling smile, but it played well.

Like crocodiles, circling, Mr. Shadow floated through the room in tandem with Mr. Singular Focus.

"Do we get to meet the seller?" Cole stroked Maddox's arm to draw her gaze and mitigate any surprised looks in case she didn't realize Van Helden was only a middleman.

"Afraid not." Their host gave an exaggerated pout. "The seller wants to remain anonymous."

Her poker face didn't falter. "Too bad." She sipped the golden bubbly, seemingly at complete ease.

"Nonsense," Van Helden said. "Then I wouldn't have his business. He wanted the product moved quickly. I provide legitimate buyers and establish a fair market value."

Only monsters could give death a fair market value. Cole swallowed his opinion and slid his hand to Maddox's back.

With exaggerated flair, Van Helden clasped his hands. "So fortunate you were able to attend." He spun, facing the others, and strode to the center of the room near the dining table. "Mr. Reinhart." He indicated the stocky guy. "Mr. Kassar." He swept a hand toward the lethal fellow, who looked ready to slit a throat. "And Mr. Reznikov." Van Helden looked in Cole's direction. "Since the bidders who are still breathing have arrived, the auction shall commence."

Slipping his hands in his pockets, Kassar stepped toward the table near Reinhart. "I propose we weed out the government agent first." His gaze homed in on Maddox.

Something visceral clawed through Cole, clenching his muscles, setting his pulse on fire.

How in the hell could Kassar know an agent was here?

Indignation lit Van Helden's face. "My staff have been vetted and with me for years, and I screened the bidders personally. All are legitimate and clean."

"Did you screen her?" Kassar asked, staring at Maddox, his accent heavy.

"And I believe you said *that* Reznikov isn't the one you invited," said his Bond villain companion.

Yep, those two were going to be a problem.

Van Helden threw a disillusioned glance at Cole and Maddox. The four guards in the room lifted their weapons as they closed in.

Raising his palms, Cole steered Maddox behind him. Based on the way her feet stuck to the floor, he gathered she had reservations about using him as a shield.

She was going to be a problem too. *Great.*

"I'm offended by your implication," Cole said. "My family is well-known. Doesn't get more legitimate than a Reznikov." He camouflaged a nervous breath with a cool smile.

Maddox stepped around Cole, holding her glass of champagne as if she had nothing to fear. "Kassar is the faceless arms dealer. Anyone who has been in this business long enough knows that no one has any idea what he looks like. Mr. Van Helden, can you verify this man is in fact who he claims? Two bidders have already been killed, and an attempt was made on my brother-in-law's life. Maybe this man wants to *weed* out one more competitor with this insane allegation."

Nice point, but she needed to get with the program. There was no shutting down Cole's protective instincts, so she damn well better let him, starting by staying behind him.

Van Helden stared at Kassar. "Can you prove your identity?"

"I have millions at my disposal, ready to be wired in payment for product you're selling." Kassar's eastern European accent rang through clearly. Slavic. "I have proof of funds. Do they?"

All eyes zeroed in on them. A palpable tension rose in the room.

Van Helden pressed a button under the dining table. A panel on the wall beside the piano lowered, revealing a state-of-the-art computer system. "Mr. Reinhart's identity and financials have been verified. Mr. Kassar and Mr. Reznikov will both provide proof of funds before we proceed."

Cole adjusted his bow tie, gliding back in front of Maddox. "If Reznikov money wasn't good, you wouldn't have invited us. I find this all rather insulting." He played the outrage card without overselling it.

Van Helden snapped erect as though someone had pulled a string through his spine. "Mr. Kassar raises a valid concern. Your wife hasn't been vetted, and for that matter, your brother was invited. Not you. An interested buyer, whomever he may be, I welcome. A government agent, not so much. I wish to see your financials. Now."

"Once we win the bid," Cole said, "you'll have all the proof you need with our payment. Shall we get started?"

The white-haired man narrowed his eyes, a rosy pink darkening his cheeks. "I don't think so." He waved to the armed guards already converging in a tight formation. "Take them below. Separate them. I don't want them talking to each other and ironing out their stories. I'll deal with them after the auction."

"Do keep a special eye on *her*." A maniacal grin illuminated Kassar's face—the first flicker of emotion he'd shown. His companion held them with a beastly stare.

It was a cold burn in Cole's gut. Somehow, Kassar knew for certain Maddox was an agent—officer. If there was a fucking leak in the Gray Box, that meant serious trouble for them beyond their current predicament.

The four thick-necked thugs with guns surrounded them, and Cole's hands clenched to fists. With the guards clustered and poised to quash resistance, a move now would work against them. Maddox cupped his forearm, giving him a clear sign not to act. She must've assessed the situation the same.

The guards directed them toward the staircase he'd seen earlier. Right side of the room near the bookcase. Cole put his hand to Maddox's lower back and edged forward. Two mercs cut in front, leading the way below. The other two covered their six, one nudging Cole with the barrel of an MP7.

As they descended in single file down the narrow, spiral staircase, Cole slipped the pen from his pocket and held it close to his leg. Maddox took her lipstick from her purse and tucked it into her bra.

The stairs opened onto a smaller sitting room, outfitted with the same luxury as the one above. An additional security guard was posted. Two against five. The guards had their weapons attached to slings over their shoulders underneath their jackets. Wouldn't be easy to get his hands on a gun, but the odds needed leveling.

"Take her to Van Helden's quarters," said the biggest guard, nodding at the two goons closest to Maddox. "We'll secure him in the gym."

Cole grabbed her forearm with his free hand. "My wife stays with me."

The one who'd spouted orders, standing at six five and at least two-twenty of pure muscle, pushed right up to Cole.

"It's okay, darling. Let's do as they say." Maddox put her hand to his chest, throwing him a stern look.

This wasn't the time for her to prove she was a badass secret agent. Five capable, armed men surrounded them. Two more on the deck above, no idea how many other guards were on the yacht. They still didn't have eyes on the bioweapon, and that creepy motherfucker with the damn Joker grin was roaming loose upstairs with his serial-killer sidekick.

"You're staying with me," Cole said.

"I hope you gentlemen don't mind," she said, removing her shoes and holding them low. "These heels are killer."

Maddox's thumbs moved so quickly, Cole barely tracked her flicking the little black end caps from the tips of her heels, and at the same time, she stepped closer to stand over them. Her hands blocked the guards' angle of view.

"I'll be fine. They'll verify this is all a mistake soon enough. Trust me." She kissed his cheek. "See you soon."

How could she expect him to let her go off alone with a freaking merc?

Microseconds ticked down. A blueprint of premeditated violence floated into place. Clear. Precise.

One of those slimy meatheads put his hand on her arm.

Declaration of war.

Cole swiveled, facing the big guard. He thrust the pen into the soft sweet spot under the guy's chin, up into his mouth. Once. Twice. Then he jammed it hard into the throat.

The big guy staggered. Blood spurted beneath his chin and a garbled noise bubbled out of him. He toppled backward to the floor.

In his peripheral vision, Cole glimpsed Maddox in motion. Grasping both shoes in her left hand, she'd whirled on the guard behind her, ramming the base of her right palm up into his nose, hard and fast. Then she followed up with a swift fist to the solar plexus. The man doubled over, bleeding and breathless.

Keep moving. Don't stop. His heart pounded off the rails. He popped the guard closest in the throat with a snap punch, compressing the windpipe. A game-ending blow. The guy was done.

The guard to his left lifted his gun. Cole grabbed his necklace and lunged, whipping the steel ball bearings across the guard's gun hand and lashing at his head.

Gasping, eyes bulging, the man stumbled, his bell properly rung.

With the heel of his foot, Cole struck the guy's knee. Bone snapped. The wheezing merc dropped. Cole slammed his knee into his face, sending him crashing to the floor.

No time to wrangle the gun loose from the strap, he spun to help Maddox.

The guard who'd passed her to head for Cole had pivoted back, realizing she was a serious threat. Bad move. She walloped him with the heels of her shoes. Face, throat, hands that'd lifted to protect himself. Once he was bleeding and on the defensive in full retreat, she threw a swift front kick to his head, propelling him toward Cole.

Cole sent an elbow sailing hard into the side of the guard's head. The man jerked and dropped in a boneless sprawl.

As Cole unclipped the HK MP7 from the sling strapped to a fallen guard, the merc behind Maddox recovered from the solar plexus hit and lunged for her.

No way for her to stop the tackle—basic physics. Checking a larger opponent coming quickly would be tough.

Everything happened at lightning speed. The shoes slipped from her hands. She struck his shoulders downward with her fists and flowed into a guillotine hold—locking her forearm up against his trachea. Fast, she moved so fast. Using the momentum and his substantial mass to her advantage, she drove her knees into his abdomen as they went to the ground. She rolled straight back and flipped him over with her legs while keeping an iron grip on his throat.

His neck snapped.

Basic physics.

Admiration swelled in his chest. She *was* a badass warrior. Fearless. Deadly.

Probably a bit sick, but her skills were a total turn-on.

He offered a hand, not that she needed his help from the floor.

"We're blown. Are you guys getting this?" Maddox said in the mic hidden in her necklace, clutching her right side as if she'd been injured, though he hadn't seen her take a hit. She nodded, listening to whoever responded in her ear. "They're inbound."

"Good. Things are about to heat up."

She pressed a hand to her ribs.

"Did you get hurt?"

"I'm okay." She unclipped a gun from one of the guys on the ground and whipped toward Cole, eyes ablaze. "The next time I tell you I'll be fine, you need to trust me and do as I say."

Really? She couldn't wait to give him shit. "Duly noted."

More armed guards stormed toward the glass doors on the far side of the room. Cole grabbed Maddox by the arm and yanked her behind a sofa as the doors opened.

She glared, pulling her arm free. "I know how to take cover."

"I can't help it. Don't ask a man not to act like a man."

"Don't ask an operative not to do her job. You're worse than Castle."

Now that was crossing a line. "Hold on a minute—"

Ear-shattering gunfire erupted. Bullets tore through the room.

14

INTERNATIONAL WATERS, ATLANTIC OCEAN
7:42 P.M. EDT

Poised in readiness, Aleksander waited for the moment to strike. The rattle of thunderous gunfire from the deck below peppered the quiet of the parlor. A shameful amount of ammunition wasted. A talented security team would've ended this by now.

Even if she was a Gray Box agent.

Incredible. The Gray Box was supposed to be a myth. Like the boogeyman. Something the Americans made up and leaked to scare terrorists and others who operated in the underworld.

Van Helden patted his tuft of cottony hair and adjusted the glasses on the bridge of his rosy nose. The little man reminded Aleksander of the frantic white rabbit from *Alice in Wonderland*. He was only missing a pocket watch.

"We'll begin the auction immediately," Van Helden said. "The opening bid is $5 million. The winner will transfer the money using this secure network." He indicated the computer near the piano.

Aleksander pulled his e-cigarette from the jacket of his tux and twirled it between his fingers while Val swept up alongside Reinhart's personal bodyguard.

Two security guards posted outside exchanged words and rushed into the parlor. "We need to assist downstairs, sir."

"Go! Go!" Van Helden waved a feverish hand, his cheeks deepening to the color of bruised tomatoes.

The guards hurried away as the barrage of gunfire downstairs intensified. From the sound of it, four different weapons were currently in play.

Van Helden lowered his head, rubbing his bushy white brows with trembling fingers.

Rotund Reinhart sipped champagne as if this were a normal day, while his security guard tensed on alert. Both men would be nothing more than speed bumps.

With no new guards posted outside, their window to strike opened.

Ejecting the blade from the e-cigarette casing, he spun on his heel and slit Reinhart's jugular in a smooth, fluid stroke.

His son sliced the security guard's throat.

The guard dropped before anyone could blink. Reinhart's champagne flute crashed to the dining table. Blood flowed from the German's throat, saturating his white shirt, and he collapsed, his head striking the table on the way down. The resounding thud echoed in Aleksander's stomach. The air was fragrant with the scent of death mixed with gunpowder wafting from the lower level.

Mouth agape, Van Helden clutched a fist to his chest. He scurried back as if retreat were possible. "She was right about you. You're not Kassar."

Aleksander stalked the white rabbit, cornering him

against the piano. "Yes, she was. But I was also right about her. So let's conclude our business quickly. I need to be on my way." He clutched Van Helden's brachial plexus—the tender group of nerves between the neck and shoulder running from the spinal cord—and pressed the tip of the bloody scalpel to his eye socket, beneath the frame of the glasses. "Where is it?"

Shaking his head, Van Helden's eyes went wide with terror. His jaw went slack.

A simple squeeze, the right amount of pressure, and the white rabbit gave a shrill shriek. His fear-stricken gaze swung to a pair of cabinet doors below the computer console.

Aleksander shoved him toward it. Trembling, Van Helden scampered to the cabinet, throwing panicked glances over his shoulder. He flung the doors open, scuttling aside.

"Go set the explosives on the helm, remote detonation, and meet me at the helipad," Aleksander said to Val, who nodded.

Aleksander strode to the cabinet and peered inside. A safe. A McClain cipher lock safe.

He had enough C-4 explosives in the heels of his own shoes to blow it, but given the nature of the contents, he couldn't take the risk.

Van Helden inched toward the second set of glass doors. Aleksander swooped down with such speed, the poor man cowered.

"Open it." Aleksander grabbed and squeezed the brachial plexus again, digging his thumb in.

Van Helden's face contorted in agony, and a

high-pitched yelp squeezed from his lips. "I can't. If I do, this will ruin me. My reputation is invaluable." With more pressure, he screamed again. "I'll only open the safe once payment hits the offshore account of the seller."

This persistence was quite vexing. "Open it. Now. Or I'll take away more than your reputation. Things you'll miss. A finger. An ear. Your tongue."

The stiff puff of hair didn't move as Van Helden shook his head, eyes bulging, cheeks flaming red on his otherwise pallid face. "I haven't stayed in business this long by caving under intimidation. You *will* transfer $5 million to the offshore account of the seller *and* a $1 million penalty to my personal account for bringing a weapon. Or my men won't let you off this boat alive."

Aleksander wanted to applaud the guy. He had more nerve than expected but failed to calculate the complication of the two agents below distracting his men.

Something excruciating was needed to quickly shift the rabbit's perspective.

Aleksander knocked the man's head against the safe and held his skull there. He inserted the scalpel inside Van Helden's ear. Slowly, ever so slowly, he pressed until the blade pushed through the spongy membrane of the eardrum.

Van Helden's gut-wrenching cry lifted the hairs on Aleksander's arms. The anguished scream stretched into a blubbering howl. When blood flowed and his wails deflated to wretched sobs, Aleksander smiled.

"Please, please. I'll open it."

Aleksander withdrew the blade.

Van Helden scrambled to enter the code, and the safe door unlocked.

A black metal case sat inside. Aleksander snatched the case and took it to the table. He lifted the lid. A foot-long silver canister was cradled in the center of the case.

Clutching his bloody ear, Van Helden said, "Transfer $5 million to the seller's account and $1 million to mine. Or I won't call the helicopter pilot back. It's your only way off the yacht."

Fascinating. "Or I could shove this"—Aleksander lifted the bloody scalpel—"into your other ear."

"You could, and I'd make the call, but you'd never know if I gave my pilot the correct code word. I have many fail-safes in place for such circumstances." The man shuddered from fear or pain, but fierce determination blazed in his bloodshot eyes. "And I leave with you. I suggest we hurry with the transfer."

Time was of the essence, and Van Helden was turning out to be an obstinate nuisance.

Aleksander had already paid $1 million for the information about the auction and dossiers on the arms dealers, $250,000 for the tip on the Gray Box agent, $100,000 for supplies, and $50,000 in transportation.

But bringing a global giant to its knees was priceless.

Aleksander only needed to keep his total expenditures below $10 million. In the grand scheme of things, $6 million on top of what he'd already spent was a win. "You have a deal."

15

Hot bullets whizzed overhead, showering the room in shell casings. The booming sound reverberated up Maddox's spine.

She and Cole took turns squeezing off rounds as they fell back to the doors leading to the starboard walkway. Gunfight 101: shoot and move if you want to live. The furniture offered limited coverage, but the high-velocity barrage would eat through it in minutes. Cole gave her the go-ahead with a nod and then snapped the submachine gun up to his shoulder. She maneuvered low behind a large cushioned chair while he laid down suppressive fire.

Rising into a crouch, she flipped the selector to full automatic and sprayed the opposite side of the room with another volley, keeping the shooters ducking long enough for Cole to pull back farther. At times like this, she missed the built-in silencer of her Maxim 9. The difference in decibels was drastic. Suppressors should be standard government issue to prevent hearing loss.

In the confined space, the noise was deafening. Her eardrums were going to ring for days.

Guards expertly advanced wide on either side of the

room. Once they were close enough, they would try to hit them from the flanks. She had to make every bullet count.

HK MP7s spat copper-jacketed lead at her from the left and right, forcing her down.

Cole tossed a heavy, round wooden dining table on to its side, and she maneuvered behind it as he shot at the guards. Her heart jackhammered in her chest. Frenzied breath burst from her lungs, but her thoughts were steady, clear.

The quick staccato of automatic gunfire grew louder, drawing closer. She and Cole had to run for it soon.

She ejected the buckle from her belt. A four-inch rectangle of pure flashbang power. She pressed it to activate the device and hurled it across the room. "Stun grenade. Five seconds."

A blinding light would flash and a deafening bang would temporarily incapacitate the security team.

Protecting his eardrums with his fingers, Cole closed his eyes and hunched over her, as if to cover her from shrapnel spray.

Cole knew there wouldn't be any fallout from a flash-bang, but she didn't see the harm in letting him shelter her with his body. Not that she could've stopped him if she had tried.

His insistence to do things his way had gotten them hemmed up in this gunfight. If he'd listened to her, trusted her, they might've been able to take out the guards quietly. They'd have ended the auction going on upstairs by now.

She covered her ears and shut her eyes.

His heart thudded in a wild beat against her back.

On a mission, she never considered how much she wanted to make it through alive. Such thinking impaired judgment, and fear led to indecision. For the first time, making it out alive—with him—was all she could think about. Precisely the thing that could get them killed.

The ear-piercing boom rocked the room. Cole grabbed her hand and they made a break for it.

They burst through the door outside. A steady, high-pitched noise whistled in her ears. She grasped the railing, sucking in a shaky breath. A blanket of ashen clouds blocked out the moon. The sea was an endless stretch of stark black.

Their plan had disintegrated the moment Kassar had outed her.

Damn it. Had Cole been foolish enough to trust Ilya with the truth? The bastard wouldn't have hesitated in ratting her out, but he would've contacted Van Helden. Not another bidder.

Lights from an inbound helo pierced the darkness.

"ETA one minute," Castle said in her ear. She'd never been so happy to hear her brother's voice. "Harper got a facial recognition hit on the man posing as Kassar. He's Aleksander Novak, also known as *the Ghost*. A hitman who takes impossible, high-profile jobs. A CIA officer died getting his picture. Lover Boy is right. Stay away from him."

Castle agreeing with Cole on anything was reason enough to give her pause, but if she were a guy, Castle wouldn't dare ask her to stand down.

Cole shoved her up against the side of the yacht, shielding her from incoming fire.

Bullets whizzed by them. Some ricocheted off the metal rail. Sparks erupted in a riot of tiny flashes. She was off her game, needed to get her head fully locked back into this. Now wasn't the time to worry about how her cover had been blown or to get mired down by feelings.

Cole returned fire, taking out the guard.

Rotor blades hacked the night air. Gunfire echoed from the top deck. There must be more guards near the helm. The helicopter hovered over the bow of the yacht. Castle's unmistakable juggernaut frame and the strapping figure of Reece rappelled out of the chopper on black ropes, shutting down hostiles on the upper level with a controlled ammo spray.

Maddox spun toward the stern and ran for the staircase leading to the auction room. A bullet narrowly missed her head, blowing out a window behind her. Ducking, she pressed on. Running barefoot in the storm of a gunfight was never good, but she had no other option. Her shoes were still in the sitting room.

More bullets pinged the side of the yacht. Not slowing, she glanced over her shoulder.

Cole was pinned with his back pressed to the hull, popping off shots. "Wait! Maddox!"

The roar of gunfire swallowed the rest of Cole's words. Her heartbeat pulsed in her throat, washing over her ears. She dug for numb detachment.

The stairs came into sight. She had to get back to the main deck, make sure the smallpox-M didn't make it off the yacht. She checked her ammo while moving. The mag held thirty to forty rounds. She was low. Ten left. Enough, if she was shrewd.

"Maddox, where are you?" Reece asked in her ear.

"Starboard side. Headed to the saloon. Main deck. Cole is under fire on the level below."

"Roger. Castle's coming to you. I'll help Cole."

She raced up the stairs and rounded the corner. Rushing through the glass doors of the sitting room, she came face to face with the Ghost.

Aleksander lunged, swinging the heavy metal briefcase against the woman's hands, throwing off her aim. A volley of bullets shot out the glass, shattering the doors into a million jagged pieces. He knocked the gun from her grip and smashed the case into her torso. The force sent her scuttling backward. Dropping the case, he seized her throat.

Her eyes bulged as she struggled to breathe, grappling with his wrists to break free. He tightened his grip and slammed her head against the wall. Her lips parted in a stunned gasp, but she was formidable and recovered quickly like this wasn't her first knockdown, drag-out brawl.

Too quickly.

She thrust a knee up into his groin. Then the heels of her palms struck his temples.

A lightning shard of pain blasted his head, and agony pulsed in his crotch. Aleksander staggered back, groping for her throat. He only managed to rip the necklace from her chest.

She slammed a bare foot into his gut, driving him from arm's reach. Winded, he clutched his chest. Something hard smashed against his head. A blinding white ache exploded.

Despite his skull throbbing under the dagger of pain, he forced his feet to steady. His vision cleared. He saw her frantic gaze sweeping the floor.

Swallowing the weakness of his body, he tapped the manic fury inside. The wellspring of hate fueled him, and his demon fired him up inferno-hot.

He spotted the gun at the same time as she did, and they both made a move. She threw a marble obelisk at his head, swatted a lamp at him, knocked chairs in his path to slow him down. She was something else, a real scrapper. In the lead, she dove, landing inches from snaring the gun, her fingertips nipping the butt. He pounced, pinning her face down, his elbow curled under her neck in a hammer lock.

Wicked satisfaction pooled in his belly, flooding his chest. He wrenched her away from the gun, tightening his hold. Trapped on her belly, she was helpless. He could snap her neck, be done with her, but it'd constitute the most serious provocation for the Gray Box to settle the score. And males never took losing a female well. The way the man with the scar had stayed glued to her side as if bound by a gravitational pull stronger than any other force on the planet. Aleksander knew such love, such passion. Scarface had also moved like someone well versed in the deadly arts. A worthy adversary.

Watching them reminded him of his love for Sonia.

And what a man would be driven to for the sake of revenge.

The time had come to take as many American lives as possible, in their capital no less, as retribution for the loss of his family. He couldn't afford to be in the Gray Box's backyard with pissed agents and Scarface hot on his heels seeking vengeance.

"Remember this mercy, Agent Maddox Kinkade." In a few seconds, she'd black out.

She scratched and clawed his arm, refusing to give in despite her insurmountable disadvantage. *Admirable*.

"Shh." He tightened his grip. "Don't fight it."

The white rabbit darted from under the piano and scrambled from the saloon.

Kinkade reached up, groping the top of her head, and yanked out the metal clip fastening her updo. Her hair fell around her shoulders.

Light glinted off the long object in her hand.

She jammed the sharp rod into Aleksander's arm and stabbed, again and again.

Arresting pain ripped through his bicep. Growling, he forced himself to clutch the wrist of his injured arm and support his hold on her throat. Enough fun and games, playtime was over. He applied pressure up from his elbow under her chin, shutting off her oxygen. Her body weakened and went limp.

Heavy footsteps thundered into the room, glass crunching under heels. One man running.

Aleksander released her and leapt for the gun. Scooping it from the floor, he rolled, spun up onto his knees, and fired. Scarface dove behind a sofa, taking cover. Aleksander jumped to his feet, seized the case with the bioweapon, and whirled to lay down suppressive fire.

But there was no need.

As suspected, Scarface was maneuvering between the furniture. Not to sneak up on Aleksander but to reach the woman. His woman.

Oh yes, Scarface cared more about her than chasing him or retrieving a deadly bioagent. Still, he fired, slowing Scarface's attempts to see if she was dead or alive.

Aleksander ran over the carpet of glass and rushed up the stairs.

The ping of ricocheting bullets swept closer. A helicopter was setting down to land on the bow, ropes dangling. More agents. Probably crawling over the yacht like cockroaches.

He glimpsed the bomb Val had set on the helm. Small, but the impact would be huge.

Holding the case, he dashed to the helicopter. Van Helden was already inside. Aleksander climbed in and Val handed him the detonator. As they lifted off, he spotted two men wearing protective tactical gear and carrying guns. They cleared the port side of the yacht, noticed Aleksander's helicopter, and opened fire.

"Three. Two. One." He hit the button. The bomb exploded, tearing through the helm, spraying metal and fire faster than the speed of sound.

As the flames spread, so did Aleksander's smile. He leaned back in the plush seat, exhilarated, bolstered. For there was no greater high, no better drug than winning.

16

Dust and smoke clogged the air. Maddox's eyes stung, and her throat burned.

She clambered to her feet. The spinning room came into focus. Shattered glass covered the floor to her right. Flaming pieces of metal and smoldering debris littered the deck. Black smoke wafted from the upper level. Unbearable heat pressed down through the doorway.

I'm alive.

A wave of dizziness bowled her over, and she stumbled. Her bare feet sank into the thick, soft carpet. She shook off the disorientation and found her bearings.

"Maddox!" Cole rushed to her from the other side of the room. Ash dusted his hair and clothing. "Are you okay?"

"Yeah. Fine." Minutes ago, she'd been at the fingertips of death, but now she was…fine. Nausea churned in her gut. Her head swam in a dense pool of muck and her legs wobbled, knees threatening to buckle.

Cole roped her into a hug.

"Are you hurt?" She pulled back, inspecting him.

"The explosion knocked me against the wall, but

nothing serious." He rubbed the back of his head. "I lost Kassar."

Shaking her head, she lowered her gaze and turned away. "Not Kassar—he's a hitman named Aleksander Novak. Shit. Van Helden got away too."

She scanned the room. Reinhart lay on the floor, his head in a puddle of sticky, dark blood, his bodyguard beside him. "Castle? Reece? Where are you guys?"

Her chest tightened in a cold clench, then she grabbed her throat. Her necklace was gone. They couldn't hear her.

The bomb. What if they'd been close to the helm during the explosion? Or worse, on it?

"Cole—"

"Let's go." He was right behind her as she pushed through the other set of glass doors out toward the bow of the yacht, where the Gray Box helo sat on the second helipad.

Spokes of fire roared overhead, back by the helm. Plumes of black smoke billowed. Flames lashed out, bright red and orange, licking the night sky. The heat bearing down on them was intense.

Castle and Reece hustled down the steps. Soot and smoke clung to them, their tactical gear singed. They'd been too close to the blast.

"Oh my God, are you guys okay?" She rushed to them, clutching each of them by the arm. Castle had scrapes on his face. Reece's shoulder had exposed pink flesh.

"We're walking and talking. We're solid," said Castle. "But the blast fried our comms."

"Your shoulder, Reece." Maddox glanced at the bruised area.

He winced and wiped his face clean of expression just as quickly. "Looks worse than it feels." A familiar phrase they used to distract from injuries. "Is the weapon contained?"

"No." Maddox shook her head with disgust. "Aleksander Novak—the man posing as Kassar—got away with it."

"Damn it." Castle pounded the air with a fist. "We had him in our sights. If it hadn't been for the explosion, we could've taken the helo out."

They made their way toward the helicopter.

"You okay?" Reece asked her. "Sounded like you were caught in the thick of a nasty scuffle. We lost your comms right before the explosion."

Cole snatched Maddox by her arm, bringing her to a stop. His grip was so tight, it nearly hurt. "I told you to wait for me." He jostled her with a firm, unnerving shake. "He could've killed you."

Everything flooded back in a rush. The pressure. The pain. The fear.

She'd clawed, fought. Prayed. Her airway shut off.

Remember this mercy, Agent Maddox Kinkade.

Oh God, the Ghost knew her name. She didn't want that man to know anything about her. She shuddered, unable to speak one word about the fight that had nearly claimed her life.

She was broken out of her thoughts by Cole cradling her face in his hands. He caressed her cheeks, his eyes wide with concern. "I told you to stay away from that scary motherfucker."

For just a second, she wanted to fall into his arms and take a deep, long breath. Admit she'd been scared.

Terrified. But there was no room to be soft. She slapped Cole's hands away.

Castle clamped a palm down on her shoulder and yanked her gaze toward him. "And I told you to listen to Lover Boy." Castle eyed Cole. "This once. Just to be clear."

Allowing the job to become personal was always a mistake. Yet there was no other way to take this sexist bullshit. "I'm more than your little sister." She glared at Cole. "And I'm more than your…"

His what?

His past.

The only reason they were standing side by side in the present was because of this mission. Not because he needed her. Or had come to find her. Or had bothered to pick up the phone.

She wrenched free of their grasps. "I'm an operative like you, Castle, and you, Reece."

"Don't drag me into this chauvinistic crap." Reece raised his hands. "I know you can handle yourself, Maddox. You can shoot, stab, and snap necks alongside the best of us. I've got no issue with you covering my back on anything."

Castle eyed him. "Not helpful."

Reece cut his gaze back to Maddox. "I've got your back. Without question."

She gave a nod of appreciation for the support. She could rely on ever-ready Reece, no matter what.

Castle heaved a deep breath. "You're a good operative, Maddox. Solid as they come. I've only worried about you on a mission twice. Your very first time, you had your cherry plucked on a real nasty one. You proved you could handle it. The only other assignment to concern me is this one." He shot a steely glance at Cole, then looked back at her. "I warned you the same as I would've Reaper or Reece. Novak killed a really good officer. The things he's reportedly accomplished took serious skill. I'm talking sharp. We need to take him as a team."

Castle thought of her as *good*, *solid*. She'd had no idea, since he steered clear of her for some reason. Her chest filled with the kind of warmth she hadn't felt since their father had given her an attaboy.

She wanted to give Castle a hug, but they weren't big on mush. "We'll take him as a team."

"And I'm a part of the team," Cole said, "until this is done."

His sloppy phrasing slapped her three different shades of wrong. "And then what? You run off? Fake your death again, only better this time so I can never find you?"

"Maddox." He looked downright flustered, like he wasn't sure *what* he planned to do.

"Well, somebody kind of had that coming," Castle said.

Cole stepped in to face off with her brother.

She moved in between them. "Get on the helo. Now."

Reece was the first to move, cutting the tension.

They boarded and put on headsets. Their helicopter was a fine piece of machinery but lacking luxurious amenities.

"Are comms open?" she asked through the microphone.

"Internal only." Gideon piloted the helicopter into

the air. "Do you want me to open a secure channel to the Gray Box?"

"No." What she needed to say, she didn't want anyone back at headquarters to hear. "My cover was blown."

"Novak sounded like he suspected one of you was undercover." Castle's gaze bounced between her and Cole, seated beside her.

"He knew it was me," Maddox said. "He knew my full name and expected me to be there."

"What do you mean?" Reece pitched forward in his seat across from her.

"At first, I thought Cole might've said too much and Ilya got word here somehow."

"I'd never." Something cold and ugly snapped in Cole's eyes. "I'm not the one who can't keep a secret."

A low blow she deserved, but she couldn't get sidetracked again with their personal mess. "Castle, we may have a leak in our office."

Her brother's face twisted into a frown. "Not possible."

"I can't think of another explanation for what the Ghost knew." As much as she wanted to come up with something. The thought they might have a mole made her sick.

"The chance the Gray Box is compromised is next to nil. There has to be another explanation." Castle's gaze wandered as if he was trying to think of one.

With the highly sensitive nature of their work and access to classified information from multiple agencies, the Gray Box had the most sophisticated security there was. And their operations facility was housed six stories below ground and had every safeguard imaginable to prevent interception of communication.

"We shouldn't jump to conclusions," Reece said. "What if there's some next generation tech, some new spyware? Hackers come up with crazy things every day."

"The bunker is shielded," Gideon said. "No electromagnetic signals can get in or out. We can even take the hit of an EMP."

Shielding from an *electromagnetic pulse* was no small thing. A high-energy EMP could drop a Boeing 747 from the sky.

Cole gave a low whistle like he was impressed. "No one is hacking into your sandbox."

External spyware sounded farfetched to her too. Besides, Sanborn had only decided to send Maddox to the auction mere hours ago. There wouldn't have been any digital record of a plan to send her in.

"Anything is possible," she said, not wanting to believe one of their own was a traitor. A leak would mean they were screwed on so many levels that it scared her.

"But only one scenario sounds probable right now," Cole said. "It might be a bitter pill to swallow, but it's not so hard to believe. You're a bunch of professional liars. Right?"

Maddox ignored the jab.

For a few, the Gray Box was a second chance, but for most, it was the end of the operative line. No other options. And for someone getting twitchy under the anvil of desperation, maybe treason was a different form of freedom. An alternative that outweighed loyalty or duty or honor. And the reality was they did lie and deceive for a living. They were all quite good at it.

Castle scrubbed a hand over his face. "Let's assume you're right and we have a leak. If the mole knows we're on to him, it'll be that much harder to plug. We need to keep this close-hold."

"The fewer people you trust on this," Cole said, "the better."

"Did Lover Boy just say I was right?" Castle folded his arms across his chest.

"No." The word stabbed the air. "I only said you weren't wrong."

"I agree." Maddox stared at her brother, knowing he was going to fight what she had to say next. "I don't think we should tell Sanborn."

"Sanborn needs to know," Castle said as if issuing an order rather than making a suggestion.

If Sanborn wasn't the leak, she'd be the first in line to tell him.

"If we have a mole, it could be anyone," Gideon said, echoing her thoughts.

A frosty calmness settled over Castle, sending a chill creeping over her skin. "Not him. Not the DGB."

She didn't want to entertain the idea either, but someone inside the Gray Box had just jeopardized this mission and their lives. Someone they trusted without a doubt before tonight.

"Castle, you sound awfully certain," Cole said, "like you hold him in high esteem, but what do you know about him?"

The one person who knew Sanborn the best was Knox and he was deployed.

Sanborn was tight-lipped, epitomized discretion, kept

their black ops pitch-black. In the intelligence community, he was respected and feared. Their boss knew so much about government dark arts, it was piss-your-pants scary, which also meant he'd know everything about how to cover his tracks.

"I know he keeps his distance because getting too close to us would cloud his judgment," Castle said. "He has to make tough calls and sometimes, he needs to bring down the hammer if we step out of line. I know he wouldn't sell out this country for money. I know I can trust him with my life. With your life." Castle stabbed the air in her direction.

"That snazzy suit of his wasn't simply tailored," Cole said. "The perfect fit, handcrafted stitching around the lapels, working cuffs—it's custom. Expensive. And he's wearing a Tag Heuer watch. A chump change government paycheck didn't pay for that."

Sanborn was always impeccably dressed, but she had never examined his clothing under a microscope. Cole made a good point that civil servants weren't rolling in dough.

"The DGB is the very antithesis of an open book. I don't know anything personal about him," Reece said. "Do you?"

"He was married for a long time," Castle said after a moment of silence. "Janet let it slip once that his ex-wife bought those suits, the cuff links, and watches he wears. When he talks about marriage, it's with fondness, like he doesn't enjoy being single. I know the Gray Box and his reputation are all he has." He squeezed one hand in the other. "He'd never risk losing or damaging either."

"Maddox almost died tonight." Cole rubbed the back of his neck. "Trusting the wrong person, someone who has most likely had special training in deception, could get all of us killed. You can't afford to take that chance."

Her brother rolled his eyes.

"There's too much at stake." Maddox stared at Castle. "We need to find Novak and retrieve the bioweapon. Then we'll tell Sanborn about our suspicions that we have a mole. That's the safest, smartest play. Am I wrong?"

Castle's jaw hardened, Adam's apple bobbing as he met her eyes. "You're not wrong."

17

The adrenaline high had drained from Maddox somewhere over the Atlantic on the helicopter ride. Fatigue was sludge clogging her veins.

Her bruised ribs hurt. Sitting in the conference room, her only comfort was from the baggy running shorts and V-neck tee she'd changed into and a couple of aspirin. The frosted walls pressed in on the room. She squirmed in her seat, anxious for the briefing to get underway.

Janet circulated around the table, refilling coffee cups, handing out her homemade jam thumbprint cookies and slices of zucchini bread the guys gobbled by the fistful.

Maddox sipped her coffee, clutching her sore neck. A hot shower would do wonders, but that luxury would have to wait.

"The drone tracked the helicopter from the yacht. It landed at the WMN-TV heliport," Sanborn said.

He'd been ticked they'd lost the bioweapon, but his obvious concern for their welfare, his relief they were alive, had been overwhelming. Undeniable. Her gut was sure that Sanborn could be trusted with the full truth, with their lives, but listening to her head was for the best.

"The news station?" Gideon asked.

"Yeah." Cutter yawned. "The one right next to the Department of Homeland Security and the National Presbyterian Church."

"The drone tracked Novak and his companion after they exited the building but lost them somewhere in the square," Sanborn said. "We only had one drone, so we also lost the helo and Van Helden, which means we have no link to the seller. Willow managed to get a tail number and she's trying to track down the helicopter."

For a second time, the Ghost had slipped right through their fists.

Harper rushed into the conference room and handed Maddox two folders. "Thick one is everything on Aleksander Novak. Slim one is everything unclassified, the way you asked."

"Thanks." Maddox guzzled more coffee and opened the thick folder.

Sipping coffee from a flag football mug, Sanborn gave Harper the nod to begin. She tapped the screen on the table, bringing up a picture of the Ghost.

A phantom vise tightened around Maddox's neck. She massaged her throat, trying to erase the sensation of asphyxiation, of dying. No air. Choking. Fear throbbing in her heart.

Remember this mercy, Agent Maddox Kinkade.

"Aleksander Novak. Born November 4, 1969, in Berat, Albania. Served as a sharpshooter in the Albanian Special Forces. Married Sonia Shehu March 9, 1987. Son Valmir, born later that year. Daughter Mila born 1995."

Harper clutched a pen, fingers strained bloodless, disgorging facts about his military service without any notes, validating her reputation as the *factinator*. No other analyst could sort through copious amounts of data, stringing together the relevant pieces and memorizing it, in such astonishing time.

Maddox fingered through the thick file while Harper briefed everyone.

Novak had a pristine military record. Special Operations Battalion, most elite unit in the Albanian Army. One of the finest sharpshooters in his battalion, broke records for number of kills, known for going deep and staying out in the field for long periods. Several early promotions. Commendations and decorations up the wazoo.

"There was a photo of the son as a young boy in his file," Harper said. "I ran it through age-progression software. Ninety-five percent probability he was the man with the Ghost on the yacht."

"Any idea about the current whereabouts of his wife and daughter?" Sanborn asked.

"No, sir."

"How does a highly decorated guy in special forces go from the fast track to becoming an assassin stealing a bioweapon?" Maddox wondered out loud. They were missing something.

"Harper, what kind of discharge did he get?" Castle asked.

"Honorable, with thirteen years of service. He had just reenlisted the year prior. After he left the army, he fell off the grid with his family. There's nothing on him until the CIA started tracking him as the Ghost."

"It doesn't make any sense." Maddox shook her head.

"He reenlisted three times. That was a career for him and he was one of their best. Why would they discharge him after he'd just signed up to do four more years?" She looked around the room, but of course everyone was stumped the same as her.

"Lifers don't just quit," Reece said. "And distinguished lifers aren't honorably discharged right after re-upping. There's more to the story. A lot more."

Maddox rolled her shoulders, trying to relieve the tension in her muscles. "Harper, reach out to the Albanian Army under the guise of Homeland Security and try to find out why he left."

Harper nodded and sat, strumming her fingers on the desk. Sanborn flicked a glance at her hand.

Catching the look, she cleared her throat and started playing with her necklace. "That's all I have."

"From the deep web video, I estimate that if the bioweapon is released out in the open," Doc said, "say on the street, depending on the wind speed and direction, it would infect those within a one-hundred- to two-hundred-yard radius. If this was deployed in the air system of a contained air-conditioned environment such as a mall, there's no telling how many could be infected. If the weapon sold had a larger payload than what we saw on the video, that changes things again."

Doc brought up a startling pictograph on the monitor, showing potential branches of infection based on exposure and contact.

"We know this new strain takes five days to kill a person," Doc said, "and in the initial four hours before someone knows they're sick, they'll infect everyone they encounter. The old vaccine immunities will be irrelevant. The worst-case scenario is if it's deployed in an international airport. It could spread to any city in the world within a day and we'd have a pandemic within weeks. I'm talking a potentially species-threatening event."

"Goodness." Cutter leaned back in his chair, horror stamped on his face.

"We're not going to let that happen," Gideon said, cool and detached, chewing on gum.

Castle scooted his chair back, rested his elbows on his knees, popping his knuckles. He'd broken that hand once—either on a SEAL mission or, more likely, a drunken fight. "We're going to find him and shut him down."

"Get your after-action reports done," Sanborn said. "Then get some rest."

Almost everyone got up, gathering their things to leave. Reece and Gideon exchanged a prolonged look. "I'll talk to her," Gideon said. Reece nodded and left.

Gideon gestured to the hall, and Maddox followed him.

"What's up?"

He cleared his throat. "The background check Cole ran." His gaze shifted away from her. "Dug up Privé. Clinic in Canada."

Her breath locked, but her mind spun.

"The Agency never found it," he said, still not looking at her. "The Gray Box never found it."

Thanks to her father pulling strings to have it buried. Although apparently not deep enough.

"It's your business. Changes nothing. Yeah?" He put a hand on her shoulder, meeting her eyes.

Ice-cold. As usual. Thank God, there wasn't a flicker of pity.

She nodded.

He gave her shoulder a squeeze, planted a peck on her cheek, and headed toward the black ops section.

She stood frozen for a moment, humbled.

They'd fought and bled together, would die to protect one another, partied hard to release the pressure from work, and got each other through real-world crap. Right after his wife died, Gideon had crashed on her sofa for a month. Maddox had helped him pack up his wife's things, been there to listen, even at three in the morning. And Reece's divorce had wrecked him in a profound way. He'd sold most of his stuff, and what he couldn't sell, he'd burned. He'd moved into a camper at an RV park and shut down some part of himself she still hoped to reach. They picked up the pieces together, made the toughest times bearable.

But for Gideon and Reece not to report knowledge of something that could result in the revocation of her security clearance and, at worst, theirs too for withholding such information went so much deeper than her battle brothers looking out for her. They were violating an oath they'd taken, for her sake.

Maddox ducked into the conference room. Cole lingered, looking at her. She sat and forced herself not to get drawn in by the electric intensity he radiated. Or the magnetic appeal of those dark eyes and the jagged scar that didn't make him less beautiful but more.

"We wouldn't have gotten into the auction without you." She kept her tone formal. "You went above and beyond."

That was framing things lightly. She'd endangered his life twice, in asking him to see his brother and again at the auction. The biggest threat to him was her. She couldn't let anything happen to him because of this operation.

"I appreciate everything you've done. You deserve a medal. Really."

So much more needed to be said, so many questions begged for answers. What had he been doing for nine years? How could he be so cruel to let her think he was dead?

But it'd all have to wait.

"Maddox." Cole grasped her hands, held her captive with those eyes. "We need to talk."

"This isn't the time or the place." Her tongue was thick and heavy. She freed her fingers and balled her hands in her lap, fighting a shiver at the loss of heat from his palms.

"You need to rest. Even your boss ordered you to sleep. Come on. Let's get out of here."

He put a hand on her leg, and her thighs clenched. The hot gleam in his eyes was a warning. To be fully vested in the mission, she had to be divested of him. For a little while. He was a distraction, dulling her edge. His presence was a constant reminder that she was a woman, who'd once fallen. Madly. Deeply. Completely.

Loving him, wanting him, her anger over being abandoned by him tinted every thought and emotion in his presence. Like beet juice on fingers, clothes, teeth. Leaving a troublesome stain.

And that had almost gotten them killed today. Trying for a do-over with him while tackling this mission was suicide at best. Worst case, a species-threatening event.

She'd been greedy once, and everything had ended in disaster. She couldn't have it all. Not then. Not now. This time, she had to make the sacrifice. "Do you remember the video of the guy who died slowly, painfully?"

His gaze fell. "Of course."

"I'm responsible for this mission. I lost the bioweapon. If we don't find Novak—"

"I get it." He raked a hand through his hair, free and flowing past his collar. "But there's nothing more you can do tonight."

She had the Novak case file to go through. A chance to get inside his head. The Ghost and his son posed a serious threat on American soil. Her personal drama couldn't be a factor.

"Let's go to your place." He slid his hand up her thigh. "We'll talk—or not talk—and rest."

Doubtful the four-letter word they'd indulge in would be either *talk* or *rest*.

The chemistry between them crackled in the air, on her skin, like an effervescent tongue licking up her spine. He was probably still wired after the yacht, wanted to wind down in another way. Not that she blamed him. Stress coiled tighter than an overwound watch spring in her muscles and she ached for release. But the job came first.

Rubbing her stinging eyes, she shook her head. Her throat went painfully dry. "Look, I know I owe you for helping us, but this isn't the right time. You can sleep at my place, since we haven't fixed your Russian problem yet. I can crash at Gideon's or at Reece's. We'll settle up after I'm done with this mission, if you're still around."

Cole getting his closure had to wait. He'd delayed the conversation nine years already. A few more days to be free of her wouldn't kill them.

18

Settle up?" As though there were a bill between them she could possibly pay. "You don't owe me for helping you." Rising, he grabbed his helmet.

After almost being put in the grave by sniper fire and nearly losing Maddox—to bullets, at the hands of Novak, and to a bomb, all in one day—he didn't know what to do with the avalanche of emotion threatening to blanket him. A restless energy vibrated in him, an anxious fear that closure and severing the ties that bound them might be a pipe dream.

And for a man who feared very little, he didn't want to delve any deeper.

What he wanted, needed more than sleep and food, was to be close to her, skin to skin, grateful they were both breathing. It wasn't about sex, releasing the pent-up storm. Not entirely anyway.

He needed to hold Maddox, feel her heart beating steady against his chest. He missed the ecstasy of intimacy. A connection beyond the physical through the flesh, a sense of peace, of absolution that he'd only found with her.

A respite from this shitstorm would do them both good.

While she stood, ready to be rid of him.

She squared her shoulders, the glacial wall redrawn. "We have unresolved stuff, outstanding issues," she said as if talking about a damn business transaction.

"That we do." He pressed up on her, backing her against the table, making the nature of one part of his business clear.

Her hands flew to his chest, keeping their bodies from colliding.

"I need to see this thing with the bioweapon, with Novak, through to the end," he said, making the second part of his business equally clear.

Tracking down Novak and his son was going to be dangerous. They were predators, deadly beasts like Cole. If they put their hands on her, hurt her, killed her—

Stiffening, she skirted around him. "Thank you for helping us. For risking your life. I know it wasn't easy for you, and I appreciate it, but your role in this is done."

Her professional dismissal bit him to the bone. She was trying to heave him to the curb yet again. "You may be done using me, yanking my chain like I'm a junkyard dog, but I'll let you know when I'm finished with you."

Her eyes stayed guarded, her posture defensive. "What's that supposed to mean?"

He didn't have the faintest clue, but he'd be damned if he'd let her talk to him like that. He wanted to sink his teeth into her, bite back, and it'd sounded good. "Means I don't need you for a safe place to sleep, but I'll see you soon."

As Cole strode out of the conference room, Maddox's heart sank.

Part of her wanted him to stay, to fight harder, but it was best he left. Every time he drew close, much less touched her, she reverted to a young girl—hopelessly in love, far too eager to worship at the altar of his body like a fanatic disciple.

She was different. Stronger. She had to be, had to shake this off. Catching Novak was all she had the strength to handle, so she sat and opened the file again. Time to dig into his military record.

Gaining acceptance into the Albanian Special Forces program was a painstaking, grueling twelve-week process. Evaluations tested navigation and marksmanship. Marches with sixty-pound rucksacks for physical endurance. Psychological testing to see who wouldn't crack under torture. They cycled through twenty-four-hour nonstop periods of physical drills and tasks. And that was just to get accepted into the program.

Afterward, candidates underwent a rigorous fourteen-week training process, learning survival skills, honing their sharpshooter and hand-to-hand combat techniques. As a final test, candidates were left in a remote area of the country without food, water, or gear. To graduate, they had seventy-two hours to evade capture by a team sent to hunt them and return to base undetected.

Jeez. Everyone on Maddox's team had survival and evasion training to varying degrees, but she'd never tracked someone with this type of specialized skill set. And time wasn't on her side.

Words blurred on the page. She had to pack it in.

She stood, her bones leaden with exhaustion. A dark emptiness chipped away at her, abrading her gut. What if she couldn't get into Novak's head? What if he slipped through their fingers again?

Doubt was static whirring in her mind. She needed sleep. After solid rest, she could tackle anything. She knocked out her after-action report, omitting details that'd indicate they had a mole, locked Novak's classified file in her desk, and took the unclassified version with her.

Turning to take the elevator, she spotted Harper coming out of the restroom, headed to the analysis section.

"Hey, Harper."

The analyst stopped, smoothing back the hair of her tight bun. "What do you need, Maddox?"

"It's pretty late. Why don't you go home and sleep?"

Not that she appeared to need any. Harper looked flawless and alert without a hint of makeup. She wasn't classically beautiful but had a captivating face and enviable stamina that defied her fragile frame.

"I went home earlier for a break, and just now, I got to thinking," she said without making eye contact in her odd-bird way, "about Novak and his son and it hit me. I can run my facial recognition program through the city's video surveillance system."

"That'd be helpful. How many cameras are we talking about?"

"Couple of thousand scanning streets, sidewalks, parks, rooftops. Another thousand in the Metro, and I can tap into some private security cameras scattered throughout the area as well."

"How soon to get it running?"

"I came back to get started writing the algorithm." Harper's fingers wiggled wildly, tapping the side of her leg. "I'll plug into the public and private feeds available and get real-time video analytics I could cross-link."

"If you find something, make sure you contact me first."

Harper usually worked behind the scenes on missions, but Sanborn was using her more and more these days as an analytical point person for operations. On those occasions, she tended to walk information to Sanborn before notifying the tactical team leader, against protocol. A protocol Sanborn didn't enforce with *her*.

He made lots of allowances where she was concerned. Harper kept her distance from everyone, especially operatives. It was as though she was only comfortable interacting with Sanborn.

"You don't want me to go to the DGB first?" With her bright eyes widening, she had the innocent look of a porcelain doll.

"No. I need you to follow protocol. This mission could succeed or fail based on how long it takes Tactical to receive relevant information. Updating the DGB is my job. Okay?"

The reasoning was sound, unquestionable, yet Harper stared at the wall as she hesitated.

She needed a nudge.

"I know you wouldn't want to do anything to hinder our efforts or inadvertently tank this op."

Whether a traitor or an introvert, there was only one logical response. "Okay," Harper said.

"And work on this task alone." Whoever the leak might be, they were a single point of failure. Reducing layers would increase transparency.

Harper nodded.

Maddox took the elevator up to the main level. She glanced at her smartwatch. Almost 3:00 a.m. Her stomach growled. She'd kill for a juicy burger loaded with cheese and bacon, but she'd nuke something lean and mean, then crash. She pushed through the heavy door, walking outside into the chorus of cicadas.

Mother Nature had the humidity cranked way too high for this hour. Six cars remained dispersed throughout the quiet parking lot, Knox's truck blanketed in darkness at the far end. Stretching her neck, Maddox rolled the bunched knots in her shoulders as she walked. The small, shady lot was a far cry from Langley's color-coded, amusement-park-sized one.

She hit the unlock button on the key fob. The headlights popped on, casting their familiar spray of light, and she stopped dead in her tracks.

Cole lay on the hood of the truck, arms folded, head resting on the windshield. Her heart flipped over in her chest. No way he'd spent two hours waiting for her.

Tenacious beyond belief. And sexier than sin.

Unreal.

The glow from the lights outlined the sweet rolling curves of his wiry physique. Long legs, tight torso, broad shoulders. Seeing him in action on the yacht, laced with lethal power, had filled her with awe in the moment. The recollection now stirred a slow burn of desire more potent than a double-shot of whiskey. Top-shelf.

Once, years ago, he'd taken on three punks who'd made the mistake of trying to mug them. He'd put them in the hospital. One in intensive care.

A born fighter.

Half of her wanted to knock his delicious body off the truck's hood, send him packing. The other half wanted to do dirty things to said delicious body.

"I hoped you'd be long gone," she said.

As she crossed in front of the headlights to the driver's door, he tossed something to her without looking. She caught it.

A white paper bag from her favorite twenty-four-hour burger joint. Her insides softened, and she salivated, even if her heart cringed at potential clogged arteries.

"Fries are cold, but the fully loaded burger should hit the spot."

The man could still read her mind after all this time, and it annoyed her worse than a nest of riled hornets. "For all you know, I'm a vegetarian these days."

He roared with laughter, so rough it grated her skin. Swinging his long legs over the side of the truck, he sat up, clutching his stomach, choking on that gut-deep laugh as if what she'd said had been the most preposterous thing in the world.

It kind of was—she'd never give up meat, but he didn't know that. After he'd disappeared, her whole life had changed. She'd changed.

He patted his chest, amusement dying to a sultry chuckle, nettling her to roll her eyes. "That'll be the day"—he squeezed out another chortle—"when you don't want a good piece of meat in your mouth."

Heat smacked her cheeks. She wrenched the door open and climbed inside, slamming it shut. He was talking about a burger, right?

Sounded so raunchy, so slip-n-slide kind of nasty.

Her thoughts took a vivid nosedive into the triple-X gutter and her sex clenched.

He opened the passenger door and hopped up into the cabin. "I believe the proper response when someone brings you food is *thank you*."

Shaking her head at her oversight in manners, she set the food on the floor with the file she'd been carrying. "Sorry. Thank you. I'm starving and tired and—"

"Stressed." He angled toward her, resting an arm on top of the bench seat, dark hair falling across his collar. "I'm no stranger to your cranky side, and I don't scare easily."

No, he didn't. She'd always admired that about him. His strength. His boldness. The fierce determination that had kept him out here waiting for hours. But she preferred when he used his superpowers for good and not wickedness against her.

"How did you get back through the gate?"

"Sanborn granted me temporary access," he said.

"I'll have to see about getting it revoked."

He scooted closer along the seat. A dizzying kind of panic skittered through her with no console between them. The masculine smell of him cut through the aroma of food, stirring a different hunger.

"You should go wherever it is you plan to sleep," she said. "It's late." Her body fluttered with traitorous sensations in protest.

"That really what you want?" The gravelly heat in his voice sent tingles to her thighs.

His gaze dropped to her mouth, and her tongue tied. She wanted to say *no, it isn't*, but also wanted to scream in outrage. Alive and well all this time, and he'd never contacted her. No phone call, no email. She had a mountain of issues to sort through. Everest-level shit. Tackling it now would strip her bare, leaving her nothing for the mission and the fight with Novak.

"Why are you here?" Her voice was barely audible. "What do you want?"

He inched closer, his proximity a dangerous tease. "You've got my gear."

Her gaze fell to his backpack on the floor near the passenger's door, but he hadn't glanced at his bag once. He was staring at her.

The scorching look burning in his eyes threatened to incinerate her resolve.

"We survived today. Makes me appreciate what's right in front of me." He dragged his knuckles down her bare arm.

Awareness tickled every pore of her body.

His face dipped, drawing near, unhurried. Testing the boundaries between them. Pushing the primal button, driving her toward one of the four evolutionary *f*'s.

Fight, flight, feed, or fuck.

He brushed his lips across the corner of her mouth, along her jaw, his stubble scratching her cheek. He pressed a searing kiss to her pulse point.

Her heart stumbled a beat, then knocked like crazy. So loud and hard, she swore he'd not only feel it but hear it—a rap against a door she longed for him to open, letting her into that bittersweet place where sensation flowed like milk and warm honey in the promised land. Where she'd do anything for another taste of him. Where only he could make her come undone.

He cupped the back of her head, his fingers curling in her hair. Licked the tender spot on her neck below her ear. His breath rough on her throat. The quiver in her chest spiraled, and if she hadn't been sitting, her knees would've buckled.

His mouth glided over her cheek to her parted lips, and he kissed her. He tugged her onto his lap, pulling her hips to straddle him. She wrapped her arms around his neck, caressing his tongue with hers.

Need unfurled in her belly, a warm, silken thread loosed from its spool.

No question she wanted him.

He kissed her hard, almost brutally. Desperately. Deep and long, he drew the breath from her body, filling her with his.

Years of loneliness and yearning flared, making a pulse thud between her legs like a heavy heartbeat. She squeezed her legs against his hips, longing to be closer.

His mouth didn't give a second for retreat. His lips so hot on hers, she melted. He stroked her inner thigh, his fingers inching higher and higher. Until he slid his hand into her baggy shorts and tugged her thong aside.

Her craving for him gathered in a painful knot in her core. She throbbed for release, growing wet at the nearness of his fingertips. Anticipation shivered over her skin.

"Want me to stop?" The low words were rough as sandstone.

"No," she breathed. Starved.

Pure male satisfaction splashed across his face.

His callused thumb rubbed the sensitive button of nerves between her legs, featherlight, and a finger slipped inside her.

She arched against him, softening, yielding in ways she'd forgotten. Cole had been her first, not her only, but the one who'd made her tremble with want and beg for more.

He nipped her bottom lip, playful, eliciting a sigh, and plunged a second finger in her slick wetness. She clenched helplessly around him, rocking against his hand.

Blood rushed through her ears. Everything inside her wound tighter, swelling, contracting. She was so aroused and ready, she feared stroking his ego by coming from two minutes of foreplay.

She lifted her hips away from his hand, pulled down her shorts and underwear, working them off her legs in a frenzy. Unzipping his jeans with trembling fingers, she freed the beautiful, heavy length of him. He made a deep sound of approval in his throat. His flesh nudged against her, hot, hard, and seeking. She ached with a gnawing emptiness.

"Are you sure I shouldn't go wherever it is I plan to sleep?" A ghost of a smile on his lips as he threw her words back. "It's so late."

"Smug doesn't look good on you."

"Sure does feel pretty damn good."

He was under her skin, stamped on her soul, branded

on her heart. To her shame, she needed him, needed the sweet friction that would leave her a sweaty, sated mess.

She curled her fist around his shaft. From the thick base to the engorged crown, she palmed him, ran her thumb across the slippery wetness on the tip, driving a guttural groan from him. She stroked herself, bathing the hard length of him in the slickness of her desire.

"Does that feel better than smug?" she taunted.

He grabbed a fistful of her hair and pressed his mouth to her ear. "Fuck yeah."

She popped open the glove compartment and fished out a condom from her purse. Their gazes locked as she tore the wrapper and quickly rolled it on him. She rose on her knees and took him deep inside.

The fullness, the pressure, startled her body. She splintered around him. Rocking her hips, she took him deeper. He pulled her tee off, unclasped her bra, and stilled. His eyes were trained on her bruised abdomen.

"I'm fine." Better than she'd been in years. Afraid the wary look in his eyes meant he'd bring things to a halt, she tugged his shirt up over his head, desperate for his skin against hers. "Really. I'm okay." He clamped his mouth on a nipple and flicked the pebbled peak with his tongue. She arched on a wave of pleasure. He caressed and suckled and licked and kissed her with gentle possession and violent tenderness.

And the world condensed to this. Connection. Communion. Cole.

He clutched her waist and brought her hips down while he pumped his in a frantic rhythm.

She planted a hand on the roof for leverage, taking

him as quickly as possible. That sweet place was in reach, the one that would sate the grinding ache.

"Cole," she whimpered, milking him hard. Her voice was packed with the urgency blooming inside.

She loved this sensation of tumbling toward relief as he caressed some deep part of her soul.

He gasped, his body tightening with hers. Slipping a hand between them, he rubbed her throbbing clit, and she shuddered in a riptide of spasms. He swallowed the cries from her mouth and took charge of the rhythm, bringing her hips down hard and fast in a driven fever to his own release.

The pleasure was so blinding and raw, it hurt.

Breathless and limp, she drifted everywhere and nowhere. Settling back into herself piece by tenuous piece. She cupped his face and kissed him. This time, aching for him to be hers again, rabid to find what had been lost. She showed him how much she still loved him, opening herself to him.

He caressed her cheek and jaw in a touch so tender, she yet again unraveled. More vulnerable. This sensation of being tethered to him was everything.

Then she looked at him, both of them panting, and it turned wrong.

His gaze hardened, pain tattooed across his face as if a kiss had somehow wounded him, and her smile fell. He dragged the pad of his thumb across her lips, wiping her mouth.

Her whole body constricted. He pulled out of her, slowly and gently. She rolled off him, loathing the volatility between them.

He sat back, staring out at the dark parking lot. Goose bumps scattered across her skin, and she was dying to know his thoughts.

They cleaned up with tissues from the glove box in silence.

Lowering his head, he hauled in a long, broken breath before he wrapped the condom in Kleenex and discarded it in his bag. They dressed in the awkward quiet.

To her surprise, he gathered her against the side of his body with one arm.

She wanted to snuggle against his warmth, but even this small intimacy was a soap bubble, iridescent and captivating and bound to burst.

They were so far from being right with one another. Thinking about what the future held for them was terrifying.

"Enjoy the burger and get some sleep." Grabbing his bag, he hopped out.

Before she'd collected her brain enough to wonder where he planned to sleep, the roar of his bike reverberated, setting her teeth on edge, and he drove off.

The idea of going home to an empty apartment and an empty bed made the loneliness of her empty life echo through her. It sucked. Big time.

She kept spare clothes and toiletries in her locker, and the sofa in the break room wouldn't be too hard on her back for a few hours. She took the burger and the file and shuffled back inside the building.

19

GRAY BOX PARKING LOT, NORTHERN VIRGINIA
9:46 A.M. EDT

Face upturned to the blazing sun, eyes closed, ankles crossed, Cole leaned back on his bike in the Gray Box parking lot. He adjusted the Glock holstered under his arm, doing his best not to melt in this godforsaken heat wave.

He'd replayed last night in his head a hundred times. Not the bits about them nearly dying. The juicy bits about making love with Maddox, holding her like she was still his. And that final, tender kiss she'd given him that had shifted the tectonic plates of his reality. How it'd soothed him and destroyed him at the same damn time.

He didn't know what in the hell to do with it all, but he was done bullshitting himself.

His desire to see her, to be with her, had never waned. For nine miserable years, what-ifs had plagued him, keeping him up at night. What if she had moved on? What if she loved someone else?

He rubbed his chest at the sudden ache.

A couple of hours ago, he'd swung by her place, but Knox's truck—Cole spat on the ground—was already gone, so he had headed straight for the spy center. Despite how she'd baited and hooked him and tried to toss him aside, he understood what she and her covert crew were fighting for. As worthy causes ranked, hers topped the list.

When Maddox left to track down the Ghost, he'd be with her, regardless of her insistence that he sit this out. She was smart and bold and more badass than he had ever imagined, but he couldn't let her face Aleksander Novak without him.

A low creak squeezed from the front doors. Adjusting his Ray-Bans, he pitched his head forward and opened his eyes. Maddox and Reece came into view as they approached, followed by Castle and Gideon.

Her riot of curls was roped back into a ponytail, tension cascading off her stiff shoulders.

"Good morning, sunshine." He tossed the words like a softball, as if the chasm of unresolved pain and anger separating them didn't exist.

Her feet stuttered. Must've caught her off guard using the pet name she used to love.

Somehow, *sunshine* didn't fit her anymore. He needed to look up the name for a monster star that burned ten million times brighter than the sun. That's what she was now.

"What are you doing here?" Her sharp question cracked the air like the lash of a whip.

"Since you didn't revoke my access, I figured you came to your senses about letting me help." The only thing he knew for certain was that he was going to help her stop Novak.

Whether she liked it or not. Even if it was the last thing he ever did.

"I told you," she said, "you're done. I can't allow you to risk your life helping us again."

Allow? Did she really think she could stop him?

She wore her bossy pants well, but he didn't take orders.

Smiling, Cole adjusted his sunglasses. "I guess you forgot. I'm a member of the band."

She folded her arms. "Well, we can do just fine without you, Ringo."

Chuckling, Castle gave a nod of approval. "Now, that's the first sensible thing I think I've ever heard you say about Lover Boy."

Gritting his teeth, Cole let the "Lover Boy" crap slide. If he let Castle see it bothered him, the fucker would only give him more shit.

"Nah, you're giving him way too much credit." Reece rested a forearm on Maddox's shoulder, half-cocked grin showing pearly whites. "He's more of a Pete Best."

Gideon scratched his trim, blond beard. "Who?"

"My point exactly." Reece's grin deepened to a bright smile.

"I'm not asking permission. I'm helping you catch this guy." Cole thrust his helmet toward her. "The bike is faster, and we don't have time to waste."

"We're not getting more tactical support from in there." Castle threw a nod at the Gray Box. "I'm sure he can do something useful—carry your gun or fetch you a coffee."

Cole rolled his eyes behind his sunglasses.

"An extra body on this would be good," Gideon added, "but we can manage without him. Your call."

With eyes narrowed, Maddox evaluated the situation.

Cole waited. He had the perfect skill set to assist, and a man like him was worth two extra bodies. A smart boss would make the right call.

Finally, she took the helmet. Attagirl.

"We're burning daylight," she said. "Reaper, follow Harper's lead on the helicopter, and locate Van Helden. Castle, Reece, news station. See how our Ghost got clearance to enter the building. Lover Boy and I will follow the lead at the taxi company."

They nodded and headed for their vehicles.

Buttoning her jacket, she stepped closer to him. "Give me your phone. I'll load the team's personal numbers and a couple of Gray Box lines in case you need them. Don't discuss anything classified on an open line."

Her bossy pants were hot.

He handed her his cell. "You left your place rather early. I'd hoped you'd get more sleep."

"Never went home." She loaded numbers in his phone. "I keep spare clothes here. Showered in the locker room. Grabbed some winks on the break room sofa."

She stiffened.

Her brows drew together and eyes snapped up. "You went to my place this morning?" His silence must've been confirmation. "Why?"

Hell if he knew. To talk? To fuck? The woman had him tangled in a tizzy.

"What lead at the taxi company?" He pulled his spare half-shell helmet from his backpack and put it on, buckling the strap under his chin. He was a safe driver, one of the best, but in the unlikely event of an accident, he'd rather Maddox have the full helmet—better protection.

"We got a facial recognition hit on a public surveillance feed. Novak got in a taxi on Massachusetts and Van Ness last night. Alone. We have a partial plate of a Yellow Cab and need to track down the driver, see where Novak was dropped."

Cole swung his leg over his bike and sat. "As you said, we're burning daylight."

She climbed on behind him, put on the helmet, and gave him back his phone. He fired up the engine, and she clutched his waist. Her hands on his chest had untimely desire humming through his body stronger than the full throttle of the bike.

He missed the carefree days when they'd ridden for pleasure. Took long walks through the Dulles terminal, eating pizza. Instead of thinking him crazy or cheap, she'd understood and appreciated that the airport was one of America's greatest works of modern architecture. Eero Saarinen's greatest design. He could go on for hours about the beauty and chaos in the story of a structure, and she'd listened without boredom, no complaints.

Maybe it'd been the same reason he didn't groan and roll his eyes whenever she wanted to watch some black-and-white flick. Or how she'd sit beside him when a boxing match came on, make a bowl of popcorn, and spout off stats she'd learned. Everything between them had been easy. No fight they hadn't been able to overcome. The two of them in sync. A lifetime ago.

Now, despite the fact that they'd reconnected in the biblical sense, she didn't scoot her pelvis up against his ass, didn't nestle her legs tight along his hips the way she once had.

Things between them were complicated. Tainted. Broken.

And it wasn't all her fault.

Any path forward was murky as smog and littered with land mines. He still harbored deep-seated resentment for her betrayal. She was pissed at how he'd handled the fallout and left her behind. And there was her chosen profession to consider.

A real shit sundae with a spy cherry on top.

———————————

Torture.

Maddox sat on Cole's bike, doing her best to maintain a healthy distance from his body, knees splayed. Then he started taking hard turns, forcing her to press against him, wrap her arms tighter around his waist, legs hugging his. Her pulse revved along with his engine, stirring her mind, bringing up images and sensations from last night. Like this was a game.

A distracting game of torture.

Cole sped into the lot alongside the little Yellow Cab Company across from the National Arboretum and parked. There wasn't a single yellow taxi, despite the name. For some unearthly reason, they were orange and black or red and white.

Before the kickstand was in place, she hopped off the bike, desperate for space away from him. And longing to have all of him at the same twisted time.

Stuffing the tangled emotions into a *save for later*

compartment, she removed the helmet and steeled herself. She walked around the squat mud-pie building with its faded orange accents and distinct adobe-clay facade.

Cole was on her heels when she opened the front door. A ding from a bell announced their entrance.

The stale odor of cigarettes and mildew almost made her turn back. A pocked-face guy scratched his potbelly, sitting behind a desk littered with balled-up fast-food wrappers. A headset covered one ear, mic reaching out to his chapped lips. "Where you headed?"

"We've reached our destination." Cole strode up to him, taking point as if he were in charge, and bravely set his helmet on the guy's desk. No telling what might crawl into sight.

The man's piqued gaze bounced from the helmet, up between Cole and her. "What? You don't need a cab?"

The phone rang, and he lifted a swollen hand for them to wait. "DC Yellow Cabs." He dragged a finger down the screen. "You headed to the airport, Mr. Morris?"

Maddox wrangled an impatient sigh, resisting the urge to snap her fingers and ask the guy to rush through the call.

"No problem, Mr. Morris. A car will be there in less than thirty minutes."

As the man lowered the receiver, Maddox curled her helmet under her arm, stepping up to the desk. "We need the driver of the cab with plates ending in Papa, Charlie, Bravo, one."

"Huh? What you say?"

Cole rested his hip on the filthy desk. "The lady said, *p* as in pizza, *c* as in cookie, *b* as in burger, one as in 'us boys only have one sausage to yank.'"

"Who are you? You guys got a warrant?"

She stayed quiet. What useful skills had Cole picked up besides incapacitating someone?

"We're from Rubicon Security. Your driver picked someone up at the corner of…" Cole looked to her.

"Massachusetts and Van Ness, around eleven thirty last night. We need to know where the passenger was dropped off."

"We'd truly be grateful." Cole pointed a finger at him. "What's your name?"

"Pete."

"Yes, Pete. We'd really appreciate the assist."

Pete's scrunched face didn't suggest cooperation was forthcoming.

"Have you ever had a thin-crust pizza from Bistro Italiano?" Cole asked.

"Nope." Pete shook his head.

"A Neapolitan-style crust. The sauce is perfection. Buffalo mozzarella. I'd be happy to arrange a delivery of one loaded with your favorite toppings as a sign of our appreciation."

Stubby fingers danced across a computer keyboard. "You don't need to talk to the driver. I can look it up for you. All right, let's see. Pizza. Cookie. Burger. One."

Surprise ticked through her. Cole was pretty good at this.

"That was Rodney's car," Pete said. "He dropped a passenger at the Hotel Monaco at 11:46."

Her chest cramped. She was suddenly light-headed, her equilibrium knocked sideways.

Pete scratched his belly. "It's located at 700—"

"We know." Cole's voice was quiet as he exchanged a knowing glance with her.

At Hotel Monaco, they'd shared their first time together. He hadn't pressured or persuaded her into it. She'd been ready and eager. Inside suite 303, surrounded by candles and rose petals, he'd taken her virginity lovingly and with such scorching intensity, he'd branded her as his forever.

Averting her gaze from Cole's burning eyes, she moved from earshot outside and called Castle on her encrypted Gray Box cell phone.

"Our Ghost was dropped off at the Hotel Monaco last night. It's 700 Foxtrot Street November Whiskey. We're headed there now."

"TV station is a dead end," Castle said. "One of the security guards scrubbed everything. No record the Ghost landed or entered the building. We'll meet you at the hotel."

Through the glass door, she watched Cole throw a couple of twenties on the desk and scrawl something on a piece of paper for Pete. Then he came outside, up close to her.

Too damn close.

The heat radiating from him slid across her like a second skin. Her chest throbbed, pulse pounding in her head. She turned, facing the flesh-colored building, refusing to show him how his proximity affected her, and dialed Gideon.

"What's your status, Reaper?" she asked.

"I located the helicopter at a local charter company. I'm going to squeeze the owner for any information."

If anyone was good at squeezing a person to make them talk, it was Reaper. Formally trained in interrogation and assassination, he was the ruthless type who'd push—or pull off fingernails if necessary—to get the information.

"Okay." She filled him in on the hotel and called Harper at the Gray Box. "It's me. How long would it take you to hack into a hotel's guest registry?"

"I don't know. Depends on the firewall encryption and—"

"Hotel Monaco. DC. I need the registered names and room numbers for any guests who checked in between eleven thirty and midnight last night. Also, tap into their security camera feed and run the facial recognition program for our targets."

"I'm on it."

Stabbing the phone with a finger to end the call, Maddox turned, headed for the bike. Cole put one hand on the wall, blocking her, and with the other dragged his knuckles across her jaw. The searing contact nearly stopped her heart.

Oh God, if she looked up at him, it would be her undoing.

His mouth caressed her hair, his warm breath against her ear. "Maddox—"

She shoved the muscular barrier of his arm out of her way and strode toward the bike. One foot in front of the other. The squeeze in her throat almost made it impossible to talk, but she swallowed past it. "Let's go."

Maddox craned her neck, looking up at the splendid Corinthian pillars of the neoclassical building as Cole pulled in front of Hotel Monaco.

What had once been their special place. They had come here many times, to be alone together, away from his parents' house or her roommates in her Georgetown dorm.

Squirreled away in the hotel, they'd talked about everything from their childhoods to their hopes for the future, had fed each other room service, swathed in a sense of completion, lying curled naked around one another for hours after making love. Always intense. Threaded with passion, like their souls had been sewn as one with adamantine strands.

The helmet became stifling. She needed to get it off. Needed to breathe.

Cole parked in a spot ahead of a line of taxis.

Heart racing, she ripped off the helmet and raked in a breath. She dismounted the bike and gripped the hard seat of the motorcycle until the ground beneath her feet stopped teetering. Across the street stood the National Portrait Gallery. Home of the Kogod Courtyard, where Cole had strolled into her life.

He'd been so freaking cute. Wild, midnight hair. Warm, penetrating eyes. A disarming smile. He'd strode up to her like he was capable of taking on the whole world to get anything he wanted.

His bad-boy hotness, heck, just talking to him had made her crazy-giddy.

She'd accepted everything he had offered—lunch, a ride on his bike, a smoldering kiss she'd remember until the day she died—even though he was trouble.

The kind of trouble that gave her father nightmares.

Pivoting, she looked back at the hotel.

This was ground zero.

A dull ache echoed through her.

Cole gripped her, and she realized she was shivering. He pried the helmet from her rigid fingers. "I've got you."

At those tender words, something inside her snapped, and she jerked away. "No. You don't." A fierce whisper. "You let me go. You let me grieve. You let me fall."

"Maddox." The shock on his face would've twisted her soul in knots if the icy anger sweeping through her hadn't been doing such good work numbing her. "I'm sorry."

Such feeble words meant nothing, changed nothing between them.

She shrugged. "It doesn't matter. I've got a job to do."

Squaring her shoulders, she zipped up her steely composure. Head in the game. Zero tolerance for one sloppy drop of maudlin mush.

She met his gaze and didn't flinch at the grief in his eyes. "We need to find Novak." Her tone was pure business.

His face strained with messy emotion, but he gave a

firm nod. "Do you have a picture of him to show the hotel staff?"

"Harper loaded our phones with one."

Cole glanced around. "Why do you think he chose this hotel?"

The ten-million-dollar question. A dozen similar hotels would put him in walking distance to the U.S. Capitol, the White House, museums, but he'd chosen this one.

"Let's go try to find out."

A few long strides brought him to her side.

Despite how crazy he made her, having a lethal, capable man such as Cole on her team was a definite plus. He'd give his all, which equated to more in one day than some operatives mustered in their careers.

They headed up the steps toward the entrance shaded beneath a crimson awning. As they reached the door, he cupped her elbow, stopping her. "It's possible he's already released smallpox-M inside and could be on his way out of the country."

They could be walking into a hot zone. She'd prefer a bullet if given a choice between the two. After Novak escaped from the yacht, he could've gone anywhere, but chose DC. There were other hotels far closer to the television station where the Ghost had landed. And instead of deploying it right away at the station or a nearby hotel, he'd taken a cab thirty minutes across town. Novak had chosen this hotel for another reason.

"I've got to take the chance. This is our only solid lead. You've risked too much already—you don't have to come in. I wouldn't hold it against you if you waited out here. No one would." Other than Castle.

"Where you go, I go. Whatever is waiting inside, we face it together."

Cole was doing a number on her, testing her in new ways.

Damn it. One little sloppy drop of warmth slipped through. Just one.

She had to hunt an assassin in possession of a lethal weapon. She needed to stay hard. Be that hunter and stalk her prey.

Cole opened the door, leading the way inside. They strode across the marble floor into the understated grandeur of the quaintly elegant lobby. It left her as awestruck as the first time.

A couple lounged on a crocodile leather sofa in front of a cold stone fireplace. A woman carrying shopping bags strolled toward the elevators beneath opulent, emerald-green crystal chandeliers. Staff chatted as they headed down a walkway along a wall of mirrored glass.

The hotel had almost two hundred rooms. The Ghost could be in any one of them. Or worse, if he wasn't here, then anywhere in the city.

Maddox approached the front desk, still scanning the lobby. Cole stuck to her side.

A young woman greeted them with a cordial smile. "Hello, how can I help you?"

"Is there anyone available who worked the front desk last night—between eleven and midnight?" Maddox asked.

The woman shook her head. "No, sorry. We did our

shift change at six this morning. Is there something I can help you with?"

Unease whispered down Maddox's spine. She glanced over her shoulder. Two men in suits strode through the lobby, griping about a business merger. The couple on the sofa cuddled, oblivious.

She pulled out her phone and brought up the picture of Novak. "Have you seen this man? He's the subject of an ongoing investigation. It's critical we find him."

The elevator on the left pinged and her heartbeat quickened. The doors opened. A man and woman pushed a baby stroller off.

"We suspect he checked in late last night under an assumed name," Cole said.

Maddox turned back to the young woman behind the desk, who shook her head at the picture. She brought up a photo of the Ghost's son, Val. "What about this man? Have you seen him?"

The receptionist peered at the picture for a long moment. "He doesn't look familiar."

They'd have to wait for Harper to hack into the hotel system.

Maddox spun on a sigh, doing another sweep of the lobby.

A man wearing a baseball cap pulled low, sunglasses, blue long-sleeved shirt—despite the ungodly heat outside—and carrying a backpack did an about-face, pushed through the front door, and hurried down the steps to the street.

She got that palpable sense that something wasn't right. Like maggots slithering in her gut, lice crawling over her skin. She'd only caught a glimpse of the man, not even a full profile. But the way he moved triggered her well-honed instincts, urging her toward action.

Snatching her phone from the receptionist, Maddox ran to the door. She dashed down the steps and whirled 180 degrees, scouring the street. Ditching the button-down and cap would alter his appearance, but there hadn't been time.

One man caught her eye. He was slender and had a hat, but it wasn't Novak.

She ignored the pang of knife-sharp frustration and scanned the opposite direction. Stepping wide around a woman walking a dog, she spotted a flash of blue. To the right, headed north on F Street toward Seventh. Long-sleeved shirt. Navy ball cap and black backpack. Right height and build. He had the cagey walk of a predator on the loose.

She needed to see his face.

Her palms itched as she marched closer. She lengthened her stride, but restrained the impulse to charge toward him. The last thing she wanted was to spook him into running. She needed to cross the street at the first break in traffic and follow parallel to avoid detection.

And almost at once, it was too late.

The man glanced over his shoulder, checking his six, and sunlight bounced off his sunglasses. The profile was a dead ringer.

A cold jolt of adrenaline raced through her.

The Ghost took off like a bullet fired. She bolted after him, with Cole sprinting at her side.

Novak plunged into the congested traffic on sprawling

Seventh Street. Bobbing and weaving around cars, joggers, people on bikes, buses, he never broke his stride. Horns blared and tires screeched as cars braked. The man had mind-boggling speed and agility. Zero fear. He pushed down the lengthy stretch of sidewalk along the Capital One Arena, shoving pedestrians out of his way.

Maddox and Cole skirted around traffic, holding up hands to get oncoming vehicles to slow. They were losing him. Novak glided down the street, extending his lead.

A biker clipped Cole, and he stumbled, pitching forward, hitting asphalt.

She didn't slow. Getting hemmed up would crush their chance to capture Novak. They had to cut through the congestion of Penn Quarter.

The Ghost pounded past the arena, headed toward H Street. He was closing in on the bustling Gallery Place mall, the hubbub of Chinatown, and Metro stations teeming with passengers.

The odds that he'd lose them escalated with each second. The hotel had been their one good lead. If he got away now, they might not get another.

Cole pushed up alongside her, recovering lost ground.

Digging until her thighs screamed, she fought through the fire shredding her legs, the ache nibbling at her side. Shoppers filtered in and out of Gallery Place ahead—an abundance of stores, restaurants: too much collateral damage if this went sideways.

The sweltering sun beat down, turning the streets into an oven. Her jacket trapped the slick sheet of sweat on her skin. She gritted her teeth and blocked it all out.

The heat. The burn. The dread.

Weakness.

A businessman on his cell drifted out of a bar and grill on a collision course with a killer. The Ghost barreled into him, sending the guy spinning hard into the street like a wobbling top. His briefcase flew into the air, and the poor suit crashed into a cyclist, bike bell zinging, planting them both face-first into the blacktop.

She stayed locked on the Ghost.

Steady.

Maddox dragged in thick, short breaths condensed with humidity, like breathing through a straw.

The path cleared of pedestrians. Cole broke away at a dead sprint, pulling ahead. She pumped her arms, driving her legs harder, forcing her body to go faster still. The tall, rectangular signpost for the Gallery Place Metro station on the corner of H Street stood erect like a beacon.

If the Ghost made it into the station and on a train, they could lose him for good.

21

F STREET, WASHINGTON, DC
12:21 P.M. EDT

No thought of how far he'd have to run, how long he had to push, Cole held a singular focus: *catch the Ghost*.

To keep Maddox safe, he had to reach the devil first.

Extending his stride in a flat-out sprint, Cole gave it everything. His shoulder hurt like hell.

He was gaining on him. Less than thirty feet, chipping away at the distance with every hot lungful.

Just ahead was the Gallery Place Metro—one of the busiest stations in DC. A throng of passengers streamed in and out of the cavernous entrance. The Ghost wove between people, darting to the left then right, flowing like a stream of water around stones.

Don't lose him. Stay close. Almost there.

Cole knocked a man out of the way and slipped through a narrow opening in the pedestrian herd. The entrance cleared ahead, and there was Novak.

The Ghost zipped past the station agent, Metrorail vending machines, and vaulted over the turnstile in one fluid motion. Steamrolling forward into the musty air and under the fluorescent lights of the station, Cole hopped the turnstile.

Maddox's pounding footsteps weren't far behind.

Cole cut to the east side of the Metro station, keeping sight of the Ghost. Escalators to the trains on the lower level were around a corner. Hopefully, passengers lining the moving staircase would slow Novak down.

What if he deployed the weapon in the station or on the Metrorail? The virus would spread fast with no way to contain it.

Novak hesitated at the escalators and snapped a glimpse over his shoulder, not looking the least bit winded. Their eyes met, and that freakish smile hitched up Novak's mouth. In a flash, he whirled, facing the escalator.

Then he jumped onto the wide metal panel running between the escalators and slid down.

Shit!

Breathless, Cole reached the escalator and peered over the side. Down a long, steep descent running several stories below ground. Really fucking long and very steep.

Sonofabitch. Novak had no limits and kept pushing the line. Cole hated heights, but that lunatic was getting away, and Maddox was closing in. No time. No time to think.

He vaulted onto the steel divider flanked by the two escalators.

"Dude, you're crazy," quipped a teenage kid getting off.

It felt a hell of a lot crazier than it looked. With the constraints of the narrow panel, Cole was forced to roll onto his side as Novak had done. Maddox's pounding footsteps drew closer. Not giving himself a chance to chicken out, he let go and gravity took him.

In a lightning rush, he zipped down cool, smooth steel feetfirst.

"Cole!" Maddox's voice echoed overhead.

His jackhammering heart blasted into his throat, followed by his stomach. He slid down the tight divider like a slick stone. The faces of gawking onlookers were a blur. He braced, leaning back against the steep, eighty-foot decline. He almost swallowed his tongue.

To control his breathless descent, he thrust his forearms out to the sides.

Bad idea.

His sleeves dragged against the rubber handrails, the friction turning his quicksilver slide into a jerky ride. He feared flipping over the side onto the steel teeth of an escalator.

Weightless, helpless, he drew his arms in close to his body.

Not every Metro in DC had bumpers. The puck-sized discs didn't stop a fall, only turned a person into tenderized meat by the time they reached the bottom. He was grateful not to face any here.

The ground below was a desperate hope rushing toward him, coming at him fast. But it was the longest eight seconds of his life. Wild exhilaration wrestled with fear.

Fear was better.

It'd keep him sharp and hungry. Keep him alive.

Novak reached the bottom and glanced up at Cole before disappearing in the direction of the Red line.

Swooshing off the metal panel, Cole's feet stumbled finding the floor. The electric surge rising in him was akin to being born again. He fell to one knee and sprang forward, following the trail of twisting heads and necks craned over shoulders.

The corridor spilled onto the westbound platform. People stood shoulder to shoulder. Jam-packed with kids, from teens to middle-schoolers, in a patchwork of yellow, green, light-blue, and red T-shirts.

Damn it. Summer camp field trips.

Across the tracks, the eastbound side was worse. He glanced at the inbound train sign overhead—three minutes ETA.

Three minutes before the Ghost could be lost in the wind.

Dim lighting in the concave tunnel turned needle-in-a-haystack into finding a needle in a pine forest, at night. Red LED lights lined the bumpy tiles along the edge of the platform but did nothing to brighten the landscape. Chest heaving, he slowed his breathing while scanning for a dark ball cap, black backpack. Anyone in long sleeves.

He shouldered past people, weaving around a huddle of kids and chaperones in light blue T-shirts that read *Ride the Summer Wave*. Every ten steps, he checked his rear, ensuring he hadn't missed the Ghost, somehow overlooked him in the sea of passengers.

Maddox made it down, rushing onto the eastbound side across the tracks. She scoured the platform.

Cole pressed forward. Most bodies stayed stationary or paced one to two feet within a localized space. He caught glimpses of one person with a blue ball cap and backpack. Drifting slowly. Snaking around shifting figures. Cole bulldozed his way to the thin male.

Metallic bitterness coated his tongue. He clasped a hand on the man's shoulder and wrenched him around.

A wide-eyed young man with olive-toned skin stared back. "Hey, buddy, what's your problem?"

"Sorry." Cole raised his palms and backed off.

Red LED lights across the tracks on Maddox's side flashed. A train was coming.

Two minutes until his westbound train arrived. He stepped up his pace through the milling flock of people, wiping his sweaty palms on his jeans. His sixth sense, the electric worm, carved a wriggling path from his skull down his spine, fizzing and spitting sparks across his nerve endings.

The rumble of the eastbound train resounded. Cole glanced back to see lights and Maddox peering down the tunnel at the inbound train. Dread churned his gut.

He faced forward and caught the Ghost's steely gaze at the other end of the same platform. No baseball cap. The maniacal grin on full display. A moment. Less. A millisecond. Cole pushed toward him, storming through the gaggle of day campers.

Novak made his move. A bloodcurdling scream rent the air as the Ghost leapt off the platform, arm locked around a woman, hauling her over the side along with him. He let go of her and dashed across the westbound tracks, avoiding the electrified third rail.

Bounding over a strip of lighting in the middle, Novak rushed across the eastbound tracks. He jumped, pressing his hands onto the platform, and lifted his body with the fluidity of a gymnast. The flat-faced train whizzed into the station on the opposite side, concealing Maddox and the Ghost from sight.

Red lights flashed on Cole's platform. He ran to

help the fallen woman. Elbowing anyone in his way, he rushed to the far end.

The eastbound train on the other side stopped and the doors opened.

Cole swept paralyzed gawkers to the side and reached down to the plump woman in the light yellow T-shirt, *Pirates and Princesses Summer Camp* written across the front. Out of his peripheral vision, cowering children shrieked and whimpered.

"Come on." He beckoned to the stunned woman clambering to her feet. "Take my hand."

Chimes dinged from the train across the way, and his skin prickled. Doors were about to close.

"Let's go, lady," he snapped at her, trying to get her moving.

Lights of the approaching westbound train on his side did the trick.

A horn blared, kicking the woman into action, hustling to the platform. She grabbed both his hands and he held tight to her forearms and heaved. Thankfully, she was lighter than she looked, but his back still protested. A black kid in his late teens, with headphones on, helped him tug her the rest of the way up onto the platform.

"You okay?" Cole asked.

She nodded, and tears streaked down her cheeks. Covering her face with her hands, she broke into sobs. Yellow T-shirts gathered around her, and Cole shot to his feet.

The train on the other side pulled out. The steel cars vanished down the dark tunnel. He swept a frantic gaze over the platform. Empty.

Cole's blood drained from his head as a hot ball of panic burned a hole in his gut.

Maddox and the Ghost were both gone.

Cole grabbed his phone.

——————— ———————

METRO, WASHINGTON, DC
12:46 P.M. EDT

On the crammed train, Aleksander slid between passengers, working his way to the car door. Folding around people, smooth, fluid, he didn't draw a single glance.

He grasped the door handle and looked over his shoulder.

Lovely Agent Kinkade had hopped onto the seventh car. She was trapped well behind him, since he'd made it onto the third from the front.

Two minutes. That's how long she had to close the gap before the train pulled into the next station. Before he disappeared.

He glided onto the second car, sliding the door shut.

She wouldn't make it. Despite valiant effort. She was a determined fighter.

It'd been a shock seeing her in the lobby and a disappointment to find her companion glued to her side, Scarface ever bound in gravitational orbit around her.

Following his instincts to split up and have Val stay at a different hotel with half their supplies paid off. Luck was on his side. But how did they find him?

He'd been careful, kept a low profile.

Yet as he'd returned from scouting the location he'd chosen, there she stood in the hotel lobby. Seeing her caught him off guard in the most exquisite way, and he'd faltered.

A mistake he wouldn't repeat.

Pressing forward, he snaked past passengers, maintaining his lead. The train slowed into the Judiciary Square station. He skated around three teenage boys to the opening doors.

He'd lose her, but she'd keep coming. And along with her, several agents and, of course, the man with the scar. He disliked having his hand forced, but it left him no choice. The situation must be remedied.

The doors opened. Aleksander leapt out, zipping through the shuffling exchange of passengers, and darted for the staircase. Grasping the railing, he peered over the side. Agent Kinkade pushed through the crowd, sandwiched in the muddle of people. She looked up, catching his gaze. Stilled, as if debating, then drove on. Ever onward, Kinkade.

He pounded up the steps to the main Metro level and dashed to the staircase leading outside. Sunlight cut through the artificial glare of the station. Warm, fresh air ripe with good fortune caressed his skin.

The natural choice, the smart one—the one Agent Maddox would expect—was for Aleksander to turn right, head east three blocks to the bustling Union Station.

A person could disappear in the yawning maw of the transportation hub that spat out multiple exits. So easy to be swallowed up in one's pick of Metro or commuter rail lines spread across eighteen platforms and twenty-two tracks and at least ten different bus lines. Better than the Americans' Baskin-Robbins thirty-one flavors. Sweeter too.

But his choice was one of necessity, and Agent Kinkade had no way of knowing that. She would assume she'd lost him in the bowels of Union Station. When she emerged from the Metro, she'd follow instinct and look in the wrong direction.

He sprinted through the National Law Enforcement Officers Memorial and veered hard to the south. Under different circumstances, he would've chosen east, removed his shirt and donned a new hat from the options in his bag, and strolled, blending in.

This was the hand he was dealt. He would play it. To win.

Hitting E Street, he then darted south, heading back to the hotel.

He yanked off the long-sleeve top, revealing a simple white T-shirt, and threw on a green bucket hat, tightening the cinch cord under his chin.

Five hundred yards. A breeze. He blasted across Fifth Street, dodging cars and joggers. Bristling energy, sharp and electric, drove him. So close now. He would not be denied. Val would be at his side, and together, they'd usher in the four horsemen.

Aleksander dashed through the traffic on Sixth Street, ignoring the symphony of honks and squawking brakes. One more block.

Holding a steady stride, he coasted.

His body nimble, his limbs light as air.

Slowing, he strode into the restaurant on Seventh. The hostess at the front smiled.

"I'm meeting someone," he said, winded. "There's my party now." He pointed, gliding past her. Cutting through the lunchtime bustle, he breezed into the Hotel Monaco, which connected to the restaurant, and headed for the staircase.

Two men stood at the front desk. Both had been on the yacht, not appearing damaged from the explosion. Agents. Cockroaches.

Aleksander enjoyed playing cat and mouse, but it was time to return to the top of the food chain where he and his son alone did the chasing. He raced up the stairs to the fourth floor, taking off the hat and glasses, and whipped the door open. Rounding the corner, he hurried to his room. He popped the key card into the slot. Green dots illuminated, and he slipped inside.

At the safe, he entered the code and retrieved the canister of smallpox. The rest of the equipment he needed to execute his plan was with Val in another hotel. The suitcase he pulled from under the bed contained everything he required for now. He stripped, changing into black pants, a generic white dress shirt, and the hotel staff jacket he'd lifted during the distraction of their shift turnover earlier this morning.

In the bathroom, he dragged a washcloth over his face and applied the disguise he'd procured—along with the rest of the items in the suitcase—from his contact.

Here in Washington, DC, with enough money, he could get almost anything as easily as ordering room service. Almost. The specialized access credentials and equipment Val was modifying for the next step of the plan could only have been obtained thanks to the assistance of the industrious information broker, Daedalus. The man was a fount of intelligence, thanks to his bevy of spies, and his access to resources was staggering.

The black wig Aleksander shifted in place itched, but as problems went, that was nil. A glued-on chevron mustache, cotton balls stuffed in his mouth between his teeth and cheeks for a jowly look, and a pair of glasses transformed his face into one even he didn't recognize.

He tossed what he could into the suitcase, his blood pressure rising over this willy-nilly scramble. The room door slapped shut behind him when he left. Hunching his shoulders, he carted the wheeled suitcase down the hall. Turning his left foot inward altered his gait, adding a subtle limp. His nerves were strung as tight as his garrote around a target's throat. He had to hurry.

Timing was everything.

The two agents from the lobby rounded the corner, coming from the elevator. The big, bald one held out his hand, and the other handed him a generic taupe key card attached to a chain. They must've swiped it from housekeeping.

Lowering his gaze and rolling his shoulders into the hunch, Aleksander strode past them. Not a second glance from them in his direction. They suspected nothing.

He slapped the button for the elevator. Getting a new burner phone was next on his list, followed by contacting Daedalus. He needed information on Agent Maddox Kinkade. Fast.

Planning and adaptation were his strengths. Seeing the *how*. He and Val had time to deal with this contingency.

The elevator chimed. The doors opened. Ducking in, he tapped the lobby button.

His plan for the biological weapon had come together easily. Such a brilliant target. It was as though the gods had set the gift of glorious vengeance in the palms of his weary hands. His retribution would be recorded as the greatest tragedy in American history. A hammer blow to the country's stability, showing the entire world the fragility of their security.

He strolled off the elevator, spotting Agent Kinkade and Scarface at the far end of the compact lobby. Scarface had a hand pressed to her cheek, anxiety etched across his features.

Aww, the lovers. How grateful they should be.

Aleksander would redefine their meaning of fear.

Scarface threw his arms around the pretty Kinkade in a strangling hug. Her hands lifted as if to reciprocate, but she hesitated.

Fascinating. Aleksander slowed but didn't stop moving.

She broke free of Scarface, shaking her head and stabbing a finger toward the elevator. His face blanked.

Trouble in paradise? If not, there soon would be. A thank-you gift from Aleksander.

Agent Kinkade answered her phone, making a beeline for the elevators, Scarface plastered to her side. Lowering his head, Aleksander quickened his hobbled gait.

They crossed the lobby toward him. Dark excitement shot through Aleksander, tingles racing over his skin.

"Harper, slow down. Wait. He came back to the hotel?" Kinkade looked at Scarface, gaze passing right over him, as they hurried to the elevator. "What room?"

When they passed, Aleksander had nearly brushed her arm. He savored the thrill of this win.

He was tempted to glance back at her. The need was a tangible ache in his teeth, but the risk wasn't worth it. He'd look into those exquisite eyes again soon enough.

On his terms.

22

GRAY BOX HEADQUARTERS, NORTHERN VIRGINIA
3:10 P.M. EDT

Tension rolled through the conference room in a cresting wave. A charged silence pressed in. Failure and frustration were in the air, a smell as real as sweat and stale coffee.

Maddox massaged her temples, elbows propped on the arms of her chair. "Please, run us through how we lost Novak in the hotel one more time."

Harper stood at the foot of the black glass table, rubbing her hands, delicate features pinched tight. "I tapped into the hotel security feed using the facial recognition program, as well as the Ponte restaurant connected to it. At 1:13 p.m., Novak entered the restaurant. He crossed into the hotel at 1:14 and hit the fourth floor at 1:18, entering room 416."

"Doesn't your network have a notification system when you get a recognition hit?" Maddox asked.

A deer-in-the-headlights expression froze on Harper's face. "Of course."

"Then why didn't you notify us the minute he set foot on the premises? Castle and Reece were on-site."

Her brother slammed a fist on the table. Harper jumped and a hand flew to her necklace, thumb stroking the pearls. Reece shook his head, bitterness etched on his face.

Cole sat beside Maddox, arms folded, eyes narrowed.

The sole unreadable one in the room was Gideon. Perched against a wall, he stood with hands in his pockets, chewing a wad of gum. His arctic gaze locked on Harper, his face an irksome blank slate.

Harper swallowed hard as if she had something lodged in her throat. "I was on a break."

"Pretty damn convenient." Castle's voice was so caustic, Harper winced.

"Or coincidence." Gideon's tone was rock-steady.

"It's just me working on this. You didn't want me to get any help." Harper plowed through her words in a strident rush. "I had to pee and get coffee. I haven't slept. I've been working all night. When I got back to my desk, I saw the alert flashing. Novak wasn't on the monitor in real-time. The program looped back to when he was first picked up entering the restaurant, and I called you. I was only behind by four and a half minutes."

"Only." Castle expelled a breath.

"We're all tired and on edge." Maddox sipped coffee, forcing herself to calm down. Pissing off their best analyst wouldn't improve the current situation. "Earlier, you mentioned Novak left the hotel wearing a disguise."

Harper nodded. "A black wig, glasses—"

"Burgundy hotel jacket." Maddox's stomach dropped to her toes. The Ghost had doubled back after she lost him in the train station, then had the gall to stroll right by her and Cole.

"Yes." Harper rolled her pearls between her fingers,

brows drawn together. "On the playback of the hotel video, he passed all of you."

Castle popped the knuckles of his bad hand like he needed to hit someone.

"Can you run a picture of Novak in the disguise through the program?"

"He kept his head lowered. I'd need a full facial shot, but I can try."

Maddox stifled the expletives prickling her tongue. "Review the footage for any leads. Also rustle up whatever you can on Kassar. We have details on how Blackburn and Callahan were taken out, but nothing on Kassar."

"Okay." Harper hurried from the room.

This was a major hit, but Maddox couldn't let the setback derail the team's focus. "This isn't over. Not until we find Novak and the bioweapon."

Reece adjusted his cap, propping the bill up with a knuckle. This one read *I Drink Coffee for Your Protection*. "Harper's slipup can't be ignored."

"Especially in light of your mole problem." Cole raked dark hair back from his face. "How well do you know her? Is it possible she left her desk to give Novak time to get away?"

"She keeps to herself, doesn't associate with anyone here," Maddox said. "Harper was away from her desk at a critical moment, but it was also her idea to modify her facial recognition program to tap into the video surveillance system. And she took it upon herself to access the private security feed of the restaurant."

Cole removed his riding jacket. "It could be a feint. Distract someone by getting them to focus on

one hand while you're winding up to take them down
with the other."

"Did you see her as she explained?" Gideon took a
seat. "That was no feint."

Maddox didn't get the sense Harper was faking her
jitters either, but the fact remained there *was* a traitor. A
fool with no ethics, no conscience, who was bartering
classified information and risking national security but
sooner or later was going to get caught.

"Harper could be the leak, or she could've made a
mistake," Maddox said. "I lost Novak in the train station.
Looking at this case from the outside, I'd be under suspi-
cion too." Taking ownership of her failure cut like a
switchblade. "But Cole is right. It's a problem."

"Let's keep Harper and bring in Cutter or Amanda,"
Castle said. "Checks and balances."

Both were solid analysts, but if Maddox had to pick,
it'd be Amanda hands down. She was a crackerjack analyst
and a great friend and could be relied on in a pinch.

"Do you want to resource some of this out to
Rubicon? I can talk to my boss, Donovan."

As simple as Cole made the idea sound, it was the
exact opposite. One didn't farm out classified work to
noncleared personnel. It would mean allowing them
to process highly sensitive information pertaining to
national security in a facility that wasn't cleared to
handle classified material. They'd have to go through
the proper red tape, which would take time they
didn't have.

One thing for Sanborn to allow a single essential
civilian in with a nondisclosure agreement, but there was

no way their boss would green-light something of such magnitude under the table. They could all go to prison.

Before responding, she shot Castle a questioning glance to see how he read the idea.

An expression of utter disbelief that she'd consider it washed across his face. "Fuck. No."

Yeah, he didn't like the prospect of prison either. "We go with Castle's idea. It's the smart play." Redundancy beat hedging the wrong bet.

"Of course it's the smart play. It's my idea," Castle said.

Cole leaned in, resting a hand on her arm. "Nice to see your brother hasn't changed." He flashed a casual, lighthearted smile, as if the world wasn't about to end.

The warmth in his face caught her off guard, and she smiled back, longing to recover the years they'd been cheated.

Wretched years that had changed them both, for better or worse.

Forcing her gaze from his, she looked at Gideon. "Please tell me you have good news." She grabbed a bottle of water and took a sip.

"I've got Van Helden," he said, deadpan. "Sitting in an interrogation room."

Maddox choked, and Cole patted her back.

"How?" was all she managed.

"After Van Helden landed at the helicopter charter company, he booked a private jet to Dubai. The man spent the night in a luxe suite at the Four Seasons. I found him chilling in a posh lounge at Dulles International, waiting to go wheels up in an hour."

"Holy hell." She straightened in her seat. "Why didn't you start with that before we got into the Novak snafu?"

Gideon chewed on his gum, detached demeanor locked tight. "I worked him over a little. Didn't take much."

Reece shifted in his chair. "Did he give up the seller?"

"Never met the seller. Van Helden offers a blind system for any skittish clientele. There was a specified site, date, and time for Van Helden to pick up the bioweapon along with specific instructions for the auction process. The seller gave him a list of the arms dealers to be invited, date of the auction, and the international account number for the wire transfer of payment."

The team exchanged can-this-crap-day-get-any-crappier looks.

"And here's the kicker," Gideon said, his icy, pale-blue eyes sparkling.

Apparently, it could.

"The auction room was wired. The seller saw and heard everything."

Cole groaned, rolling his eyes. "With that system, how does a skittish seller know Van Helden won't just steal their product?"

"Van Helden may be a criminal, but he prides himself on not being a cheat. He's built his business on his reputation."

"At least there's one less black-market middleman out in the world," Castle said.

"No-go on sending Van Helden to the Hole."

The Hole was the super-spook maximum security facility so highly classified, the only Gray Box personnel to know where it was located were Sanborn, Castle, and deputy director Knox.

"Sanborn made a call to arrange Van Helden's transfer. Ten minutes later, the director of national intelligence called."

The Gray Box only reported to the DNI and the president.

"Sanborn has to cut him loose. Looks like either the CIA or NSA is protecting him as a confidential informant. They're working something and need Van Helden to hook a big fish. Sanborn is on his way to the White House to find out specifics and update the president on our status."

Cole unleashed an appalled snicker, leveling the room into silence. "Van Helden is just as bad as those scumbag arms traffickers, not to mention whoever decided they wanted to sell a bioweapon. And you guys are letting him walk because of some filthy interagency deal?"

"Sometimes, we let the lesser evil walk in order to protect the greater good," Castle said.

Incredulity gripped Cole's face. "You guys are no better than—"

Maddox rested a hand on Cole's arm and squeezed. "This is going to be a long day." She needed to shut this down. They had to pull together, not tear each other to pieces. "We have a lot of work ahead of us."

Janet strolled into the conference with a platter of sandwiches and crudités. She was a godsend, greasing the wheels to keep everyone moving. "Should I plan dinner too?"

She'd already fed them breakfast, and this spread would carry them through. Hopefully.

"No," Maddox said. "Don't trouble yourself. Thanks."

"I have a fresh pot of coffee brewing." She grabbed the old pot and left.

"Reece, do another search through the stuff we found in Novak's room," Maddox said. "See if we missed anything."

They'd done a thorough sweep of the room before leaving the hotel, bringing back everything they'd found. In the closet, she'd discovered the tux the Ghost had worn at the auction and the empty metallic case the bioweapon had been stored in. That at least told them the cylindrical canister they were looking for was sixteen inches long.

Reece had canvassed the bathroom, collecting the contents of the wastebasket. Cole had found a copy of the *Washington Post* on the desk and had brought it to the conference room.

"On it," Reece said.

"Castle," she said, catching him with a sandwich in his hand, "before you stuff your face, we need to know what's within a one-mile radius of the hotel. He chose to stay at the location for a reason. We need to figure out what it is. Prep a threat matrix for each potential target. Prioritize anything high-profile or time-sensitive. Task an analyst to help. Not Harper."

As much as she hated bringing in a second analyst full-time on this, they had little choice. She wanted Amanda, trusted her the most in analysis, but a mole in the small organization meant the traitor was going to be someone they trusted. Better to let Castle choose, a random pick.

"Agreed." Castle rose. "But just to clarify, you are not the team leader."

Suppressing an eye roll, she smiled. "I believe Sanborn called you—and I quote—*backup*."

"Backup with three years seniority."

Another damn challenge. She was in charge and if this op went south, it would rest squarely on her head and her record. But she could throw Castle a bone here and there if it meant he'd cooperate. "Agreed. You're the senior person on my team."

"Reaper, can you compile a spreadsheet of the Ghost's past known contracts? Types of targets he's taken out, any special skills he might have had to use to pull off the jobs."

One assassin looking at another might be helpful for a different perspective.

"Sure." Gideon dug into a sandwich and sat, logging in to an individual screen on the smart table.

Sensing Cole's stare on her, Maddox glanced at him.

Once they had regrouped at the hotel after losing Novak on the train, he'd given her a breathtaking bear hug, and for a split second, she'd forgotten how their ugly past had poisoned any hope for a future.

A dangerous moment of hesitation.

Time to establish boundaries and set him straight about his place in this mission.

"You should hydrate." She took one of the last ham sandwiches. "It'd do you good to get a bite away from here. You're not used to working in a place with no windows. It can drive you stir-crazy."

"Take a break with me. You need one. Clear your mind for a few minutes."

"I can't." She tensed and considered stepping into

the hall for what she needed to say next, but being alone
with him right now wasn't a good idea. "Cole," she said,
lowering her voice, "this thing between us is a distraction.
You've no idea how hard I work to measure up. I've
sacrificed, suffered, bled to be here. I'm good at what I do,
but out there, I need to be objective. Not emotional." An
operative. Not a woman. "You have to back off."

If she wasn't a good operative, she was nothing.

Cole hardened his jaw and shot a glance at Gideon, as
if uneasy they weren't alone. Gideon ate while working.
He was listening, of course, but appeared oblivious.

"There's no putting me on a leash," Cole snapped.

Another one of those dog references he threw around
like she thought of him as a pound puppy.

"And with this thing between us," he continued,
"there is no backing off."

"Then you need to walk away from this." Not just
for the sake of the mission or herself but to keep him
safe. *God, what if something happened to him out there, at
Novak's hands?* Her stomach clenched at the thought.

Cole popped to his feet, his expression mulish. He
looked fierce and as pigheaded as ever. "That's not happening. You're pissed I hugged you in the hotel when I saw
you were safe. It wasn't wrong, even if it was ill-timed.
We didn't lose him because of a hug. Don't forget, Novak
slipped by Castle and Reece too. Novak was just better
than us today. Your inability to find balance with me
being a part of this equation is your issue, not mine. But a
word of advice—practice until you can."

He snatched Novak's copy of the *Washington Post* off
the table.

"I'm taking a break." Cole stormed out of the room.

Balance had never been an issue. She didn't allow her personal life to invade work. Her world was simple, small, sterile...because he hadn't been in it. Now the lines were blurring.

Practice until you can. When did he start talking like a Chinese fortune cookie?

The sudden tightness in her chest was an irksome weight.

Janet breezed in with a fresh pot of coffee, plugged in the carafe, and marched out with the pep of the Energizer bunny.

"You're right," Gideon said, typing on the virtual keyboard, not looking at her.

"Thank you." The validation was a relief.

"But he was also right."

She stiffened, not seeing how that could be the case. And quite frankly, right now, she wasn't inclined to try.

———————   ———————

GRAY BOX HEADQUARTERS, NORTHERN VIRGINIA
5:30 P.M. EDT

In the bathroom, Maddox pressed a cold, wet paper towel to her eyes. Two minutes of this while taking deep breaths was the best quick refresher.

The door opened and closed. Based on the sound of the shoes—a quiet rubber sole—on the tile and the cadence of the step, it was Amanda. Instinct prodded her to look and find out for certain, but she had another minute to go.

"It's just me," Amanda said, entering a stall.

Her friend knew her well. "Thanks."

Maddox let her shoulders relax and absorbed the cool sensation penetrating her eye sockets, clearing her mind.

An image of Cole popped into her brain—him lying on the hood of the truck like he owned the world. He was right. She did need to take a break, the physical kind with him, only not now. She blocked him out.

Amanda flushed and washed her hands.

Maddox tossed the paper towel away.

"You look stressed to the max," Amanda said. "Are you pulling another all-nighter here?"

"If I have to, but…"

Thoughts of Cole boomeranged back. She always shared her sexual exploits with Amanda. The intimate details of making lo…what she'd shared…with Cole last night were private, but not saying anything to one of her closest friends was like having the juiciest secret tap-dancing on her tongue. If she didn't drag it into the light, acknowledge it to someone else, did it really happen?

"But what?" Amanda asked.

Maddox shrugged. "I'm kind of hoping to get another *workout* in later." She couldn't hide the grin that stole across her lips. The tingle in her fingers and the stupid kick of her heart were confirmation: it had indeed happened.

"Another? With who?" Amanda eyed her speculatively. "The badass-looking hottie?"

Maddox's grin spread to a deep smile.

"Omigod, you've already had sex with him?" Amanda gave her a playful nudge. "You work fast."

"It's a long story. I'll tell you about it, over lots of wine, once this mission is done."

"I can't believe you've been holding out on me. You know I have to live vicariously through you." Amanda sighed. "I miss sex. Correction. I miss good, steamy sex. Especially the early morning kind, when you roll over, half asleep, and one touch leads to another until you're both wide awake." She tipped her head back and did a little shimmy.

Memories rolled in, threatening to carry Maddox to a place she wasn't prepared to go, where lust and love inextricably entwined. She remembered how good it'd once felt to fall asleep curled in his arms, covered in the scent of him. In the twilight, how his touch could rouse her from the throes of slumber, loose a sigh, get her aching and wet when they were barely even awake.

"The ultimate stress reliever." Amanda fluffed her hair and checked her face in the mirror. "If you've finally found a man you want to do the *mambo* with more than once, do not hesitate to lock down that totally lickable man. I bet early morning sex with him is *hot*."

With her heart stuck in her throat, Maddox couldn't respond.

They walked down the hall with Amanda chatting about how she sometimes missed her ex but was ready to find someone new who wouldn't mind a ready-made family. She was lucky to have little Jackson—the cutest boy with a heart of gold. One day, the right guy would come along and fall for them both. If anyone deserved love and happiness, it was Amanda.

Maddox peeled off with a wave and went into the conference room. While she poured a cup of coffee, the demands of the job settled back on her shoulders.

She dropped into a chair and reviewed the compiled data on Novak and the freelance contractor jobs accredited to him. All high profile, tough shit to pull off. One job stood out. A hit on a female assassin in Prague. In fifty-plus contracts, only one had been a woman. No children. He seemed to have some sort of code.

Remember this mercy. Icy spiders crawled in her belly, and she shuddered.

No collateral damage was another trademark of Novak's. Even the car bombing at a casino in Philadelphia—only Callahan and his guards had been killed. A less-skilled operator would've taken out innocent bystanders as well.

Over and over in his file. Complete control, one woman, no children. It meant something important about him, but what?

Cole strode through the conference room doors, holding up a newspaper. His features were laced tight with determination. "The *Post* we took from the Ghost's room. One section was missing. This one. Events section for the weekend."

"The auction was moved up a day. Novak's original plan might've been conceived expecting to get his hands on the weapon today, Friday night. Maybe he wanted to use it at an event over the weekend, since he's waited and didn't deploy it already." She grabbed a highlighter and flipped open the paper.

Potential targets had already been highlighted with notes beside each one giving an approximation of how many people would be in attendance.

"You did this?" She blinked one too many times.

"I can do more than crack skulls."

"I know you can." He'd graduated summa cum laude from Georgetown and had been working on a master's in architecture at MIT before their lives went to hell. He could do anything. Maybe even leap tall buildings in a single bound. "I'm just surprised."

"As a member of the band, I've got to carry my weight, right? I wanted to be helpful. To you."

More dreadful heat warmed up long-frozen cold spots. "Thank you."

Gideon peered up at her from the monitor, but she avoided meeting his eyes.

The conference room door swung open. Castle led the way. In tow were Reece, Harper, and Cutter.

Harper held two folders clutched to her chest and sat on Maddox's left side with her gaze lowered. "I was gone from my desk for ten minutes, thirty-seven seconds." Her tone was hushed. "The time allotted for a break during an active operation is fifteen, but it was still my fault Novak got away. I'm sorry. I'm the best analyst here. You didn't have to assign Daniel the threat matrix. I'm more than capable."

Folding her hands, Maddox dug for the right diplomatic words. "It's not a reflection on your ability to do your job. It wasn't fair to ask you to work around the clock without help. You need to be able to go to the bathroom, eat, sleep. We all need breaks." Cole's admonishment rose in her memory and she shook off the rising irritation. "We wanted to keep the footprint small on this. It's my fault, not yours. You've been doing a great job."

Harper reared back, surprise washing over her face. "O-okay."

Maddox glanced up to find Gideon staring with the focus of a microscope. His sharp gaze bounced between her and Harper.

The hairs on Maddox's arms raised. She ran her tongue over her teeth, unsettled by the intense look that made him appear as if he were chiseled from dry ice. Cold and untouchable. One would never guess that when he let loose and cracked a smile or laughed, women in the vicinity dropped their wet panties. And he used that smooth charm like any other weapon in his arsenal.

After Maddox gave him a thumbs-up and a head nod, his attention shifted. Odd, he wasn't friends with Harper. No one was. He never interacted with her—he went out of his way to avoid her. So far on this mission, he'd barely spoken five words to the girl.

Harper handed Maddox both folders. "The first one is everything I could find on the death of a man in Costa Rica who we suspect was Kassar based on the wife's statement taken by police. The second file is the additional information about Novak's military record. I'll brief everyone in a moment. Also, we don't have enough of his disguised face to run the image through facial recognition." Harper stared at the conference table as she spoke.

"But we tracked the taxi he took from the hotel," Cutter added.

Harper's gaze zeroed in on Mr. Gung Ho. "I tracked the taxi while you sat looking over my shoulder." Her shaky voice was a notch above a whisper. "I discovered the auction and I've been working this mission from the beginning. We wouldn't have this operation if it wasn't for me. You're just latching on midstream."

Seeing Harper riled up was a first.

Cheeks flaming rosy red, the analyst pulled her lips inward as if she wanted to swallow them. She tilted her head down. "The taxi gave us nothing. He was dropped off at Union Station."

The bastard. Maddox had assumed that after Novak lost them at the Metro, he would've headed for Union Station—the most practical place to escape—but there hadn't been any sign of him on the street. For him to deliberately take a taxi from the hotel to Union Station, when he must've known they'd later track it, meant he was toying with her.

Harper and Cutter stared at one another like they were about to rumble, armed with notepads and laser pointers. Although Cutter was in his late twenties, fit, and had hand-to-hand combat training, Harper seemed fired up hot enough to claw out his eyes.

Territorial wars in the Gray Box weren't uncommon. They were a small outfit, most of them were as close as family, and no one was in this for glory—Cutter not included. But everyone wanted to make their mark. On this case, Maddox didn't need the waters any muddier.

"Harper, you need analytical backup on this, but the record will reflect you're point analyst."

"Okay," she said in a low voice, sounding appeased.

Yes, the woman would get the glory of a win or the disgrace of a failure. A more cunning analyst would've preferred a blurry line.

"I reached out to the Albanian Army," Harper said, "like Maddox asked, and tracked down a retired colonel who had been friends with Novak. They enlisted around the same time. During the Kosovo War in May 1999, Novak's family was being transported in a refugee convoy." Tapping a digital button on the glass smart table, Harper brought up an image of a truck convoy in a woodland area. "The men and women had been separated. Wife and daughter in one vehicle, son in another. A U.S. aircraft attacked, acting under incorrect intel that it was a Yugoslav military convoy. Fifty people were killed, including his wife and daughter."

Harper stared at the screen rather than making eye contact, fidgeting with her pearls as she spoke at high speed. "NATO and the US issued an apology for the airstrike, amongst others. We made a lot of mistakes during Operation Allied Force, including the accidental bombing of a refugee camp. Novak was so vocal about his hatred for America and the unnecessary, brutal loss of innocent lives that he was discharged."

"He wants vengeance," Maddox said. "This is personal for him." A vendetta fueled by grief complicated the hell out of the situation. "Deploying the bioweapon in the nation's capital would suit Novak's motives perfectly. Where do we stand on a threat matrix?"

"We've got a shitload of threat scenarios to comb through," Castle said. "He picked a prime spot with that hotel. Easy walk to the White House, National

Mall, National Gallery of Art, National Portrait Gallery, Capital One Arena, Washington Convention Center. Hell, there's even a Walmart Supercenter."

"Great." Maddox chugged more coffee. They could find him. They just had to be smarter.

Castle and Harper went through the threat matrix, detailing various scenarios. Cutter chimed in at every opportunity to offer his two cents, garnering a death stare from Harper.

The Ghost most likely had already picked his target, with a possible contingency site. They had to separate the wheat from the chaff.

It'd only take one piece of information, the right one, to steer them to whatever Novak was planning.

While listening to the threat scenarios, Maddox reviewed the information on Kassar's death. What Harper had found substantiated her hunch about Novak's personal code. Kassar's wife and daughter were found bound but otherwise unharmed. It fit. Novak valued the lives of children, had a tendency not to kill women, and avoided unnecessary loss of life.

Understandable, considering what had happened to Novak's family. She fingered through the new file on Novak, stopping on the date his family had been accidentally killed. May 26, 1999. The anniversary of their deaths was just over a month ago.

She was close to something, felt it in her bones, but what?

Hours had passed by the time Castle and Harper were done and Cutter had finished his litany of interjections. Maddox's stomach was clawing like an angry cat for food. She should've taken up Janet's offer to bring in dinner. As much as she wanted to eat, they had to cross-reference the events section in the *Post*.

The weekend leisure guide that'd been missing from Novak's paper could possibly indicate when and where he planned to act. There was also an equal chance he'd wait until the heat died down, but who'd want to tote around a biological weapon any longer than necessary?

Facts about Novak and dates from the file cycled in her mind. She turned back to the page regarding the accidental bombing of the civilian convoy. America had acknowledged the mistake and issued an apology with *deep regret* on June 29, 1999.

Novak didn't have the opportunity for his revenge to coincide with the anniversary of their deaths, but this was the next best thing.

Tomorrow was June 29.

The knots in her gut tightened. The date was significant enough to outweigh Novak lying low, but it was best not to draw too much attention to it. Their leak might give the Ghost a heads-up. Better to seem as if they were simply following procedure. They were focused on time-sensitive, high-profile events anyway.

"On the calendar for tomorrow," she said, "a concert at the National Gallery of Art, summer cinema series at the Washington Convention Center, comedy show at the Capital One Arena, and charity event at the Hirshhorn Museum."

"And there's a heads of state dinner at the White House," Harper added.

Too many pieces of the puzzle. They needed to issue

a warning order, a precautionary message giving only the essential elements of information to help the FBI and Secret Service to take the necessary safeguards.

Sanborn waltzed into the conference room. "How's it going?"

"It's possible Novak might deploy the weapon sometime this weekend," Maddox said. "We've picked key locations as possible targets, but we have to issue a warning order, running through the DNI's office down to the Secret Service and FBI."

"I've already given the Secret Service an unofficial tip-off." Sanborn sat at the head of the table. "I'll make it official when I make the calls and issue the warnings. Narrow down the threat matrix as much as possible. Then get food and rest. Hit this hard at the crack of dawn."

Famished and fatigued didn't skate across the surface of how she felt, but they had to press on. She rubbed her temples, sneaking a glance at Castle. He gave a subtle shake of his head. He must've been thinking the same thing.

"Sir," Castle said. "Maddox and I'll disseminate the message and make the calls."

"No need to tack on extra hours of work. Use the time to refuel. You're useless running on fumes. I know for a fact that you, Maddox"—Sanborn pointed a stiff finger at her—"got three hours of shitty sleep in the break room last night. Castle"—that finger swung to her brother—"you came back at zero five hundred, which doesn't have you sitting much better."

"You know a lot," Cole said. "You ever leave this place? Or do you live in your office?"

"Where I live and how much sleep I get don't matter.

Nor are they any of your business, because I'm the one responsible for these operatives. You'll go home and get rest. That's an order."

"Castle and I are staying to make the calls." This mission wasn't going to earn her any brownie points with her boss. "That's our responsibility."

No one outside their circle of five could be trusted.

"Give me the room." Sanborn's tone turned to molten steel. "Except Castle and Maddox."

The room cleared.

Sanborn let the door shut, his flinty gaze cut between them.

"It's pretty darn clear you're keeping something from me. There were discrepancies in the after-action reports from the auction. Minor things. Enough for me to get the impression something was omitted. Then you asked Willow to go directly to you with any updates. A straightforward by-the-books request, I assured her."

Of course Harper would've gone to him, but on its own, the request wouldn't have raised a flag.

"Now this unusual insistence to issue the warning order." Sanborn stood, pressing his knuckles against the table, his face a thundercloud. "Taken as a whole, this reeks."

In the bloated pause, Maddox refrained from looking at Castle.

"Someone better start talking, or this conversation is about to take an ugly turn you'll both regret."

"We need autonomy on this one," Maddox said.

Narrowing his eyes, Sanborn visibly tensed, his mouth thinned. "Why?"

"This is a tricky situation with the Ghost," she said. "For us to bring this guy in, this is how we need to do it."

"Not sufficient for my blessing. Try again."

"If it wasn't mission essential," Castle said, "we'd never leave you out of the loop. Never."

Sanborn folded his arms, drawing in a deep breath. "If I'm not in the loop on everything and this goes wrong, you two would take the heat, alone. Career-ending heat."

Their jobs, being members of the Gray Box, were for many of them the only things left in their lives worth fighting for. Sanborn was testing them.

"Roger that, sir." Castle nodded with a grave expression. "Understood."

Sanborn eyed Castle, his prize protégé. The air pressure in the room rose, and the stare became frighteningly intense. "What aren't you telling me?"

Trust was a commodity they couldn't afford to waste on the wrong person. She wanted to bring him in on this. Sanborn was loyal to his people and his country. But they couldn't take the chance. Needed to be textbook about how they proceeded.

"*Topaz*," Castle said.

The codeword for a prior operation a few years back, where Knox and Castle had gone so dark, Sanborn thought they might've gone rogue. Their after-action reports—which were need-to-know, leaving her clueless about the specifics—had explained their reasons.

"This is similar to *Topaz*," Castle added.

The silence was deafening as Sanborn weighed everything.

"We're tip of the spear, and sometimes, we have to operate outside every box to get the mission done. Request granted. But—" Sanborn stabbed the table with a finger. "Do. Not. Fail. And once this is shaked-and-baked, you owe me a debrief with crystal-clear transparency. If I'm not one hundred percent satisfied with your mission-essential explanation, you won't be fired. You'll both be disavowed." He strode out of the room.

A sinking sensation swept through Maddox. If you were disavowed from the CIA, MI6, Mossad—take your intel flavor of the day—a black ops program might scoop you up. To be disavowed from a deep-black off-the-books unit was to virtually cease to exist. No work history. No 401(k). You became nobody with no past. The only thing worse was a whitewash—where you literally ceased to exist.

"Don't," Castle said.

She looked up at him. "Don't what?"

"Second-guess this. The minute you do is the minute we give Novak battleground advantage."

Novak already had too much working in his favor. Castle was right. Yet again. "Topaz?" To say more, to ask the question burning her tongue, would insult her brother.

"The op had nothing to do with a leak."

All she needed to hear. "I'll write up the warning order. You start making the calls."

23

VIENNA, VIRGINIA
9:56 P.M. EDT

Holding a bag of Chinese takeout, Cole picked the lock to Maddox's door. The pungent smell of shrimp lo mein and Peking duck prodded him to hurry. Fifteen seconds.

Yep, he was just that good. In truth, it was his Z-wave gadget doing the work, but after the shitty day they'd had, he was taking the credit.

He set out the containers of food in the kitchen and rummaged for a wine bottle opener. *Bingo*. Of course she had one. He opened a robust bottle of Brunello and searched for a decanter. Score, yet again.

Candles strategically placed in the living room sat untouched, collecting dust and purely decorative, but he lit them anyway. He slipped off his jacket and holster, aching to scrub off the grunge from the day.

Using her shower would smack of presumption. But the wretched smell of his body offended his own nose, and the last thing he wanted was to turn her stomach during dinner.

She might kick him out, had every right to, but he sensed she needed him and maybe he needed her too. Exactly what for, he wasn't certain.

When she disappeared on the train with Novak, he'd almost lost his mind. The thought of that creepy animal hurting her or—*good God*—worse had filled him with a terrifying sense of loss and an overwhelming need to hurt the Ghost.

Swallowing his taste for violence, he kicked off his boots and stripped.

Being in this grinder of danger and the revolving close brush with evil had a way of clarifying one's priorities. He didn't come to Maddox's place for sex, though a physical release after a hard day would be nice, and she was the only lover who kept pace with his appetites and satisfied him on a level that'd have him sounding like a Hallmark card if he examined it deeper.

Years ago, she'd always been eager to have him, to experiment sexually, which had just been the icing. The cake had been her generous heart and sense of adventure, how she didn't care he came from dirty money and made him feel as if he could walk on water when she looked at him with that sparkle of awe in her eyes.

And she had really loved him, so much it'd left him breathless.

There was no way back for him and Maddox. Might not be a way forward either.

All he knew was to heal their wounds, they needed the salve of remembering what it was like to belong to each other. They'd found that for a dazzling moment in the parking lot. The intensity of it, the searing heat, the soul-deep comfort had startled him senseless.

They needed that feeling again, a sense of connection, but this time without the physical. She had a tough, grueling job and after such a rough day, he wanted to show her tenderness and the warmth of being there at her disposal.

To give her whatever she needed—a decent meal, a glass of wine, a hug, an understanding ear to listen to her frustration over losing Novak, even space and some alone time. He crossed his fingers she didn't need the latter, but he'd give it.

He brushed his teeth, appreciating the feminine sight of makeup and frilly skin care products neatly organized on the counter, and stepped in the shower—not giving a damn about presumption.

Hot water soaked him, loosening his tight muscles.

He eyed the vast assortment of pricey-looking Lush products from gels to scrubs to shower bombs. Selecting one at random, not caring if he smelled like a bouquet of flowers or a damn sugar cookie so long as he was clean, he scoured off the defeat of the day, letting it rinse down the drain.

Smiling, he remembered how Maddox used to talk to herself in the shower—full-blown conversations. Her quirky way of working through a problem, preparing to tackle something tough. He used to joke that she was a total nutjob, albeit his nutjob, and she'd countered that it was a sign of higher cognitive functioning.

Bet as a super spy, she nixed having out-loud conversations with herself.

Steam had engulfed the small bathroom by the time he stepped out. Grabbing a towel, he dragged it over his head, through his hair, and down the length of his body.

Damn, he was starving. If she didn't get back soon, he'd be tempted to eat without her. Which would make him a royal asshole, since she was working to stop a psychopath with a vendetta. Seeing her in action and understanding what she was fighting for made him fall a little deeper in love and in lust. Her prowess was an undeniable turn-on, but his objective tonight was clear.

Throwing the towel on his shoulder, he sauntered into the living room.

The distinct click of a round being chambered in a gun stopped him cold.

Maddox crept into the living room, holding her Maxim 9. Her heart tripped into her throat, body drawing tight.

Cole. Naked.

Sleek with ripped muscle. A living, breathing weapon. And wet.

Her mouth went dry.

She lowered her gun, clearing the lump from her thickening throat. "Is this going to become a habit? You breaking in?"

"Not if you give me a key."

She threw him a sideways glance. Cole stood in all his unabashed glory with a towel draped on his shoulder. And every inch of him was indeed glorious.

She caught sight of lit candles in the living room. The smell of Chinese food pierced the haze of arousal twisting through her. Decanted wine sat on the counter.

What was next? Barry White? "What is this? A date?"

"I hate labels. Too restrictive."

Fathomless dark eyes searched hers. Damp hair black as night. Those wiry muscles. The delightful length of him.

The tug of war between wanting him and being furious with him was exhausting.

"Labels are good." She took off her jacket and holster. "It's important to define things. That way, you take medicine and not poison."

"This isn't a date. We both just need to decompress."

Sounded like an idea she wanted to indulge in. She was strung tight as piano wire with tension and needed to loosen up. They'd been in a real pressure cooker for the past two days. Her body screamed for an outlet, the kind of release only a man like him could give.

"I thought we could take a breath, eat together," he said. "Maybe talk instead of fight."

Or maybe like last night in the parking lot, neither *talk* nor *food* was the four-letter word at the top of the agenda. "Candles. Dinner. Wine. None of this stuff is involved when I screw someone."

He flinched. "You used to appreciate a little romance."

She'd lost her appreciation for many things after he had left. "Well, things change."

"It's just stuff, Maddox. Candles to help you relax. Blow them out." He shrugged defined shoulders. Bare shoulders. Everything was bare. "Food to bring your blood sugar back up. You get so damn cranky when it drops, but chuck it in the trash."

Smelled too darn good to throw away. Better than something from her freezer.

"I thought the wine would please your tongue." He licked his lips.

And she wet hers, looking at the length of his arousal. Wine wasn't the only thing that would please her tongue.

"It's a nice Brunello," he said, "but you can pour it out."

With her government paycheck, she couldn't afford such a splurge. The wine was a keeper.

He wrapped the towel around his waist, covering up the sight of his beautiful cock.

Maybe they weren't on the same page.

"I didn't come here to screw, Maddox. Sorry I gave the wrong impression."

Yep. They definitely weren't on the same page. A problem she'd have to remedy.

"What do you want?" he asked. "To start with."

A graphic list formed in her head. For starters, she wanted the flirty dirty talk he used to pour into her ear, making her wet with his foul words and raunchy descriptions of what he planned to do to her. She wanted his mouth on her breasts. She wanted his rough fingers in her hair. She wanted his hard, hot body grinding all over hers. Oh yeah, she wanted.

"A glass of wine?" he clarified, casting a glance at the counter. "Some food? A foot rub?"

She chuckled. "Since when do you give foot rubs?"

Folding his muscled arms, he looked downright delicious. She was tempted to lick him all over, and before the night was over, she just might.

"As you said, things change." He held her gaze.

"It's been a long, sweaty day." She hadn't showered since 6:00 a.m. in the locker room. "I'll get cleaned up first."

"No need on my account. I'd prefer to smell you as you

are." His fiery gaze held hers captive, making her tingle with awareness. "But whatever makes you comfortable."

She narrowed her eyes, wondering what happened to the brazen man who would've had her cornered and stripped naked by now. The man who turned her on like a faucet, taking her from zero to abso-fucking-lutely ready and wet with a few dirty words. The man who took control and drove her wild, the one she'd craved for years and needed tonight more than anything else.

Why in the hell had he gone all soft and sensitive?

She strode up to him and yanked his towel off, letting it drop to the floor. Staring at his erection, she backed up to the wall in the living room. "How about that *massage*?"

A wild playfulness she recognized danced in his eyes.

He knelt on the floor in front of her and unlaced her tactical boots, removing them along with her socks. He propped one of her feet on his thigh and massaged the knots of tension from the soles. His hands were so talented, his fingers so skilled, so darn good, she sighed.

"Where did you learn to do that?"

"I've learned lots I intend to show you."

He rubbed the other foot, his gaze holding hers, softening her in ways she didn't quite like. They could have sex without it meaning anything. If she wanted to satisfy a basic, primal need without the entanglement of messy emotions, then she needed to eliminate the intimacy of foot rubs and kisses and treat him the way she did other men who'd passed through her bed. Men she didn't see twice.

Like meat.

"That's not the body part in need of a good…hard… *rub*," she said.

"No?" He inched higher, kneading her fatigued muscles one at a time, turning her stomach to warm jelly. "Better?" He gave a devilish grin that would've been irresistible if it hadn't been infuriating.

She gritted her teeth. "Warmer, but not quite there."

"Tell me what you need." His fingers worked up to her tense thighs. "I can't give it unless I know what it is."

On the inside, she squirmed with impatience, but she wasn't about to show him how desperate she was to have him. "Take an educated guess."

"I've become many things over the past few years, but a mind reader isn't one of them." His grin spread to a taunting smile. "Guessing is like gambling. I prefer certainty."

She'd forgotten how much fun foreplay and sex had been with him, the erotic games they'd enjoyed, how they'd tantalized and excited one another.

Maybe remembering wasn't the best idea.

Without fanfare or the hint of a seductive striptease, she took off her pants and underwear and kicked them to the side, exposing herself to his heated gaze.

She leaned over, bringing her mouth close to his. "How's that for certainty?"

"Warmer, but not quite there."

A small smile escaped her, and to her surprise, the tension in her shoulders eased.

"I'm going to need something verbal." His rough tone tickled an itch she hadn't been able to scratch for almost a decade. "Explicit. I need one hundred percent confidence what I think you mean isn't a figment of my own naughty desires."

Did he really expect her to crown him the winner of this tête-à-tête and say the words regardless of how hot it was making her?

"What do you need from me?" He kissed her inner thighs, spreading them wide, teeth scraping her skin, making her nerve endings thrum. "Hmm?" He hummed as he palmed her where she was growing wet and hungry to have him, and she shivered. "Tell me, and it's yours."

The hard heel of his hand rubbed against her and his fingers teased, featherlight.

Her sex clenched in happy anticipation, but he dropped his hand.

Whatever game he was playing, more than sex was at stake, and she refused to let him get the best of her as he'd done last night. "I'll tell you, but first I need you to say, *I win*."

"All right. *I. Win*." He gave a slow, smooth smile and winked.

To hell with it. If giving him what he needed to hear was going to give her what she needed to feel, so be it. "Yes." A heated whisper. "And more. Okay?"

He flashed a triumphant grin, sexy as sin, and molten liquid pooled low in her belly on the wave of her own victory. This was a win-win where no one had to lose, but his smile was a tad too smug.

"Bite me, you egomaniac."

"I'd rather eat you."

Her toes curled into the carpet.

"Would you like that?" he asked, low and husky, his darkening eyes searching hers.

She clutched a handful of his damp hair, bringing his head back and chin up. "I'd like fewer questions and more action." Their gazes held, challenging and smoldering. The draw to him was primal. "Rough, naughty action." She let him go with no care for being gentle.

"I like it when you're bossy and explicit. It's really hot."

His head dipped to the soft notch between her legs. He clutched her hips and smelled her, long and deep. Crazed butterflies took flight, winging about her belly.

"You smell so good, makes me want to taste you everywhere. Spread those gorgeous thighs wider for me."

Loving it more when he was bossy and explicit, she did as he told her with a little thrill uncurling inside.

Then his mouth was on her so fast, she didn't have a chance to take a breath.

She arched off the wall from the shock and pleasure.

This time, he didn't tease. He licked and suckled and dragged his tongue along her seam, pressing all the right buttons. He was great at this and used to do it a lot when they'd been together. Not just because she'd loved it, but in his enthusiasm, he'd showed how much he really enjoyed it. A tough warrior yet a generous, attentive lover.

She writhed and whimpered, her fingers clutching his hair as if to pull him away while her palms cradled his head closer.

He brushed his lips across her inner thigh, nipping at her flesh.

"More," she breathed, barely able to utter the single syllable.

"Say the magic word," he ordered in a sinful tone that had her melting.

He was driving her crazy with desire. She'd say anything, even throw a *pretty* on top.

"Please."

His husky laughter sent delicious vibrations over her. His fingers slid inside, stroking and scissoring. He threw her leg over his shoulder, and his hand gripped her bottom, urging her onto his greedy mouth.

She was at the brink, close, but not close enough. He latched onto her clit with his mouth and sent his wicked tongue over it, silk and sandpaper at the same time, and sucked hard. It tipped her over the edge and her body let go in an uncontrollable shudder.

He dragged her quivering body to the floor and trailed a path with hot kisses on her hip bone, stomach, breasts, throat.

Before his lips reached her mouth, she rolled on top of him and skimmed her cheek across the line of soft hair from his belly button to the patch of dark curls between his legs. She took him in her mouth, determined to give as good as she'd gotten. The scent of him, the familiar taste permeated her senses. Hearing his gritty, guttural sounds filled her with a joy she'd never experienced with another, the power rush of owning his pleasure, absorbing the raw urgency in each blunt fingertip pressing against her scalp.

"God, you're incredible."

Breathing him in, she swallowed more of his length, letting him tickle her throat. She remembered the way he liked it. How much pressure, when to squeeze the

something she hadn't realized she'd been starved for. It wasn't sweet and tender. This was all-consuming.

He molded to her, driving into her with heartrending intensity. A reckless energy she was powerless to fight built in their rhythm, tightening her muscles. She shoved her hands in his hair and kissed the hell out of him, licking into his mouth and sucking on his tongue. He tasted of mint and longing and *her*.

Her breasts grew heavy and swollen. The need to have all her clothes off, for their bodies to touch everywhere without restriction, was overwhelming. Cole must've felt the same way. In seconds, he had her shirt and bra off. No finesse, no control. His breath fanned her throat, and he pinched her nipple, coaxing a cry from her lips.

"You okay?" The words were gentle, and he slowed, grinding his pelvis against her, but didn't stop the inexorable drive into her. "I don't want to hurt you."

"Don't hold back." She caressed his face, running her thumb over his lovely scar. Not that scars were pretty, but everything about Cole had always been perfect. Because it was a part of him, and he'd been hers. Once. "Let it hurt."

His grip on her tightened, his rhythm quickening, his strong thrusts growing urgent. She clenched around him as they melded into one another. This man was the only one to give her a safe space to let herself feel soft and sexy. To lose control regardless of the consequences. Free from the responsibility of her actions. To delight in the heightened sensation, the wild heat in her body, which had been numb for so long. Sex with him was hotter, better than any one-night stand.

Tension, sweet and thick as honey, gathered in her core. "Harder."

He hooked one of her legs behind her knee with his hand, raising it to her chest, and powered deeper into her while putting his other rough hand in her hair.

"Look at me." The banked fire in his eyes was scorching. Like he wanted to set her soul on fire too. "You're so damned beautiful. So beautiful, it hurts."

He made *beautiful* sound special, as if he saw more than a pretty face or nice body. As if everything about her was exceptional, and he was the luckiest man in the world to be with her.

His hips pistoned against her, and she drove hers up with equal fervor. The slick, fierce friction of their bodies made the need for release brutal.

He rutted on her. Hard. Fast.

And she loved the rawness of the way he took her. The untempered heat of his touch, threatening to melt her to nothing.

She gripped his shoulders, her nails scraping his back, writhing under him, struggling to take more, needing more. Arousal churned through her body, pressure deep in her belly built to a throb, her sex clamped around him and she came even harder and faster, shattering like glass.

He grunted against her neck, his body growing taut as he followed.

The sensation of him coming inside her without protection, the deeply intimate and satisfying nature of it, tempted her to forget her broken heart and how terrified she was to risk it again.

Time stood still in that moment.

Her short breaths grew shallow. The sweaty weight of his body pinned her to the carpet. He brushed his lips over her mouth and kissed her. A tender peck, as if testing for something. He licked his lips and kissed her again, softness stroking her, triggering a wash of agonizing memories.

She twisted her face away, not wanting *this*…blistering sweetness. Tenderness would have her losing her way, losing her common sense, or worse, her heart.

"Maddox." A silken whisper. "Please."

She shoved his chest. He pulled out of her, collapsing in a heap on the floor, his breath in tatters. His arms curled around her, drawing her back against his chest in a spooning position, their bodies stuck like magnets.

Loving him hurt, but the pain was a skinned knee compared to the agony of losing him.

This Band-Aid needed to be ripped off and thrown away. She couldn't bear to drag it out and tried to pull up, but he wouldn't let her go and kept his arm locked around her waist.

In another life, things would've been different, but this was their reality: ugly and mangled and ruined.

She shoved his leg and smacked the granite of his arms. Still, he held on.

"Let me go, or so help me—"

"What'll you do?"

She threw an elbow into his side. Not hard, but the force knocked the breath from him and the sound of his groan made her reel in surprise.

His grip loosened, and she sat up.

"I'm sorry." She brought her knees to her chest, covering herself. "Are you okay?"

"Yeah, it kind of tickled," he said in a strained voice.

Naked beside him in the spent aftermath, she was too exposed, too vulnerable. She hurried to the bathroom, raced through the fastest shower of her life, and put on the thickest pair of sweats she owned.

She stared at herself in the dresser mirror, wanting to crawl out the window instead of facing him. Part of her wanted him to stay and the other part needed him gone. She didn't want to hurt him, but she didn't want to get raked over the coals again either, as collateral damage in his twisted efforts to find closure.

Meat. She needed to treat him like meat to hold it together.

She strolled into the living room and took a firm stance. He sat on the sofa with the towel wrapped around his waist, met her gaze, and gave her a warm, devastating smile.

Her willpower faltered, but it didn't break. "I want you to leave."

He recoiled as if she'd slapped him, knocking the smile from his face. "Not like this. Let's sit and eat. We don't have to talk." He raked a hand through his hair, looking off balance. "Let me hold you. We need to be close right now. To let ourselves feel this, without being afraid of it."

He wanted her to soften in his hands, to be okay with whatever *he* decided when it was convenient for *him.* Her heart wasn't a yo-yo he could throw away and reel in however he pleased. She had a backbone forged in fire, and there'd be ice-skating in hell before she became any man's plaything.

"I don't do chitchat and dinner with meat." The words prickled her tongue. She didn't mean it and saying it pained her, but this was about self-preservation. "It was a great fuck. Thanks."

Hair-trigger reflexes brought him to his feet. The fierce expression on his face scared the shit out of her, leaving her a new kind of breathless.

24

VIENNA, VIRGINIA
11:37 P.M. EDT

Did she call him *meat*? Like he was nothing more than sex to her?

Maddox was the essence of his soul, the reason Cole drew breath. His world only made sense when she was at the center of it, and there had been a time, impossible to disregard, when he'd been the same to her.

The disrespect she threw at him, casual as a salutation, cut him to the bone. He wasn't going to accept her treating him like meat, in the same manner she should never accept him doing the same. It was beneath them.

She was angry and had a right to her tough-girl posturing.

For any chance of healing, though, she had to work through the anger like he had, and together, they had to wade through their mess.

If she wanted him to leave, he would, but there were things he needed to say first.

"No matter what happens between us, I'll always be more to you than meat. A good fuck? Hell, yeah." He gritted his teeth and got up close to her. "But so much more. I'm in there." He put a finger to her chest. "I'm in your blood and under your skin."

He curled his hands around her shoulders, and she flinched but didn't pull away.

"It's the same for me—you're like a drug," he whispered across her lips. "A habit I can't seem to kick."

Nine years without her had been worse than dying. He was hooked on her, had it bad, and he knew it now.

"And I'm a drug for you too."

Trembling in his hands, he sensed how she struggled between giving in to him and ripping out his heart.

The fire in her gorgeous eyes was searing and ready to burn him. "You're like poison—"

Cupping her face, he seized her mouth in a deep kiss, consuming her vicious words. No delicacy, just a wild, desperate rush to connect. She pushed at him, but fortunately in that moment, desire beat anger, and her mouth opened to him. Her tongue sought his with equal urgency, and finally, her fingers curled in his hair, holding him close.

Their colossal screwups filled the dark crevices between them like plastic explosives ready to blow apart any chance they might have at a future.

Still clutching her with one hand, he pressed the other to her cheek and tore his lips away.

"I love you, Maddox."

Stark silence fell.

Her eyes narrowed, and she shoved at his chest. Hard. "Do you expect me to swoon and fall into your arms like some sentimental sap because you uttered those three little words?" She shoved him again. "If you love someone, you don't let them think you're dead. *For nine years*. You've no idea what losing you did to me, how it wrecked me." Her chest heaved, eyes turning glassy. "All this time, I thought I'd killed you. Thought I'd destroyed our future. But every day you were alive, choosing not to be with me, you were the one killing us. *You* buried us!"

She slammed a fist against his chest, and he took it, keeping a hold on her.

Two days ago, she'd held back, hiding what she was capable of physically. No doubt if she wanted to kick his ass, she could. He'd take that too—a fist to the chest, an ass kicking, getting hit by a speeding semi—whatever was necessary to hash this out and see where they stood once the dust settled.

"I was a stupid girl who made a horrible, tragic mistake." Her voice broke into a sob, fracturing his heart. "What you've done, for nearly a decade, letting me mourn and grieve for you, was deliberate." A tear slipped from her eye. "While you moved on."

He hated the time they'd spent apart and how he had hurt her by leaving. More than anything, he hated the wall separating them. He was a fighter—born and bred—and the only thing that could stop him from fighting for Maddox was death.

Even then, he'd find a way.

He needed to tear down the wall between them, beat it down brick by brick with his bare hands if necessary. "I never moved on from you, honey. After that shitstorm of violence and death, the things I had to do—the blood on my hands—changed me forever. It gutted me."

She stilled, meeting his eyes. The fight in her was slipping, her body softening. He loosened his grip on her arms.

"I couldn't look at myself in the mirror. The man I was died. Nikolai Reznikov, his dreams, his passions—everything died. Even my face was taken from me." He threw a hand to his hideous scar.

In one fell swoop, his life had collapsed in on him. The only thing to survive the ashes was his love for her. He staggered away under the brutal burn in his gut that inevitably came with dwelling on the past and dropped onto the sofa, putting his head in his hands.

She sat on the floor with her back to the couch and the coffee table between them. "You don't know what I went through after you left."

"I know about the clinic."

"But you don't know why I was there." She lowered her gaze as he braced himself. "Before you left, I found out I was pregnant."

His thoughts derailed. He drew in a strained breath. "What? Why didn't you tell me?"

"My mom suspected I was pregnant before I did. The smell of fish started making me sick, and I complained everything tasted like metal. She made me take a pregnancy test. I was terrified when it was positive. We were too young, not engaged—but it was yours, so I was also thrilled."

Sharp memories swarmed him. The way she'd stopped drinking soda because she said it was like sucking on pennies. The time she'd gotten sick in a seafood restaurant. "How far along were you when I left?"

Her gaze shuttered. "Close to three months."

His chest constricted. "Why didn't you tell me after you found out?"

"Mom asked me not to. You would've dragged me to city hall and married me."

That's precisely what he would've done. Although he was only twenty-four and she not yet twenty, he wouldn't have hesitated.

"My mother said that if I gave everything serious consideration for a couple of weeks, really thought it over, she'd be my ally in whatever decision I made. Even if it opposed my father."

Of course she'd agreed to that. Cole knew exactly where Castle got his imposing frame, self-righteous attitude, and explosive temper. Maddox would've been crazy to refuse her mother's offer.

"I wish you had told me. I get it. I do. Taking your mother's deal was the right call, but what was there to think about?"

"Binding myself to you and your family forever. That's what a baby would have done. Forever with you was what I wanted. But forever with Ilya?" She shook her head. "I hadn't considered what our kids would be subjected to around him. And what if my father was right and your family didn't pull out of organized crime? What would it mean for our children?"

Shutting his eyes, he raked his hair back with his hands. She never would've asked him to walk away from his blood, even if it was to start a new family with her. He'd been naive and shortsighted. He hadn't considered the danger his family posed to creating a new one, the hazards he'd subjected her to by bringing her around them.

"I never should've exposed you to my family. Never should've put you in a position where you had to have secrets from your father." He scrubbed a hand over his face. "Did you consider having an abortion?" He didn't blame her. How could he?

"No. Never." She met his gaze. "I had a miscarriage. I was six months pregnant when I lost the baby. Twenty-four weeks."

A chill scraped his soul. At six months, women showed, felt the baby kick, rubbed their bellies, started shopping. She must've seen it on a sonogram, heard a heartbeat. Things he'd missed, like watching her belly grow heavy with his child.

He'd almost been a father. Oh God, he'd lost more than he ever knew.

They both had, but she'd borne the brunt without him.

He got up and sat on the floor beside her. "I'm so sorry." Tucking hair behind her ear, he ran his thumb down the side of her face tentatively, hoping she'd let him get closer. "So far along—is that normal?"

She brought her knees up to her chest. "I'd been cramping, but the doctor said it was normal. Until it wasn't. Castle was home on terminal leave from the navy and found me sitting in a pool of blood. He rode with me in the ambulance, held my hand in the hospital."

The loss of their baby, her sorrow, his failure tore him to shreds. They'd almost had a child. Been a family.

Tears leaked from her eyes. He pressed his lips to her cheeks to catch them and wrapped his arms around her. She put her head on his shoulder, accepting the small comfort.

"Cervical incompetence, the doctor called it. My body couldn't carry the baby." Her voice thickened.

"The doctor said my condition could be treated for next time, like our baby was replaceable. First, I'd failed you by opening my big mouth, then I failed you by letting our baby die. It was all too much, and it broke me."

He ached for her. Combing a hand through her hair, he rubbed her back, slow and steady. Beneath her tough exterior, she was fragile and bruised. The vulnerability she shared with him was precious, and he cherished it.

She'd carried this around far too long and it was time for her to shed this burden. "You didn't *let* our baby die. It wasn't your fault, honey. Stop blaming yourself."

"Our baby weighed one and a half pounds," she said, her face soft, voice soft. "They issued a stillbirth death certificate. I named him Kinkade Reznikov."

Tears pricked the backs of his eyes, and his heart bled with hers. "That's a good name."

He wanted to erase the pain of the past, make it better somehow. Apologize for not having the strength and good sense to come back for her. But *sorry* couldn't undo what had been done.

Some scars never went away.

"After I got out of the hospital, I couldn't bear seeing a baby or a pregnant woman. I'd have panic attacks, sometimes a complete breakdown. Then I stopped leaving the house."

Seeing young couples in love, families with small children, had been hard on him, but he couldn't imagine how much harder it must've been for her, compounded by thinking he was dead. He'd been clueless, safe in his ignorance.

Fate had dealt them a shitty hand, but her worst of all.

"My father took me to the *spa* in Canada. When I got back, Castle gave me sneakers and a fully loaded MP3 player. Took me on a run every morning, even on weekends. Never talked to me about any of it. About anything. We just ran together until the day I started running alone."

No wonder Castle hated him. The man's vehemence was justified. Cole had abandoned her to deal with hell, alone.

He put his forehead to hers. "I should've been there for you, at your side, every step of the way." What he wouldn't give to have made different choices.

She pulled out of his arms and eyeballed him. "What happened to you? Where did you go?"

"Ended up in Alaska. Needed to recover. Physically. Mentally." His soul hadn't started healing until he saw Maddox again. "The wilderness was good. Took random jobs, some I'm not too proud of."

Hard work at the lumber mill had satiated the animal inside during the day. Drinking whiskey and cage fighting had lulled the beast into submission at night, till even that wasn't enough.

"If you had a boyfriend," he said in a low voice, "or husband who put his hands on you one too many times and you wanted him in the emergency room instead of getting stitched up again yourself, I was your guy for hire."

Looking at him with hooded eyes, she seemed to measure each word on a scale of belief.

"Everything I tried to make myself feel better made me feel worse. So I told myself no more bloodshed. No drinking." If he continued, she might want to cut off his dick, but he needed it out on the table. "No boning chicks whose faces blurred together and names I didn't care to ask." Women interested in fucking the mysterious guy with the ghastly scar who'd helped them out of a jam. He never spent the night, never bought them dinner. Heck, they bought him drinks.

He'd been something awful back then.

Her gaze fell, face twisting into something painful that hurt his heart.

"Did you ever fall in love?" she asked, not looking at him.

"You're the only one who has ever gotten in. You were my first thought every morning. The only thing on my mind as I tried to sleep. Not being with you tore me apart."

"Not enough for you to come back for me."

"I'm not going anywhere." He drew closer. "I'm here, Maddox."

"For how long before you bail? What if there's another shitstorm? Are you going to cut and run? Leave me behind again?"

"We're in a shitstorm right now, and I'm here. Fighting for you. Fighting beside you."

He was risking his life for her. If that wasn't proof he loved her, what was?

A crestfallen shadow fell across her face. "Nine years ago, I would've followed you through that violent hell. And to the wilderness. But you were able to leave me. You were able to stay away, when nothing would've kept me from you. And if it wasn't for my job as a *scum-sucking spook*, I still wouldn't know you were alive."

The words hit him like shrapnel. His mouth went bone-dry, and any response withered on his tongue.

"What I know for certain," she said low, "is you want closure. To be free of me."

Shit. "I didn't mean it."

Her watery eyes narrowed. "When you looked me in the face and said it, you meant it. I felt it. In my gut. In my heart. Because you wanted to hurt me, and you did."

Double shit. He had meant it, had let stupid spite color his words. "I was an angry idiot for saying it. I don't mean it now. I don't want to hurt you." He'd rather tear out his own heart.

"You used to be reliable, steadfast. True as a compass. Now you're this messy seesaw. And I don't know which way the wind is going to blow with you."

There was nothing he could say; no words would convince her. He had to show her, after this thing with Novak was done.

He put his hand on her shoulder. She cringed, and it was a kick to the chest.

"It's late." The words were like broken glass in his throat. "I'll go, let you rest." He dropped his hand. Sleep deprivation dulled the mind, slowed reflexes. Going up against Novak, they needed their faculties sharp. Space for her to breathe and process everything wouldn't hurt either.

"No need for you to go to a hotel. You can sleep on the pullout sofa."

His gut burned. "No." He lowered his head. "I don't need your pity pullout."

He went to the bathroom for a quick clean up, dressed, and gathered his things.

When he reemerged, she was still sitting on the floor, resting her head on the sofa. One word summed up how she looked: drained. He hoped she'd ask him to stay, in the bed. Knowing it was better for her if he left.

He grabbed the blanket draped on the sofa, covered her, and went to the door. "You didn't fail *me*. I failed *us*. I was young and foolish, and I made a lot of bad decisions. Being angry at you, never coming back for you was the biggest mistake. I forgive you, Mads, for the things you set in motion all those years ago, for the death of my father. None of it would've happened if I'd had better judgment. I only hope one day, you can forgive me."

Not that he was worthy of absolution after the cruel penance he'd forced them both to pay, but to free her heart from the burden of the past, so she could move on, love again, find happiness, and really be with someone.

Even if that someone wasn't him.

She deserved a full, rich life with all the things she desired.

He wanted to be the man to give it to her, but maybe that wasn't possible. Maybe his apologies were years too late and not nearly enough.

Maybe what they shared was toxic, damaging, too unhealthy to continue, and they'd both be better off with a fresh start.

But one thing would never change.

"I love you, Maddox. Always have, and I'll keep on loving you. With every last breath."

Whether it was enough was a question yet to be answered.

He ducked into the empty hall, feeling hollowed out
and raw, pressed the top button on the smartcode lock
to activate it, and gave the knob a last twist to be sure
she was safe.

25

Aleksander sat hunkered low in the van, staring at the black Kawasaki Ninja motorcycle. The same one had been at the Hotel Monaco.

Now it sat outside Agent Maddox Kinkade's apartment building like a harbinger of death.

The one-page file he'd received on her stated she was unmarried. The bike could be hers, but intuition told him it belonged to the man with the scar.

Not surprising to find him here, but Aleksander's current contingency plan didn't involve Scarface. Not in this phase.

Aleksander might need to determine a new *how*.

The front door of the apartment building closed with a heavy thud. Scarface descended the steps and strolled to the sports bike. Aleksander smiled as he watched the man put on a helmet, swing his leg over the bike, and rev up the engine.

Adjustments to his plan wouldn't be necessary after all.

A resounding roar pierced the night air, and Scarface zoomed down the road, out of Aleksander's way. Aleksander gave Val a knowing glance and climbed from the van. In a hushed click, he shut the door. He tugged the leather gloves tighter and brushed hair from the new blond wig over the top rim of his glasses.

Crossing the street, he did a quick three-sixty scan of the area and slipped into the darkness alongside the building. The shadows beyond the pools of streetlight concealed him, directing his steps.

He took up a position by a tree beside the pond separating him from the apartment building and stroked the device in the pocket of his smoke-gray coveralls.

Her apartment was on the second story, third in from the corner.

Light filtering through the vertical blinds shifted and flickered. A television. Balconies with iron railings and no screened patios provided the best-case scenario. Now, he waited for the right moment to strike.

VIENNA, VIRGINIA
4:40 A.M. EDT

No air. Tightness around her throat. A chilling darkness rushed up.

Maddox jackknifed awake, clutching her chest, raking in shaky breaths. She was alive. Safe. Her racing heartbeat steadied.

She looked at the television in her living room. An infomercial for an omelet maker. She must've fallen asleep on the sofa, dreading a cold, empty bed.

Cole had been so impassioned last night. Almost

convinced her. She wanted to believe him. Believe in his love. Trust he wanted to stay, for her, with her. Could they really have a second chance?

It terrified her to hope. One thing about him hadn't changed—he was still an *all or nothing* sort of man. He would press and knead until she gave him everything. If she opened up, fully gave herself to him, and lost him again, would she be able to recover?

No sense dwelling on it. She glanced at her smart-watch. 4:45. Time for a quick run, nothing lengthy, and then she'd hit the Gray Box. If their assumptions were right, this was probably their last day to find and stop Novak.

The Ghost wasn't going to make it easy. If anything, he'd up his game. Big time.

She turned off the TV and got dressed. Lacing up her sneakers, she couldn't get Cole out of her mind. The sex had been better than she remembered. Red hot.

Wasn't it supposed to be the other way around?

Time erased any negatives, sharpening the memory of the good to a ridiculous standard. So when you slept with your presumed-dead ex, you were disappointed.

Except their connection had been seamless, like they'd been one again. Raw, primal, off-the-charts good. Probably the lust-induced hormones muddling her mind.

At least they'd cleared the air. She knew about his dark exploits in Alaska, and he knew about their baby. If they didn't have any secrets, learned to forgive, maybe a future was possible.

VIENNA, VIRGINIA
5:15 A.M. EDT

Aleksander received Val's text.

Agent K on a run with a dog.

According to the information in the dossier, she jogged every day. Clockwork, predictable. Not even 6:00 a.m., and she was out on a run.

Aleksander jumped atop the railing of the lower-level patio. The duffel bag on his back rustled like tissue paper crumpling. He hopped, grasping the second-story wrought iron balusters, and hoisted himself up.

His arm muscles didn't shake, not a quiver. A twinge tickled the bicep Kinkade had stabbed. He'd taken pharmaceutical-grade painkillers to mute the biting ache, along with amphetamines. The theft had garnered him enough medicine to propel him through tomorrow when this would be finished.

He landed on her balcony with a harsh crunching underfoot. A layer of pea gravel covered the floor. The loud sound would've alerted her to his presence. If she'd been home.

Clever, Kinkade.

The lock on the sliding door was a keyless double bolt system. Speed bump.

He was prepared for such hiccups. Using the glass cutter, he set to work. In two minutes, he squeezed his hand through the small hole and unlocked the door. He yanked open the slider and dipped inside.

Silencing the light clatter of the vertical blinds, he locked the door. He spread a thin layer of odorless Loctite glue around the edges of the hole and replaced the cut glass. With the blinds concealing evidence of the breach, she wouldn't notice unless she came close enough for inspection.

There had been no mention of her owning a dog in the single sheet of information. If the canine was hers, Aleksander was ready. He set three poisoned doggie treats behind the club chair. In the event a pooch didn't go for the planted bait, he had more in his pocket wrapped in cotton pads. Delicious smelling, quick-acting, and potent.

Light as air, he crept into the bedroom. Her bed was perfectly made as if she hadn't slept in it, drawers to her bureau half open. Yesterday's clothing scattered on the floor.

He tucked the duffel bag away under the bed, dropped down into push-up formation, and squeezed out a steady fifty.

Moving up into cobra pose, he stretched in the yoga position, keeping his shoulders low and away from his ears. Downward facing dog. He pushed through his hands, elongating his spine and legs. Vertebrae popped. He held the pose, breathing, focusing.

Then he relaxed on the floor and slid underneath the bed.

He played out the scenario. Not once, not twice, but over and over. He had to see it sharply, precisely, and it'd be reality. Clean. Fluid.

The burner phone in his pocket hummed. Without

looking, he knew it was Val texting. Kinkade was on her way up.

A faint conversation in the hall. Female voices. One older. The apartment door clicked open and slammed shut. Footsteps. Light. Only hers. The kitchen faucet ran.

Silence. Glass tapped granite.

Footsteps approached the bedroom. Sneakers and bare calves crossed the threshold in front of the bed. She hesitated and turned, standing still.

He controlled every movement, every breath, didn't blink.

She drifted into the living room and didn't move. Seconds later, she checked the closet.

Good senses.

Lowering his eyes to the carpet, he slowed his heartbeat, reeled in his energy to a level as stagnant as moss. Deflecting her intuition with his stillness.

She spun on her heel and went into the bathroom, leaving the door ajar. A toilet flushed and water from the shower started.

Taking a breath, he slid out from under the bed and darted into the corner across from the nightstand. He eased the device from his pocket and switched it on.

The bathroom door opened wide. "Cole?" She stepped into the bedroom in her bra and skimpy panties, looking toward the living room. "You can't keep breaking in like this."

Aleksander swooped in as she pivoted. Her head didn't make it over her shoulder for a glance behind her. A blue arc of electricity crackled across the metal prongs, buzzing like a trapped wasp.

He jammed the stun gun into her ribs.

One hundred thousand volts of electricity flooded her body.

A scream strangled in her throat, her face contorted in agony. The way she shook, rapid and violent, unsettled him. Suffering was unnecessary. She was only an annoyance he needed to contain. A pest.

He shut off the stun gun and caught her shuddering body.

Soft. Shocking how soft a woman could be. The memory of softness had long evaporated.

Gently, he laid her on the bed. Scantily clothed wouldn't do. He wasn't a sadist. Peering into the open bureau drawers, he found stretchy pants and a T-shirt. He took the syringe from his other pocket and flicked off the green cap at the foot of the bed. That breadcrumb would be the first thing Scarface would see when entering the room later. The stun gun would be the second.

Aleksander found a delicate blue vein in her arm and depressed a mix of ketamine and midazolam, two powerful sedatives that when combined reduced the risk of unfortunate respiratory effects. An elementary score from a local veterinary clinic.

Noting the time, he dressed her down to socks. A small kindness where she was going. Although they were adversaries, he bore her no ill will.

In fact, this was goodwill. He snickered at his joke.

This was merely a means to securing his vengeance. She was Scarface's weakness. The weakness of the men around her, if they cared for her. He'd scratch their weakness, make it bleed. While her men scoured the city in desperate search of her, chasing his planted clues, spinning their wheels away from Aleksander, he'd be free to do what was needed.

The time of retribution was at hand.

He lifted her warm, limp body into his arms. Her head lolled toward his stomach, and he wanted to brush her hair from her face. He tucked her in a folded embryo position inside the extra-large duffel bag—the perfect size for her slim frame—and zipped it closed.

Kneeling, he slipped his arms through the straps, rolled to his hands and knees, and stood. He adjusted the weight of her on his back, gaining his balance. As he shut the apartment door, the one directly across the hall opened.

An elderly black lady with a rust-colored mutt stood in the threshold. The dog yipped at him, and the woman glared. "Who are you?"

"Picking up a donation of old clothes for Goodwill."

"Oh, I'm surprised that sweet girl didn't tell me. I could've given her some stuff." The dog barked and jerked at the leash.

He kicked a warning at the animal.

The old woman tugged the fleabag inside the apartment. "Come on, Herman, let the man go. We'll run our errands later."

Aleksander headed for the stairs.

"Isn't it a little early in the morning for a pickup?" The elderly woman's voice faded behind him.

He trudged down the quiet steps into the sticky air.

Val had moved the van, parking on the same side as her building but not directly in front. After opening the rear doors, Aleksander eased the bag off, setting it inside.

The grumbling thunder of a motorcycle rent the air. He didn't need to see the bike to know it was Scarface.

Didn't these people sleep?

No. How could they if they hoped to catch someone like him?

Sure enough, Scarface rolled the rumbling motorcycle ten yards behind the van as Aleksander shut the door. The metallic clink of the kickstand struck the ground.

Aleksander reached into the top of his coveralls, grasping the handle of his silenced SIG P320 subcompact.

Limping to the driver's door as if hobbled, he vectored his senses in on Scarface. Not simply his gaze from the corner of his eye or his hearing. He tuned in that sixth sense anyone in his business—or theirs, for that matter—needed to stay alive.

He'd prefer to use Scarface as the firebrand. Nothing like a distraught lover telling an impassioned story to churn the others up, reel in the focus and emotions of Maddox Kinkade's fellow agents. But there was a fine line between success and failure. They needed to be incensed and distracted, but if Scarface so much as hesitated going inside, dared look in Aleksander's direction with brows drawn, Aleksander would have to kill him.

Scarface's heavy footfall hit the steps, bounding to the front door of the apartment building none the wiser. Aleksander hopped inside the van. Val started the engine and pulled off.

Satisfaction spread in a slow, sweet smile.

26

VIENNA, VIRGINIA
6:07 A.M. EDT

Cole strode down the hall to Maddox's apartment. Three days ago, he'd been the most miserable son of a gun on the planet. Had a gaping hole where his heart should've been.

Today, he could walk on water, move mountains. Just because *she* was back in his life. Hell, it might take him moving a mountain to clear the path for a future with Maddox, but he'd do whatever was necessary.

Sleeping at the two-star hotel twenty minutes away had been an exercise in restlessness. He'd tossed, not quite able to get comfortable, as if his body needed hers pressed beside him to relax. And during the uneasy shut-eye he'd managed, he dreamt of her.

Not one of those pleasant, frolicking-on-the-beach dreams. The specifics escaped him, but it had centered on finding Novak, keeping her safe.

An African American lady, looking to be in her late seventies, plodded out of the apartment directly across from Maddox's with a cute pooch in tow. Her keys clattered as she locked her front door.

With the elderly lady watching, he knocked on Maddox's door rather than use his usual method of entry. The dog eased closer and sniffed his leg.

"Herman likes you. Surprising if you're the one who has been putting his hands on that girl. Giving her all those terrible bruises." She yanked the dog away. "Not that it's any of my business." The lady shuffled slowly down the hall. "Knock again. She's home. A guy was here picking up a donation."

A cold tingle sparked in the back of his head. "What guy?"

Glancing over her shoulder, she shrugged. "A man from Goodwill. Knock again. She's there."

Forget knocking. He reached for his tools, but the worst thought slammed into his mind. He tested the doorknob. It turned freely.

His shitstorm detector redlined. He threw the door open, scrambling inside.

"Maddox?"

At the sound of the running shower, his heart settled a little. He swept the apartment. Living room. Kitchen. Her jacket, gun, two cell phones, and keys were on the counter. The slow churn of sick dread in his chest spun faster.

"Maddox?" He tore into the bedroom and froze. A pale-green plastic cap like one from a hypodermic needle lay at the foot of her bed.

His stomach pitched. He stepped around her bed. On the carpet near the nightstand was an empty syringe and stun gun.

No, no, no.

"Maddox!" He stormed into the bathroom, flinging the door wide.

A dense bank of steam blanketed the room. He

charged through the muggy cloud and wrenched the shower door open.

Empty. The shower was empty.

An achy tightness seized his heart. The world teeter-tottered, flashes of darkness blotting out the light. He grabbed the glass door, steadying himself, and shut off the water.

His gaze fell to her sneakers and jogging clothes piled in the middle of the tile floor. He rushed back into the bedroom, stopping in front of the syringe and stun gun. The air in his lungs turned coarse as sand.

They'd been apart five hours. Five.

This couldn't be happening. But it was. Fucking Novak. Had to be.

He pinched the bridge of his nose, struggling to think. Shutting his eyes, he cleared his mind. The neighbor mentioned a man had come to collect a charity donation.

Cole had seen a Goodwill van on the street, the back of a tall guy with a sad limp. The early hour was odd, but he'd dismissed the guy, paid no attention because of the limp. And because he'd been fixated on seeing Maddox.

He dashed to the kitchen and grabbed a Ziploc bag. Using a paper towel, he threw the syringe inside. Novak didn't kill her—he would've left her body—but that animal had drugged her with something. He needed to know with what.

He scooped up her things from the kitchen and tossed them into his backpack with trembling hands. Slamming her door shut, he careened down the steps of her building.

The older neighbor lumbered down the outer stairs.

She plodded one careful step at a time, lining up both feet, then tackling the next. Her dog ran up to him and sniffed his legs again.

"Excuse me, ma'am," he said. "What did the Goodwill guy look like? The one at Maddox's apartment."

Her eyebrows raised in contemplation. "Well, um, tall and thin. White. Blond. Eyes like a fox. Crafty, you know. Wore glasses. Herman didn't like him. That man tried to kick my baby." She shuffled another step. "Oh, and he had a strange accent, something foreign."

Fear and fury thickened in his chest and clogged his throat. He jumped on his bike, turned the engine over, sped off.

The Ghost had been at her damn apartment. Somehow found out where she lived. Had touched her a second time. Had taken her right under his nose.

Zipping down the street on his bike, he rode by pure instinct, his gut pulling him to the Gray Box. He clawed through his mind for details he'd disregarded earlier.

White van. Fucking Goodwill had been written on the side. What was the license plate?

X-ray, Lima, Delta. The last three parts of the Washington, DC, plate were XLD.

How had Novak gotten close enough to use the stun gun on her? Maddox would've put up a fight, stayed out of reach, but there wasn't any sign of a struggle in the apartment. Why take her instead of killing her? What was he doing to her right now?

A three-ring circus of terrors spun in his head, and he cranked the turbine-powered bike into overdrive.

At the Gray Box gatehouse, the guard waved him in.

Screeching to a stop in front of the main building, Cole killed the engine. He raced up the steps, yanking off his helmet, and burst through the front door, setting off the metal detector.

Two guards behind the front desk took a defensive stance, eyes narrowing to slits. One guard raised a hand of warning. The other reached for something under the counter. Most likely a gun. "I'm going to have to ask you to stay where you are, sir. Please raise your hands."

Cole marched toward the desk. A red laser beam of light hit his chest, stopping his feet.

A sniper. Hidden somewhere on the top floor. Cole was in his sights.

Cole raised his palms. "I need to get in. I have to speak with Castle Kinkade. It's urgent."

"I'm sorry, sir. But we can't let you in without an escort."

"This is an emergency. Maddox Kinkade has been abducted. I need to speak to Castle."

Why weren't they listening to him?

They'd seen him before with Maddox. He was on their damn list.

The security guards behind the desk exchanged a quick glance. One picked up a phone and made a call. The other said, "Sir, I'm going to have to ask you to wait outside."

"I've been here before. With Maddox Kinkade. You know who I am. Cole Matthews."

"Sir, you're emotional and armed. I'm going to have to ask you to wait outside."

Cole glanced down. With his arms up, the holstered

Glock was visible. Damn it to hell. He hadn't been thinking about the gun, and he had a knife sheathed at the small of his back and another in his boot.

"You need to step outside, sir. Castle Kinkade will be up shortly."

Turning, Cole kept his hands in the air. His heart was a merciless hammer beating against his rib cage as he stormed outside.

Rage revved through him full throttle. Unable to contain the blistering steam, he stalked back and forth on the pavement. His fists shook at his sides. His body wired, he was keen to bring the Ghost serious pain. To break every bone in his body.

Leaving her had been a mistake. He should've protected her, above all else. That was his one job. He was supposed to protect her. He should've followed his gut.

Damn it! What had that maniac done to her? What if…

No. No *ifs*. He'd find Maddox. He'd get her back. He'd find the Ghost, too, and put him down for good.

Ferocious thoughts of violence battered his brain.

Castle, Reece, and Gideon rushed outside.

Cole clung to the thinning threads of his sanity. "He took her."

"What happened?" Castle steamrolled up to him. "Who took Maddox?"

The hot tang of bile spurted up Cole's throat. "I was just with her. Most of the night." He stalked in a circle, the words flying from his mouth. "I left for five fucking hours. When I got back, she was gone. The shower still fucking running. That bastard!"

"What the hell are you talking about?" Castle grabbed Cole by his jacket.

This was Cole's fault. He'd left her alone. Five hours. Long enough to give the Ghost a chance to take her. To hurt her.

If he'd been there, the way he should've, this never would've happened.

"I-I-I didn't think she wanted me to spend the night. So I left." He should've swallowed his pride and slept on the stupid pullout. Then she'd be safe right now. But she needed space.

Stupid. He was so stupid.

"Wouldn't let you spend the night?" Castle's face twisted into something beastly. "Did you fuck my sister?"

The hot bite of those words ate through the panic, gave the thrumming fury a way to vent.

With a swift downward blow, Cole broke Castle's hold and gave him a vicious shove, sending the big guy stumbling back. "It's none of your damn business. You're not hearing—"

Launching a right hook, Castle swung wide. Cole dodged it, but Castle followed up with a power punch, clipping him.

Pain stabbed his rib cage. Cole fought through it, throwing a jab. A sharp reflex. His fist smacked Castle's chin, throwing Maddox's brother off balance. Sweeping a leg out under Castle and snatching the tough guy's wrist, Cole flipped him over, hurling him to the ground.

Then he stepped back.

"I'm ready to stomp someone's face in! But I'd rather it not be yours, because I need your help to find

Maddox. That maniac drugged her. Took her! Do you understand? She's gone. And I don't know where. Help me find her."

Growling, Castle climbed to his feet.

Reece swept in front of Castle. "Look, man, Cole is right. I get you're pissed at this dude. I gather he hurt Maddox pretty bad back in the day, gives you a right to be angry. But you need to table this shit. We need to work together to find her. Once we do, she'll handle her issues with Lover Boy."

"We're on the same side." Gideon clasped Castle's shoulder. "We're all fighting for the same thing."

Castle scrubbed a hand over his face, regaining his composure. Jaw tight, he finally nodded. "Let's go inside. Find my sister."

27

In the conference room, Cole told the story twice. Once for the guys and a second time when Castle thought it best to bring in Sanborn, Harper, Amanda, and Cutter.

"You said you saw the van, right?" Harper asked. "Did you get a plate number?"

"I did, yeah." Cole nodded. "Partial. X-ray, Lima, Delta. A District of Columbia plate."

"We might get lucky," Harper said. "Land a hit from a traffic cam."

"I'll run the plate." Cutter hopped to his feet and shot out of the room like there wasn't a moment to spare.

The doe-eyed analyst's expression of furrowed brows and pinched lips mirrored Cole's, but for different reasons. His appreciation for the kid's gusto was slow to rise.

Everyone's motives had to be questioned, offers to help examined, suggestions scrutinized. First, Novak knew Maddox's name and that she would attend the auction. Next, he found out where she lived somehow and kidnapped her.

A compelling argument that an insider was helping him was snowballing.

"Cole, walk us through everything again." Sanborn

stroked his smooth chin. "Slowly. We're missing something. I know it."

How many times did he have to go over this? Replaying it wasn't helping. It only made the vein in his head throb harder. Maddox was out there somewhere, Novak had the upper hand, and they were wasting precious time. The longer it took to find her, the lower the probability that they ever would.

And it was Cole's fault for being too prideful to sleep on a sofa.

He gritted his teeth, hating himself. "I left her place a little after one in the morning."

"Stop." Sanborn lifted a hand. "Close your eyes. What cars were parked on the street? Was the white van there?"

Closing his eyes, Cole retraced his steps. "Yes. The van was parked further back across the street, but I didn't notice anyone inside. I wasn't focused on it."

"Okay." Sanborn folded his hands. "So the bastard was there, waiting. How did he find out where she lived? I still can't understand that."

Furtive glances were exchanged. Sanborn's eagle-eyed gaze seemed to notice, but he said nothing. The silence dragged, the tension in the room building along with the pressure in Cole's chest, prodding him to vomit the truth.

You have a mole. Someone in the Gray Box sold her out like a commodity. Not once, but twice. Someone entrusted with classified information violated that trust and stabbed her in the back.

He put his elbows on the table and pressed down hard while biting his tongue.

Janet breezed into the conference room with a pot of coffee and a large box of doughnuts. She set the box down and plugged in the electric carafe. "Should I notify Mrs. Kinkade about…what's happened?"

Castle shook his head. "I don't want my mother to worry. She doesn't need to know. Not yet."

Their mother, Susan, was a sweet woman who wore her heart on her sleeve and doted on her children. Knowing what had happened to Maddox was a cruel burden she didn't need to carry.

Janet nodded and left as Cutter hurried back into the room and sat.

"Negative on the plate. The Goodwill van probably hasn't been reported stolen yet, but I have a search running through traffic surveillance cameras."

They needed to catch a break, some lead to help them find Maddox.

"How did Novak find out where she lived?" Sanborn asked again, slowly, softly, not dropping the issue. "Any ideas?" He gave Castle a pointed look like he saw right through him.

Castle stared back, his face deadpan, his eyes hard.

Moments ticked by. It was like there was a time bomb ready to explode in Cole's chest.

"Maybe he doubled back to the hotel a second time after taking a taxi to Union Station," Cutter said as if he was thinking as he spoke. "He could've watched from across the street in front of the museum, followed the team back to the Gray Box. Then waited for her to leave and trailed her home."

Sanborn cocked his head and straightened slightly. "Where would he wait without being seen and still be able to have a line of sight to identify her clearly?"

Cutter shrugged. "Hell if I know. It's just a theory, boss."

Reece flipped his cap around backward and leaned forward. "The woods across from the access road that leads to the front gate. It's possible he hid there, with a motorcycle, and watched through a night-vision device. With his training, that would've been right up his alley. When he spotted her, he could've trailed her with no lights on until she hit the highway. It was late. She was tired and may not have noticed."

Sanborn held a poker face, didn't blink. "That is a solid theory," he said with a bite in his voice.

Since Novak had her name, he could've paid a talented hacker to track down where she lived, the same way Cole had. It was also possible someone from the Gray Box called Novak, told him when she was leaving and what vehicle she was driving, making it easy for him to follow her.

A more insidious thought crawled inside Cole's head. What if someone in this building, in this room, had simply given Novak her address?

His stomach soured.

"Cole, we need to establish a timeline," Sanborn said. "When did you get to her place?"

"It was just after six." Cole shook his head, berating himself again. "I parked behind the Goodwill van." That maniac had taken her right in front of him. His insides squeezed like something in his chest was going to burst. "Novak shut the back door and limped around to the front. The pathetic little hobble threw me, caused me not to think twice about him."

And Cole had been too distracted by the anticipation of seeing Maddox, had lowered his guard and let situational awareness slip.

"Her neighbor came into the hall, said she knew Maddox was home because a guy had picked up a donation. When I asked for a description, the lady mentioned a foreign accent."

The air thickened with each detail repeated, and Cole's anxiety swung back toward panic.

Reece clasped one fist, relaxed his fingers, and clasped the other. Over and over. Gideon chawed on gum, like a former smoker itching for a hit of nicotine. The analyst, Harper, jotted every word on a notepad. Elbows perched on his knees, Castle stared intently at the table. But Sanborn's expression was serene, his gaze soft and unfocused as if he was visualizing everything Cole described.

"The front door was unlocked," Cole said. "Her gun, jacket, cell phone, and car keys were on the kitchen counter. She'd picked up her clothes from the living room floor from earlier. The cap to the syringe was right in front of her bed. It was the first thing I spotted. The syringe and stun gun were on the other side near the bathroom door."

The Ghost had taken her by surprise as she came out of the bathroom.

Had she let her guard down, too, thinking it was Cole breaking in yet again?

The thought weighed him down with guilt, and his heart twisted. "The shower was running. The bathroom full of steam. Her sneakers and clothes were on the floor."

"Stop," Sanborn said. "Was the bathroom floor wet or dry?"

Cole raked his memory. "Dry."

"He got her before she stepped into the shower. No signs of a struggle?"

"None." And she would've put up one hell of a fight if she'd had the chance.

Harper scooted forward. "When I undress, my necklace is the last thing I take off. Did you see her watch in the bathroom or bedroom?"

Cole shook his head, trying to keep track of the various streams of thought. "Her watch?" If relevant shit had slipped his focus, it was pretty much guaran-damn-teed he didn't remember anything about a watch. He pressed the heels of his palms to his eyes and combed his mind. "Toothbrush, hand soap, towel. Box of tampons. No, I don't think I saw a watch."

"What difference does it make? How can it help?" Amanda asked, her face riddled with anxiety, her mouth pinched.

"Maddox has a smartwatch. She wears it every day," Harper said in the quiet, dry tone that only changed if Cutter was getting under her skin. "If the watch wasn't in her apartment, it means she still has it on."

"Where are you going with this?" Sanborn asked.

Castle slapped the table. "You're a genius. Her watch has a GPS chip linked to her smartphone. If we have her phone, we can locate her."

Oh, thank God. Cole could breathe again.

"Wouldn't the stun gun have shorted out the watch?" Cutter asked.

"This isn't a Road Runner cartoon where electricity races over Wile E. Coyote," Gideon said, and Cutter rolled his eyes. "Stun guns have a very high voltage to penetrate thicker layers of clothing at the point of contact. But the amps, the amount of juice they use is pretty minuscule. Not even high enough to short-out a pacemaker. Novak would've gotten Maddox where there's a big bundle of nerves close to the skin. Stomach, neck. Her muscles would've absorbed the energy, disrupting her central nervous system. Incapacitated her for a minute, two at most. That's why he drugged her."

Amanda squeezed her eyes shut as if picturing the same horrible thing playing in Cole's mind. The pain Maddox must've felt as Novak had gotten her in the stomach or neck. Cole pressed his fists against his thighs.

"Thanks for the science lesson, Golden Boy." The sarcasm in Cutter's voice rang clear as a bell.

Gideon's jaw hardened.

Reece let out a low whistle, flipping off his cap and setting it on the table. "Kid, you've got some nerve calling Reaper that. Having an *Annie* spot on the team, you REMF, hasn't earned you the right to razz this operator."

"I might be a *rear echelon motherfucker* right now, working a desk as an *analyst*," Cutter said, "but I've bled in the field with some of this country's finest." He straightened his suit jacket with a huff.

"Enough." The single, fiery word from Sanborn ended the squabble steeped in history Cole wasn't privy to.

"Unless he used the stun gun directly on the watch," Harper said, not the slightest bit derailed, gaze glued to the table, "it should be functional."

"What are we waiting for?" Cole ground out, fighting for patience. "Let's use the GPS to find her."

"It's not that simple," Harper said. "Not unless someone knows her password. It took the FBI weeks to crack into the smartphone of a terrorist, and I've never hacked one."

A deflated sigh resonated through the room, and for a moment, Cole didn't know if it came from him or Amanda or them both.

"Our firewalls are more stringent than the NSA's Utah Data Center because you designed them." Gideon chewed on his gum in a slow, steady rhythm, head lowered. "I bet the only reason you've never hacked a smartphone is because you've never tried. You're smarter than any FBI techie or analyst. If anyone can do it fast, it's you."

Gideon never once glanced at Harper, and she sat with her doe eyes wide and face flushed, looking totally spooked.

You would've sworn it was either the first time the guy had ever spoken to her, or she was terrified of him. Both seemed plausible. They moved in opposing currents—where one went left, the other went right. Even now, they sat at opposite ends of the table.

"O-kay. Can you do it or not?" Cole hit the glass table with his palm.

Harper flinched, snapping out of her daze. "I've never tried."

"Do you know how?" Cole raked his hands through his hair.

"In theory."

Her iffy expression didn't inspire the confidence

needed to keep him planted in the damn chair any longer. Cole sprang to his feet and stalked the room.

"Does anyone know if she enabled the iOS option on her phone?" Harper asked.

"What?" Cole didn't know the difference between iOS and DOS. Based on the heads shaking and shoulders shrugging, the others didn't have an answer either.

"On a smartphone, typically a person picks an alphanumeric passcode between four to six digits long. With a simple four-digit code, there are about ten thousand combinations and it could take a few hours. The iOS option allows for a thirty-seven-digit code. It'd take weeks to crack."

His hands clenched. "We have hours! She has hours!"

Harper cowered as if the anger in his voice had smacked her with physical force.

"Settle down." Gideon's ever-steady tone took on an edge. "This isn't helping."

Cole nodded. "I'm sorry. I didn't mean to yell."

Harper clutched her pearls and wrapped an arm around herself. "I have a program where I can run personal data to help pinpoint a code faster. Most people pick passwords for their private laptops and cell phones from personal identifiers. If I had more information about her, it would speed up the process."

The news was shifting from iffy to not too bad. "Collectively, those of us in this room probably know everything there is to know about Maddox."

"First, I need to do some NAND mirroring."

"What's that?" Castle asked. "No geek speak."

"The smartphone only gives you ten attempts at

entering a password before you're permanently blocked. I need to clone the NAND chip where the encryption security is onto a field programmable gate array chip and remirror the FPGA every nine tries, so I can input an infinite number of passcodes until I find the right one."

Hope welled, and Cole prayed Novak wasn't hurting Maddox. "I don't care how it's done, Harper. Just do it."

28

SOMEWHERE ALONG THE POTOMAC RIVER
9:52 A.M. EDT

A headache jackhammered Maddox's brain. The foul smell of decay and mold smashed through the dissipating drowsy haze. Dryness caked her throat like she'd swallowed sawdust.

She sat against a wall, wrists bound above her head and ankles zip-tied together. Her heart lurched as details came back in a brutal rush. Electric blue light crackling. The grip of excruciating pain—a hundred fists twisting. The pungent scent of ozone.

Novak. It had to be.

Pressure built behind her eyes, her vision clearing. She was in a room. Decrepit, wide space. Broken windows. Walls smeared with black soot and grime.

A whisper of death brushed her hand, creeping, creeping down her forearm. Prickles slinking over her elbow, tickling. Goose bumps raked her clammy skin. She looked up at her wrists, bound to a rusty metal bar bolted to the wall.

Prickly, black straw-like legs crawled on her bicep, inching closer to her face. Not into her shirt. Not in her hair. Not in her ear. *Please.* She jerked, yanking down hard on the bar.

Novak drifted into sight, stealthy and eerie as a nightmare.

Terror slithered in along with him.

He knelt on the debris-covered floor beside her. "Ah, you're awake." He swept the spider off her arm into a pile of rotted wood.

Sweat matted her hair to her forehead and cheek. Panic cramped her chest as she stared into his empty, dead eyes. "You don't have to do this." Good, her voice sounded steady, calm. Even though her heartbeat was a feral, desperate roar in her ears. "We'll back off."

"Don't lie. Not to me." He gestured to his chest as if offended. "I hold you in high esteem. Don't take that away." His words rolled in a social tone like they were colleagues or business competitors, instead of sounding like the madman he was.

"What do you want?" Trembling, she tamped down the fear—of spiders, of Novak, of dying. She scanned the room for Novak's son but didn't see him. "Why are you doing this?"

"I suspect you have answers to both questions."

He wanted revenge for his family, and she'd gotten too close at the hotel.

"Are you going to kill me?" She wasn't ready to die, not here, not a victim. But if he was going to kill her, why hadn't he already? A bullet in her head would've been easier than holding her hostage. Unless he needed her for leverage.

"I don't want your life." He tilted his head to the side, staring at her. "I want you as bait."

Bait. In less than three days, she'd gone from A-team

operative on the rise, to agency tool being worked like an asset, and now damn bait. *Liability*.

"I've every confidence your scarred-face man has the Gray Box stirred into a frenzy to find you. But I needed to galvanize their sense of urgency. So I made a little phone call."

A smug smile played at his lips.

Her breath caught and held.

Screwing with her team by nabbing her wasn't enough. This sick bastard wanted to play on their testosterone and alpha-male instincts—both of which, when dialed too high, became as volatile and unstable as nitroglycerin.

Cole would do absolutely anything to find her.

Gideon, Reece, and Castle would be torn, their judgments clouded, but they'd stick with the mission. They'd better. The ethics they lived by dictated it.

Novak was a pro, but even pros made mistakes. Maybe whatever call he had made was traced.

"I know what you're wondering." His eyes narrowed, and that grin turned taunting. "The call was untraceable. I used a scrambler. Bounced the signal from one cell tower to the next."

Novak stayed one step ahead of them. She'd expected cunning and skill, but how in the hell had he found her? He knew her real name, but she wasn't listed. She'd been careful about safeguarding her identity and whereabouts to the point of paranoia.

"On the yacht, how did you know who I was?" He'd gotten inside information from someone. She needed to know from whom. "How did you find out where I lived?"

His spooky smile deepened with sinister joy. She'd have nightmares about it for weeks—if she lived that long.

A ragged breath rocked through her chest, and she fought to steady it, to focus on this tiny window of opportunity. She had to shake the tree to get some fruit. "Who is your informant in the Gray Box?"

"The only person I know who works for the Gray Box is you." He touched her nose with the tip of his gloved finger.

She jerked her arms against the restraints, turning her face away from his touch.

"But…I have an expensive friend." He leaned into her face, and she recoiled, pressing the back of her head against the wall. "A powerful information broker with little birdies everywhere."

And one of those birdies was their mole, feeding this broker intelligence, which he was in turn selling to this soulless animal.

"Does your friend have a name?"

"My friend has many names. And many ears and eyes, everywhere."

She gritted her teeth through the frustration souring her stomach. There had to be something she could get out of him. The smallest nugget might lead somewhere. "Where am I?"

He craned his head back, looking around. His face was close enough for her to sink her teeth into one of his ears. She could hold on and do her best to rip it off. But then what, with her hands and feet tied?

"Someplace that'll make it very difficult for your men to find you." He flashed that creepy-crawly grin. "But after a long search in all the wrong places, I'll send them to you." He angled his head toward her, those dead eyes stuck to hers. "And then you can go home and sleep in your bed tonight. Safe, but knowing you failed."

She swallowed the vitriol burning the back of her throat.

This wasn't over. Not yet.

He wasn't going to win. She refused to let him.

"You don't have to hurt anyone else." Reason wouldn't work on Novak, but she had to try and talk him down, get him to rethink a bloodbath. "Taking more lives won't bring back your wife and daughter. Killing innocent people isn't justice."

"*Justice,*" he scoffed. "Justice isn't possible. I want vengeance. I want to punish this country. It'll be slow and painful. It'll rip out the heart of every citizen as I make them watch. This mighty nation will be glued to the television, helpless to look away, powerless to stop it once it has begun."

"That's what makes you a monster."

"I want to hurt and humiliate your government. I want your leadership, the heads of the most powerful country in the world, to feel small and helpless to defend their own. Just as I felt small and helpless to protect my family. If that makes me a monster, then yes, I suppose I am."

Everyone could be baited with the right hook. If she pressed the right button, he might let something slip. "If your wife and daughter could see you now, do you think they'd be proud that you're about to kill innocent women and children as payment for their deaths?"

"Save your breath, Agent Kinkade. Or I'll have to

find something in this room to use as a gag. Something filthy and rotten you wouldn't like in your mouth."

He grabbed her chin with gloved fingers, and that sickening vulnerability gripped her even tighter. Novak wrenched her head to the right. A black leather-covered finger pointed to a dead rat in the corner. Maggots crawled through its decomposing flesh.

Bile inched up her throat. She gritted her teeth, grateful her belly was empty, or she might've heaved.

Scrunching his face in mock disgust, he *tsk-tsk*ed. "Silence is best. If you keep talking, you might make Levik angry. He already wants to kill you, but…" He shook his head.

Who in the hell is Levik? His son's name was supposed to be Valmir.

"Your death isn't necessary. In fact, it would work against me in many ways." He stood and dusted off his knees. "Once I'm gone, feel free to scream until your lungs burn. There's no one around for miles, and help will not be on the way anytime soon. Now, I must leave and prepare for tonight."

"Why didn't you kill me on the yacht? You could've snapped my neck. No problem."

He stared at her for a long, hard moment, a haunted look in his eyes. "Death is not easy. You look at a man like me, contemplate the things I've done, and assume that killing is simple. You assume I'm a monster."

His face wrinkled with such tortured emotion, if he had a heart, she would've sworn it was aching.

"Just as the murder of my wife and daughter shall soon become a problem for your country, killing you would've been a problem for me. I don't want your scarred-face *monster* nipping at my heels for the rest of my life. Make no mistake, he is the kind of man who would go to the ends of the earth, through all nine circles of hell if necessary, for his vengeance. I wish you a long life with your monster, Agent Kinkade, but if I ever see you again, I will kill you."

Her blood ran cold.

Novak pivoted, practically floating away as he strode from her sight, not making a single sound.

29

GRAY BOX HEADQUARTERS, NORTHERN VIRGINIA
10:33 A.M. EDT

Cole prowled behind Harper at work on her dual-monitor computer setup, watching her fingers whiz across her keyboard as she tried to hack Maddox's smartphone. Every time she glanced over her shoulder at him, he paced and somehow ended up hovering again.

Raking a hand through his hair, he floundered for an ounce of patience.

Nothing moved fast enough. Not Harper's flying fingers. Not Cutter sitting ten feet away, hunting for more information that might help. Not Reece, who was out searching the Goodwill van they'd found abandoned on Route 1 off I-495. Not even Janet brewed more coffee fast enough.

And for some reason, the mind-numbing palette of this underground facility—with its subdued blue partitions, lifeless beige walls, and corpse-gray carpet—reminded him of an upscale funeral home. He was suffocating in it.

Turning, he marched over to Harper and went to tap her on the shoulder.

"Wouldn't do that if I were you." Amanda handed him a cup of coffee. "She has this thing about being touched." She nodded in Harper's direction. "But don't let her know that you know. She tries to keep it hush-hush. The three of us learned the hard way." Amanda waved a sweeping finger at Doc and Cutter, who both chatted with Janet while she refilled their mugs. "We don't talk about it with the others. And she'll work better if you don't loom. I guess you haven't noticed, but she needs her space."

The analyst gestured to the layout of their section. Harper sat far removed, working in a corner—actually, facing the corner with her back to everyone, wearing earbuds—while the other three had their workspaces in close proximity on the opposite side of a round confer-ence table.

This wasn't his day for noticing the little things. "Thanks. For the heads-up and the coffee."

"No problem." She gave a sympathetic smile. "I hope black is okay. I didn't know how you take it."

"Black and strong is perfect." He wondered if Amanda Woodrow was in Maddox's inner circle. Clearly, one existed. If you were on the inside, Maddox called you by your first name. If you weren't, it was simply Harper, Cutter, Doc. "Hey, to Maddox, are you Amanda or Woodrow?"

"You're asking if we're friends." She waved for him to follow her over to the section near the televisions.

Taking a gulp of coffee, he trailed along.

"I see you've picked up on the inner dynamics around here," she said. "Operators form a tight bond pretty fast. They're out in the field risking their lives together. They tend to keep a little distance from their intel analysts. Operators live or die by the intelligence they get, and having a clear line is a good thing, but we're all pretty friendly and socialize. Except for Willow. The one exception to the name rule is Reece. He was Delta Force for so long, I think it makes him uneasy if you call him John."

Interesting to know, but it wasn't an answer.

She must've seen the question lingering on his face, because she gave a soft smile and nodded. "I'm Amanda to Maddox. She recruited me from the DEA. I was an operative until I had Jax. Staying in black ops as a single mom wasn't realistic, even with help from my parents."

Cole glanced over her shoulder at her desk and spotted a picture of a cute little boy with sandy curls, maybe four or five. No doubt the artist of the colorful illustrations pinned to the partition wall framing her monitor.

Off to the side of the main aisle, Janet stopped to talk to a passing man Cole hadn't seen before. Tall, slim, wore glasses. They were barely within sight at this angle and would've been concealed entirely from the rest of the analysis section by the partitions. She brushed something from the front of his shirt. A split-second gesture, so fast that if Cole had blinked, he would've missed it. Whether friendly, motherly, or something more, he couldn't tell. The guy looked fifteen to twenty years her junior.

"Incoming," Amanda whispered.

Cole pivoted, following her gaze to a svelte woman, polished from her platinum-blond haircut to her body-hugging dress and daring, sky-high heels. She sashayed by like she owned the place. The cougar eyed him, long and hard, as if he were a bowl of thick cream she wanted to lap up.

He faced Amanda. "Who is that?"

"Sybil Parker, insider threat monitor," she said low. "She and her two underlings are the only ones here Sanborn didn't hire and can't fire. They keep an eye on personnel, communications, networks—make sure no one is looking at porn or sending out classified information on an unclassified open system."

"Who monitors her?"

Amanda shrugged. "I guess no one."

The tall, slender man walked past in front of the wall of televisions, headed in the same direction as Sybil Parker.

"He works for her?"

"Yep. Minion numero uno Ricky Olsen."

"Are he and Janet good friends?"

Amanda's brow creased at the question. "Odd thing to ask. No. The Jedi and Sith can never be friends."

Perhaps it was nothing and he was reading too much into the small gesture between Janet and Olsen. He wouldn't be able to think straight until they found Maddox.

Something flashed in Amanda's light-brown eyes. "You're the guy from the picture in Maddox's locker. The one she won't talk about. I didn't recognize you before." She lowered her head. "I asked Maddox once if she ever wanted to get married and have children."

Cole leaned in, riveted, needing to know. "What did she say?"

"With all her heart. She wanted nothing more every single day."

The answer filled him with gripping sorrow and

unexpected hope. One day, he wanted to give her that. More than anything.

Amanda sipped her coffee. "I asked why she wasn't out there making it happen. Working isn't living. You know?"

Yeah, he knew all too well. He gave a nod.

"She told me it wasn't possible because the only man she had ever loved was dead. That it was her fault. And if he was no longer able to have those things, then neither could she."

It was a meat cleaver to his heart. He'd been such a damned fool.

Amanda rested a light hand on his shoulder. "We're going to find Maddox. I know it."

His throat closed, chest tightening. He nodded, wanting to take her words and cradle them in his hands. Man, he needed to believe.

"You should eat something," Amanda said. "To keep up your energy."

Wasn't possible. Not while that psychopath had Maddox locked up somewhere and Cole didn't know if she was in pain, gagged, or even conscious. The visuals were killing him. His hand clenched with impotent anger, utterly powerless in this holding pattern. He thirsted to end Novak, but the only thing that mattered, really mattered, was getting her back safe in his arms. "I can't eat. Not until I find her."

Harper spun in her chair, plucking out her earbuds. "Maddox didn't use iOS. I'm close in terms of hours, not days. The personal data helped. I should be able to crack it."

The tension in his body eased a hair. Maybe the

universe was on their side after all, but he had no idea
what to do with himself for hours.

SOMEWHERE ALONG THE POTOMAC RIVER
11:05 A.M. EDT

After Novak left, Maddox heard a door slam closed and a
car drive away. Silence reigned in the dilapidated building for nearly an hour, she estimated. She was alone.

The fuzziness from the drugs finally lifted. Maddox's
thoughts cleared, and her mind scrabbled for a way to
escape. She swung her legs to the side, tipping herself
onto her knees. The angle twisted her arms, pinching
her rotator cuffs.

The old metal bar ran about twenty feet in length,
bolted to the wall at both ends. Brackets spaced every
two feet reinforced the bar's anchor to the wall. She
tugged hard. The zip tie cut into her wrist. The bar didn't
move, but something clanged. She yanked again. The
bracket three inches to her right jangled. She shimmied
closer, knees grinding into fallen bits of plaster.

Curved in shape, the four-inch-long rusted bracket
wobbled on the pair of screws holding it in place.

Gripping the side of the bracket between her wrists
and the flex-cuffs, she shook it, loosening it from the
wall. Over and over. The corroded edge of metal
scratched the soft flesh on the inside of her wrist.

The top rusty screw popped out enough for her to

grasp with her thumb and index finger. She unscrewed it, bit by bit, until it slipped out. She set to work on the next one.

Death had spared her for a reason. Maybe it wasn't her time yet. Maybe she was meant to stop Aleksander Novak. The Ghost was scared. Kidnapping her was an act of desperation.

The second screw popped out and the bracket fell into her hand. She scooted to the next metal bracket and tipped the flat edge of the loose one to it. She honed the dull edges of the metal in her hands, sharpening it.

This job was one uphill battle after another, bringing her nose-to-nose with evil, reminding her life was fragile. At the end of the day, there had to be more for her than this cold, hard fight for the greater good. The work was honorable, but it was difficult, sometimes scary shit. She needed balance.

The one person she'd been most intimate with, closer to in heart and soul than any other, had offered her comfort and warmth. He had risked his pride in admitting he loved her still and always would. In return, she'd said awful things and hurt him.

If she got out of here—*fuck that!*—when she got out of here, she was going to stop being terrified. Of loving Cole, of losing him, of getting hurt again. Professionally, she faced every threat, endured the grind, worked her way through the fear to get the job done. She had to stop being a lowly coward with him, owed it to herself. He deserved better—along with an apology for how she'd pushed him away.

She put the bracket between her teeth, pressed the

edge to the zip tie, and, bobbing her head back and forth, sawed the bracket across the plastic restraint. Bitter flakes of rust hit her tongue. Getting out of there to stop Novak was her sole focus.

No way in hell would she allow herself to be rescued. *I won't be the weak link in the chain. Not today. Not ever.*

30

GRAY BOX HEADQUARTERS, NORTHERN VIRGINIA
11:15 A.M. EDT

Cole paced in the break room, the one space in the facility he'd seen drenched in vibrant colors. Art deco paintings hung on the ferocious yellow walls, their mind-boggling waves and splotches of organized chaos in myriad saturated hues. An absolute riot of color.

The rest of the facility with its laid-back tones and cushy vibe was nauseating. This was the one room he managed to tolerate.

Castle strode into the room, wearing the same heavy expression that Cole carried. They eyed each other. Cole stilled, waiting for the answer to his unspoken question. Castle gave a quick, tight-lipped head shake.

No news.

Cole's nerves frayed a little more. "Someone in this damn dungeon helped that psycho kidnap her. You understand that, right?"

Castle narrowed his eyes and his jaw hardened. "Yeah." His gaze darted to the hall, where one of Parker's minions strolled past.

The pixie-faced woman with short, spiky hair must've been Nicole Tully, based on what Cole had learned from Amanda. Nicole worked midday hours, afternoons through the evening, and picked up the swing shift when necessary.

He glanced at the clock, noting it seemed a little early for her to be in.

The ITM section was supposed to monitor the digital activity of Sanborn's people, listen to phone calls, ensure the transmission of data was aboveboard. But did they have access to personnel records and personal information they didn't need to do their job?

Once Nicole Tully had passed, Castle glared at Cole. "Lower your voice about that issue."

"Issue?" Cole said in a harsh whisper. "How about major fucking problem? Or deep shit?"

Castle opened his mouth to say something, snapped it shut, and poured a cup of coffee. The son of a gun said something under his breath. It sounded like *I won't be baited*.

After a long draw from the mug, Castle said, "I'm not the enemy. Trust and believe I'm itching to take out my frustration on you just as much as you are on me. But the only person that'll help is Novak. Not Maddox."

Cole went back to pacing, grinding his teeth over the fact that Castle, of all people, was the voice of reason.

"Look, I don't like you any more than you like me," Castle said. "For now, let's put our crap on the back burner. Why don't we call a cease-fire, okay?"

Sweet Jesus, more words of wisdom from the big lug. What was next? A bolt of lightning striking six stories below ground?

"Yeah, okay. We both love her. She wouldn't want us fighting."

Castle froze, his jaw twitching as if he wanted to say something ugly and sharp. But he only clucked his tongue.

"I do love her." For this truce to be real, there was a lot Cole needed to say. "I know you don't believe me because I left and didn't come back for her. You have every right to hate me for that. I hate myself for it. I know how you helped her when she lost the baby." He swallowed his pride in an effort to be a better person. One worthy of Maddox. "Thank you for being there for her. She needed me the most then, and I failed her. I told her what happened to me. One day, I'll tell you too. I think I owe it to you."

Castle's eyes widened. He looked stunned. Confused. In a flash, it was gone, and Mr. Tough Guy nodded.

Cole let his admission settle between them for a few seconds and dove right back in to the pressing matter at hand. "What are you doing about the *issue*?"

"We're not sitting around twiddling our thumbs. It has to wait. Our hands are a bit full—"

"There you are." Doc rushed inside the break room. "Castle, I was just in Sanborn's office. He got a call from the director of national intelligence and wanted me to find you."

"Is it about Maddox?" Castle and Cole asked in unison.

She shrugged. "He didn't say. I'm sorry. Only that you needed to get in there."

Castle set his mug down and took off.

A revving sensation ticked up in Cole's chest, and he had to move. He ate up the room in one direction with long strides, turned, and went the other way.

Doc watched him with a sad smile that he'd rather

not see. "This waiting can't be easy. How are you holding up?"

He stopped, whipping his gaze to her, and folded his arms. Was she shitting him?

Standing there with a poor-you expression, using a come-sit-on-my-sofa-and-chat tone, wearing another bohemian I-wanna-make-the-world-better blouse with stupid flowers, and oozing a not-so-in-the-closet hippie aura, she was dead serious.

It was brutally obvious Doc was trying to be nice. The woman seemed sweet as pie, but he needed to be as far away as possible from *nice* and *sweet*. So he was stalking back and forth like a caged wild thing surrounded by this maelstrom of color.

His throat grew dry as he fumbled hard for the right words, since he didn't want to offend anyone else who was trying to help.

Before he could say anything, Castle came back with urgency like he had news, but from the grim expression on his face, it wasn't good.

"Did something happen?" Cole asked. "Did someone find a lead?"

Castle's gaze dropped a moment, and when it bounced back, his face had hardened to ice. "That bastard called the DNI's office. Novak boasted about having Maddox, said he buried her somewhere up to her neck on the bank of the Potomac."

Doc's sharp gasp cut through the sudden roar thundering in Cole's head.

The words sank into his brain, connecting slowly. Once they added up, something inside him unraveled, and it took his last shred of control not to lose it completely.

Scrubbing a hand over his bald head, Castle said, "We have until high tide to find her—9:00 or 10:00 p.m.—or she'll drown."

"Oh no." Doc pressed a hand to her throat.

To bury Maddox, torture her—unable to move, trapped with the knowledge the water would rise, wash in with the tide, drawing up her neck, creeping past her mouth, covering her nose—was unconscionable.

Drowning wasn't a pleasant way to go. Right up there with being burned alive.

Red-hot rage boiled over inside Cole. His body was desperate to expel the frustration building. He spun and kicked a chair, sending it flying across the room.

Doc covered her mouth with a shaky hand.

He shut his eyes and saw Maddox. Buried, alone, afraid. This wasn't something he could fix, talk his way to a solution, fight with his fists. This was purgatory with a countdown to hell.

His nerves quivered with fury and, beneath it, fear. The pressure welling in his chest deepened. For an instant, he thought his heart might burst. He doubled over, grasping his knees.

Think. He was no good to her unless his brain functioned. "Any trace on the call?"

"No. The Ghost was quick. Clean," Castle said. "Reaper is firing up our helicopter."

The Goodwill van had been abandoned where Route 1 connected to I-495. At the eastern border of Virginia, along the Potomac, but Novak was too clever to bury her there. Without knowing if the Ghost had gone north or south after ditching the van, Maddox could be anywhere. The Potomac stretched for miles.

Cole stood upright, regaining his composure. "I'm getting on that chopper."

"Of course." Castle nodded.

"Harper is close to hacking into the phone. Contact us in the helo when she does." Everything was taking too much time. And Maddox was running out of it. She couldn't die. If she did, the world wouldn't be worth living in.

"Yeah, we can patch in. No problem. We're going to find Maddox." Castle gave a sharp affirmative nod. "Then we're going to kill Novak."

"The Ghost is mine. I get to kill him." He wouldn't do it quickly or painlessly with a bullet. He needed to take out that monster with his bare hands.

"Roger that."

SOMEWHERE ALONG THE POTOMAC RIVER
11:37 A.M. EDT

Maddox popped the hard plastic zip tie securing her wrists. The tightness in her chest eased. She spat the rust from her mouth and worked on the zip tie binding her ankles.

She tugged at the strap of hard plastic as she sawed through it. "Come on. Damn you."

The zip tie popped, freeing her ankles. With only a pair of cotton socks on her feet, she treaded softly around nails, puddles of sludge, and rusted pieces of metal.

When Novak had snuck up on her with the stun gun, she'd been in her underwear. He'd dressed her, shown a strange mercy. He was deadly, ruthless, but there was more to him.

Sections with piles of rusted mechanical parts carved up the space between wide-open bays. Gaze glued to the ground, she slipped carefully around trash as she made her way to the window. The last thing she needed was something stuck in her foot.

The view from the third floor was nothing but trees for 180 degrees. Where the hell was she?

Most likely Virginia, possibly Maryland. Novak could've even driven to West Virginia.

She checked her smartwatch. GPS was offline. *Great.* She wasn't near civilization. She gazed out the window, determining which direction to head. About a mile out, beyond a loose cluster of trees and patch of grass, was a gray-blue slash of water. A river. The Potomac or the Shenandoah.

If she followed it, eventually she'd run close to a town with connectivity. In sneakers, the trek wouldn't be a problem, but in socks, no telling how many miles, the terrain would eat up her feet. Not that she had a choice.

A small animal squeaked behind her, followed by a pitter-patter of critters, larger than rodents. She spun in the direction of the noise. Anything could be hiding in the rubble of this abandoned building.

She tiptoed down the staircase. A splinter in her foot

could do enough damage to slow her down, and a gash would put an end to the journey before it started. On the first floor, trash, shards of metal, and broken glass riddled the ground in a mosaic of landmines—degrees of pain—from the staircase to the busted entrance.

To avoid frayed pieces of metal and shattered glass, she stepped into a cool, sticky puddle. The same black sludge she'd seen throughout the building. As she walked, the gummy substance left dark, tacky spots behind like little stamps of misery.

Thirst scratched at her parched throat. The only thing keeping her stomach from rebellion was the determination pooling in her veins as she inched toward the tree line.

Never one for the outdoors, a pure city girl, Maddox had never been happier to reach the forest. She treaded lightly, scanning the area. The tacky gunk saturating her socks stung her skin worse than salt in an open wound.

Leaning on a tree, she peeled off the socks. The soft grass was a staggering comfort.

She trekked through the grass. Rugged pieces of bark and rocks bit at her feet.

A violent thread of determination coiled in her core. She checked her smartwatch. The phone still didn't work, but maps were online. West Virginia. Miles from a town. Following the river south looked like the best route.

The more distance she covered, the more the unforgiving terrain rubbed her tender feet. The bubbling rush of the river was a welcome sound, opening a world of possibility in her chest. Clenching her teeth through the pain, she used the trees to steady her footfalls. All she wanted was a soothing bath, a hot meal, to take a break from the grind. She was running on fumes but summoned her anger as fuel.

The Ghost had the upper hand again. If she didn't get out of these woods and stop him, he'd succeed in unleashing a deadly virus. And that wasn't an option.

She quickened her pace, coiling the thread in her gut ever tighter.

31

For the three hours they'd been in the air, with no sign of Maddox, Cole endured ten thousand hells. He was on the verge of coming unhinged.

Gideon's steely composure never wavered. The guy was so guarded and laser focused, there was no attempt at reassuring chatter between them. Cole was grateful for the silence and the guy's ice-cold poise lowering the temperature of the cockpit by ten degrees.

The Potomac flowed through Virginia, Washington, DC, Maryland, up to Pennsylvania and West Virginia. The roiling river was over four hundred miles long and as much as eleven miles wide where it flowed into the Chesapeake Bay. Some spots along the bank were shrouded by trees, forcing them to do a second pass to be certain they hadn't missed her.

"Good news," Castle said over the headset linked to the radio.

About time. He needed good news. "Did Harper get into the phone?"

"I'm putting her on now."

The airwaves went dead, crackled with static, then Harper said, "I got in."

Cole clenched his hands, heart skipping beats. "Where is she?"

"She's moving south slowly along the Potomac, West Virginia. I'd say by foot based on the speed. Not running, and much slower than the current would be pulling her if she was in the water. I'm sending the coordinates now."

"Moving? Are you sure?"

"Without a doubt. The watch is moving. You guys should be able to vector to her position."

A chorus of hallelujahs blasted in his head. "Thank you, Harper. Thank you."

"Let me know if you need anything else."

Thank God. He wouldn't need the shovel in the back to dig her out if she was above ground. His chest stayed heavy as if his lungs were made of iron, refusing to let in a full breath until he had eyes on her.

Gideon altered direction, taking a hard left turn. Cole's stomach flipped.

He kept his hands curled into fists as they headed northwest. His nerves ran right on the edge. The coordinates were buried in a forested patch. Based on the trajectory of her signal, she was headed toward a clearing, where Gideon vectored to land.

Cole glimpsed her wending past trees adjacent to the river. Ripping off the headset, he threw open the door and jumped from the helo before Gideon touched down.

Maddox stumbled from the tree line, limping, her hair a windblown tangle of curls. He dashed across the field, unable to get to her fast enough.

A sad smile broke over her smudged face. She reached for him, and he hauled her to him so powerfully, they collided. He crushed her against his body, lifting her from the ground.

The rest of the world dissolved in a rapid rush of relief. Everything that was knotted inside him unfurled, and he held her tight, so tight.

Nothing would keep him away from her ever again. Not her anger, not her hatred, not her stubbornness. She was stuck with him. Whether she knew it or liked it.

Keeping his death grip on her, he showered her with kisses on her mouth, eyes, cheeks, his fingers curling in her hot-mess hair. He was overstepping, putting her mission on hold, and for once, she let him.

"I don't know what I would've done if I lost you," he said in her ear.

"Think I'm letting you off the hook that easily?" Pulling back, she met his eyes. "No way. You've got some making up to do. A decade's worth, mister."

"Just a decade?"

"At least."

A penitence he was eager to pay. He set her down and stroked hair from her face.

She cupped his cheeks. Their gazes held, with tears in her eyes. "I pushed you away because I was scared. I was hurting and lashed out. I'm sorry for not making you feel like I wanted you to stay last night. I did, but I was a coward."

"Honey, you are the bravest, strongest person I know." Her courage and persistence put him to shame. He was staggered by her. "I gave you cause to be guarded, to be scared. But I swear, I'll never give you another reason to doubt me."

Every day, he'd prove his love, if she gave him the chance.

He gathered her in his arms again, for just another moment, allowing them both to appreciate the contact and the comfort. With Gideon watching and the wind whipping up nearby from the rotating helicopter blades, it put tangible pressure on them to get moving.

Breaking the intimate hold he craved, he put an arm around her shoulders.

She took a step and tried to mask a wince. He looked down at her bare feet, bloody and blackened. His heart gave a soft thump.

He scooped her into his arms and carried her to the helicopter.

"How did you escape? Novak called the DNI, said you were buried up to your neck somewhere along the river and we had until high tide to find you."

Sheer horror gripped her face. "He wanted to mess with you. Get into your heads so that the only thing you guys could think about was saving me instead of finding him."

"Well, it worked. I've finally decided how I'm going to kill him. It's pretty gruesome, so I'll spare you the details."

"You can't kill him. We need him alive. He might have information about the mole."

There was more than one way to catch a mole. Novak was as good as dead. And it wasn't up for debate. "Let's get you home and cleaned up."

"I can't go home." She shook her head. "Besides,

there's no time. I have clothes at my office. We should go there."

They hopped into the back of the helicopter, and Gideon cracked the first smile Cole had seen. *Sheesh*, the guy really was far too pretty. Redefined the meaning of fair.

"You done messing around? Can we go catch a ghost?" Gideon asked, his severe hardness falling back into place.

"Absolutely." She flashed a fatigued grin.

Cole sat beside her, his arm draped around her and her head resting on his chest. Gideon radioed the Gray Box, giving them an update. Over the headset, Maddox filled everyone in on the true details of her abduction and confinement.

Her tone, the way she spoke about the Ghost had changed, fucking softened. Compassion resonated in her voice.

Didn't she understand? One couldn't have sympathy for a rabid dog.

You just had to put the beast down.

She guzzled two bottles of water, and he wished he'd brought more.

Gideon set the helicopter down in front of the Gray Box so Maddox wouldn't have to walk from the hangar, but Cole had no intention of letting her walk at all. He helped her from the chopper and lifted her into his arms, carrying her to the entrance.

"When we get inside, you have to put me down. I can walk."

"I know you're a badass secret agent, but your feet are pretty cut up."

"Badass operations *officer*."

"My point is I get that you're capable, but think about the mess you'd make in that glossy polished lobby. If not for your own sake, then spare someone else from cleaning up your blood."

She sighed. "All right, but just to the elevator."

They entered the building, and the metal detector blared.

One of the guards hustled to their sides. "Officer Kinkade, are you okay?"

"I'm fine." She motioned to get down.

Cole adjusted his grip on her, locking her body to his. She grimaced, not hiding her annoyance. Giving her a wink, he smiled.

In the elevator, she struggled to stand. "This is embarrassing. And sexist. Put me down."

"Your feet are bruised and bleeding. If this were an alternate universe and you were a dude, I'd still carry you. I'm not letting you walk. Once your feet are bandaged and you have shoes on, you can go back to being Xéna, Warrior Princess. Until then, I'm carrying you. End of discussion."

She had a backbone of steel and her independence was admirable. He just hoped she recognized that everybody needed someone to lean on from time to time.

The fiery rebellion that he loved so much set her eyes aflame. "I'm only interested in fighting Novak today. You win for now, Hercules."

"Hercules? You see me as a mere demigod? I was thinking more along the lines of Superman."

She chuckled. "You're aiming high."

"I sure am and have been ever since I met you." He tilted his head and kissed her, soft and quick. She was safe in his arms. His heart swelled and filled. This was happiness. "I love you, Maddox."

As he waited for her to say the words back, he could feel the coiled tension in her body. Her muscles had been tight since they found her, understandably. They had to track down Novak. This might be an inappropriate time to pour his heart out, but their lives could end in a haze of smallpox-M today. And if her job was always this level of crazy, then every moment had to be treated as *now or never*. But he tucked away his irritation and impatience, set on not pushing.

They still had heavy baggage, and the mission had to come first. The magnitude of her job pressed in on him as they headed toward the subterranean facility. To do her best, she had to leash certain emotions. When she was ready, in time, she'd say the words he longed to hear.

She combed her fingers through his hair, and her eyes were deep and vulnerable. "Last night, I didn't mean it when I called you *meat*. You could never be that to me."

"I know." And he did. There was no need for her to tell him.

"I was trying to protect myself, but it was selfish and wrong to say it. There's no justification for disrespecting you like that." She brushed her mouth across his. "I may have grieved and mourned, but I never let you go."

"And I hope you never will."

Her lips parted, and they shared a breath. In the shallow space between their mouths, want and need and—without a doubt in his hopeless mind—love rippled. Those emotions flamed and spread through him the closer they drew before she caught his bottom lip, licked the top, sinking inside. He absorbed the tender friction, the sweet warmth. She wrapped her arms around his neck, her fingers diving into his hair, and flattened her breasts against his chest as they both tried to get closer, feeding off the blooming spark.

Arousal drizzled through him, every part of him coming alive with her soft, lean body pressed solid to him.

The elevator stopped, and the heavy doors opened.

They eased their mouths apart. He smiled at the longing that gleamed in her eyes.

"Let's get moving. We've got work to do," she said.

He planted a kiss on her nose. "Yes, ma'am."

Cole carried her down the walkway, and she directed him to the female locker room. The entire team, including Cutter, Amanda, and Doc, intercepted them before they made it that far.

Once the flurry of exclaimed relief and questions slowed, Maddox held up a hand to silence them. "I'm fine. My feet look worse than they are."

"Let me take a look at them," Doc said.

"Thanks, but I just need a med kit and to get cleaned up so we can get back to work."

Just like his warrior princess. She wouldn't have it any other way.

Everyone parted like the Red Sea, and Cole pushed through the door of the locker room.

"You can put me on the bench by the shower."

Gently, he set her down and cupped her cheek.

"They have the essentials in here," she said. "But I

need my canvas bag from my desk. It has a change of clothes and my running shoes."

"I'll be back in a minute." He stood to leave, and she grabbed his hand.

"Thank you. For coming to look for me. Finding me. I said awful things to you last night. I'm sorry."

"I deserved all of it." He'd tell her a hundred times he was going to be there for her, but she had cause to doubt him. He had to put in the work and show her. "I'll be right back."

He kissed her cheek and left the room. Posted like sentinels, the others stood in the hall.

"Could someone grab her canvas bag from her desk and a med kit for her feet?"

Harper motioned to go grab the stuff, but Cutter raised a hand, stopping her. "I don't mind errand boy work. I'll go."

"Thanks," Harper said, more relaxed than Cole had seen her. Maybe she was warming to the guy.

Cole gritted out the details of Maddox's ordeal, bringing the whole crew up to speed.

"Sounds like whatever he's planning is happening tonight," Sanborn said, "if he only needed us out of the way for the day. Let's reconvene in the conference room and reevaluate the threat matrix with fresh eyes."

Everyone dispersed, except Sanborn and Castle.

"We fixed your problem with the Russians," Sanborn said.

"Who is we?" Cole asked.

"The United States government. We gave them the whereabouts of three unsavory individuals the Russian

Mafia wanted far more than you. And we made it clear to the ambassador here that Nikolai Reznikov is dead. And you, Cole Matthews, are an American citizen and protected asset. The message was acknowledged and the trade accepted by the Kremlin."

And long may Putin reign. Tightness in Cole's chest loosened. The Bratva didn't fear the United States government, not even here on American soil. But they wouldn't risk crossing Putin. "Good thinking to appease them with some bigger fish. Thanks."

Sanborn nodded. "It's the least we could do for your help." He strode off.

Castle clasped Cole's shoulder. "You did good finding her." His hand fell as his gaze frosted. "But it doesn't change my opinion of you."

"Duly noted." Maddox's opinion was the only one Cole cared about.

"When I found out that you were alive, I almost killed you myself. That's the first time I've ever let personal feelings come before the mission." He shook his head as if still troubled by it. "Setting up Maddox to find Cole Matthews, without letting her know you were alive, was the hardest thing I've ever done. Sanborn was testing me. To see if I could do it. I almost caved."

Emptiness mowed through Cole. She'd said that she didn't know he was alive before seeing him in person, and he'd doubted her. "This isn't a game. Maddox isn't a toy I'm playing with. I love her. I'm not going to hurt her again."

"That remains to be seen." On that sweet note, Castle turned and walked toward the conference room.

Castle's gruff manner rubbed Cole like pumice stone, but her brother's protectiveness and love for her had been beautifully transparent. Castle had cause to hate him. Cole needed to work on building a relationship with him as well.

Cutter returned with her bag and medical kit. "Do you need anything?"

"Any food around here?" Cole's appetite had kicked in with gusto.

"Janet is always bringing in stuff." He beamed. "Homemade empanadas and snickerdoodles are in the conference room."

"Great." Sounded good to his stomach. He took the bag and kit, then knocked.

"Come in," Maddox said.

Pushing through the door, he spotted her, seated on the same bench. This time, she was clean, hair dripping wet, body enveloped in a towel.

Her head hung low, shoulders hunched, saddled with emotional sandbags he wished he could remove. Had it been the ordeal of the day? Novak? Or was she still weighed down by everything between them?

She didn't meet his gaze as he sat beside her. Staring at the floor, she clasped the bench tightly as if hanging on to keep from tipping over.

"Let me look at your feet." He patted his lap and held up the med kit.

Swinging her legs, she swiveled and put her feet on his thighs. Scrapes marred the soles of her feet, alongside red bruises that were going to turn purple and a few deep cuts. He drenched some gauze pads with antiseptic and dabbed the bottoms of her feet. She flinched but didn't complain.

She was strong and courageous, and he was the luckiest damn bastard in the world. She had a tough job, one he was starting to admire, and Novak wasn't making things any easier. Emotion was a complication she couldn't afford, and he finally understood why.

He wrapped gauze around her feet as best he could without making it too bulky to pull on her shoes. "Finding Novak is the most important thing and I know you need to clear your head of everything else to focus on bringing him down." His gaze met hers. "I just want you to know that I'll do whatever I can to help you. I've got your six out there. I let you down before when you needed me most. It'll never happen again."

"Thank you. For having my back, for understanding, for risking your life by helping me with this."

"It's the least I can do. I don't deserve you. Or a second chance at happiness with you. But I hope one day you'll forgive me."

Her warm hand caressed his cheek. "I forgave you while I was held prisoner in a warehouse, forced to face the truth. It's foolish to hold on to the pain. We've both paid for our mistakes. It's time to move forward, but…"

She dropped her hand and lowered her head.

"There's something I never told you." She met his eyes. "I didn't like going to your house and being around your parents."

He blinked, caught completely off guard. "Why? My parents were always nice to you. My mother loved you."

"I thought the feel of your house, the atmosphere, would be different from mine, but there was a similar underlying sadness. A heaviness in the air from all the secrets and pretending that everything was normal when it wasn't. At the time, I didn't fully understand it, but looking back, I see that our families were two sides of the same coin. I don't know what a second chance would look like for us. What kind of atmosphere would we create together? We're not the people we used to be. We're both a bit damaged."

"We have changed, but it's like time has made us an even better fit for one another." He took her hand in his. "Some scars don't go away." He ran her fingers along the jagged line on his face. "But they can all heal. If our love can survive the last nine years, it can surmount anything."

The locker room door creaked open. "They have the threat matrixes loaded," Harper said. "They're waiting to go through them with you as soon as you're ready."

"We'll be right there." Maddox pulled away, easing to her feet, and went to the bench with the canvas bag. Nodding, Harper left.

The right words to convince her were lost to him.

They belonged together, always had, always would. They were inevitable. It was simple to him, but it wouldn't be that clear-cut to her. For now, they needed to find and stop Novak. He needed to believe that the rest, they'd work through together.

GRAY BOX HEADQUARTERS, NORTHERN VIRGINIA
4:15 P.M. EDT

Maddox loaded her gun in her shoulder holster, clipping handcuffs and an expandable steel baton to the rig. She stuffed a tube of tear gas gel in her pocket and grabbed the anti-inflammatory pain reliever from the med kit.

On the way to the conference room, she popped the pills, washing them down with water. She nabbed a seat inside next to Cole and suppressed a sigh of relief as she got off her feet.

Cole rested a hand on her knee as he inhaled a couple of empanadas.

Doc hung up the phone in the back of the room and sat. "That was the CDC. An unidentified male with an Eastern European accent called and told them to prepare for large-scale containment of a facility that would soon be attacked by a smallpox weapon. He claims he'll notify them of the location once it's too late to stop it."

Maddox's stomach dipped, tension weaving in her chest.

"Why would he show his hand by contacting the CDC?" Cole sat up in his chair, wiping his mouth with a napkin.

"Wouldn't he want this disease to get out and infect as many people as possible?" Reece asked. "This doesn't make any sense."

"It's brilliant." Maddox put her forearms on the table and folded her hands. "Makes perfect sense."

Sanborn took a seat at the head of the table. "Enlighten us."

"Novak made it clear to me he wants America's punishment to be slow and drawn out. He said he wanted to rip out the hearts of the citizens by making them watch." She met the curious gazes around the room. "When terrorists hijacked planes and crashed them into the World Trade Center, it was the worst attack on U.S. soil. The imagery of those planes hitting the buildings played on a loop, devastating us each time we watched."

Maddox swallowed back the sorrow that always welled whenever she thought of it.

"Now imagine a public facility where people have gone for entertainment gets quarantined because of a biological attack. No one in or out except the CDC doctors in hazmat. Smallpox-M takes how long to kill a person?"

"Five days," Doc said.

"Five agonizing days of waiting. News cameras posted out front, headlines about the impending gruesome deaths, with pictures and details of what it's like to die horribly, not just from smallpox, but from this amped version of smallpox-M. No vaccine. No treatment. No chance for survival. Imagine the footage of body bags coming out, played on a loop for weeks afterward." Goose bumps raised the hairs on Maddox's arms.

"Dear God." Doc put a hand to her stomach.

Maddox roped her hair into a ponytail, tugging an elastic band around the damp curls. "That would be the ultimate win for someone like Novak."

"A win we're not going to let him have." Castle pounded a fist on the table and exchanged a nod with Cole.

What the hell was that about? They were barely allies and would never be buds.

"Has the threat matrix been refined?" Maddox asked.

"Yes." Harper hit a button bringing up a color-coded matrix. "The charity event at the Hirshhorn Museum is expected to have a hundred and fifty participants. The concert at the National Gallery of Art can seat two hundred and fifty. The show at the Capital One Arena can hold almost twenty thousand. But forty thousand are expected to attend the cinema series at the Washington Convention Center."

"Shit." Reece rocked back in his chair and looked at his watch. "The concert starts in less than two hours, but won't he go for the larger numbers?"

Maddox scanned the matrix. "Not necessarily. What do we know about these events?"

"The Hirshhorn will be a list of who's who in DC, bringing in big dollars for charity," Sanborn said.

Socialites and millionaires. A distinct possibility. "The concert?"

"Classical music. Local musicians," Cutter said. "Folks from all backgrounds. It's free."

"It's still early enough in the day that children could be there." Maddox took a sip of water. "I don't think it's the concert. I think he'll avoid killing children. Women, too, if possible, but that doesn't look likely."

"The Washington Convention Center will have the biggest draw. What's playing?" Gideon asked.

"It's a marathon of the Jurassic Park films," Cole said, looking at her. "If you're right about him, he won't hit the movie series. Kids and teens will be there in droves."

"Are you sure, Maddox?" Sanborn pressed his fingers into a steeple below his chin. "You know what's at stake."

Everyone stared at her, waiting. Nothing was certain. Her heart squeezed. She couldn't get this wrong. She needed all the pieces in play before she answered. "The show at the Capital One Arena is a comedy act, right?"

"Comedian Dez Dax is performing at seven," Harper said.

Reece hiked an eyebrow. "That's not a comedy show."

"What do you mean?" Maddox folded her hands to keep them from shaking.

"It's Dez Dax. Dr. Sex." Reece swept his hands out dramatically as if she should understand.

"He used to be a comedian," Castle said. "Parlayed his skit about how to pick up a woman and have guilt-free sex into motivational speaking gigs for men. He's crazy popular. Has great advice." Castle was a womanizer who didn't like attachments. He certainly didn't need help in that department.

"So only men go to his shows?" she asked. This could be it. The break they needed so badly.

"Smart women would go to hear the techniques this guy espouses," Cutter said, "so they don't fall prey to it, but his stuff is geared toward men."

"The Ghost was a floater," Maddox said, thinking out loud, "bouncing from place to place. We have no idea if he knows enough about American culture, much less this Dax guy, to understand the perfection of the target. But a big draw event with no children and practically no women couldn't get any better for Novak."

Cole put a hand on her arm. "There was a big article about Dax in the *Washington Post* Novak had in his room. It's going to be a sold-out show. Dax is breaking record numbers, at Madison Square Garden in New York, now here. I'm sure it's been mentioned on TV too."

Her pulse pounded. Novak's profile pointed to this. But what if she was wrong?

"Is the show the target, Maddox?" Sanborn folded his arms. "What does your gut say?"

This fit everything she knew about the Ghost. This event made the most sense. "I think he'll hit the Dez Dax show. The arena is across the street from the hotel where he was staying, which would explain why he chose the Hotel Monaco. Novak would consider a job clean if it only took out men, but he'd settle for a high percentage."

She wished there was a way to confirm they were on the right track.

Scrubbing her thoughts, she searched for any overlooked details. "When we found Novak at the hotel, he was coming back from somewhere. He'd only leave the hotel for something critical like supplies or to—"

"Scout the target location," Castle said, finishing her sentence.

Maddox nodded. "Is there any way to go back through the surveillance footage around the arena for about two hours before Cole and I arrived at the hotel?"

Harper smoothed back her bun, even though not a single hair was ever out of place. "I can hack into the digital feed of the arena's security cameras and play those back." She was on her feet as she spoke, already moving toward the door.

"We need to know how to disarm the bioweapon." Maddox glanced at Reece, hoping she wouldn't need his demolition skills on this one. "Just in case."

"If I can see the wiring and it doesn't have a bi-layered backup trigger, I can disarm it. No problem."

Then why did that sound like it had the potential to be such a huge problem?

"The CDC has a portable biocontainment recepta-cle," Doc said. "But it's large and heavy and, despite the name, isn't very portable."

"Have the CDC bring it with them and we'll position you close by," Sanborn said.

"Sir." Maddox looked at Sanborn. "The Capital One Arena is huge. Twenty-five thousand square feet. A lot of terrain for five bodies to cover. We could use Cutter and Amanda out there." They both had field experience and were qualified with a firearm.

Sanborn stood, pushing his chair away from the table. "Request granted. Don't get this wrong. Recover the bioweapon. Capture or kill Novak and his son." His voice was gritty and raw and carried the force of a hammer. "And when this is over"—he pointed a stern finger between Castle and Maddox—"we're going to have a come-to-Jesus heart-to-heart."

"Roger that, sir." Castle rocked back in his chair, shoul-ders relaxed, his face the epitome of picture-perfect calm.

Sanborn clenched his jaw. His otherwise smooth aplomb remained intact as he strode out of the room. He had the power to tank their careers, but there was no way around pissing him off at this stage. They couldn't run the risk of tipping their hand to anyone that they knew about the mole. Not until Novak was in custody and singing like a canary about his expensive, powerful broker friend and all his little birdies.

Maddox looked around the room. "Tonight, we don't stop until we have Novak."

"Hooah," Reece said, letting the Army Delta in him show.

Standing, Gideon threw a stick of gum in his mouth. "Let's go catch a ghost."

32

CAPITAL PARK HOTEL, WASHINGTON, DC
6:30 P.M. EDT

Aleksander dabbed the spirit gum—a special adhesive for skin—on his eyebrows, cheeks, and chin. One strip at a time, he applied the false facial hair, transforming his brows into bushy black caterpillars. He layered thinner pieces on his jaw for the appearance of a beard.

With the dark, shaggy wig, he was a different man in the mirror. He buttoned his white shirt and took the press credentials from the bathroom sink, slipping one of the badges that'd get him and Val entry to the building around his neck.

He passed Val in the bedroom suite. His son flowed through his dance of tai chi poses, honed muscle flexing beneath taut skin.

Focused. Disciplined.

The watch with the hidden garrote looked good on Val's wrist. As if it belonged.

Aleksander double-checked the canister he'd tucked inside the professional television video camera. Both the media passes and camera had come from his contact at the TV station. Such credentials had come in handy in the past, providing access to almost anywhere. The inside of the camera was the perfect concealment for a gun, but rather than stowing a firearm, he'd had Val adjust the interior to store the bioweapon.

He strolled to the window and put in his earbuds.

Played Berlioz. *Symphonie Fantastique.*

Nonstop traffic flurried across the streets. Preoccupied people absorbed in their shallow lives packed the sidewalks like mice in a barrel. The frenetic pace of the city energized him. Or it was the booster from the medicine fortifying his bones, charging his system to a razor's edge.

He felt invincible.

Would be nice to see the Gray Box giving their last-ditch effort to find Agent Kinkade. Or to have one more update from the broker, but twelve hours from go time, he always went dark and terminated communications.

The Capital One Arena was a mere four-minute walk. This city offered many tempting targets, but the death toll of women and children at most exceeded his stomach-churning threshold. The success of this Dez Dax and his sold-out show in New York City had been splashed across the newspaper on the flight from England. Nothing personal against Dez Dax, but reading about him again in the entertainment section of the *Washington Post* cemented the target. As close to perfection as possible.

Tomorrow, he would lay Levik to rest. Val planned to buy a boat and do some sailing. His son loved the ocean. With his demon gone, Aleksander would quietly retire in the Seychelles. Sonia had wanted to honeymoon there, but they couldn't afford it on his military salary. He would've loved to have shown her the islands. Just once.

He wished he had a picture of his beautiful ladies. In this business, such personal items were a liability, but he wanted to see his Sonia and Mila as they'd once been. Happy and smiling.

Instead, he was cursed to see them lying on the ground in an assembly line of carnage. Easier for family members to identify their dead. Dismembered limbs set in a pile.

He'd sworn an oath to his family, and shortly, he'd make good on it. With those agents out of the way, how could he possibly fail?

33

CAPITAL ONE ARENA, WASHINGTON, DC
7:00 P.M. EDT

The playback of the security feed at the Capital One Arena confirmed Novak's survey of the location. It was possible the Ghost might've scoped out more than one place for the bio attack, lining up the arena as a backup. The city was ripe with potential targets, but Sanborn agreed the video combined with Maddox's hunch about the demographics at the Dez Dax show was a solid lead.

Doors opened to the general public one hour prior to the seven o'clock show time. With four entrances to the Capital One Arena, Maddox had assigned Castle, Gideon, Amanda, and Cutter to cover them. Doc was positioned in an unmarked van with a CDC unit and the biocontainment receptacle—a three-hundred-pound, hermetically sealed container that resembled a safe.

The rest of the team had taken point inside an hour ago. In coordination with arena security, they'd have eyes on everyone entering the facility.

Cole and Reece gathered around Maddox in a corner to the side, out of the way of the horde of men pouring into the entertainment center. She pulled a cap down over her hair. "Remember, I want Novak and his son alive," she said over comms to the entire team, with headquarters tuned in, not wanting to elaborate over the open channel, since someone listening was their mole.

Once they contained the bioweapon, they would clean house. Novak and his son were the only ones who could steer them in the right direction of the leak in the Gray Box.

She looked at Reece. "The ventilation system is the easiest way to disperse the weapon throughout the facility. Find someone in maintenance. Make sure access stays locked down."

"Will do." Reece took off.

She folded her arms and faced Cole, bracing for an argument. "We should split up to cover more ground."

"You know what I'm going to say. Let's not bother fighting. I stay with you."

With her injured feet and Novak having gotten the drop on her not once but twice already, she was in no position to gripe. They moved deeper into the arena by the concession stands in a spot with the best vantage point of the elevator and stairs, keeping their backs to the wall.

She didn't limp, but her gait was unnatural. Soreness raked her swollen feet with each step. She should've seen if Doc had anything to numb the bottoms of her soles.

Cole took a position within arm's reach, the side of his face with the scar obscured by a vendor display and the communications earpiece Sanborn had authorized concealed by his hair.

The place teemed with men from early twenties to midforties, even a few who looked eligible for an AARP membership. The crowd's kinetic energy grated on her senses. The noisy frat boy environment, rife with the odor of beer and greasy junk food, was right up Castle's alley.

She scanned her sector to the right while Cole surveilled left.

Masculine gazes zeroed in on her, licking the length of her body. She garnered smiles and winks, unsettling her stomach. Despite her low profile, she was attracting too much attention.

Cole followed the gaze of the gawkers and sidestepped in front of her, shielding her body without obstructing her line of sight. It worked. The guys seemed to cease noticing her.

"This is Delta. I found one of the maintenance mechanics," Reece said over open comms. "Access to the ventilation system is restricted. We're heading there now. I'll stay posted, ensure no one gets through."

"Copy that."

The minutes ticked past, drawing closer to showtime, and the crowd thickened.

Maddox scrutinized the faces who passed, her palms growing clammy, stomach rolling with jitters.

The Ghost could transform himself into almost anyone. Safe to assume his son could as well. No one could be dismissed. But whatever they looked like, regardless of their disguises, they'd need to get the canister inside the building through security, clearing a bag check.

"Alpha here," Maddox said. "Has anyone spotted a guy with a package or a bag, something that might take extra time clearing security?"

Everyone posted at an entrance checked in with a negative response.

Fifteen minutes to showtime. They were missing something. The Ghost was well prepared and wouldn't risk waiting until the last minute to get in position.

A woman in a business suit accompanied by a man with a television camera got in line at a concession stand. They both had press badges hanging around their necks.

Novak and his son had landed at the WMN-TV news station and had been inside the building for several minutes. A TV camera was large enough to house the canister.

"Bravo," she said to Castle, "is the security liaison still with you at the F Street entrance?"

"Yeah, why?"

"Are the media expected to be here tonight? If so, why haven't we seen any reporters come in?"

The line fell quiet as she waited.

"Shit," Castle said. "Reporters started arriving at seven thirty. They were invited by Dez Dax and he plans to give round-robin interviews after the show. There's a separate entrance for the press. Head of security didn't think to tell us, because the general public can't get through it. All reporters have to show valid credentials."

She gritted her teeth. "If they have a list of attendees, ask if WMN-TV is on it."

Gut-wrenching silence. Anxiety pulsed through her in time with the seconds she waited.

"One reporter and a cameraman from WMN-TV."

Maddox's spine prickled. "Homebase," she said, addressing Harper back at the Gray Box, who was tapped into the arena's security. "Find the camera feed for the press entrance. Rewind. Novak and his son came through sometime within the last twenty minutes."

"On it," Harper said. It took less than three minutes for her to respond. "Two men from WMN-TV arrived ten minutes ago. Reporter with shaggy brown hair, beard, white shirt, black pants, glasses. Younger cameraman, blond hair, messy fringe haircut, blue shirt, black pants. Handheld TV camera. No bag. Over."

Aleksander, the Ghost, was posing as a reporter. His son, Val, had the TV camera.

"Homebase, we need to find them. Now." Her heartbeat quickened as she eased away from the display, sweeping the crowd.

Cole stiffened, shoulders straightening, every muscle poised for action.

"Doc, reposition inside the garage connected to the arena," she said, praying it wouldn't come to a quarantine. If it did, the facility would be sealed with twenty thousand of them inside.

"We're moving now, prepared to initiate level-four biocontainment if necessary."

Phantom fingers formed a fist and pressed into Maddox's gut, stirring her to move. She strode through a throng of men flowing in from the street toward the stadium and concession stands, making her way to the stairs for a higher vantage point.

Cole entered the mass of people funneling deeper into the complex, toward the center of the arena by the elevators. He glanced back at her as if reluctant to put too much distance between them. She gave a hand signal for him to continue the sweep, hoping he understood that sometimes, having her six meant following orders.

This time, he didn't hesitate. He gave a nod and pressed on.

She climbed the stairs, sticking close to the wall, scanning the crowd.

Cole did a pass of the elevators and met her gaze. He gave the negative sign. She held up her index and middle fingers and gestured to the level above. He acknowledged with a nod.

"We're going to sweep inside the stadium." She went higher.

"I found them," Harper cut in. "They just exited the elevator, making their way into the stadium. Section 101."

The knot behind Maddox's solar plexus tightened. Her pulse was pounding now, strong and steady, driving her to move faster. "Delta, find someone from security to ensure that maintenance stays locked down, and get inside the stadium."

"Copy," Reece said.

"Everyone else, hold positions at the exits. Have security lock down the press entrance. The Novaks don't get out." Maddox elbowed her way through the sluggish mass up to the landing, gritting her teeth from the pain of her sore feet.

Cole bolted past her into the crowd, knocking guys out of his path.

"Homebase," she said to Harper, "keep eyes on them. Make sure they don't double-back and slip by us."

"Okay."

Maddox squeezed through the crowd filtering into the stadium. "Out of the way. Coming through. Make a hole!"

Men staggered to the side, allowing her to pass. She dashed into section 101.

The arena lights dimmed. A bright spotlight bathed the stage. The high-voltage crowd buzzed with excitement as the opening act came out to warm up the audience.

Cole stalked left, sweeping section 100 straight down the middle, right to 101, and left to 121 along the center.

Maddox moved counterclockwise to the right, scanning up over the club sections and down the main concourse. Men making their way to their seats obstructed her line of sight. Grabbing hold of the railing, she climbed up to the club level for a higher vantage point.

She spied a man with blond hair and blue shirt standing with his back to her down the walkway on the lower level. A gaggle of men streamed across the main aisle, blocking her view, but Cole was closer with a better angle.

"Romeo," she said to Cole, "at your eight o'clock, between the main concourse section 119 and club section 226. Near the stage."

She clenched her tingling fingers into sweaty fists and backtracked clockwise along the upper level where the aisle was less crowded. She kept a fix on blondie with the blue shirt.

The horde thinned, peeling off to their seats, and a clear view opened. He had a professional television camera set on a tripod. It was Val. But where was Aleksander?

"Romeo, Tango has a camera." Maddox shoved through the crowd, weaving around people. Staying on the second concourse, she maneuvered closer to the stage.

Cole charged across the lower-level walkway, ducking past men.

"Homebase, do you have eyes on the main Tango? Where is the Ghost?"

"He disappeared," Harper said.

Shit.

Val opened the camera, pulled a metal container about sixteen inches in length from the side. Then he bent, dropping out of sight.

"Check," she said, indicating a positive ID on the bioweapon. "I repeat, Check. Delta, get to the stadium ASAP."

Cole elbowed someone hard to the side, nearly knocking a young guy over the railing.

Val homed in on the commotion in Cole's direction. He spun on his heel and rabbited from the stadium into the arena's lobby.

Cole tore past stragglers taking seats, dashing in pursuit of Val, leaving the stadium.

"Make some noise," the guy who was the opening act said, "and let me hear how excited you are to see Dez Dax tonight."

The crowd went wild. "Dr. Sex! Dr. Sex!"

Maddox raced to the nearest stairwell, flying down the steps between sections 227 and 226. At the bottom on the main concourse walkway, she hesitated. A man appeared out of the shadows and stepped into the dim light of the aisle up to the mounted camera. Shaggy brown hair, white shirt.

Novak. It was Aleksander Novak. Her insides knotted.

He tipped the canister with his toe, sending the bioweapon rolling off the main walkway under the seats. Then he looked around as if checking the area.

Their eyes met for an instant.

Maddox bolted toward him.

He smiled, that crazy-evil grin, and scrammed.

"Main Tango confirmed." She sprinted to the television camera and dropped to the ground. Without thinking about what filth she was lying on, she reached down and felt around. Her fingertips stroked smooth, cold metal. She pressed up against the back of the seat and stretched. Curling her fingers around the canister, she pulled it up.

A red timer counted down.

"Checkmate," she said, indicating they had an active bioweapon. "Delta, we have six minutes, thirty seconds. Do you read me?"

Not enough time to evacuate. It'd only start a panicked stampede. And the garage was a good mile away. Even if her feet were in tip-top condition, she wouldn't reach the biocontainment receptacle in time, and she couldn't let the Ghost slip away.

"Roger," Reece said in her ear. "I'm in the stadium. Section 115."

"Get to 119." Maddox spotted Joe Miller, the head of arena security she'd coordinated with upon arrival, entering the area and thrust the weaponized smallpox into his hands. "We have a situation," she said, ensuring the team heard over the open channel. "That's a weapon of mass destruction. Don't let it out of your sight. Only give it to Special Agent Delta."

She pointed out Reece, who was within sight and closing in.

The guard's brows shot up and his eyes widened with alarm. "What? Why is this thing counting down?"

She took off after the Ghost, down the stairs closest to the stage.

Two more guards were unconscious at the foot of the steps. Several onlookers in the crowd nearby had their cell phones out, lights illuminated, as if they'd taken video or photos of what'd happened.

She leapt onto the corner of the stage. A thousand tiny fires sparked in her feet. She ducked backstage and collided with a security guard speaking into a walkie talkie.

"Did you see a man run by?" she asked. "Dark hair. White shirt. Press credentials."

"Yeah. East hall."

Maddox raced down the backstage steps, drawing her Maxim 9. "Doc, initiate containment protocol and ensure the biocontainment box is ready."

"Okay," Doc said.

"Delta here," Reece said in her ear. "Checkmate secured. No time to attempt disarmament. Headed to Doc."

Leading with her gun, Maddox tracked the trail of stunned gazes down the east hall.

Cole chased Novak's son past concessions. Their feet pounded across the smooth tile floor with Cole gaining ground.

Val ducked into an open elevator, and the doors started to close.

Cole powered through his stride and shoved a boot

through the gap in the safety retractors. The elevator jolted and opened. Cole jumped into the cab, taking a defensive stance. He was keyed to the max.

The doors slid shut, sealing them in the metal box. Val charged in a fury, swinging a right hook. Cole swatted the punch and blocked an incoming thrust of a raised knee, then threw a fist that glanced off Val's jaw without doing damage.

Val power-drove a forearm into Cole's throat. Sinewy muscle jammed into his Adam's apple, and his skull smashed against the metal wall. His ears rang, air wheezing through his constricted windpipe. A dark heat rose in his chest, fueling his rage.

This man had helped kidnap Maddox. Helped hurt her.

Cole dug both thumbs into Val's eye sockets.

With a startled hiss, Val staggered back. Cole slapped the alarm button, jerking the elevator to a halt. He pressed in, drove an uppercut to the man's chin, knocking him on his heels.

Val's head snapped back, and Cole pushed on. Not slowing. Not hesitating. He had the Ghost's son, wanted to smash in his face, hungered to give him a beatdown.

Machine-gun-fire momentum lit through Cole. He drove his knee up into Val's body as he grabbed the man's shoulders, hauling him into the sharp thrust. Without giving an inch, Cole smashed the heels of his palms against the man's ears. Val reared back and slumped to the floor.

Cole's pulse jackhammered in a haze and his breath came hard. Hellfire pumped in his system. He slammed his boot into Val's face and body. Once, twice, and kept raining on him.

Bones cracked. Flesh bruised. Blood splattered across the floor, turning it red and slick.

"Mercy!" Val could barely raise a pleading hand. A battered heap of a man, cowering, covered in blood. "My father spared your woman. Showed her mercy."

Cole kicked him one last time, and Val slumped in the corner, knocked unconscious, before the word penetrated.

Mercy.

Mercy cut through the fog of violence and revenge, bringing Cole back to himself. What was he doing?

He stumbled away, sore fists shaking at his sides.

Alive. She wanted them alive.

What would Maddox think of him?

An out of control monster, thirsting for revenge. No better than the Ghost or his son.

Val looked like a deflated balloon, head to his chest, face bloodied, out cold.

Cole had to be better. For himself. For Maddox. She deserved better.

He turned to the control panel of the elevator and rested his aching forehead on the cool steel. The salty bite of his own blood filled his mouth. He released the alarm button. The metal box jerked into motion, and he lifted his head.

A gray flash of wire swept past his eyes and nose. His mind registered what was happening and he thrust his left hand up, but not fast enough. The garrote wrapped around Cole's throat. The vicious bite of the cord against his trachea pinched his airway closed immediately.

Val tightened the strangulation device, hauling Cole back onto his heels.

The fiber wire cut into his skin. He struggled, clawing at the thin cord, unable to get a purchase. Frantic, on pure instinct, he threw his skull backward, aiming for Val's face. Again and again—no contact. Val kept his head out of range.

Gasping, Cole kicked at the elevator panel to open the doors. The alarm shrieked, and the elevator jerked to a stop.

Cole pounded with his foot and scratched at the wire. Pushing off the door in a hard shove, he used the leverage to propel them in a surge of force. They crashed into the wall. Air left Val's mouth in a harsh rush, but his hold around Cole's throat didn't slacken.

It tightened. Too tight. A guttural roar blasted in Cole's ear.

He thrust his free elbow into the man's gut and side. Val kept his grip.

Panic swelled along with the trapped air burning Cole's lungs. The garrote stayed taut, digging into his throat. Moisture on his neck. The metallic scent of his own blood hit him.

Desperation was a hot whip lashing him. His heart a painful never-ending throb. He had to get this man off.

Now!

Or he was going to die.

Cole reached behind his back, shoving his hand in the paper-thin space between their bodies, and pulled his Browning blade. He twisted his hand, rotating his shoulder, and plunged the knife into flesh. And he didn't stop stabbing until the garrote loosened and slipped free.

Three distraught service workers hovered around the entrance to the Washington Wizards locker room. One had a broken nose. He cupped his bleeding nostrils, his head tilted forward.

"Did a man run in there? Glasses? Dark hair?" Maddox asked through ragged breaths.

The three nodded. "Some crazy guy. He hit Mike when we told him the locker room was off-limits."

"Is there another way out of there?"

"No."

"This is Bravo," Castle said over the comms. "Exits are locked down. We're headed into the stadium."

"Find Romeo. I'm at the locker room." Maddox threw open one of the heavy double doors.

The short hallway was clear.

She crept down the corridor, past the Wizards' silver emblem on the wall and framed pictures of players in action. Pivoting left, she swept into the brightly lit, empty locker room.

Wooden cubbies lined two walls. Plasma screens hung from another and a whiteboard on the fourth. Corners were clear. No doors on the hardwood cabinetry. Nowhere to hide.

Adrenaline mainlined in her veins. She prowled around the corner to the threshold of an adjoining room. The lights were off, but she made out stacks of towels and massage tables in the darkness.

All her senses were heightened and alert. She paused and listened, straining to pick up the slightest movement, her breath controlled. There was only the sound of her blood thundering in her ears.

She eased into the shadows. Spine to the doorjamb, she fumbled along the wall for a light switch. The room was large, too dark, too silent, with plenty of objects to hide behind.

Stomach acid surged into her chest. Her grip on the gun was steady, heart rapping hard against her rib cage as her eyes adjusted to the lack of light. She found the switch and flipped it.

Fluorescent tubes flickered on and buzzed. Harsh white light bathed the room.

Novak charged her with a trash can. Slamming the hard plastic bin into her, he knocked the gun from her hands, sending her into a spin deeper into the therapy room.

Her 9mm clattered to the floor, steel skidding across the tile.

She gained her bearings and popped the retention release on the baton, flicking it with her wrist, expanding the full twenty-six inches.

Novak closed in. Blindingly fast. Boogeyman eyes raged behind glasses. He lobbed a foam roller at her head.

She ducked, sidestepping, and swung the baton, belting him with lightning strikes.

He didn't slow. Didn't seem to feel the popping bite of any of her strikes. Just kept storming forward with shocking force like a freakish Terminator. Teeth bared. Snarling.

With each startling advance, he pressed her backward. Herding her to a corner. Where he'd have her trapped. Pinned. Able to hurt her badly.

She raised her right knee high and thrust her foot out

with all the power she could muster. Her well-aimed heel connected with his groin. It should've dropped him, but it didn't. A swift follow-up kick to his gut propelled him back inches, giving her a narrow opening.

And she took it.

Desperate to put space between herself and Novak's grasp, she scrambled away from him. She spotted her gun under the massage table and went for it.

Scalding pain tore into her scalp, and she was wrenched back on her heels as he snatched her ponytail. On reflex, she reached for her hair.

He knocked the baton from her fingers and threw her against the wall. Her head bounced off the sheetrock with a crack, knocking the comms piece out of her ear.

A brutal stab of agony mushroomed in her skull. She fought to keep her eyes open, not let her knees buckle. The tang of aluminum filled her mouth. She blocked and threw punches on instinct, her aim wild as her vision cleared.

Until a vicious blow sent her sprawling.

With horror movie speed, he caught her in a rear headlock, keeping her upright on her feet. His arm was an iron band around her throat.

The natural inclination was to lean back to lighten the pressure on the windpipe. If you did, you'd be defenseless with no balance and your attacker would have you.

She shrugged her shoulders, creating a pocket of space, and tucked her chin into the crook of his elbow, clutching the inside of his arm. She pitched forward from the waist, bending at the knees, and drove a heel into his instep to get his hold to loosen.

Growling in her ear, he jerked her side to side, trying

to knock her off balance. Sounding like a deranged beast that wanted to tear the flesh from her limbs. She stepped her foot behind his, locking his leg, and popped her elbow back into his solar plexus. With the other hand, she twisted his wrist, spun out of his grasp, and, planting her free foot, torqued his arm to throw him to the ground.

The technique was precise, flawless, but he seized her jacket, yanking her down along with him. They smacked to the cold tile in a tangle, rolling, punching.

He outweighed her by a good forty pounds and was amped to a manic level. But she was strong and fast, had years of vigorous training, and she fought him with everything in her.

She jabbed at the stab wound she'd given him in the fight on the boat, trying to exploit his one apparent weakness.

Sweet Jesus! Why didn't he wince? Why didn't he show any signs of a physical deficit?

In a blink, he threw a headbutt, rattling her brain, and flipped her onto her back.

She deflected his blows and pivoted her hips forward, kicking him, driving his body further down hers. Grabbing one of his arms, she threw her legs straight up, wrapping them around his neck, and punched his other arm between her thighs. She had his head trapped low by her hips and had his free arm locked in her grip. Using her legs, she applied as much pressure as she could to his neck, shutting off his airway.

A solid triangle choke hold.

All she had to do was squeeze her thighs. Squeeze

hard. Keep her grip on his arm. Bring him deeper into the submission hold. Not let go.

His features contorted into something ghoulish. Eyes full of nightmarish determination drilled into her like hot nails. Then everything changed, and her advantage evaporated. So fast but so mind-boggling, it unfolded in slow motion.

The Ghost rose up on his knees, hoisting her entire body from the floor with him. Like a damn machine.

What kind of drug was he on?

Her heart ricocheted. The only thing keeping him from killing her was her grip on his arm and her legs squeezing his throat.

A demented smile broke through his feral snarl.

In some unstoppable wrestler move, he slammed her against the floor. Breath flew from her lips like a popped balloon. Pain and panic crashed through her, sending hope into a tailspin.

Everything in her went slack. Fingers, legs, heart. The world hazed white.

He seized her neck in a stranglehold. She was stunned, lungs straining. He had her hips locked down, but she tried to gain leverage with her legs, her heels scraping the floor. For such a slender man, he was so heavy and strong.

A scathing ache pulsed like an angry heartbeat from her head to her tailbone. Her mind spun, thoughts racing—to Cole. She loved him. Wanted to live—for him. She should've told him it didn't matter what their second chance looked like, as long as they were together.

Calm settled over her. She had to do something. Anything. Like hell she'd let Novak win.

Maddox clawed at his hands, scratched his face. All in vain. The Ghost's hands squeezed her jugular, dragging her closer to death. Darkness edged her vision.

She groped her jacket for the tube of tear gas. Her pockets were empty.

Where was it? Did it fall out in the struggle?

"I ran and I knew you'd follow," he said in a hiss of berserk fury. "Knew I'd get you alone. I swore I'd kill you, Kinkade, and I'm a man of my word."

She extended her fingers and struck at his throat. One of his hands lifted from her, and the pressure eased enough for her to suck in a clipped breath.

His fist pumped into her face with a thick, meaty sound. Her head jacked right. Light bloomed behind her eyes, ears ringing; her teeth tore into her lip and blood filled her mouth.

She was dazed, everything swam, but her fate was clear. And it wasn't good.

For one brilliant instant, she saw Cole, heard his voice.

Move, honey. Or you're as good as dead. Move!

Tear gas, she thought again frantically and patted her pants, this time in a frenzied search.

"Not with a knife or a gun. Just my bare hands." Novak clamped down on her windpipe as he leaned over her into the hold for added power.

There. The tear gas was in her right pocket.

She dug in her jeans, nails nipping the tube and slipping from the metal. With her other hand, she hit at his throat and arms and chest, each blow growing weaker. She was tiring, desperate for air.

The burn in her lungs, the unbearable pressure was too

much. His hands tightened around her throat, and it seemed as though her head might burst like a squeezed grape.

"Doesn't get more intimate than this," he said, his voice rough, barely human. He drew his face close to hers as if he might bite her. Or, God forbid, kiss her.

Worse, he exceeded her imagination.

His tongue flicked out, and he licked her cheek in one long, disgusting sweep.

Catching a grip on the small cylinder with her fingertips, she worked it up her pocket and pulled it into her palm. She closed her fist around the tear gas, thumbed off the top, and sprayed his eyes.

The best thing about the gel was no danger of blowback in her face.

Howling like a wounded wild thing, he reared back, his weight rising off her, and wiped at his eyes with his sleeves.

She raked in a coughing breath. Her raw throat burned. Calling upon whatever strength she had left, she drew her knees into her chest and kicked him full out. He toppled like a chopped-down tree.

Sucking in deep, ragged breaths, she spied the dull gleam of her gun.

He shrieked and thrashed on the floor, swabbing his eyes with his shirt.

She rolled to her hands and knees and grabbed the 9mm, leveling the barrel at him. It was then she realized she was trembling. She scrambled to her feet as he made his way up on his. When her mind cleared, the black edges around her vision lifted, and her aim sharpened.

Novak spun around, his face fierce. Their gazes

snagged. She steadied her shaking weapon hand with the other. He squinted at her with red, swollen eyes and launched forward at her with nightmarish intensity.

She wanted to blow a hole in his skull. Paint the walls with his blood and brain matter.

But they needed him alive.

She shifted her aim from center mass and shot him in the leg. He fell to his knees. Glaring, he crawled undaunted in her direction, fueled by some demonic willpower.

As he reached out for her, she put a second slug in his hand and kicked him away.

Castle barreled into the therapy room and stopped short, taking in the sight.

"Your timing sucks." She took a step, rubbery knees threatening to give, and leaned against the wall. Her insides quivered like battered Jell-O. Experience had taught her that by morning, she'd feel the ache of every wretched bruise.

Castle cuffed the Ghost, hands behind his back. "You did all the hard work. My timing is shit-hot."

"The bioweapon?" she asked, regaining her bearings.

"Reece made it with thirty seconds to spare," Castle said. "It's contained."

"Cole? Is he okay?" It was as if the universe hung in suspended animation as she waited for an answer.

34

CAPITAL ONE ARENA, WASHINGTON, DC
7:45 P.M. EDT

Cole sat in the back of an ambulance, letting the EMT flash a light in his eyes while he nursed his bandaged throat. The tech had gotten the bleeding to stop, and he was fortunate there was no permanent damage or need for stitches.

The building hadn't been locked down under quarantine, and he heard the CDC was pulling out, which meant the bioweapon was contained.

Maddox pushed through the arena doors onto F Street. His heart rolled over in his chest. She looked like the devil had chewed her up and spit her out, but she was alive. And nothing else mattered. He nudged the fussing EMT to the side, leaped out of the ambulance, and ran to her. She flung herself at him, and he caught her close against his body, his arms snapping around her like bands of steel.

Their arms twined around each other in a desperate clinch. She shivered in his arms, her head tucked under his chin. He held her tighter. Holding her had never felt so good, so precious.

Tomorrow wasn't guaranteed. He would make the most of every single day he had with her. No more regrets.

He cupped her bruised face. "You okay?" His voice was raspy. Each word burned his sore throat.

"Yeah, or I will be." She yanked back, lightly touched the bandage on his neck, and her gaze fell to his bloodied clothes. Alarm widened her eyes. "Cole—"

"Most of it isn't mine," he reassured her.

"You look awful, like you've been through the grinder."

"Me? Have you looked in the mirror?" He curled an arm around her and cradled her head against his chest.

She roped her arms around him, clutching his shirt, and a shudder ran through her. "Thank God you're okay. I can't lose you again."

"You won't." He kissed the top of her head. "Never again."

She peered up at him, her eyes misting, and nodded. "Is that Val's blood on you?"

"For a thoughtless, ruthless minute, I wanted to kill him. As though taking his life would've made me feel better, like more of a man after they kidnapped you. Then I came to my senses, because I knew you'd be ashamed of me and that you needed them alive. I tried not to kill him, but…"

She caressed his jaw, running her fingers over his two-day stubble. "You are my personal hero. And I could never be ashamed of you. Never."

He rested his forehead on hers, wondering how he had made it without her and this unconditional comfort. "Are you sure you don't want to upgrade me to superhero?"

"Don't push it." She chuckled and hugged him close. "Thank you for not dying on me." The hug tightened, rooting him in gratitude before her arms loosened, and she looked up at him. "I need you. I love you, Cole. No matter how we've changed or what our second chance looks like. I want it. I want you."

"You've got me." He brushed his thumb along her cheek.

"I think we've earned our shot at happiness."

"Yeah, we have." He glanced at his bruised knuckles. "Is Aleksander alive?"

"We have him in custody. I'll get answers out of him. We just can't let him know his son is dead."

GRAY BOX HEADQUARTERS, NORTHERN VIRGINIA
8:35 P.M. EDT

Maddox stood in the hall outside interrogation room one beside Cole.

A few more hours and this mission with Novak would be behind her, and she could enjoy the prospect of having a real life. A full life for the first time, with everything she wanted but had been too afraid to dream of.

Sanborn shook Cole's hand. "Thank you for the detailed debrief and for your assistance."

Cole pressed a hand to his throat. "Have you been able to find out who the seller was behind the auction?"

"Amanda, Willow, and Daniel are going to turn their focus to that in the morning. Willow discovered the *Le Monde* newspaper used in the proof of product video could've been purchased from any number of shops here in DC or New York. There's no way to isolate where the video was filmed. At least we have Aleksander Novak and the bioweapon. A huge win for us. One we wouldn't have gotten without you," Sanborn said. "You turned out to be an invaluable asset. I'd love for you to consider joining us."

Anytime Sanborn spotted talent, he went into recruitment mode. No way would he pass up a chance to add Cole to his prized collection.

"I can guarantee fulfilling work far beyond what you're doing in the private sector, where I suspect you're underutilized and have to put up with a fair degree of bullcrap. As a bonus, you'd get to see a heck of a lot more of Maddox than you will otherwise. Picture an adrenaline-filled deployment somewhere sandy together."

Cole smiled at Maddox, raking his long hair back, and her heart fluttered. He was so kick-ass cool, she wanted to kiss him.

"Thank you for the tempting offer. But you can't afford me, and I'm not taking a pay cut."

She hiked an eyebrow. "What kind of paycheck do you bring home?"

"The sweet six-figure kind."

Her breath caught. "How sweet?"

"Probably three times what you're making."

"Sorry, sir," she said to Sanborn. "But he can't quit."

The three of them shared a light chuckle.

"I should probably be the one recruiting for my boss. Donovan Carmichael could use some of your black ops folks."

"Donovan and I go way back from our former days at the Agency. He'd love to get his hands on my people, but I pity the person foolish enough to poach from me." Sanborn gave a wolfish smile.

Cole raised his palms in a hands-off gesture.

"I'm afraid you can't sit in on Novak's interrogation," Sanborn said. "You're free to go, but Maddox will be done soon if you'd like to wait for her in the conference room."

Cole cupped her arm, caressing her with his intense gaze. Her face heated, and her soul sighed. She was so thankful and ecstatic to have him back, and she'd show him every day.

"I'll wait," he said.

She nodded. "See you in a few."

Sanborn opened the door to the viewing room that looked in on the interrogation cell through one-way glass. "Daniel, escort Cole to the conference room. See that he has anything he needs to be comfortable."

As Daniel Cutter joined them in the hall, he looked the happiest Maddox had ever seen him. Almost satisfied for once. Working the case with them must've been a boost. Maybe the guy would tone down his gung ho style.

The entire team had pulled together, unlike any other op, to get this mission done. Made them tighter, stronger than ever. Ironic considering there was a mole in their midst.

"Novak keeps asking for coffee, food, and to see his son," Cutter said.

Sanborn's lips flattened into a tight line. "Let Janet know to get him something."

"Sir," Maddox said, "Novak is in pain and uncomfortable and I'd rather keep him that way until he starts talking. I need some concrete answers first."

"Okay." Sanborn nodded and gestured to Cutter that it was okay to leave.

Cutter chatted with Cole on their way to the conference room, passing Nicole Tully, who carried a microwaveable meal, looking the same as she always did, probably headed to the ITM section.

No one appeared any less innocent or guiltier. No one was the slightest bit out of character, as if they were on edge from harboring a terrible secret. Since the yacht, she'd made a list of everyone in the Gray Box, checking it twice—*was it him, or maybe her?*—but none of them struck her as the traitorous type. They were some of the best spies in the world and couldn't tell who the liar playing them for fools was.

And that made their predicament horrifying.

"Maddox, you and Castle owe me an explanation." Sanborn's voice was firm and coarse.

She braced herself. "Sir, if you don't mind letting me question Novak, I think everything will become clear."

"All right. But I expect full transparency."

Maddox gathered her thoughts, took a deep breath, and entered interrogation room one.

Sitting in a chair, Novak clutched his bandaged hand. His wrist was handcuffed to the bolted-down steel table. His face was scratched and bruised. Weary eyes reflected the dissipation of adrenaline and whatever he'd been hopped up on.

She sat across from him. "If you're in a lot of pain,

Doc can give you something." In an hour or two, they might consider giving him a couple of acetaminophen tablets.

"No. Just hot coffee and something to eat."

"First, you need to answer a few questions. We know why you wanted to kill all those people. What we don't know is who helped you along the way. Who is your mysterious, powerful friend? Who leaked my name? That I would be at the auction? Where I live?"

A laugh came out as a snort. "What do I get in return? Needs to be more than food and coffee."

"Depends on the value of your information."

He sat silent, staring at the one-way glass like he could see through it with the sheer power of his mind.

Maddox's thoughts offered up a hundred ways for Gideon to torture him, but with Novak's training, he'd resist. Not break. "What do you want in exchange?"

"Immunity. For me and my son."

She folded her arms. "You don't strike me as a snitch. Why are you willing to give up your source?"

"Boils down to survival. I want immunity. My son's freedom."

"Let me hear what you have to bargain with."

"From time to time, I use an information broker. Powerful. Well-connected. Fast. Always reliable. He's provided me with the intelligence I've needed to pull off several jobs. He notified me about the auction for the smallpox weapon. I paid him a considerable sum for information on all the buyers. His person on the inside *here* told him you'd attend the auction and warned me not to attend, since it was a trap."

Acid grated the back of her throat. "Tell me about the mole in our agency."

"I don't know who it is, only their code name. But it's someone close enough to you, Maddox Kinkade, to send my broker detailed information about you, at my request, in under eight hours."

Her nape prickled. He could be lying. "Exactly what detailed information was provided?"

"Besides your home address? Marital status. Habits, like a predictable morning jog, rain or shine. Vices. Such as frequenting Rocky's Bar with your coworkers. I could delve a little further." His voice dipped to a whisper and that creepy grin swept over his face. "But I don't know if Scarface is listening. Hearing how you pick up men at the bar might upset him."

A chill turned her heart to ice. She wanted to look away—hell, she wanted to crawl under the damn table and shrivel into nothing—but she held his entertained gaze.

The unsettling details he knew didn't narrow down the suspects. The ITM section had access to personnel records and could've easily looked up her address. Her marital status and predilection for jogging, sometimes doing so on the grounds here, were common knowledge. Everyone went to Rocky's, including Sybil Parker's minions and topside security.

The Gray Box employees got a discount because Rocky was the sister-in-law of one of the guys deployed and the team looked out for her.

Maddox never hid the fact that she left the bar with men on occasion any more than the others did when they picked up women. They never boasted, but they did share tidbits during typical office banter in the gym, break room, never thinking it was a weakness an eavesdropper might exploit. The only one who didn't screw and tell was Gideon.

"I can't give you the mole, but I can give you the broker. Not only how to make contact, but how to lure him out into the open. If you have him, you'll have your mole." His grin spread, and he even dared to chuckle. "And I say that knowing whoever is selling your secrets is worth far more than me and my son. In the immunity deal, there can be a stipulation that if I don't hold up my end, the deal is null and void. But once I've given you proof, we must be freed at once."

Cocky bastard.

"It'll take time to verify any evidence you give us."

He lifted a finger and wagged it back and forth, rattling the chains attached to his cuffs. "This is nonnegotiable. I can have a microchip delivered with information you can act on immediately. Then my son and I are to be released, not handed off to another agency." His smile slipped, and his eyes flickered for the first time with a hint of genuine fear. "Not the FBI, not the U.S. Marshals, not local police. The broker has people everywhere. I doubt we'd survive the transfer, and if we did, it wouldn't be for long."

"You expect me to believe this broker has a vast network of spies embedded throughout the intelligence community?"

With a snort, Novak shook his head. "He turned someone in here. An agency that isn't supposed to exist." His tone all but screamed *you idiot, doubt me at your own peril.* "You've no clue what you're dealing with. The magnitude of it. How far the broker will go to protect his empire."

Her cautious skepticism evaporated. This was bad, as bad as it got in their line of work.

"Why so glum, Agent Kinkade? You should be preparing to celebrate with the information I'm going to give. Instead, you look like you're going to a funeral."

This catastrophe could very well bury the Gray Box, ruin the U.S. intelligence community as a whole, and destroy careers. Glum was an understatement.

"What's the code name of our mole?" Maddox asked.

He pursed his lips, eyes gleaming like they were playing a game.

"Tell me as a show of good faith and we'll see about getting you some coffee and food."

"Your mole is code-named Cobalt. To learn more, Val and I need immunity."

Cobalt didn't ring any bells.

"The name of the broker?" she pressed.

He flashed that taunting, superior smile she hated and made a show of zipping his lips.

Maddox stood, squaring her shoulders. "Let me speak with my boss."

"I want to see my son."

"Once we finalize the deal, we'll put you in a room with him."

"Ticktock, Agent Kinkade."

Shutting the door behind her, she let out a quivery breath. *Holy shit.*

She rushed into the observation room.

Sanborn practically slapped her with his stern gaze as she closed the door. "I have a stranger in my freaking house!"

Everyone in the room froze at his raised voice. The DGB didn't yell. Never cursed. He was the epitome of smooth, unruffled power.

"And you all"—Sanborn pointed to her, Castle, Reece, and Gideon—"thought, in your infinite wisdom, it was best not to tell me and handle this on your own?" His anger was so tangible, she wouldn't have been surprised to see steam rising from him.

Maddox stepped forward. "We didn't know who we could trust. Still don't, but if the mole knew we were on to him, it could've compromised the mission."

"It was my idea to leave you out of the loop," Castle said, taking the major hit. He met her eyes, and she spotted a glimmer of friendliness. "The prime directive had to come first."

"Good initiative, *horrible* judgment. I take it Mr. Matthews knows we have a leak?"

She nodded.

Sanborn shuttered his eyes, his face grim. "Even the civilian knows." *While I was in the dark.* He neglected to say the words, but he didn't have to.

She cringed on the inside at the hurt and disappointment in his expression, in his tone.

Yes, in a way, it was an awful betrayal. Albeit a necessary one.

They still had to investigate everyone in the building, including him. Now Sanborn knew that they knew about a traitor, if he was indeed the mole—which she doubted—it'd be damn near impossible to catch him, unless the evidence from Novak fingered Sanborn irrefutably.

He rubbed his brow and glanced at his watch. "I can get the ball rolling on immunity for Novak, but I won't be able to get anything in writing until midmorning."

"When do we tell him about his son?" Maddox asked. "I lied and told him we'd put him in a room with Val. The minute Novak finds out his son is lying in a morgue, he's going to lose it."

Sanborn stared at Novak through the one-way glass and a haunted look clouded his eyes.

"He almost killed twenty thousand people, including us," Reece said. "I say we tell him after he signs the deal and we verify the microchip isn't chicken feed that'll have us chasing our own tails, tying us in knots."

Sometimes chicken feed—worthless information— glittered like gold. They had to exercise extreme caution, and verification would take time.

"So what if you lied to that monster about his son?" Reece was a good man, one of the most honest and honorable she knew, but his words belied his issues with not wanting to have children. Complicated issues that had ended his marriage.

Sanborn lowered his head. "He may be a monster and a terrorist." His voice grew quiet and gentle. "But he's also a father. There's nothing worse than the pain of losing a child." The usual cool, clinical veneer cracked, revealing real sorrow that twisted something in Maddox's chest. "Children are supposed to bury their parents, not the other way around." He swallowed, cleared his throat, and said, "I should be the one to tell him. After we know the information he gives us is legitimate."

The loss shrouding him was unmistakable. Sanborn was a father and had suffered the agony of burying a child. From the somber expressions of the others, they hadn't known either.

She might've picked up on it when he talked about her miscarriage if she hadn't been wallowing in the mire of her own convoluted emotions.

"I'm sorry." The rest of her condolences stuck in her mouth when she sensed the gazes of the others slide to her. Their unease about broaching a subject personal for Sanborn mingled with her own. "That we couldn't bring Val in alive. That you'll be the one to deliver the news."

"It's a part of the job." Drawing in a sharp breath, his face turned stoic and his shoulders went straight as a soldier's. "No one outside this room is to know we have a mole, so we can get this broker and plug our leak. Understood?"

Everyone nodded.

"We'll put our heads together and come up with a game plan. But that *we* doesn't include you, Maddox."

"What? Why?"

"Because you need downtime. Forty-eight hours."

"But—"

"Don't misunderstand. I'm hot enough to boil your grits right now for withholding this information from me. But you were almost blown up on a yacht, tased, drugged, and kidnapped, and you've been turning and burning for over a week." He put a hand on her shoulder and concern filled his eyes. "Forty-eight hours R&R. I'm not asking. I'm ordering. Don't even take the time to write an after-action report. Just get out of here. I'll recall Alistair and Ares. They'll help while you're out. When you get back, take care of your paperwork and be prepared for me to work you to the bone until we find this damn mole. Then I'm going to drag Cobalt over the coals."

35

ARLINGTON, VIRGINIA
9:27 P.M. EDT

They'd both been through the wringer, had the shit beaten out of them, and every part of his body hurt. His throat, even his fingers.

Everything except his heart.

Cole pulled his bike into the attached garage of his town house, comforted by the solid warmth of Maddox snuggled up close behind him.

The garage door closed. They dismounted, tugging off their helmets.

She smiled at him through the weariness and past the ache of her bruises. Just like that, he forgot about his pain. Hope shimmered between them, and for the first time in nearly a decade, he looked forward to tomorrow and the beautiful possibilities—with her.

"Thanks for bringing me here." She wrapped an arm around his waist. "I couldn't go back to my place after Novak. Not yet."

"I was hoping to convince you to stay with me."

Changes would have to be made to accommodate her on a permanent basis, but he was willing to turn his world inside out and reorder every priority to make her happy.

She rested her head on his shoulder, nestling closer with her hand rubbing his chest.

A tangle of need tightened through his sore body. He walked them up to his reinforced steel door, pressed his thumb to the fingerprint scanner, and entered the six-digit code. The keypad beeped, unlocking the door. With a press of the handle, they were inside.

He shut off the alarm and took her hand.

As they strolled through the first floor, she grew tense beside him with her head on a swivel, taking in his place.

"Do you want something to drink?" he asked. "Water? Wine? I'm sure I have a nice red you'd like."

Her eyes were wide, and she didn't try to hide her surprise.

Chuckling, he glanced around at the open space along with her. His place had every upgraded amenity: wide-plank hardwood floors, top-of-the-line appliances, slick quartz countertops, a built-in coffee system that elevated brewed java to the next level.

But it was also devoid of the cushy comforts of her apartment. The dining room was bare. A sixty-inch television mounted to the wall in the living room faced workout equipment rather than a sofa. A vertical climber, rowing machine, inclined barbell bench as well as a flat one, stacks of plated weights, and an adjustable dumbbell set.

Why sit on your ass watching TV when you could get in a workout?

"Why don't you have any furniture?" she asked. "Did you just move in?"

"Uh, no. I've lived here for over two years. I didn't want to waste money on furniture I didn't need."

Smiling, she shook her head. "Prudent and practical." Her voice went all sultry as she took off her jacket and gun. "Very important qualities I find rather sexy."

Good thing his weird bachelor setup didn't turn her off. Not completely anyway.

She leaned against the counter in the kitchen and beckoned to him with a finger.

He went to stand between her spread feet, wanting to erase every inch of space between them. Gliding his hands over her hips, he caressed her backside, bringing her pelvis flush to his. She peeled his jacket back, dropping it to the floor, followed by his shoulder holster and weapon.

"Are you hungry?" he asked, brushing his lips across hers.

She nodded, hauling his shirt over his head. "But not for food. Please tell me you've got a decent bed in this place and not some economy-size cot."

They both chuckled.

"I have a nice setup in the master, the best mattress and sheets money can buy."

"Of course you do. Superman's Fortress of Solitude might've been stark and efficient, but he did have a luxurious king-size bed waiting for Lois."

He hiked his eyebrows and opened his mouth to speak.

She pressed a finger to his lips, silencing him, and flashed a naughty grin.

They stared in each other's eyes for a sweet moment that had his blood pounding in anticipation before she curled her fingers in his hair and gave him a long, lazy kiss that sent a shock of heat racing through him.

Cupping her breast, he ran a thumb over her bra across a pebbled nipple.

A mewling sound rose in her throat, and she eased her lips free. "Let's shower. Then you can show me that bed. And it better live up to the high expectations I have for *my* Man of Steel." She winked at him.

Her words went right to his heart and several places farther south.

Soft candlelight flickered like fireflies, casting the bedroom in an amber glow. Maddox kissed Cole, needing another taste of him. Their bodies were a tangle of limbs, breath mingled, supple flesh melded as one. The musky scent of sex thickened the air.

"I love you. I love you. I love you." The whispered chant spilled from her lips in his ear, and she couldn't stop it, wanted him to hear it, ached for him to feel it.

They rocked against each other in the sumptuous bed fit for royalty, clutching one another, fueled by this sensual craving that never diminished. She relished the cocoon they spun in their slow, nurturing connection. Skin on skin, the thudding of their hearts vibrating through her, they were as close as possible in every way.

His warm, rough hands slid over her body, cupping the swell of her breasts and butt. Those fingers had explored her curves, every scar with such tenderness, there was no doubt he cherished her. Imperfections and all.

Her whole body tightened, unraveling in the ecstasy

they made together. In a vicious groan, he came undone with her.

The full weight of him pressed down on her, his breath ragged against her throat, his lips tracing her jawline. She smiled in his lush hair, never wanting him to move, relishing the ache. Sated and rooted in this moment, in their love, in being his from skin to soul.

He caressed her face with both hands and kissed her. "Hungry, *lyubov moya*?"

She'd never tire of hearing him call her "my love" in Russian. "Starving."

"The steakhouse a couple of blocks over delivers until midnight on the weekends."

"Sounds perfect. Along with a glass of wine and a couple of ice packs." The ache from her bruises and scrapes was setting in.

Her cell phone buzzed, vibrating on the nightstand. Groaning, Cole rolled off her, and she grabbed it.

"It's the office." Surprise was rich in her voice. She answered. "Maddox here."

"Sanborn got the thumbs-up on an immunity deal and it's being ironed out," Castle said. "But the president insists after the deal is signed that Novak is transferred into the custody of the U.S. Marshals until we can apprehend the broker."

She jackknifed up in the bed. "What? Novak will never agree to it. For the first time, I saw something that terrified him. The broker. He can't be transferred."

"It's out of Sanborn's hands if he wants the president to sign the immunity deal."

A dark, sinking sensation churned in her stomach. "I

don't have a good feeling about this." It wasn't going to end well.

"None of us do."

"I'll come in early to help oversee the transfer."

"No, you're taking time off. We thought you should know. That's all. Sanborn is recalling Alastair and Ares. They'll help. And we're going to start polygraphing everyone. Listen, get some rest and enjoy your downtime with Lover Boy. When you get back, you'll be working around the clock until our leak is plugged. Later." Castle disconnected.

She gritted her teeth and set down the phone.

Cole clutched her hand. "I caught the gist." His eyes darkened. "This mole is a serious problem. I feel it in the marrow of my bones. Is it always like this, Mads? Your job, your life?"

Inwardly, she winced and braced for some caveman speech about how dangerous her job was and how she shouldn't be putting her life on the line to get it done. "Yes."

She watched his muscled chest expand as he took a deep breath like he was winding up to say something she didn't want to hear.

"Mads—"

"Don't say it. I don't want to fight with you and I'm not quitting my job."

His eyes softened, and he caressed her bruised cheek. "Marry me."

Her breath stalled, thoughts spinning like a carnival ride.

"I love you. Till the day I die. I want to own my

future. The only one possible, with you as my wife. I want to share everything with you, have a family."

Family? A sudden flash of fear paralyzed her. "What if I can't have children?" Pressure pounded in her head. "The doctor could've been wrong. I might not be able to carry a baby to term. I don't even know how to squeeze a kid into my life. You shouldn't be deprived of that."

She'd sacrificed having a husband, children, happiness, because she'd believed her chance had died with him. But he was alive and should have everything.

"Look at me." The unyielding hardness of his tone snatched her gaze. "If we have children, it's because we both want to. We'd find a way to squeeze a kid into *our* life. Not like I can strap a car seat to a motorcycle. My living room is a freaking gym and I don't own a dining room table. But we'll make it work. Together. We'll see a specialist." He pressed his palm to her belly, and the touch brought tears to her eyes. "Or adopt. Or we'll get dogs and spoil them rotten and be those crazy dog people."

She laughed, letting the image wipe away the sadness.

"We're going to build a home and a family together. No secrets in our house, no pretending. I'm not promising perfection, but I know we'll create an atmosphere where we're safe to be messy, happy, and honest."

Belief didn't waffle and creep up on her slowly. It dropped in her gut and detonated with certainty. But she didn't want him to feel obligated.

"Are you sure you don't want time to think about who I've become and what our lives will look like? Marriage is big. You've got me. You don't have to propose right now."

"Ask me why I chose Matthews as my last name when I ditched Reznikov."

Okay, she'd bite. "Why?"

"Because I loved the sound of Maddox Matthews. It has a ring to it, don't you think?"

A bittersweet smile touched her lips. Her heart swelled, full and light like a balloon, on the verge of bursting from love. A love that had survived against all odds.

"My soul knows yours," he said. "My heart never stopped beating for you. You're a phenomenal woman and this butt-kicking super agent—"

"Butt-kicking super operations officer."

"It really doesn't roll off the tongue, honey, so I'm sticking with agent. My point is you're not going to bake cookies for the PTA. And you don't have to. We'll define our normal as we go, together. I want you as you are, Maddox. I love you now and always." Those intense eyes sparkled. "I'm committed to us. No matter what. So, will you marry me?"

They'd never forget the past, all they'd both suffered, but they'd managed the hardest part—forgiveness. What they shared was real and rare. They were better together than apart, belonged to one another, and would find a way to create the life they wanted, even if it wasn't going to be easy.

"Yes." She kissed him hard. Quick pecks of joy on his cheeks, nose, along the jagged line of his scar from his brow to the corner of his mouth. "I love you. I want to be your wife."

He pressed his forehead to hers and stared in her eyes. "For the next two days, I don't want your mind on the

Gray Box. Give me all of you, and I'll support whatever you have to do."

If the situation was reversed, she wasn't sure she could be this understanding. Danger came with her job, and she wasn't quitting. For him to recognize that and be so supportive meant the world. He was amazing.

The concern regarding Novak and the mole lingered, but Cole was this wonderful buffer. With him, she could get some much-needed space from the work that normally consumed her, compartmentalize her duty, and find balance.

She threw her arms around his neck and hugged him, tight and hard. If forty-eight hours of being completely focused on their future, on him, would earn his unconditional support in the monumental task ahead of her, ahead of them all, she was sold.

No negotiation necessary.

"You just made an offer I can't refuse."

EPILOGUE

The door to the secure holding room opened. Someone brought Aleksander a cup of black coffee, placed a box of doughnuts on the table, and left without a word. It'd taken long enough.

Three doughnuts were in the Krispy Kreme box. He would've inhaled anything but sighed with relief none were chocolate.

He took a ravenous bite into a glazed doughnut. The rush of sugar and carbohydrates gave him a jolt of much-needed energy. Stretching his neck, he sipped the coffee and gagged.

The American brew was horrid. Bitter and grainy.

A smooth Italian espresso would be better. At least it was piping hot. He took a big gulp and set the cup down.

Hopefully, they'd given his son proper sustenance, maybe a sandwich and some soup.

He'd gladly give those agents all the information he had if it meant he and Val would go free. Free to find another way to make America pay. He was bloodied and bruised, but he was not yet broken. It might take two more decades, but he wouldn't stop. *Never*. Not until he had his vengeance.

The oddest sensation permeated him, tiny hot pinpricks through his body. His skin itched, hands shook uncontrollably. Then his muscles seized in a violent convulsion.

He keeled over, his leaden arms unable to stop his cheek from slamming into the hard steel table. Eyes frozen open, he stared at the door. His heartbeat thundered in his ears and saliva pooled in his mouth. Searing flames spread through his heavy, useless limbs. He couldn't move.

A neuromuscular paralytic drug must've been in the coffee. A precise dose that still enabled him to breathe and feel the torture of it working.

Heat crawled over him, like a thousand fire ants, biting and stinging, that he was helpless to swat away. The burn, oh, the burn…excruciating. He would've screamed under this agony if he'd been able.

The door opened again, and the same person returned. This time…wearing gloves.

You? You're Cobalt?

A four-faced devil, who was willing to betray their country, lie, backstab colleagues, live a fake life filled with false smiles, pretending to be something they weren't.

Not even Aleksander had ever stooped to such parasitic depths.

The pain worsened to a corrosive sizzle in the lining of his stomach, underneath his fingernails, and his eye sockets, but it was the least of his current problems.

A gloved hand lifted Aleksander's forearm. There was a flash of something familiar—his hotel keycard. Broken. The jagged piece of plastic ripped into his flesh as Cobalt sawed across his wrist. The rough edge snagged on his skin and tore open his veins in deep vertical gashes.

In minutes, he'd bleed out.

His arm was flicked to the table like a dead, smelly fish, and his other was raised.

Aleksander would've laughed if he could've. He'd wondered countless times how he would die someday. In a blaze of glory? Falling from a rooftop? A bullet in the face? Knife to his kidney? A garrote of someone else's around his neck?

Cobalt planted the broken hotel keycard in Aleksander's hand, picked up the coffee and box of doughnuts, and hustled out of the room.

Admittedly, Aleksander lacked the imagination to envision his own coldblooded murder staged to look like a suicide.

Would Agent Maddox Kinkade buy this charade?

Doubtful. But that was Cobalt's problem—or better yet, the Gray Box's.

Surely, there was more to Cobalt's plan. Every good mole knew their luck would eventually run out. They used decoys, played the shell game with finesse, and always, always had a fail-safe in the event something went wrong. If they were smart.

Cobalt was very good, clever—*hell, I never saw this shit coming*—and had the support of the most powerful, merciless man Aleksander knew. And that was saying quite a lot.

Warmth leached from his limbs, and a deep weariness dragged at him.

Valmir? Would he be safe? His son knew nothing.

Aleksander struggled to hang on, to cling a little longer for Val's sake, but the crushing fatigue was stronger.

Bastard. *Cobalt, I'll be waiting for you with Levik down in hell to settle the score.*

Darkness was a great gaping mouth, the pitch-black closing in, seeking to swallow him.

The bright faces of Sonia and Mila floated, shining through the looming void. In a park. They were running through the woods, laughing. Val was there, too, a little boy.

The sun was warm, so bright that everything glistened. He chased them, trying to catch up. Sonia reached out her hand, fingertips so close, he grazed softness. Beautiful softness.

Then they faded, their laughter dying. Echoing.

A crashing wave of shadows engulfed him in cold, empty darkness.

AUTHOR'S NOTE

I love the Washington metropolitan area, which I currently call home. If you are familiar with the Capital Beltway, you might notice I altered some places, locations, and took a few liberties with minor details to suit the flow of the story. I did my best to retain as much authenticity as possible to depict the richness, diversity, and energy of the DMV (DC, Maryland, Virginia).

Read on for a sneak peek of the next book in the Final Hour series

NOTHING TO FEAR

GRAY BOX FACILITY, NORTHERN VIRGINIA
THURSDAY, JULY 4, 5:25 P.M. EDT

Everyone has been polygraphed," Gideon Stone said, flipping a switch to tint the conference room's glass walls opaque, "and put under surveillance." But their team was undermanned and overwhelmed, stretched to the breaking point.

"We still have nothing." Strain leaked into Maddox Kinkade's voice. "We won't win playing this long game."

Gideon sat at the touch screen table and brought up the final autopsy report, swiping through the digital pages. Conclusive results indicated homicide. A fast-acting poison that mimicked natural causes had killed Aleksander Novak, one so rare it was missed on the first toxicology panel.

Someone in his unit, someone they trusted with their lives, had murdered a suspect in custody—here in the ultra-secure facility right under their noses.

The obscene moxie that must've taken made Gideon's blood simmer.

"We need to get up close and personal with each suspect." Maddox looked around the table. "Run this to ground as quickly as possible."

Only the six people sitting in that room had solid alibis for the estimated time of death and could be relied on without question. They were a close-knit crew and had been through the thick of it together.

"Let's deal with Dad first," Maddox said.

Slim odds that Bruce Sanborn, director of the Gray Box, was the leak. Dad, as they called him behind his back, cared too deeply about his people to endanger them. Still, they had to do their due diligence and investigate everyone who had access and opportunity, including the boss.

"Dad keeps secrets locked up tighter than gold in the Federal Reserve Bank," Gideon said. "And he's the best at tradecraft."

"Who has balls big enough to take Sanborn?" Maddox asked.

"I think it's safe to say I have the biggest pair." Castle Kinkade, Maddox's brother, dragged a hand across his bald brown head. Nobody laughed. He'd proven his mettle often enough in the field, putting his ex-Navy SEALS experience to use. "But to make it fair, whoever is left last without a target should get the headache of taking Sanborn."

Across the table, Alistair Allen clicked his tongue. "Nice try, Elephant Balls." His posh James Bond accent clashed with his hipster haircut and grunge attire. "As Sanborn's protégé, you're the best choice to get close enough without triggering his Spidey-senses."

Steel-toe boots clubbed a vacant chair as John Reece threw his feet up into it. "I'm all for fair, but that's a valid point. I think you're stuck with the short end of the stick."

Castle folded his thick arms over his linebacker chest. "All right, the hot potato is mine."

"You can handle the heat." Maddox fiddled with her new engagement ring. The massive rock must've cost her fiancé a kidney. "Next, Sybil Parker. Her epic fail is the reason we're here."

Parker's position as Internal Threat Monitor was protected. The ITM and her henchmen were watchdogs, blessed with unfettered access to mission details and the authority to surveil any computer system and phone line to prevent insider threats—to catch spies. The irony.

Complicating this shitshow, the director of national intelligence had hired the ITM three-pack, and only he could fire them, making the lot untouchable without irrefutable evidence.

"I'm up for the challenge," Reece said.

"Got a death wish?" Maddox snickered. "That Praying Mantis will eat you for a midday snack. It won't be easy to play Parker. She'll anticipate it."

Reece tugged down a ball cap that read *I'm Your Huckleberry*. "No worries. I got this. I'll approach her with *serious concerns*," he said, using air-quotes, "about her nemesis."

"No love lost between her and Sanborn," Owen "Ares" Whitlock said. The guy had dark eyes, dark hair, and an even darker presence that'd make the average man wet himself. "That's catnip Parker won't be able to resist. Guess you're not an insult to our profession after all."

Reece grinned and flipped him off. "And I'll try to dig deeper into her minions."

Stand-up guy taking one for the team with Parker. Gideon gave him a two-finger salute.

"Maddox," Ares said, his voice full of grit and gravel, "you should take Doc."

No secret the man had a thing for their resident CDC scientist, Emily "Doc" Duvall, but she avoided Ares as if he had a communicable disease. Ares obviously didn't want the hound dogs he worked with sniffing around the one lady he wanted and couldn't have.

"Doc is dying to be BFFs." Maddox winced. "But it gives me the perfect in. Okay."

No one would deny Ares a favor. Going along was sure as heck easier than opposing him.

"At the top of the list after Parker," Maddox said, "is Willow Harper."

Gideon's pulse spiked, his insides doing a one-eighty just hearing her name.

"A sharp cryptologist. Talented programmer. Skilled hacker." Maddox rubbed her brow. "I don't get a malicious read from Harper, but she's a loner. A textbook red flag. And she made critical mistakes during the last op that can't be ignored. She was also the one who redesigned our firewalls." Knowing gazes were exchanged. "She could dig into our network without leaving a trace."

All true, but Gideon's intuition—or whatever he relied on to stay alive in this brutal job for ten years—protested. Willow Harper was no mole.

There was an awkwardness about her that he found genuine. Refreshing. Her modest charm hid a loneliness he recognized. But he kept his distance. She was refined and had a gift for creating elegant programs. He was rough around the edges and had a knack for terminating threats. They were different breeds.

"I can try reeling her in with my charm and repartee," Alistair said. "If a friendly approach doesn't work, I can always use a bit of pressure to crack her odd shell."

Gideon choked on the chewing gum slipping down his throat. *What the—*

"I should have a go at her," Ares said. "I'm the one who's been surveilling her."

A snowball's chance in hell either would succeed. Ares was a bull in a china shop and his atomic intimidation factor would render her mute. Alistair's crass tongue and droll facade wouldn't scratch her shell. The team couldn't squander time on the speed bumps of their failures.

"Applying pressure is my specialty." Gideon's voice was low and cool. He *was* the only one in the group trained in interrogation. The cruel kind at CIA black sites. "I'll take Willow."

The room flatlined. Everyone's attention snapped to him, wary looks surfacing.

"*Willow?*" Ares chortled. Even his grim laugh could scare someone shitless.

Gideon could count on one hand the times he'd spoken to her beyond a passing salutation. On the rare occasions he had mentioned her, it'd been by surname. How he thought of her was a different story. Letting that slip was unlike him.

Gideon shrugged. "Getting on a first name basis is logical. I'll need to get close." *Willow* had rolled off his tongue smoother and sweeter than soft-serve ice cream. Something about her inspired whimsical thoughts and deranged hope for a drop of goodness in his life.

Maddox's insightful green-eyed gaze pinned him. His best friend saw through people, picked up on the things others sought to hide, and she knew him better than anyone. He wanted to squirm under the dissection of her scalpel-sharp scrutiny, but merely flexed his jaw.

"If Harper *isn't* the leak, she doesn't deserve you on her tail." Maddox shook her head. "I've seen how you look at her. I know how you'll handle this."

Really? He didn't. Arching a brow, he waited.

"The lover angle," she said. "It's the wrong play. We don't know enough about her—whether she's into girls or guys or no one at all. And if you're her type and she's *not* our traitor, heaven help her."

He knew what she was saying. One-night stands and no attachments suited him. No one got burned. No one got a chance to see the truth about him—not since his late wife, and she'd been terrified.

"Give me some credit. I'll feel her out and determine how to play it, but the reality is *lovers* fosters intimacy faster than other methods. Yields more reliable results too."

Not that he'd ever worked a honey trap before and sleeping with Willow hadn't been on his agenda. Walking into the conference room, he hadn't even planned on getting within two feet of her, never mind taking her as a target. But after observing her the last three years—her unfaltering work ethic, how she interacted with others, avoided office politics—he had an advantage the others didn't. He knew Willow's character.

Maddox drew her dark curls into a ponytail, accentuating the striking features of her golden-brown face. "I have a hunch Harper is innocent. If she's cleared, she still has to work with you. The situation could get messy. Ugly. I don't like it."

Gideon shared her concern. There was something wholesome yet complex about Willow. He wanted to protect her, not hurt her. Out of their other choices for the job, he was the best one.

"We're at war," Castle said. "We were supposed to be impenetrable, but the enemy is embedded, has been fooling *us* for years. If this isn't resolved ASAP, heads are going to roll."

A leak inside the CIA or FBI would be bad, but this was worse. Their off-the-books unit operated beyond the black and white lines of other agencies, and at times beyond the law. They were sanctioned for direct-action on foreign and domestic soil with access to the most classified data. This was a political nightmare that could end careers, starting at the very top.

"We don't have the luxury of indulging a hunch," Alistair said. "Sometimes we do bad things for good reasons."

"This isn't really your forte, Gideon," Maddox said, pausing as if waiting for him to agree, but he held her gaze and his tongue. "Flirting and finesse," she finally added.

Gideon was good at many things and some of those began with the letter F, but only his best friend knew he couldn't flirt *or* finesse his way out of a paper bag.

To keep the others off Willow, however, he'd be willing to try.

"Are you kidding? If anyone can quickly get that

analyst to lower her guard, whether it's inside or outside the bedroom,"—Castle hiked a thumb at him—"it's our Golden Boy."

The nickname prickled Gideon's nerves, poking fun at his college days as a quarterback as well as his fair looks that had always been more of a curse than a blessing.

The guys thought Gideon was an expert pickup artist based on his appearance. In truth, he was a magnet for flirtatious bombshells and let *them* pick him up instead. He was good at asking questions, not at having bullshit conversations.

"I'm capable of getting close and finding answers without…complications," Gideon said.

"Capable, maybe, but not without complications. I'll take her instead of handling Doc."

"Our leak compromised you and nearly cost your life." Ares stabbed the air at Maddox. "Harper's at the top of the list of suspects and we're worried about her feelings? Lives are on the line, national security is at risk, and the clock's ticking. We find the mole, no matter the cost."

An uncomfortable silence settled around the room.

"Gideon takes Harper," Ares said. "You'll keep Doc."

Maddox raised both palms. "Fine." She slid her hand in her pocket and dumped a pile of memory sticks in a clatter on the glass table.

Flash-C drives. A small device that plugged into the USB of a personal computer—no ports in the Gray Box—and cloned the hard drive. Those were courtesy of Maddox's fiancé, who worked at a private security company that specialized in corporate intelligence gathering.

"Anything I should know about her?" Gideon asked Ares, as he swiped a flash-C drive.

Everyone would assume *anything not in the surveillance report* that Gideon should've read by now, but snooping on Willow's personal life was a temptation he'd resisted.

"She wrote in a notebook two nights ago. Keeps it in her bedside table. I haven't had a chance to break in and look at it with that old bulldog on patrol. And she has insomnia."

Something they had in common.

"You don't need me for the rest." Gideon threw on his jacket, covering his holstered Maxim 9, and shoved through the door before bickering kicked up over the remaining targets.

The sooner he proved Willow's innocence, whittling down the list of suspects, the better.

Muted blue partitions, beige walls, and pale gray carpet gave the interior offices a serene atmosphere. News chatter flowed from nine large screen TVs lining the main wall of Intel. Gideon glimpsed a report on a tropical depression over the Bahamas as he skirted the periphery of the open layout, bypassing small talk with the others. Only Willow was on his radar.

He spotted her nestled in a remote corner, facing the wall. She was typing on her dual-monitor workstation, automatic-fire keystrokes. A sleek, chocolate-brown bun with never a hair out of place showcased her slender neck and sophisticated string of pearls. But the vulnerability of her position—her six exposed and earbuds in—grated on his operational wiring.

Worst of all, the angle at which she sat deprived him of seeing her face as he approached.

Whenever he set eyes on her, he smiled, even if he didn't show it on the outside.

He hesitated behind her, within arm's reach. Her long, unpainted fingernails clicked keys in a blur. Lines of source code materialized. Interrupting her would be like disturbing Picasso.

In the screen's reflection, her gaze darted up to his. She swiveled, giving him her profile, and yanked out an earbud. A lithe leg extended from her pencil skirt.

She wasn't a classic knockout, but her haunting beauty knocked him on his heels.

"Yes?" Her surprised look read pure professional. "Did you need something?"

"Hey, I was wondering, would you, uh, maybe like to get a drink with me after work?"

"No, thank you."

Ouch. He blinked like a dumbstruck idiot. Willow had little reason to be interested in him. She was demure, brainy, better than he deserved, and most of all, she knew what he really was, but he hadn't expected such a rapid shoot-down.

He stuffed his hands in his jeans pockets, regrouping. "I was impressed with your work on the last op, hacking the cell phone. You helped us find Maddox. Means a lot. Can I buy you dinner as thanks? Or, uh, a cup of coffee? I know a cozy café. Good music. Great espressos."

She stared at him with those enigmatic hazel eyes, the barest flush to her porcelain skin, looking sweet enough to eat. "No need to thank me. I was doing my job. That's why I get paid."

Damn, she intrigued him. The sensation was unfamiliar. But at this rate, he'd have better luck playing Russian roulette than finessing his way past her defenses.

Willow sat at her desk, stunned. Gideon Stone was talking to her and not about a mission.

Sometimes she overheard people call him pretty, but she didn't understand why. There was a brutality to everything about him. From his black ops call sign— *Reaper*—down to his ferocious good looks: a lean face, sharp angles, bold features, and a tumble of hair the color of sunshine glinting off ice. Even his eyes were a severe blue—the palest shade, so arresting she never dared look too long for fear of staring.

Not staring was a rule she'd learned not to break, since it made people uncomfortable.

The bridge of his once-broken nose was millimeters flatter than it should've been. A slight crook hinted at the violence in his life, but the flaw added character to his face.

Humanized him.

Whenever she ventured close to Gideon, caution drummed inside her. She was likely to say the wrong thing, while he never seemed to want to say anything to her at all.

"No drinks. No dinner. No coffee." His brows drew together in a look of concentration.

What was wrong with him? Nothing ever rattled his iceberg composure.

She was the one with social issues.

Perhaps she shouldn't have said *no*, but she didn't drink alcohol, didn't exceed four cups of coffee a day unless working overtime, and it was absurd to thank her for doing her job. Right?

Did he really want to have dinner with her? Why? She'd smiled at him once, after taking a class on how to make friends, and a scowl had darkened his face in return.

"What are you listening to?" He pointed to her earbuds.

She pulled the other one out, tossing them on her desk. "Nothing." The always-on TVs and chatter from her colleagues clogged her thoughts. The high-fidelity earplugs lowered the decibels of the environment to a natural sound—clean and clear—allowing her to focus.

Gideon traded his typical grimace for a feral sort of grin. At least, she hoped it was a grin. His mouth curved up, lifting his incredible cheekbones, but the rest of his face had a strained expression disturbingly similar to the one her dad got when he was constipated.

"What type of code are you working on?" He gestured with his chin at her computer.

"Something new." Eager to discuss anything that wouldn't trip her up, she turned, pointing at one monitor. Source code was safe.

Whenever she talked too long, it was evident the motherboard of her brain was wired differently. People called her odd, peculiar. Her sisters preferred the term *dweeb*.

"I call it the Pandora Program. It'll detect and flag any internal security vulnerabilities in our operations, so

I can mitigate the possibility of us being compromised from the inside."

He stepped up behind her, resting a hand on the back of her chair. The unexpected heat from his body tickled her spine. He always looked too removed to touch, glacier-cold, but the warmth radiating from him now was undeniable.

Clenching her thighs, she was tempted to brush against his arm for the barest contact but scooted to the edge of her seat instead. "I'm about forty-six working hours from testing it."

"Wow. The program will be ready in a week?"

"Less. Three point two-eight days. I've been putting in extra hours." It still wasn't enough. They had a traitor in the unit, as everyone knew after the debacle with the dead guy. The program needed to be ready yesterday.

"You're amazing," Gideon said.

"It's just a program." Her computer alarm beeped. *Six-thirty already?* "I have to go."

She silenced the chime, saved her work, and logged off, removing her ID badge from the card reader. As she slipped on her heels, she spun the miniature globe designed out of binary digits that sat on her desk—the last thing she always did in her routine.

If only the world were as simple as the two-symbol coding system.

Snagging her purse, she stood and turned around.

Gideon's expression turned grim. "What happened to your face?" He closed in, swallowing her comfort zone like a black hole.

She staggered back, bumping into her desk, and

touched the cut on her cheek near her left ear. "It's just a nick. He threw a dish and the broken pieces went flying. It was an accident."

"Who?" Gideon reached for her cheek, and she sidestepped him. "Your boyfriend?"

Boyfriend? She'd only have one of those in her dreams. Unfortunately, she never dreamed.

"I–I'm going to be late." She scrambled into the aisle, avoiding him. "I have to go."

He strolled alongside her for some unfathomable reason. His strong physique and weightless stride—propelled by athletic grace—projected his lethal ability to handle anything.

"I'll walk you out to your car." A declaration, not a question.

Her stomach somersaulted. "What? Why?"

It took nine minutes to get from her desk to the parking lot, depending on the wait for the elevator. An extra two to her car since she parked on the far end. That meant for eleven minutes she'd have to talk. *With him.* Focus on the rules to seem nice. She wasn't unfriendly, but things got lost in translation.

Her ribcage tightened, making it hard to breathe. "There's no need to walk me out."

"I'm leaving anyway. It's no trouble." Gideon peered down at her, and the intense look in his piercing blue eyes sent butterflies dancing in her belly.

She stared at him trying to recall why it was a bad idea and tripped over her feet. *Gah!* Tearing her gaze away, she focused on what was going on around her, determined to pull it together and not fall flat on her face.

Holding center stage in the middle of Intel as she passed around a platter of fudge was Janet Price, the director's assistant. She was a Rubenesque woman, who had an effortless way of bringing people together over her homemade dishes.

Gideon stopped and joined the gaggle. Willow considered hurrying to the elevator, but pressure to follow the etiquette rule about mingling for a minute or two to avoid coming across as antisocial weighed on her. She needed to work on being socially acceptable, so she stayed.

Laughter floated in the air over the background noise of the news. Doc and Janet giggled, practically arm-in-arm and breathless over one of Daniel Cutter's Marine Force Recon stories.

On and on, Daniel went. His stories always sounded the same, not at all funny to Willow. She never got their humor.

Voracious hands shoveled chocolate into eager mouths. Chatter flowed easy as a breeze.

Willow swallowed past the tightening in her throat. Sometimes she longed to be a sail riding that wind, but usually found herself a feather adrift in it. Social codes and cues she couldn't decipher layered their conversations. There was a wall between Willow and everyone else. She didn't know how to break it down and trying was overwhelming.

Gideon swiped a piece of fudge and a slow-burning smile spread across his face. An odd tingle gathered in Willow's chest, making her toes bunch in her shoes.

"Janet," Gideon said, "these are incredible."

Everyone else chimed in with a chorus of compliments. Willow's obligated two minutes of office mingling were up. This was the perfect moment to skedaddle to the elevator. Alone.

She pivoted and nearly bumped into Amanda Woodrow, the lead analyst.

"Willow," Amanda said, smiling. "I'm glad I caught you. I wanted to talk to you."

"Not now. I need to leave." Willow rolled her pearls between her fingers, hoping her honesty didn't sound rude. Amanda was a lovely supervisor, never giving her a hard time about special accommodations, like the set-up of her workstation. Willow didn't want to offend her.

"It'll just take a sec. You're doing a great job. I'm really impressed with the counterintelligence program you're developing."

As Amanda kept praising her, taking far longer than a second, Willow got a queasy ache in her stomach. She had to end this conversation. In a book she'd read, one technique was to change the subject with unexpected flattery followed by a *farewell*. But what to say? Her gaze roamed over Amanda's desk, past colorful crayon drawings, and to the photo of her five-year-old son, finally with a full head of hair since his leukemia had gone into remission.

"I like your son's curls," Willow said, cutting off Amanda. "They're really pretty."

"Uh." Amanda's brow furrowed. "Thank you."

"See you tomorrow."

Before Willow took ten steps, Gideon stalked off from his friends, waving goodbye. He was at her side again, stirring unease in her and at the same time, a shocking sense of comfort.

What in the *Twilight Zone* was happening?

Gideon popped the chocolate in his mouth, moaning *Mmmm*, an intense look on his face, fingers curling as he savored it. Oh, she'd love to melt in his mouth like that. *Mmmm*, indeed.

But even if she managed to get through a conversation without babbling or blowing it by being herself, she'd heard through office gossip about the way he picked up women at Rocky's Bar. For one night only. Reminded her of a Broadway musical song her mom had loved.

"*One night only*," she sang under her breath, "*come on baby*."

"What'd you say?" Gideon licked the remnants of chocolate from his fingers.

"Oh, nothing." Her cheeks burned. *Shut. Up.*

"Why didn't you take any fudge? Don't like chocolate?"

"I love chocolate, but I don't eat homemade stuff other people bring in."

"Why not?"

"I don't know if their kitchen is clean, if they have cats, or wash their hands before cooking. Amanda told me her son, Jackson, sneezed in cake batter once, and she still baked it."

Willow's skin crawled with the heebie jeebies.

"Don't you have a dog?"

"Cats and dogs are different. Cats climb all over everything. But no, I don't have a dog."

Gideon nodded with another constipated expression. She bit her lip, quickening her step.

In the central hall, they passed Director Sanborn talking to two forensic accountants who'd been ordered to come here even though it was a holiday. The chief wanted to follow the money to find the leak by auditing everyone. The pressure on him was immense. Surely the director of national intelligence and the president, the only two people Sanborn answered to, were looking at this situation under a microscope.

The chief was a good man and always looked out for her. She didn't want to let him down. Hopefully her new program would help.

Gideon tapped the button for the elevator and stood behind her, where she'd have to look over her shoulder to see him. Glancing at the carpet, she slipped her purse strap across her body and peeked back to glimpse his boots. He had big feet to match the rest of him.

"Sorry I held you up at your desk." His warm breath brushed the nape of her neck, and her skin tingled.

"It's okay." She fought the dangerous impulse to look back.

"Are you hurrying off to an appointment?"

"Sort of." After the last around-the-clock mission, she'd made a promise to be home for dinner every night this week and make fresh-cooked meals.

The ten-inch reinforced steel elevator doors opened. She stepped inside with a shaky exhale and slunk to the far corner, needing a little distance between herself and him.

Gideon strode into the car. The heavy doors slid shut with a soft thud. He leaned against the side of the elevator and crossed his arms. Light danced off his hair forming a halo, but his hard body and smooth swagger spelled unabashed sinner rather than saint.

His gaze homed in on hers. A shiver chased through her down to her thighs.

"You never told me what happened to your face," he said.

"Yes, I did." Her voice was the barest thread of sound.

"You neglected to mention who's responsible."

"It's none of your business."

"You're right. I don't mean to pry. It's just that I've never seen you with a bruise or cut before. I'm concerned, that's all." He pushed off the wall and moved toward her. The stark power of his impossible-to-ignore masculinity drove her feet backward.

"There's nothing to be concerned about," she said.

"Then what happened? A guy threw something at you?"

"Not at me." Her nerves drummed. "It's personal. I don't discuss my private life with co-workers." The steel wall at her spine stopped her retreat. "And we're not friends."

He halted shy of breaching her personal space, a good foot between them, and stared down at her for so long she wondered what he'd say next, if anything. Then he gave her a sexy, lopsided grin.

A zing speared her belly. She clutched her purse against her stomach to steady herself.

"You don't have many friends here, do you?" His tone was soft as velvet.

"No. Not many." Zero friends, at work or otherwise. Her dad didn't count.

"Sounds lonely. Might be nice to let someone get to know you, spend time with you."

His warm smile spread, lighting up his face, thawing his icy eyes. Her mouth went dry, and she licked her lips. If he'd been within tongue's reach, she would've licked *him*.

"I'd like to be that someone."

Her mind pinwheeled. "Huh?" She'd heard him, but he might as well have spoken Greek.

His perfect smile dimmed. "I'm saying that I'd like for us to be friends."

She managed a swallow, loud enough to punctuate the thickening tension.

Gideon's gaze fell to where she was clutching her purse like a lifeline and back up to her face. "Do I scare you?"

"Sometimes." Big. Fat. Lie. He scared the heck out of her all the time.

She'd involuntarily memorized his personnel file. Information had a way of wallpapering itself to her mind. Age: thirty-two. Height: six-three. Weight: two-ten. Trained by the CIA. Sole Gray Box helicopter pilot. The specifics of all his assignments. She'd even hacked into the sealed parts of his record and devoured every nugget that'd been redacted. Savage details, extreme things he'd done out of duty and in self-defense. How he'd killed with his bare hands, and once ripped a man's carotid out with his teeth.

She was as frightened by him as attracted to him. What did that say about her?

He backed away at her admission. Frowning, he tugged at his shirt collar as if it'd gotten too tight and raked back his unruly forelock. She wanted to erase the uncharacteristic red dots of color surfacing on his cheeks.

"You don't need to be afraid of me." That was first time she'd heard his voice sound so low and shaky. "I'd never hurt you, Willow."

Another hard swallow. He said her first name. She didn't think he knew it. "I didn't mean it like that. I know you wouldn't hurt me."

"Is it okay to walk you to your car? I can hang back in the lobby if it's not."

Who wouldn't want a hot guy walking them to their car? It just didn't make an iota of sense why he'd wanted to. "It's okay."

The elevator opened onto the same floor. They hadn't moved. She hadn't pressed the button for the lobby and neither had Gideon. She was going to be late.

Castle, a hardnosed operative built like a howitzer, entered and hit the button for the lobby. He jerked his chin up, and Gideon did likewise.

The elevator cage crowded in, and she wanted to run off. Gripping her purse strap, she watched the floor numbers illuminate as they ascended from the sixth sublevel of the SCIF—Sensitive Compartmented Information Facility. She'd rather look at Gideon but couldn't pry her gaze from the elevator's display until the doors opened.

The elevator dinged and the doors slid open. Castle strode out first. Gideon stepped off at her side. Her kitten heels clicked across the smooth sea of concrete polished to a mirror finish. The sharp sound echoed in the austere, high-ceilinged lobby.

Castle swiped his ID card along one of the electronic turnstiles that sandwiched the metal detector and strolled outside. Gideon waved to the armed plain-clothes guards seated behind the ivory marble desk, addressing both by their first name.

Maybe it meant nothing that he knew hers as well. Something inside her deflated.

A sign embossed with *Helios Importing & Exporting* in elegant gold script hung on the wall. The business front provided a plausible explanation for the special-ized vehicles on the compound, the helicopter in the warehouse behind the main building, and credible cover story to family members for operatives traveling at a moment's notice.

She swiped her ID card. The plexiglass flaps of the turnstile retracted, and she walked through. Gideon hurried ahead and pushed the door open for her, stand-ing on the threshold. She brushed the steel frame on the way out to avoid contact with his swoon-worthy torso.

The slap of broiling heat and unforgiving humidity had her blouse sticking to her dampening skin before they reached the tree-covered parking lot.

"Where are you headed for your appointment?" he asked.

"Wolf Trap."

"Where's home?"

"Wolf Trap."

She rushed to her car. Her pulse had a wild, skitter-ing beat. He asked a lot of questions—twenty since he'd come to her desk. It was kind of nice. Answering questions was easier than racking her brain for something interesting to say. But his tone on the elevator had delved deeper toward *want to take your clothes off* than *want to grab a latte*, if she hadn't misread things—as she often did. Now he stayed two feet away as if he were the one afraid—to get too close to her.

Maybe she shouldn't have admitted that he scared her, but she wasn't worried about her physical safety with him. She probably messed up the entire conversation, acted the wrong way, said the wrong thing. *As usual.* What if he never talked to her again?

Regret burned her face. She pressed a palm to her forehead. "Tomorrow, if you need me to do research for you, I don't mind. I'm happy to help you."

He nodded, his expression unreadable, those blue eyes deadly serious. "Sure."

"No need to be my friend." She unlocked her car door. "It's my job."

"Everyone needs an ally, Willow."

What a strange thing to say. Besides, Director Sanborn was the only ally she needed.

She hopped into her older yellow VW bug and brought the engine to life with a sputtering rumble. She cranked the air-conditioning and fastened her seatbelt over her purse strap. With her hands at the ten and two o'clock positions, she pulled off.

She glimpsed Gideon in the rearview mirror watching her drive off. He pivoted as if to step away, but then lowered his head. Staring at the ground, he knelt and touched the asphalt. She turned onto the single lane dotted with twelve-inch diameter silver disks. Headed to the front gate, she noted the sign that warned against exceeding thirty-five miles per hour.

Higher speeds would activate the retractable pneumatic bollards—electro-hydraulic stainless-steel pillars—that'd pop up from the ground. One of many security features of their lockdown protocol, or to prevent hostile intrusion.

Huge shade trees lined the road up to the six-foot rebar-reinforced concrete barriers that edged the first few hundred yards of the entrance. The automatic armored gate slid open.

The traffic light changed from green to yellow. She punched the gas, zipping by the small manned gatehouse, and cleared the light as she sped down the access road to hit the highway.

The George Washington Parkway ran along the Potomac River northwest to Langley, where it bled into I-495. Blowing past the fifty miles per-hour sign on the GWP, she eased off the gas. A slight incline slowed the car to sixty. She merged onto the two-lane highway. With the holiday, traffic would either flow smoothly or cramp in a blink. She switched on cruise control for fuel efficiency, hoping for the former. Every nickel saved added up.

Drawing in a breath, she prepped for sensory triggers. She had difficulty processing certain sounds. Sirens overloaded her synapses, and the unbearable noise of metal on metal was crippling. Growing up, if an emergency services vehicle passed with sirens blaring, lights flashing, her sensory meltdowns in front of other kids had infuriated her sisters.

Her father never wanted her to drive, but she had no choice if she wanted to work at the NSA. In time, her excellent driving record had lessened his qualms.

The Parkway merged into I-495, looping the urban fringes of Virginia and Maryland, encircling DC. The southbound strip of highway construction wasn't hampering her commute, but she hated the claustrophobic effect of the concrete barricades funneling four streams of traffic into three and blocking the shoulder. Barring any jams, she wouldn't be too late.

Her car zipped up on a white minivan. She sighed, glancing at the adjacent lane to see if she could maneuver over. No such luck. She tamped the brake, but her car didn't slow. The cruise control should've de-activated, but the light stayed on and the speedometer didn't budge as her car devoured the pavement, getting closer to the van. *This can't be happening.* She'd taken the car for routine service last month, and everything had been fine this morning.

She jabbed the button and pumped the brake again. The ABS light blinked on. The distance to the minivan closed at a staggering rate. She stomped her foot and something in the brake assembly shifted this time, the spongy response giving way to no resistance.

The brakes are gone. Her heart pounded in a dizzying rush, and fear overrode disbelief.

A glimmer of light bounced inside the van. Cartoons played on two flip down screens. Kids were inside, and she was rushing toward them with no brakes and nowhere to pull over.

Panic buzzed in her skull. What was she going to do?

An opening appeared. She darted behind a truck,

despite the position drawing her further from the exit lane. Blocked on all sides, the speedometer snagged on sixty and her options dwindled to nil. Her car barreled toward the back of the eighteen-wheeler. Horror flooded her.

She jammed down on the brake, the pedal to the floor, and prayed for a miracle. Honking, she signaled to change lanes, first trying to the left, then right, but no one let her in on either side.

The distance between her and the back of the truck's high steel wall shrunk. Two hundred feet dropped to a hundred. Eighty. Forty. Blood roared in her ears. Her stomach knotted.

If no one would let her change lanes, she'd have to force her way in.

A hairsbreadth from impact, she laid on the horn and swerved into the HOV lane.

ACKNOWLEDGMENTS

First, thank you to the men and women who fight to protect our freedom. Your sacrifices are appreciated.

Writing a book is a solitary task that is never easy, but this story never would've made it out into the world without the help and support of many people. Special thanks to my phenomenal agent, Sara Megibow. You took a chance on me and found *Every Last Breath* a home. I asked a million questions that would've had other agents running for the hills, but your patience has been tireless. You go above and beyond with your encouragement, advice, and outside-the-box ideas.

A huge thank-you to my kick-butt editor, Mary Altman, for your discerning vision, infectious enthusiasm, and seeing the potential in this book. I couldn't have asked for a more diligent and understanding editor. To the entire team at Sourcebooks, from Dominique Raccah, to the art department, publicity, and sales, I would like to express my gratitude for your belief in this series.

Thanks to my critique partners and beta readers for providing invaluable feedback to make this book stronger.

Imagine Dragons: thank you for creating such amazing music that inspires my writing and motivates me during a workout.

Thank you so much to my patient husband, for allowing me to barricade myself in the office, juggling our awesome kids when I'm writing, and supporting this crazy endeavor. You guys are the ultimate cheering squad and mean everything to me.

To anyone who picks up one of my books: I'm beyond grateful that you read it and for telling your friends to read it, too. Word of mouth means the world to an author. Thank you!